# A WHITE ROOM

Stephanie Carroll

UNHINGED BOOKS

A White Room
Stephanie Carroll

Published in the United States.

Edition ISBNs
Trade Paperback: 978-0-9888674-0-6
eBook: 978-0-9888674-1-3

Library of Congress Control Number: 2013930913

Cover Design by Jennifer Quinlan of Historical Editorial
Original Painting: Lady Astor by John Singer Sargent, 1909.
Author Photo by Corey Ralston
Book Design by Christopher Fisher

*Never without Jonathan ...*

It is not that women are really smaller-minded, weaker-minded, more timid and vacillating, but that whosoever, man or woman, lives always in a small, dark place, is always guarded, protected, directed and restrained, will become inevitably narrowed and weakened by it.

—Charlotte Perkins Gilman

When we remember we are all mad, the mysteries disappear and life stands explained.

—Mark Twain

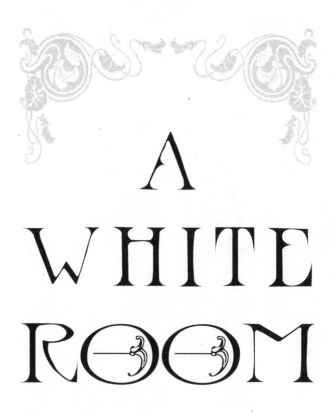

# A
# WHITE
# ROOM

# Prologue

*October 1901*
*Labellum, Missouri*

My father died with the taste of blood on his lips. To think that's why I now sat covered in blood. That's why there were red handprints on the walls, crimson footprints on the floor, and screaming streaks across my white dress.

The investigator scrutinized me, and I rubbed my hands together under the table, the blood dry and cracking on my fingertips. I had been caught, and the house smirked in triumph. The furniture trembled with joy, and the critter designs on the dishes bit their tongues, holding back cheers. Had the house won? Would it finally swallow me whole? Would my husband—still very much a stranger to me but a man who only hours ago claimed to love me—would he choose to turn me in to his colleagues waiting outside?

Now I had to choose. I could fight for my freedom—my sanity—or I could keep the promise I'd made my father. After all, it had been such a simple request made with blood-smeared lips.

# One

*March 1900*
*St. Louis, Missouri*

Florence squealed and dropped the pot onto the iron range with a loud clang.

"What's wrong?" I looked up from chopping carrots on the breadboard.

"I burned myself." Cringing, she held her hand palm up. "It hurts a lot."

"Let me see." I dunked a cloth into the cool water I had used to soak the vegetables.

Florence walked over, passing through a ray of light coming from the window. It cut through the kitchen and illuminated the dust in the air. "I thought I had enough cloth on the handle. Sin to Moses, it hurts!"

Florence and I had offered to help with supper after our father started feeling poorly that morning. It was probably just a cold, but my mother had a tendency to overreact. She'd had herself and our handmaid Kathy fluttering for the better part of the day.

I studied the puffy red streak across Florence's palm. It had reacted quickly but wasn't bubbling or peeling. Still, it was probably enough to burn for a few hours.

She winced. "What should I do? I don't want to bother Mother."

"No need." I grinned mischievously. "Follow me," I said.

We slipped out of the kitchen, skittered down the hall, and made a hard right up the central staircase. Florence hid the burn on her hand as we noisily scaled the steps, our skirts swishing and our boots clunking.

In our room, I clipped some leaves from an aloe plant I had learned how to grow in class at the university. We sat on Florence's bed, and I broke open a fleshy clipping and applied its liquid with cotton.

She squirmed a little when I touched it. "This is extraordinary, Emeline," she said.

I glanced up for a second and then back down. "What do you mean?"

"That you know things like this." Although I'd say my brother, James, was my best friend, my seventeen-year-old sister, Florence, understood and admired me more.

I held down a flattered grin. "I don't know much of anything, no more than what Mother knows. She probably has some of this in her kit." I placed the clippings on the nightstand.

Florence lifted her brown eyes. "But she didn't grow it." She used her other hand to scratch her head.

"Be careful. It took me all morning to get your hair right." Florence still needed my help to create the popular pompadour look, a style that required me to tease the hair at the crown, flip it up and back, high off the forehead, and shape the curls into an ornate bundle on top of a hidden crepe pad pinned underneath.

"Sorry." She lowered her hand.

I heard the sound of little bare feet scampering across the wood floor. It was probably my youngest sister, Ruth.

Florence shrugged. "Anyway, I think it's just extraordinary."

"I've only taken a few introductory courses. After I go to an actual nursing school, I'll really impress you."

"You're not going anywhere unless you ask."

I focused on the red skin. "I'm just waiting for the right time."

I had returned from college at the end of the year. My parents had sent me in hopes that I'd find a husband or at least acquire enough education to engage in meaningful conversation, but instead I discovered a passion for medicine. "They want me to hurry up and get married. They won't automatically say yes. If I had asked right away, Mother would have assumed it was a silly whim and refused. Then I didn't want to spoil the holidays with arguments and debates, and everyone gets so tired after the holidays, and before I knew it—"

"It's March," Florence said.

I nodded.

"What's wrong with right now?" she asked.

"Father isn't feeling well."

"It's just a cold."

I heard a scuff at the door. A little voice said, "Ahh. Shhh!"

Florence and I squinted at each other and then at the door.

Another noise, and someone whispered, "Listen."

I sighed and stood. I walked to the door and swung it open to reveal my two youngest sisters, thirteen-year-old Lillian on her knees with her hand cupped around her ear and seven-year-old Ruth standing by her side. Lillian had recently taken little Ruth under her wing, which meant trouble for all.

"Lillian, what kind of nonsense have you gotten Ruth into now?" I could hardly scold. They'd learned this from years of my own coaxing to listen at closed doors.

Kathy had clothed Ruth in a puffy lavender dress with little green and pink flowers, and her long dark hair was tied in two braids, but Lillian was still in her nightclothes, with a single knotted plait down her back.

"And why aren't you dressed? It's half past one. Mother will have a fit."

Lillian unfroze and jumped to her feet. "Are you really going to be a nurse?"

I slapped my hand to my face.

"You should help Father."

"It's just a cold," Florence interjected from the bed.

"Get in here." I grabbed Lillian by the nightshirt and pulled her into the room. Ruth followed willingly, and I clacked the door shut.

"Use a special nurse thing," Lillian said. "Then he'll let you go."

Ruth inched toward Florence, quickened her step, and jumped onto the bed with her.

I sighed. "I don't know any special nurse things. I have to go to school for that, and I didn't want to talk to you about this anyway."

"Tell Father you could fix his cold if you went to school."

"That's not a bad idea," Florence said.

"Tell him! Tell him!" Ruth interjected, unable to glean my annoyed tone.

I looked from Lillian to Ruth, hardening my face. "This is a secret. I haven't asked Father or Mother, and I don't want anyone telling them."

"That's a great idea." Lillian pointed to herself. "If I tell him, then you won't have to." She whirled around.

I snatched her by the nightshirt, grabbed her shoulder, and flung her back. "You wouldn't."

She flashed a conniving grin.

"Why? What do you want?"

"Nothing." She pursed her lips. "But if you're too scared…"

"I am *not* scared."

Florence cleared her throat, and I glared over my shoulder at her. She absentmindedly played with one of Ruth's braids. "Maybe right now is the right time."

"Are you really encouraging this?"

She sat up straight and dropped the braid. "If it will get you to do something."

Ruth's eyes popped from me to Lillian and back.

I scowled back at Lillian.

She smirked in a way only a little sister could.

An hour or so later, I had built up the nerve to approach my father. He was probably asleep having not felt well. I should just ask, I thought to myself. No, that conversation couldn't happen now, but I couldn't let Lillian tell him, either. She would, too, and she would do it in a flamboyant, ridiculous way, so my parents would never seriously consider it—how ludicrous to allow the eldest daughter to attend school instead of finding a husband. I had to show them why nursing was worth pursuing—I had to make my case to a lawyer and—worse—my mother! I should just get it over with, I thought to myself. I knew if I presented it properly, Father would understand. Mother might take some work, but if I could get Father to say yes...I held my breath, straightened my posture, and made my way down the hall to my parents' room.

Inside, a rancid smell hit me. My father was seated bent over in the bed. He gurgled a black, grainy substance into a chamber pot while my mother stroked his back. His nightclothes were streaked with pale shades of yellow from sweat.

I stared, shocked.

My mother held a glass of water to his lips. He sipped, sloshed it about, and spit. With a gentle touch on the back of his neck, my mother guided him down onto his pillow. She examined the contents of the chamber pot and then fixed her eyes on me. She beckoned me as she walked out. "Emeline?"

I hesitated, thinking it was only supposed to be a cold, and then followed her quick heels, staring at her dark hair pulled back into a tight bun.

"This is not an ordinary case of dyspepsia," she said.

"Do you think it's influenza?"

"I don't know. He says it feels like something is slicing him from the inside." She made a clawing gesture across her stomach. She stopped and turned around. "This—this isn't normal." She held out the chamber pot. The putrid-smelling contents resembled wet coffee grounds. "He's hardly eaten anything. I don't know what this is. He doesn't have anything in his stomach."

"What's wrong?" Lillian and Ruth popped out from around the corner, having been listening in again.

My mother jumped and then glared at them. "Go downstairs, please."

Their eyes shot to me.

"Go," she ordered. "And get dressed."

Lillian stopped and flashed worried eyes back before leading Ruth past us toward the stairs.

I returned my attention to my mother. "I should send for the doctor."

She took a deep breath and sighed. "No, I'll send for Dr. Morris. Go sit with him. I'll only be a moment."

I turned back and jumped when Lillian leapt out again, without Ruth this time. I brought my hand to my chest at first, not sure how she'd sneaked there so quickly, but then I narrowed my eyes and dropped my hands. "Didn't Mother just tell you to go downstairs?"

"Is Father all right?"

"I don't know." I walked past her.

"Fix him."

I turned back. "Mother's sending for the doctor."

"No. You can fix him. You know how. You can."

"Lillian."

"You can, you can." She bounced.

"Lillian," I said with enough force in my voice to stop her, "go downstairs."

She scowled at me, pushing her chin out.

"Now."

She narrowed her eyes at me before stomping down the hall, probably only to sneak back the moment I turned my back.

I returned to my parents' room and lowered myself into the rocking chair next to the bed. My father's large belly rose high and then fell. His breath rustled his droopy mustache with a low rumble. It was only supposed to be a cold. I wished I did know more nursing so I could help him. He couldn't be too sick. It couldn't be serious. What if it was serious?

I wished I were a little girl again. I wanted him to pick me up and spin me around and around. I wanted him to put me on his shoulders so I could see the city, or let James and me hang from his arms and swing us back and forth, pretending he was a giant. Sunday walks in Forest Park. Back then he'd seemed too powerful to get sick. I couldn't remember him having ever gotten sick. He'd seemed invulnerable. He was a strong lawyer who wore fancy suits and argued on behalf of the innocent. Whenever something didn't make sense, he could explain it, make it right. He knew everything; he could do anything. He was strong and protected us. He would wrestle a wild beast to protect us, and in fact he had when he stopped a mad dog from attacking Lillian when we were little. He took care of me when I fell ill, stroked my hair, read me stories, and made me laugh.

I noticed droplets of sweat along his thin hairline and was searching for a cloth when his snore broke into a wet choke. He hacked himself out of sleep and up into a slumped position.

I grabbed the glass of water from the nightstand. "Father, Father, drink this." I lifted the glass to his mouth.

He held the hacking back long enough to take a sip, but when he swallowed, his throat constricted and he spewed water all over the bed and my arm. I pulled back, and he gagged and gagged until more black tar gurgled down his chest. I stepped back, horrified. I didn't know what to do. I just stared. He wouldn't stop. He gagged, gagged, gagged until bright red blood dribbled down his chin.

Almost a month later, we crowded into my parents' room, positioning ourselves among my parents' dressing tables, a vanity, the washstand, and the bulky armoire. I held little Ruth on my hip and stood near the door. My father lay there pale and wilted, his lips stained red. Dried blood streaked the rumpled sheets. My father's condition had worsened until Dr. Morris informed us of the need to remove a tumor from his stomach. The doctor had warned us the procedure might not save him, so my father asked to see all of us together in case this was the end. I told myself this would not be his final goodbyes. He would get better. He had to. We needed him. We all needed him. He could always calm Mother, encourage me to take a risk, guide James to pursue the right and just thing, inspire confidence in Florence, and tickle giggles and good behavior out of my youngest sisters. He took care of us. He was going to be all right. He was going to get better. He had to get better.

He asked for James, who had Lillian by the hand. My brother clung to his composure, but his eyes were red. James released Lillian and maneuvered around Mother and Florence, who were sitting in chairs next to the bed. Florence clutched my mother's hand, and my mother clutched her embroidered handkerchief.

"James." My father fumbled for his grasp.

James clasped his hand and lowered himself.

"Be strong. You will need to be the head of the family," my father's voice rasped.

James closed his eyes and shook his head slightly but didn't say anything. My father squeezed his hand. James bent over and clutched my father and then retreated to a chair next to the window. He dropped his head into his hands. Lillian nudged him until he sat up and took her in his arms.

"Lillian?"

She hesitantly turned out of James' hug and inched her way to Father.

He reached out and touched her cheek. "You're the only one who can fix a smile on my face no matter how difficult my day. Don't ever stop. Take care of Ruth. She looks up to you."

Lillian hugged him and then turned around red-faced and stomped over to me.

"Watch over your mother," my father told Florence.

Stopping in front of me, Lillian lowered her brow and crinkled her nose. Her lips were tight as she whispered, "Why didn't you fix him?"

My stomach lurched and I swallowed. "I told you I couldn't."

"Bring me Ruth."

I glanced at my father. "I'm not a nurse," I whispered to Lillian. "I'm nothing." I walked past her and lowered Ruth to the bed. She crawled around our father and snuggled him.

He squeezed her with one arm. "You'll always be my little squirrel. Keep Lillian out of trouble. It's a big job, but you're a big girl now, aren't you?"

Ruth's pupils grew.

Then he reached for my hand. I clutched his and submitted to his pull. I sat on the bed and leaned forward so he could whisper into my ear. "You have to take care of them, too. James cannot do it alone. I'm going to need you to make sacrifices. You're strong enough. No matter what you have to do, no matter how extreme, you will have to sacrifice for your family for the rest of your life."

I pulled back and stared into his eyes, unsure exactly what he meant, but I didn't care. He thought he was dying and all I wanted was to make him know I'd do whatever he wanted. I would worry about understanding later. I would ask him the next time we were alone. For now, I closed my eyes and silently swore it. "I promise, no matter what it takes. I will." I stood and turned away so he wouldn't have to see me cry. I wiped the tears off my cheeks with the back of my hand.

He turned his head to face my mother, who took his hand with both of hers. Her chin quivered as tears dripped down her swollen face onto her sleeves and dress.

I put my hand on Florence's shoulder. She trembled, staring at our parents with pink eyes.

"I love you," Father said.

She sobbed harder.

Lillian was now sitting on James' lap, her arms around his neck and her head leaning against his shoulder.

"I love you." My mother kissed his hand. "I can't handle this, Charles. Please. Please don't leave me. Please, don't leave me. Please." She wept. "I know—I know I'll do something horrible if you leave me. I will. I will." She wheezed between sobs.

Ruth watched with her eyes and mouth in the shape of little O's.

My mother's words filled me with a feeling far beyond fear or pity. They made my hands tremble.

"When you feel sad," his voice caught in his throat, "remember how much I love you and how much it will hurt me if you do anything horrible."

Ruth buried her head in my father's side. She seemed unsure as to why everyone was so upset.

My mother folded over onto the bed and bawled, gasping for air between sobs, her hair coming unpinned. He always knew what to say to her. She couldn't carry out some dramatic rampage of grief if she knew he wouldn't approve. She loved him too much. She needed him—we needed him. I needed him. He couldn't die. He wouldn't die when we needed him. He was strong. He would be strong because he knew how much we needed him.

His somber gaze circled the room, meeting our eyes one by one. "I love you all so much." His voice broke and he heaved. He closed his eyes, took in a deep breath and choked on it. For the first time in my life, I watched my father cry. I watched him weep.

After the operation, my mother refused to leave Father. She sat there all night and day, staring at him. After a particularly long night, I insisted she eat something and get some sleep. I told her to take just an hour while I sat with Father.

After some time, I heard her skirts rustling down the hall. I knew she was coming back, so I left. I passed her and saw James in the hall. I quickly squeezed his hand and asked him to sit with

Mother and then headed down the stairs. As I reached the middle step, I heard my mother wail, a sound I had been dreading. I rushed back up. James hovered at the top landing, his hands hanging limp and his transfixed expression unmistakable.

I grabbed his shoulders and he nodded. I wrapped my arms around him and clung tightly to him. I let go. "Mother?"

His eyes glistened when he glanced back toward the room. I charged down the hall. My father lay still and silent, just as if he were asleep, but his bulbous belly no longer rose and fell with gentle breath. My mother hung over him, her back to me, her hands covering her face. As she brought them down, something glimmered, and I realized she had scissors in her hand.

"Mother, what are you doing?"

She drove the shears toward my father's face.

"Stop!" I lunged forward. I grabbed her, and she whirled around with a chunk of hair between her fingers. A small bald spot disfigured my father's hairline.

She held it up. "He's gone." Tears cascaded down her cheeks, and she nearly collapsed into my arms.

I grasped her as she bawled on my shoulder. I held her like that and looked down at my father's face, his swollen belly, and his sagging skin. It felt as if we stood there for a long time. When Mother released me, her puffy red face was contorted.

"I should get James and the girls," I said.

She covered her face with her hands, still clasping the scissors.

I peeled them out of her fingers and held them to my bosom. "I'll be right back."

James still stood there in the hall. He looked lost and confused. I touched his arm. "James, I have to tell the girls. Will you stay with Mother? I don't think she can handle this."

He nodded without looking at me, hesitated, and then walked toward the room.

I faltered halfway down the stairs and crumbled onto the step. My corset dug into my hips and my powder-blue skirt puffed up around me. Breathe, I told myself, breathe. I closed my eyes. They couldn't see me upset. I had to be strong for them. I could cry myself to sleep later. Father wanted me to be strong. I dabbed my eyes to make sure there weren't any tears and then fanned air at them. Just don't cry, I told myself. You can't cry. I inhaled deeply, stood, and walked into the front hall.

"Miss Evans?"

I halted.

John Dorr was loitering in the main entryway. "Oh." I jolted and looked away.

"Good day," he said. "Your servant just went to find you."

I looked at the floor, the wall, all around. I couldn't bear to look him in the eye. I always avoided those eyes. We were not well acquainted, but every woman who had been introduced to this man knew those eyes. "How do you do, Mr. Dorr?"

"I'm well. I hope you are not busy?"

"I'm very sorry, Mr. Dorr, but I'm afraid I don't—my parents cannot visit at this time. My father—"

"Yes. My father told me he's not too well. I'm here to call on you, actually. My mother—and I—thought you might need a distraction. You must be terribly busy and not in the mood to visit."

"No. I'm sorry, it's just—" I couldn't say it. Should I say it? I wondered—should I tell Mr. Dorr before I tell my own flesh? I didn't know what to do. I couldn't look at him, let alone say it.

"Are you all right?"

"My father—my—he—he's passed." I unwillingly flashed my eyes up at him. They locked with his, and suddenly I couldn't take it. "I'm sorry." I couldn't control it. It was real. I dropped the shears and brought my trembling hand to my mouth.

Mr. Dorr reached out and clasped my hand. "Forgive me. I'm so sorry. I hadn't heard. Your servant didn't say…"

"It just happened now." I gestured down the hall. "I—was—going to tell everyone."

He straightened. "Oh, dear God."

I nodded.

"Are you all right? Can—can I help?"

"I have to tell my sisters. I—I have to call for the doctor."

"Please. Let me worry about the doctor. I have my carriage. I'll go straightaway."

I lowered my gaze to the warm hand clasping my own.

"Are you sure I shouldn't stay? I can send my driver alone. I can stay."

"Thank you, but no. I'm all right." I wiped the tears from my cheeks and forced my eyes to meet his—to prove it.

"I'll go straight to the doctor." He paused. "My—my condolences."

I sank deep into his black eyes and swallowed. "Thank you."

He nodded, did an about-face, and left.

I lingered a moment until Kathy appeared behind me. "There you are, miss. You found Mr. Dorr then?"

I kept my back to her. "Kathy." I swallowed and sniffed. "I need you to gather the girls. Father…he's gone."

I felt dizzy and on the verge of hyperventilation during the funeral. Afterward, at our house, I shuffled from room to room amid swollen faces and consoling glances, trying to make sure nothing went wrong, for my mother's sake. The larger a funeral, the more that people assumed the family cared, and Mother wanted everyone to know how much we cared. Although we had a substantial parlor, people spilled out into the foyer and the dining and sitting rooms. My mother had filled the house with fragrant white flowers of every kind, and I struggled to breathe as I set out food in the parlor and checked on preparations in the kitchen. I just wanted to run away, but I had to keep an eye on Mother.

I struggled to find her in the ocean of black in our parlor. Black dresses, black slacks, black shoes, shawls, and gloves. The house itself was shrouded in black, too. We'd tied black crepe and netting around the doorknobs, hung black wreaths inside and out, and muffled the door chime. We draped my father's portrait in velvet, locked the piano, and covered all the mirrors with black sheaths.

I had wrapped myself in a black silk-and-taffeta dress with lace details that scratched at my wrists and neck. I wore a long locket necklace with my father's hair in it. Mother had made one for each of us, but I found it disturbing and planned to stop wearing it after the funeral.

I spotted my mother and weaved through mourners to get to her side. "How are you?"

She glanced up from a conversation that continued without her. "I'm fine. Thank you."

I sighed. So far nothing had been ruined. She had gone on a frenzy planning the elaborate spectacle as her last grand gesture of love, but I knew she hadn't let herself realize that he was gone. I expected an emotional collapse at any moment, and I knew that if one thing went wrong, she would crumble in front of everyone.

"Florence took your sisters upstairs."

I sighed wishing I was with them, but my sister's pure heart could calm better than mine could. "We have enough food?" My mother's droopy eyes shot open.

"More than enough." I held up my hands.

She looked all around, bobbing her head. "I should have gotten more flowers."

"There's plenty. It's perfect."

She touched my arm, her eyes wandering.

I took her hand in both of mine. "Mother?"

She looked at me.

"Let me worry for you." I released her.

A man appeared next to her to express his sympathies.

I started to search for my brother. I walked into the foyer and gazed up at the staircase, where an avalanche of flowers flowed down the banisters. I was wondering if James had gone up, too, when I heard Dr. Morris' voice nearby. "It doesn't make sense," he said. "He had more time."

I froze.

"It was quite sudden, but isn't that common after surgery?" I heard a woman with a heavy-bodied voice ask.

I turned to find the location of the conversation and saw the doctor standing on the left side of the staircase. He faced away from me but at such an angle that I could see him thrust his chin out and stiffen his expression as he gripped the glass of sherry in hand. He reached up with his other hand and scratched a touch of baldness on the back of his head. "I suppose, but there are usually signs, a suggestion as to what went wrong." He shook his head. "Something—it doesn't fit."

He didn't notice me, but I couldn't just stare. I pretended to look for someone.

The doctor sipped his sherry. "It doesn't make sense."

"What are you saying?" I didn't know the blond woman he spoke to, and her dry eyes suggested she hadn't known my father. "He was showing improvement?"

Dr. Morris ran his fingers over his mustache. "No. No. Surviving that disease is nearly impossible, but he could have lasted longer with a few more—"

A voice interrupted my eavesdropping. "Miss Evans?"

I looked up and John Dorr's black eyes entranced me.

"I can't tell you how sorry I am for your loss."

I blinked. "Oh." I took a deep breath and considered how to politely excuse him. Then I realized he gave me reason to linger. "Thank you." I stepped slightly to the side so I could face Dr. Morris while talking with Mr. Dorr.

"Your father and my father were better friends than I realized. He said he owes him all of his success."

I listened for Dr. Morris' hoarse voice. I glanced away from Mr. Dorr and spotted the blond woman.

She lifted her hand to her chest. "I cannot imagine."

"Are you all right?" Mr. Dorr asked.

"Oh, I'm sorry." I turned my attention back to him. "I'm... obviously..." I swallowed.

"Of course." He lowered his chin. "I wanted you to know if you ever need anything, I—"

I kept my eyes on the attractive young man in front of me even though I listened to Dr. Morris. "More than half the bottle was gone," he continued. "There's no excuse for using that much morphine. I clearly instructed Mrs. Evans. I'm wondering if she accidentally..." He trailed off.

I peeked over Mr. Dorr's shoulder and saw Dr. Morris lift his eyebrows and widen his eyes.

"What?" I whispered.

"What?" Mr. Dorr asked.

My mouth hung open. "Um," I fumbled. "I should thank you for your assistance...that day."

He lowered his gaze and spoke softly. "I only wish I could have done more."

"You couldn't."

"If you or your family ever need assistance, I want you to know you can call upon me."

Mr. Dorr said more, but I wasn't listening. I could hear Dr. Morris again. I couldn't help but move my eyes in his direction. "I won't mention it," he grumbled. "The situation is unfortunate enough, but to think Mrs. Evans may have been responsible..."

I suddenly felt hot and dizzy and bent forward a little, bringing my hand to my chest. My lungs constricted, and a lump in my stomach melted like butter.

Mr. Dorr reached out. "Are you..."

I tried to inhale. "I—I need—some—" I couldn't breathe.

The people around me were so close. There were so many. My corset felt too tight. The black ribbons on the staircase, the black shrouds on the mirrors, the black wreaths on the walls, and my black dress swelled and merged into the rest of the black until everything disappeared.

It felt like falling.

Then I felt my feet moving, heard my locket clinking, and felt my weight in John Dorr's arms. I saw flashes of my boots shuffling and clacking as he guided me to the right of the staircase, down the hall, and out the servants' door just before the kitchen. The bright light and cool breeze jolted me. I gulped air desperately.

Mr. Dorr stood at my side, holding me up with his left hand wrapped tightly around my waist and his right under the crook of my arm. "Are you all right?"

"I—I—think—I might faint." I breathed heavily.

My mouth salivated, nausea crashed into me in a huge wave, and my knees buckled. He tried to hold me up, but the black fell over my eyes like a full-length weeping veil, and a dizzying buzz in my head prevented me from thinking.

"I'll take her," a distant voice said.

Then the blackness gave way to light. I was on my knees, my hands flat on the ground. My stomach contracted and my sight returned. I vomited yellow bile into the grass.

I felt our servant Kathy next to me and glanced over my shoulder to be sure.

"I asked Mr. Dorr to leave." Kathy nodded. "He knew you were sick. I knew you wouldn't want him to see."

"Thank you," I said with an exhale. I wiped my mouth and cringed. I fell back onto the lawn and put my hand on my head. "Did anyone else see?"

"No, honey." Kathy dimpled. The little lines around her eyes and the corners of her lips were like creases in warm bread. "He held you up almost straight. No one noticed you looked faint."

"I don't know what happened. I was listening to…" I remembered what Dr. Morris had said. What did he say about my mother? Did he really think—no, he said my father was losing the fight. He said he wouldn't say anything. Was that right? Yes, I reassured myself. Thank God, I thought. But he told that woman—what if she spread a rumor? I panted, dizziness returning. My mother—my family—we wouldn't be able to handle that. No, she wouldn't say anything. He wouldn't say anything. They wouldn't. They wouldn't. I rubbed my cheek and slid my trembling fingers to my lips. "I was listening to Mr. Dorr and all of a sudden—"

"You're doing too much is all, miss. It's all right. No one suspects you're ill." Kathy rubbed my back. "If anyone does, they wouldn't expect anything less."

I lifted heavy eyes, heaved forward, and vomited again.

# Two

*November 1900*

My mother wept, swathed in black and bent over her writing desk in the sitting room, which she had decorated with light, cheery colors long ago. She existed like a ghost—out of place in the world of color and light. It had been like this for months.

I touched her shoulder. "Mother? Are you all right?"

She struggled between crying and breathing. "No, no, no. I'm not all right. I am not all right!" She clenched a letter between her hands.

"What is it?"

She sucked in air.

"Who wrote you?"

"My brother."

"Is he not well?"

"We have no money."

I stiffened, dumbfounded. "What?"

"The funeral expenses—I didn't realize—the surgery and medical costs and living the way we live without any income. We shouldn't have—I didn't—" She shook her head. "We are—we..." She choked on her words, but I knew: destitute, poor, hopeless.

I stumbled backward and bumped against the arm of the white sofa. "What do we do?"

"James said when he starts working he will send us a little money each month."

She told James? Why hadn't he said anything to me? "He can't earn enough to support himself and us."

"I know." She turned around to reveal feverish eyes and a red face. "We have to sell the house. We have to sell everything." She blubbered and slumped back onto the writing desk.

I hesitated. "How long have you known about this?"

She buried her head in her arms and muffled her words. "I don't know."

"Why did you let us buy mourning toilettes?" I asked. "Why did we have that huge procession? The hand-carved casket? The glass-window viewing carriage? The family plot? All the flowers and food—we didn't have to do any of that."

"I don't know!"

I took several short breaths. "It's all right. It's not your fault... but where will we go?"

"My brother."

"Uncle Robert?" I thought about the tiny house, his stuffy wife, and their two plump children. "Does he have room?"

Her head was still buried in her arms. "James is going to move into a boardinghouse, and we will share a room."

"The girls?"

"All of us."

"All of us?" Five women. "One room?"

"We don't have any other choice."

She gripped her handkerchief with one hand and clenched the other tightly on top of her lap.

I knelt and took her hands in mine, including the soggy handkerchief.

"I don't know what else to do." She sobbed harder. "I can't take care of you by myself. I can't do anything."

"It's going to be all right." I looked into her bloodshot eyes. I thought about my father—my promise. "I'll figure something out. No matter what. I will take care of us."

I rushed to the Dorrs' house. The servant asked that I wait in the parlor, a spacious room decorated with rich velvet and animal hides. Although Mr. Richard Dorr worked in the same field as my father had, he had acquired much more wealth. Over the past few months, he'd made it known that my father had helped him start his firm, now a great success. Richard and his wife, Elisa, had been wonderful after the funeral. Even though the rest of my family didn't know them as well as my father had, they stopped by regularly with various gifts of kindness. Elisa became a steady companion for my mother and saw to the rest of us quite regularly. They made us promise to come to them if we ever needed anything—anything.

Elisa glided into the room. "Emeline?" She had a sickly sweet appearance, feathery hair, and a pink nose.

I tried to greet her without revealing my panic but failed. I couldn't believe what I was about to do, but I had to—I had to if I wanted to keep my promise.

"What's wrong? Is everything all right? Where's your mother?"

"She doesn't know I'm here."

"What's happened?" She motioned to a chair. "Please."

"I can't." I gripped my hands together. "I just can't bear to be still right now."

"Emeline, what's wrong?"

"You said I should come to you if we ever needed anything."

"Of course."

"I'm afraid we need a great deal right now."

"Emeline, tell me, what is the matter?"

"We've run out of money."

"What?"

My cheeks flushed. No one spoke of money in polite company. "We're bankrupt."

"But—your father…"

"My mother has never had to handle finances, let alone…She didn't think. She wanted to honor my father. She—we had that elaborate funeral and procession. The doctor's bill alone." I caught Elisa's eyes. "We have to sell our house."

Elisa lowered herself into the chair she had offered me, her hand to her chest.

"James is going to move out. My mother is going to take us to her brother's house."

"Emeline, I'm so sorry. You know we will do whatever we can to help your family during this time. We can spare a little money, but—"

I shook my head. "That's not why I've come."

She lifted her gaze.

I inhaled deeply. "Do—"

"Emeline. What gives us the pleasure?" Richard had entered the room wearing a dark blue smoking jacket. He was a tall, slender man with little hair remaining on the top of his head.

"Good afternoon." I lowered my chin and curled my toes inside my boots. "I'm so sorry if I've disturbed you."

He lowered himself into an oversize chair. "Not at all." He glanced at his wife and observed her solemn expression. "What's this about now?" He talked with an unlit pipe clenched between his teeth. He pulled out a pack of matches.

"Dear, I'm afraid Emeline and her family are having some troubles." Elisa leaned forward and glanced at me, unsure whether it was her place to tell him.

Richard ripped off a match and prepared to strike it.

"I'm afraid we have—we're—the doctor and funeral expenses were too much. We have nothing left." I paused. "We're losing our home."

Richard's face fell. "I'm so sorry to hear that."

I nodded rigidly.

"Do you need money?"

I shook my head. I knew no loan could be enough to last, and we had no means to repay. I had to ask for much, much more—so much that I had to give something in return, and I had only one thing to give.

"How can we help you?" Elisa clasped her hands.

"There is something you could do."

"Go on." Richard struck the match and it burst into a little flame.

"It would help us not just now but long term as well."

Richard lifted the match to his pipe.

"And I know my father would approve and be eternally grateful."

"What is it, Emeline?" Elisa asked.

Richard started to puff.

I pursed my lips and exhaled. "Could I marry your son?"

Richard's pipe drooped.

Elisa brought her hands to her mouth, so only her wide eyes showed.

They must have thought me mad. Like most girls aware of John Dorr, I considered him beyond my reach. He had nearly black hair, which he wore slicked back, and he kept his face clean-shaven, a new trend that revealed his sharp cheekbones. His strange features gave him an almost-sinister type of beauty. An intriguingly handsome man from a well-off family, he should have been taken long ago, but his arduous education and antisocial tendencies gave him rare opportunity for courtship. His parents surely had high expectations of a bride, but the past few months had revealed the extent to which Richard Dorr felt indebted to my father. It wasn't much, but I had made a promise to do whatever it took.

Richard cringed and rapidly waved the match out. "What?"

I put my hands up. "I know it's outrageous to ask, but if I were married, I could take some of the pressure off my mother. She wouldn't have to care for me, and I could send her a little money each month, too. Perhaps they could afford something—a tenement."

Elisa lowered her hands.

I wondered how they saw me in that moment. Was I still a twenty-three-year-old girl with feathery-fawn hair, a girl who had attended university, who came from a well standing, middle-class family? Or did I appear frazzled, desperate, and poor? I gulped. "I know, I don't have anything to offer your son or your family, no dowry, but I can offer my promise that I will be the very best wife to him."

They stared at me, hardly blinking.

"I've had no other prospects. I refused suitors while at Grantville." I failed to restrain my tears as I begged. "If I became a Dorr, I could help my family. You would be rescuing them from destitution." I stopped myself.

Elisa blinked, her mouth open. "Emeline—I—I don't know—"

"My father wouldn't have wanted this for us. Please. I will be the best wife. I will sacrifice for him. I will honor him for the rest of my days. I will do anything to make him happy. Please."

Elisa's mouth froze open.

Richard lowered his eyes and then brought them back to me.

"Emeline? I—" Elisa shook her head.

It was too much to ask, and I knew it. I felt my cheeks flush. "But…I understand. I'm sorry. I should never—I—I—have to leave." I rushed into the foyer, scrambled for my coat, and fumbled with the double doors.

"Emeline, wait!" Elisa said, but I could not stop.

I fled.

I tried to forget my embarrassment for the next few days but relived the scene over and over until my mother approached me Saturday afternoon. She entered the sitting room timidly while I read next to the warm fire. Her voice trembled and her eyes glistened as she informed me that Elisa and Richard Dorr were calling with their son. Her bottom lip trembled and she clenched her hands, unaware of any courtship, unsure of my sentiments. Then I smiled, and she assumed the rest. I watched her body and mind sink with relief for the first time since my father had died. She reached out, clasped my hands, and pulled me off the sofa. "A wedding, my daughter will have a wedding."

I hopped with her in a little circle until she dropped my hands and started pacing. "It will have to be small, in mourning, of course, and soon, within a month."

My eyes shot wide open. A month?

"Oh, and with the holidays, but that's good. It's good. Everyone should be happy to come for a Christmas ceremony and to see you before you move so far away."

"Far away?"

"The Dorrs said their son's job opportunity in Labellum will not wait for any honeymoon, and don't you worry, I won't make any problems for you, dear. I won't say one word. I will make no complaints, even if they don't want a ceremony at all. I don't care. You are getting married!" She reached toward me but pulled back and held her hands under her chin, under her growing grin. "Your father would be so proud."

I nodded along with her assumptions, but inside I wondered, where's Labellum?

After the Dorrs left, I sneaked outside and sat on the front steps of our house. It felt haunted by the lonely feeling of a home that wouldn't be ours for much longer. We lived in a red brick house with white-framed windows flanking the front double doors. I folded my arms, not having brought a coat. I embraced the bite of the cold as a form of martyrdom. There still wasn't any snow, but the icy air nipped at my nose and reminded me of days spent playing rosy-cheeked in a white childhood wonderland long ago.

I heard the door open and close, followed by footsteps. I stiffened and straightened. I felt someone standing next to me.

"I believe congratulations are in order?" he said.

"Last rites sound more appropriate." I looked up at my brother. He chuckled.

"It's not funny."

"I thought it was clever." He handed me my black coat.

James wore his black frock coat over gray trousers. He squinted out at the street as a horse and carriage clip-clopped and rattled down the road. "I figured I'd come out here and tell you to stop pouting."

"I'm not pouting."

"Uh-huh."

I sighed. "How did you know?"

"Emeline, you can fool Mother and Mr. and Mrs. Dorr and him, but you can't fool me." He knew me too well.

"I don't know what else to do. It's going to save our family."

He grunted and dropped down next to me. "I thought all girls wanted to get married."

"Maybe I'm not a girl."

"I always thought you were built for railroad work."

I squinted one eye at him with annoyed amusement. "I would think I'd be a well-dressed lawyer—like you." I poked him.

He laughed at the assault. "Yes, you are probably too weak for hard labor."

We chuckled and then simmered down, submitting to the depressed state lingering around our home. The breeze rustled the branches of nearby oak trees, little dead leaves still clinging to them.

"Did you see him?" I asked.

"He seems fine enough, a little bit gangly, but other than that…"

"He's so quiet. I'm afraid I'm going to be bored."

"Boring is good." James' voice lifted.

"How's that?" I folded my arms atop my knees and laid my head down.

"Boring is better than obnoxious. Boring means you'll be married but not irritated."

I admired James' soft boyish features and realized that his confidence made him seem very grown up. "Maybe I want more in marriage than to not be annoyed."

"I thought you didn't want to get married?"

"I don't."

"Why is that again?"

I tilted my head and narrowed my eyes at him.

"Well? Is it something about him?"

"Promise you won't laugh."

"I promise nothing unless under the threat of torture."

I gave him a stern look, the kind only an older sister can give—a look that threatened torture.

"All right, all right, I promise."

"I kind of wanted...to work."

"Work?"

I lifted my head. "You know, work, like what you'll be doing soon."

"At a law firm?"

"No." I hesitated and blushed. "I kind of wanted to be a nurse."

"Really?" He grinned.

I gave him another look.

He raised his hands in defense. "I'm not laughing." He put his hands down. "I didn't know you liked medicine, is all."

"I couldn't tell anyone, could I? Mother would faint."

"So you weren't going to really pursue it."

"No, I was. At Grantville College I took classes. A lot of women are doing it." I talked fast, excited. "I was waiting for the right time to ask...Father. He would have let me, I know it. Just...didn't work out."

James lowered his eyes.

"I don't know." I covered my face with my hands and then tore them away. "Obviously, I'm not going to be a nurse. I don't mind John Dorr, or I didn't until today. The problem is, I don't want to move away from everyone. I never would have—it's all a huge mistake." I clenched my eyes shut and shook my head. "But I can't take it back." I leaned over and wrapped my hands around James' waist. "I don't know what to do. I want to stay with you."

He put his hand on my back. "Emma, you know we could never stay together forever. I'll probably get hitched soon, and then where would you be?"

I didn't answer.

"You'd just be a burden. Our family needs this. You're doing the right thing."

"He's going to take me away, though. I'm going to miss everyone so much."

"Even the three hens?" He snickered. He'd come up with the nickname for our three sisters because they had the ability to appear perfectly calm and together until something excited them into a flurry of noise and feathers.

I smiled at the thought and smacked his knee. "This is serious!"

"You know you'll visit us, and when I've gotten settled into the firm, I'll come out to see you all the time."

"Really?" I moved my head closer to his chest.

"Yes."

I sat back up.

"I know you're scared, but Emma, this is what people do. You get married. You have children."

"*You* don't have to."

"Yes, I do." His face hardened. "If I lived out on my own and didn't get married, I would starve to death, but not before traipsing around in trousers full of holes."

I held back a giggle. "What?"

"I don't know how to do any of the 'secret' stuff you and Mother do. If someone threw me in a kitchen with everything I needed and a set of detailed instructions, I'd cook my own hand."

I laughed, nodding. "But you are moving out alone."

"And you can't get mad if my trousers are uneven at your wedding."

I chuckled a little.

"You need someone to take care of you, and John Dorr needs you to take care of him. I know he's not everything you hoped for, but at least he's not horrible. Just think what you could end up with if you don't get married now."

I raised my eyebrows and wondered what type of prospects I'd face as a destitute woman living in one room with my mother and three sisters.

"My point is, maybe you're just a little scared. I'm sure if you give this John Dorr a chance, he'll end up just fine, and if he doesn't…" He stood and pulled me up by the hands.

I popped up. "Yes?"

"I'll come get you."

# Three

January 1901
Labellum, Missouri

My eyes moved across the steamboat passengers. Death lingered on the tip of everyone's tongue, and everyone was clad in black crepe and taffeta. What an odd time to be newlyweds. I looked at John and considered him, clinging to the hope that affection would grow with time. I touched the ring he had given me—a tiny pearl atop a gold band surrounded by a circle of white opal spheres. Florence had eyed it after the ceremony. "Emeline?" she said as her smile turned. "Pearls mean tears."

John had recently graduated law school, and his father wanted him to mentor under a friend, Mr. Lewis Coddington, who had a firm in Labellum, Missouri. On January 28, 1901, a few weeks after our private ceremony and only six days after Britain's Queen Victoria had died, my new husband and I sat silent and still on a steamboat bound for the distant town. Not only were my family and I in mourning, but people all over the world were mourning the queen. A marriage was supposed to be a happy occasion, but the dark curiosities surrounding death twisted the minds of everyone around us.

We docked at the edge of the little town, nestled between two bluffs that gave it the appearance of a hole in the side of the world. I had lived in the city for my entire life, and now my best option was to live in a hole. We plodded off the boat, and John led me to our surrey, a plum-colored boxy carriage with a fringed canopy top and bench seat. The gray-haired driver made sure the horse clopped through town quickly.

"Just wait until you see the window molding." John went on and on about the house he had found. "Oh, and the parlor. It truly is an architectural wonder!" He had explained that the previous owners had left all their furniture and decorations. I didn't know why anyone would abandon their furnishings, but I imagined it was a sad story. Still, if the house was lovely, I knew I could be happy. The town was tiny and my husband a stranger, but I could be happy running a beautiful home. It was the one thing I would have authority over. I'd always detested my mother's décor. Whenever I complained about it, she reminded me that when I got married, I could decorate however I wanted and I didn't have to use a single thing she had chosen. It wasn't as if I could—those things were all gone now.

"We're getting closer." John held himself up to see how far away we were, but the rocking surrey pitched him back onto the seat.

I observed him as he grinned, bobbing around to see past the horse and driver. At least he was twenty-five. Women in my situation had often found themselves married to fifty-year-old widowers. I hoped he thought well of me. We hadn't had much time to become acquainted during a brief engagement that got swept away with moving arrangements and the holidays. I hoped he didn't find my apparel unappealing. Unlike those who might mourn the queen for a few weeks, I would wear blacks, purples, and eventually white mourning garb for almost another year because of my father's death.

"We're here! We're here!" John shouted and unsuccessfully tried to stand again.

I lifted my head and sat taller to see, struggling to glimpse through trees flashing past. When I finally laid my eyes on it, I saw a structure that was not what any home should be. The driver veered right at a break in the trees and took us on a straight path toward the monster. When we stopped, John jumped off to fiddle with something before offering his hand to help me out. If he had offered it immediately, I wouldn't have taken it because I'd been stunned into stone, staring at the bizarre construction before me.

"It was built in 1880," John said. "A gothic revival, I believe."

I unfroze and remembered that it was supposed to be a happy day, but the only thing I could say reflected my disenchantment. "It looks...dark."

"What do you mean? It's white." John reached out his hand, and after a brief hesitation, I grasped it and stepped out, drawing up my skirt to prevent a snag.

How could a white house seem so dark? The entire building, apart from the russet wood-shingled roof, was red brick painted over with a pasty white. The red base seeped out from beneath the blanched masquerade. It was overbearing, like a fortress. A fortress bloodied by war and then disguised as a house by some conspirator or...perhaps...the house itself.

A ring of broad- and slender-trunked trees circled the house and then thickened into woods. Winter had stripped the trees naked and covered the forest floor with a rug of decay. I imagined a splash of sunset color in the fall, the broad leaves turning orange, yellow, and a blazing red before blanketing the ground with a sea of fire. But now skeletons lingered all around.

John raved about the structural design, but it wasn't a marvel—it was a catastrophe. Structurally sound at best. The anterior stuck out farther than the rest, and the sides jutted out like broken, lop-sided hips. The front doors were abnormally located to the right rather than in the center. My gaze drifted above the front doors to a slender and strange gothic window with intricate crown molding on the right hip of the house. Its twin faced out of the uneven left wing. The front had two windows so close together that they could have been one if there hadn't been a thick piece of frame between them.

"Is that the parlor?" I pointed at three-paned bay windows on the bottom floor.

"Uh, yes. The two tall windows above it are our chamber." John lugged a trunk off the surrey with the help of the driver.

"And the other windows?"

They eased the trunk to the ground. "More rooms."

"The porches…they're peculiar."

"I think they were additions."

The Greek-revival columns on the porches would actually have been quite attractive if they'd been a part of another house, but they didn't match a gothic revival—they only amplified its awkward state. The right porch had a few steps leading up to a small landing and the front doors. The bay windows completely interrupted the porches, separating them from each other. The left porch sat higher and stretched farther back, but because it had no steps, there was no way to reach it. I pictured some awkward little man deciding to build the porches and columns on a whim, having always desired a Greek revival and it being popular to remodel to one's own desires. People generally did so with the aid of a profes- sional to guide them, though.

"All right, let's go inside." John picked up two bags and led the way.

I walked behind, staring in wonder.

John opened the front double doors, releasing light into a long narrow hallway with a door directly to the left and a door facing us at the end. I'd assumed the awkward little man's whim had been applied only to the exterior of the home, but once inside, I realized he'd had more vigor than that. I peered down the hallway. "Where are the stairs?" In most homes, the stairwell was the first thing you saw, and many people took pride in the magnitude and luxury of theirs. It was a mark of station.

"They're around the corner." John dropped the bags next to the coat rack and hung his hat.

I detected the musty smell of cedar, lamp oil, and dead flowers.

John grasped a small oil candle lamp with handles in the shape of snakes from the table next to the coat rack. It had a flat top and a rounded base that came to a point in front in the style of a genie lamp. John sparked the flame, but it was the middle of the day.

"What are you doing?"

"You want to stumble in the dark?"

I shook my head. "It's daylight."

"There are no windows in the hallway, and I would prefer we left the doors closed unless someone is in a room."

"What?"

"It's a big house, and we don't want to lose each other. This way I'll always know where you are."

I shuddered. "Yes, but what a horrible way to live."

"I'm sure you'll find it quite convenient once you get used to it." He glided down the corridor. "Besides, it's only in the hallway."

I didn't follow. I stood in the gloomy passageway with a heavy feeling in my abdomen and an urge to whirl around and run home. "What about gases? The rooms have to be aired to prevent toxins from building up."

"You can air them daily if you must." He stopped at the first door on the left.

"What about the cost of oil?"

"Let me worry about the expenses." He motioned for me. "Come along then."

I stepped forward, hesitated and then went to him.

"This is the parlor." John opened the door on the left to an oversize room. The bay window faced out front. Cobalt wallpaper darkened the room, which brimmed with outdated bric-a-brac. Little figurines, jars, bowls, and statuettes crowded every table, shelf, and ledge. Such clutter had been stylish in my mother's day, but I intended to be liberated from it. I crept in and approached a bowl resting on a silver stand with four swirly legs and two twirling arms that rose over the basin and down slightly, as if intending to plunge into some life-giving liquid. My fingers followed the metal curves around and around. Most of the bowl was a tempting yellow, but it also had pink at the bottom left. The shade drifted upward like smoke, fading from pink to mauve to indigo and finally to yellow. I supposed it was intended to mimic a flower, but the edges of the bowl rose at two spots and formed what resembled the ears of an owl. I touched two circular indentations buried in the yellow like eyes. There was a beak, too, where the silver stand came to a point in the middle. It was as if someone had plucked the head off an owl and mounted it on a metallic forest.

My eyes dropped to the table that the bowl rested on, and I realized that the knickknacks distracted the eye from tangled table legs and bizarrely designed chairs of various sorts, none of which matched. Everything in the parlor was like that! The cabinets had winding appendages like tentacles. They burst out at all sides and darted back in toward the body but failed to make it before twisting all the way around and zapping back out again. Inanimate objects had hidden eyes built right in. Faces were embedded in every hunk of wood that could be found. The arms of chairs were carved with animal heads, paws, and claws. They gaped and smirked. Beady eyes peeked out from every crease and corner. Some were meant to be creatures, but others were just ambiguously lifelike. These peculiar things transformed the room into a murky woods filled with unknown beasts, and I felt lost in it all until I spotted another means of escape.

On the wall to the right, opposite the bay windows, I noticed a second parlor door. "Where does that lead?"

"You'll see." John motioned for me, and I weaved between the furniture to get back to him. He shut the door and led me down the hall. "The sitting room." John opened the door, and I nearly leapt, shocked by the bright pink wallpaper. The room was littered with ornamental chairs and tables, along with a writing desk and a prairie cabinet. It, too, had bric-a-brac and ruffles sprinkled over every tabletop, shelf, and ledge. Thousands of white and pink doilies drowned every table and chair and the little pink sofa, too. It reminded me of an ocean of pink goo. I was certain that if I were to sit in it, I would suffocate in a warm flesh-colored swamp. Everything in this room must be sold, I thought.

John closed the door. We turned left and faced another long corridor with two doors on the left and one on the right. The stairwell opened up like a cavern at the end, the first few steps exposed and then swallowed into the wall as they curved around.

John went to the door on the right first. "This here is the library and my study." He opened the door to reveal shelves of books, leather armchairs, reading tables, and a heavy wood desk with an overbearing chair like a dark throne. A narrow back rose to a point higher than any man's head. The chair was fashioned from a strange wood that looked cold and hard like metal. It was painted a blackish brown and bore sharp, elaborate etchings.

He closed the door and pointed across the hall at the first door on the left. "That is the parlor again, the door you asked about."

"We could have gone straight through?"

"I don't want to make a habit of taking shortcuts. These corridors are here for a reason."

I dropped my shoulders but tried to appear agreeable.

He opened the second door on the left. "The dining room." Inside was a narrow room with wood floors and wainscoting. The upper section of the walls had been covered in maroon wallpaper. High-backed chairs surrounded a long dinner table. A sideboard, a third the table's size, sat against the right wall, along with a rolling server and a cabinet topped with green decanters. I would be especially keen on ridding the room of its unrelenting nature theme. The chairs had insects carved into them. The table swirled with vines. The silver and the servers were shaped like salamanders and leaves. The pitcher even had a leaf for a lid. The decanters were made of bright, glowing green crystal, as if each had its own little fairy imprisoned inside. John shut the door.

Then he pointed to two doors to the right of the basement

stairs. "That's the bath chamber and the servants' entrance, which leads to the outhouse."

I opened the bath-chamber door to find a claw-foot tub, but oddly the feet looked like those of a crow or a raven, not a bear or a lion. An equally dark washstand, basin and jug accompanied the tub, with black birds flying in spirals around the jug and spreading to the basin as if plunging to their deaths.

"Shall we see the upstairs?" he asked.

"The kitchen?"

"It's in the basement." He pointed to the right of the staircase, where an even smaller set of stairs twisted down into a dark chasm.

"Down there?"

"Yes. You've seen houses like that in the city, I'm sure."

I had seen houses like that. Usually, the lady of the house never stepped foot in the kitchen because the family had cooks, butlers, and servants. My family hadn't even that many servants, so a newlywed couple certainly couldn't afford to pay poor souls to go down there.

"It's a marvel, really. Most homes around here don't have them because of the high water table, especially being so close to the river. Apparently, this property is on a slant and there's natural drainage. It is prone to leaks but stays cool for food storage. I'm told you can even keep ice down there in the summer."

"Wonderful."

"Come now, upstairs."

We scaled the constricted staircase. It twisted right after the first five or so steps and disappeared behind a wall. Once it turned, there were white walls on both sides and a low ceiling. It felt as if they leaned inward. After two more rights, we reached the landing and another dark hallway so narrow it couldn't be decorated with little tables or flower pots as most hallways were.

We passed a door on the right and one on the left. "Those rooms are furnished, but we have no use for them." A final door faced us at the end of the hallway. The staircase had circled around, and we were facing the front of the house again.

"And this is our chamber." John opened the door to reveal, finally, an agreeable room. It had pale wood floors and white walls. The furniture was plain, well crafted, and made of a nearly black wood. The white and mother-of-pearl statuettes and elegant wall hangings were also lovely. I tried to go in, but John closed the door before I could. "Let us get the rest of our things."

"Oh. All right."

We walked down the hall back to the stairs.

"Well?" John asked as we crept down the stairs. He probably expected me to join him in his ravings.

I forced a smile. "It's…unique."

"That is why I chose it."

"It's just not to my tastes. I'm sure I'll feel better once I redecorate."

"Redecorate?" John stopped in front of me in the middle of the stairwell.

"Yes. Redecorate." I felt hot and uncomfortable halted in the cramped space.

He turned around, scrunched his face, and shook his head. "No."

"Pardon me?" It felt as if the walls were creeping closer.

He folded his arms. "I don't think you should redecorate."

"But why?"

"We were lucky to find a home furnished and decorated. That is why I bought it."

"But it's—it's awful." I regretted saying it as soon as John's expression wilted.

But then his features hardened into a look of stern resolve. "I am sure you will come to like it with time." He continued down the stairs.

I felt the weight of disappointment. Not only was John forcing me to live uncomfortably in every way, but he was also wrenching away the one thing I controlled. We had descended all the way down the stairs and entered the hallway when I finally dismissed my mother's warnings to keep complaints to myself. "John?" I stopped next to the dining room.

"Hmm?"

"I don't think I will like it with time."

He turned at the end of the hall and rubbed the back of his neck. "My father and Mr. Coddington went to great lengths to find a home that would require little from us, as a wedding gift. We should be grateful."

"I am grateful, but decorating and making a home a sanctuary is a wife's duty. I want to create a sanctuary for you."

"I'm already happy," he said. "I don't need you to do anything. You should be thankful to get so much when you hadn't even a dowry."

My muscles stiffened and my mouth fell open.

He motioned for me. "Come on." He disappeared around the corner, and the hall went dark except for a tiny glow reflected on the wall where he'd just stood. I remained. I wanted to resist, refuse, but I had no dowry and nothing to stand on. He had accepted me when I had nothing to offer. He did me a favor. I had no right to make demands—a slave to circumstance. I never wanted to leave that spot and face reality, but I feared the sound of him calling for me when he noticed I wasn't behind him. I missed my family. I wanted to go home. I blinked and fanned air toward my eyes. I couldn't be upset by this, I told myself. My mother was right. I shouldn't have objected to him. He was right—the house was finished, and I would be grateful. I would be happy with time. I would show John my thanks. From this point on, I was going to be a perfect wife.

I swallowed hard, forced my feet to budge, and quickly rounded the corner. "Forgive me?"

"Of course," he said cheerfully while swinging the front double doors open and letting in the stinging white light.

We spent our first night in our new house silent and awkward. John had purchased a few provisions, but I needed to visit the general store. We ate dinner in silence, probably because we felt so tired from our trip. I gave up trying to start conversation after one or two questions were answered with only a single word. I wasn't in a mood to talk, either. John would feel more inclined toward conversation tomorrow. After dinner, John stood and I collected our dishes. He picked up the snake lamp from the table and moved in his stately manner toward the door.

"Where are you going?" I asked.

He turned back. "To the study. I'm meeting with Mr. Coddington in the morning, and I want to be prepared."

"But—" I stopped.

"Yes?"

"I—um, forgive me. I don't think I—" If I had to go down in that basement alone in the dark, I would die of fright.

"What?" he asked.

"I haven't been down to the kitchen yet. I'm afraid I'll…trip."

He pointed behind me. "Just lower the dishes in the dumbwaiter. Get them tomorrow."

My eyes followed the direction of his finger to the shaft built into the wall with a pulley mechanism for transporting items to and from the basement. "Oh, thank you."

He left without responding.

While I placed dishes and other items in the dumbwaiter, I wondered what we would do after this. We were both tired from our journey. Nerves crept around my belly when I thought of sleeping in the same bed with him. I had never been in a bed with a man. I picked up my glass of water from the dining room table, took a sip, and put it back down. I stood there for a moment, not moving. I didn't swallow the water, just held it in my mouth. I was afraid. I felt uncomfortable about sitting next to John, let alone sleeping in the same bed with him, being naked with him. I was scared, but a little excited, too. No matter what, I was going to be a good wife. I couldn't be what I wanted to be in life, but this was the dream—women wanted to get married, not work until they found a man. I—we were going to be happy. I swallowed and nodded to myself.

I used the pulley to lower the dumbwaiter down the shaft to the kitchen. When I heard the thump at the bottom, I felt unnerved, as if the noise had disturbed something down there. I would have to go down there the next morning. What if there were no windows and the place was dark as night all the time? I shuddered. I tried to cast out the thought, but when I faced the table and the empty dining room, a sense of misery crept up the shaft from the basement and out like smoke to envelop me. I froze but soon forced myself to edge my way to the door.

I peered down the hall and spotted a glow from the study. I took the dining room oil lamp, grasping the handle shaped like a strange woman with insect-like wings stretched out below the bone-colored glass cover. I exited the room into the dark hallway, the basement entrance just behind me. I felt as if whatever I'd awakened in the basement might reach out and try to snatch me as I slunk past it. I threw myself into the library and exhaled, having reached safety. John popped his head up and acknowledged my entrance with a puzzled expression and then returned to shuffling through some papers in a leather briefcase. When he found a particular document, he pulled it out and placed it on the desk.

I controlled my breathing. "Shall we retire for the evening?"

He lifted his eyes, papers in both hands. "Uh—I've only gotten started."

"Oh, of course."

He shuffled through more and then started organizing them into two piles.

"But you must be exhausted."

He kept his eyes on the papers. "Uh—yes, I am, but I have to be prepared." A cigarette burned in the ashtray. He picked it up and took a long, hard draw.

"What better way to prepare than to be fully rested?"

He exhaled a stream of smoke. "But I also need to be prepared."

I started to feel as if I were intruding. "Very well." I lingered a moment. "Um—can I help?"

"No." He sounded irritated. "You can manage on your own, can't you?"

"Of course." I noticed I was fidgeting with my wedding ring. I immediately stopped and clenched my hand tightly. Unaware of another option, I reentered the dark hallway. The lamp's glow illuminated the area around me and the first step of the twisting stairwell. I stopped just before the stairs. I scrutinized the hole leading into the basement. I took a deep breath and decided to hurry. As long as I could make it to our chamber and shut the door quickly, I could escape this frightening sensation—this feeling that my presence had disturbed something here.

I stepped forward and began to scale the steps. I curved right and entered the middle part of the stairs, where the top and bottom steps were hidden around corners. I felt as if I were completely enclosed, turning and twisting. The walls seemed to contract. I felt trapped. I felt as if the house had locked me in a box—a coffin. I climbed faster. Finally, the light disappeared into darkness ahead. I had reached the landing.

Our chamber was at the end of the dark corridor. I walked stiffly and quickly, my eyes flicking back and forth as the lamp's light reflected off a doorknob on the right, then the left, the right, the left—door after door of rooms that would remain empty and silent. The sensation of eyes watching me swelled. I tried to calm my heart. I tried to laugh at my foolishness, but it didn't work. How my sister Lillian would have teased if she'd seen me so ready to take flight for fear that a beast might appear out of thin air. Finally, the light reflected off the doorknob at the end of the hallway. I reached, turned the knob, stepped in, and shut the door. I made sure not to peek back, for fear of what I might see.

I sighed, relieved, feeling as if I had shut out the rest of the house and was at last safe. Although I was disappointed that John chose not to join me straightaway, I was somewhat glad. I could undress alone and be ready in my nightclothes when he arrived. I just needed to complete my task before he entered, which might have been at any moment. Unfortunately, I could not undress with speed. I was used to having a handmaid assist me, and I wore a full toilette that day. I removed layer after layer—skirt, petticoats, my decorative jacket, my shirtwaist, my corset cover. My corset seemed to take a half-hour to get off. John, however, did not appear before I was able reach the last layer, my chemise and drawers. I quickly put on my nightdress.

I left the lamp lit for when he came. The tiny glow comforted me. It made the room soft and safe. I explored the room, touching and examining things. The chamber felt light compared with the rest of the house. The statues and wall hangings were simple and colored in various shades of white. With the yellow glow from the lamp, though, everything appeared shiny and gold.

I slipped into the bed and lay there awake waiting for him despite my exhaustion. Perhaps I was too anxious to sleep. Any fears I'd had were replaced with a sense of expectation. Perhaps whatever happened this night would remove the invisible barrier between us.

I felt strange in this bed. I missed my bed. I missed my home. I missed my world with light and people and St. Louis. I missed the echoing sound of carriages in the narrow streets, the sight of people walking their dogs, and the vines creeping up intricate brick homes in the Central West End. I missed the feeling of knowing there were hundreds of people just outside my door. I'd never felt alone. I'd felt safe. I sighed. I wished he would come up.

Finally, I heard something and hushed my thoughts so I could listen. There were the sounds of footfall. John could be treading down the hallway or climbing the stairs. I waited. The door would open at any moment. I should hear the doorknob squeak. Maybe he was coming up the stairs and hadn't quite made it to the door. I waited. I listened to the house shift under someone's weight. He was coming. But then the noise stopped. Nothing. I heard shuffles, creaking, and even footsteps several times, and several times I could have sworn it was John on his way, but nothing happened. No one was there. I hoped no one was there.

As I lay there, I felt terribly alone, like I had made a horrible mistake. I missed my family. I missed my younger sisters, the way Ruth giggled at everything, even if it wasn't funny—she was so little. I missed Lillian's antics and Florence's friendship. I missed my mother's voice. Who would have guessed such a thing? I missed how much she cared. I especially missed my brother. Only two years younger than me, James was my confidant, my best friend. I missed his encouragement. He reminded me of my father. I missed the smell of my father's cigar and being able to hear him sneeze from down the hall. Always sneezing. He wasn't there anymore, though. None of them were. I couldn't go back if I wanted to. With that I closed my eyes and chose to abandon consciousness rather than cry.

I woke up when John entered. I had no idea how long it had been, but my stomach leapt with excitement, and then I froze in fear. I didn't sit up or move. I remained on my side and listened to him undress. I heard him drop his shoes with two soft thuds and place his cuff links on his dressing table with two clinks. A yawn. A belt buckle. I did nothing but listen as he changed into a pants-and-shirt sleeping suit. It was a popular new garment for men, inspired by some type of exotic sleepwear from Persia or India.

He slipped into the bed, and I stiffened with uncertainty. I wondered, should I tell him I was awake? Should I wait for him? What was it that I was supposed to do? I certainly couldn't initiate without knowing. If I didn't know, did he know how to begin? He must have known, for I surely did not. Should I reach for his hand or his lips? Or should he reach for me? My panic returned, and I lay wide awake. What was to happen? What was I supposed to do? What—then I heard a noise. I listened. John was snoring.

# Four

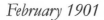

*February 1901*

$\mathcal{B}$eing married to a handsome man and living in your own home was supposed to be the dream. I felt like a stranger pretending I'd been invited. I'd once thought John would never have agreed to marry me if he had not cared for me, but I wasn't so sure anymore. I had expected our first night to be far more…romantic. We did eventually have our night together, but it was not as I had anticipated. We undressed with our backs to each other and did not speak a word. Our exchange felt awkward and uncomfortable, and we avoided each other's eyes. I wasn't sure what I had expected— perhaps I'd thought it would be more…loving.

After that, every day felt the same. I woke up intent on being the finest and most cheerful wife so that I might satisfy my husband and make him fall in love with me, and every day I failed. It began at five in the morning when I rose by candlelight, slipped into my dressing gown, and started breakfast while John shaved and dressed for work. John always sat at the head of the table, at the end closest to the door, and read as I brought breakfast up from the basement, tray by tray, through the dumbwaiter. He poured coffee from the pitcher with the leaf-shaped lid and ate oatmeal with his vine-inlaid spoon while little frogs and critters snickered at him from his plate of ham and eggs. He didn't acknowledge me when I sat next to him. As Mother had taught me, I was to amuse with discussion. Why else had I received an education, she would say. The task, however, was something of a challenge with John. I didn't know why, but he rejected the act of conversation.

"How is work?"

"Hmm?" He glanced up and then returned to his reading material. "Oh. Uh—fine." He managed to always have something in need of reading while we ate. At first the material seemed reasonable—the newspaper or files for work. As time went on, however, I noticed that his reading seemed less and less obligatory. Once he spent an entire meal reading a church bulletin. He spent twenty minutes reading a two-sided sheet of paper no bigger than a folded napkin. He must have reread it five times, every minute or so flipping it over. Our meals rapidly evolved into a match I could not win. No matter the question, he responded only with short awkward answers, some of which didn't even address the question. He absolutely refused to speak more than a few words until he swallowed his last bite of food. Finally, he'd stand, announce his departure for the firm, and leave without any farewell—not a kiss on the cheek or a touch on the shoulder. He didn't even say goodbye.

He was my husband, and I wanted him to act as such. I wanted to be held, to be touched. I prayed I would do something to please him, to rouse some affection. Sometimes I imagined what it would be like if he came home and swept me up, spun me around, and kissed me over and over as if he had done nothing but miss me all day. Oh, how I longed to earn a kiss—a real kiss. I wished I could initiate such a thing, but a lady would never do that—would a wife? I didn't know. I didn't know what to do. Even if I knew how to go about it, I didn't think I could get John to stay in the same room with me long enough to make such an attempt. He worked all the time. He was never home. It certainly made it easier for him to avoid speaking to me.

When he left in the morning, my day of tedious redundancy began. My handmaid, Mrs. Lottie Schwab, couldn't be a live-in because she had a family of her own, not that we could afford a live-in anyway. We couldn't even afford to pay Mrs. Schwab for the whole week. Although wealthy, John's father believed we should start out on our own, with little help. I believed that had more to do with me than with family tradition.

When Mrs. Schwab didn't work for us, she picked cotton or fruit for local farms. The hard outdoor labor had tanned and aged her once fair thirty-four-year-old skin. That's why upper-class women avoided the sun. When we first met, I observed brown freckles all around her nose and cheeks. I usually saw freckles on pale women with luscious red hair. Mrs. Schwab had a mix of thick brown and blond strands, like hay. At the time, I assumed she failed to clean her face and requested she be sure to bathe before entering the house. She made no rebuke. The next time I saw her, she reminded me of my request by promptly informing me that she had bathed. Her southern accent never failed to reveal her true feelings no matter how careful she chose her words. I felt awful but figured it would be cruel to explain my mistake and why I had made such a demand. I thanked her instead.

Although I hadn't been impressed by Mrs. Schwab when we first met, I found her quite the amusement. Her German surname reminded me of the word *suave*, but Mrs. Schwab was clearly un-refined. She was expecting, but continued to work despite the fact that she had begun to show. This wasn't abnormal among working class women, but polite society considered such a delicate condi-tion to be a private affair and even deemed it an inappropriate topic for open conversation or polite correspondence. Middle and upper class women went into confinement or took a lying-in pe-riod. They withdrew from the public and dedicated most or all of their time resting for the sake of the child and public decency. Mrs. Schwab, however, continued on as she grew larger and struggled to maneuver herself, often knocking things over with her bulging abdomen. John grumbled and deducted the cost of the items from her pay. I didn't mind, as I hated everything she broke, so I slowly stopped informing him when certain objects were no longer with us. Mrs. Schwab helped me three days a week, and even though we didn't speak much, her presence, or lack thereof, determined the mood of the day.

First she'd help me into one of my dreary mourning dresses, cinching my corset, pulling my skirt closed over the layers of petticoats, and assisting with high-collar buttons. She'd also help me with my long hair, which I wore in a pompadour with curls, twists, and tucks atop my head. Then I'd have her open all the doors downstairs to let the light out of the rooms. She'd clear away the dishes and lower them to the basement using the dumbwaiter. Next she would empty, clean, and refill the jug and basin in the bath chamber. She'd then go to the dungeon to wash the dishes and remove the ashes from the coal-burning stove.

"The dungeon" was my nickname for the basement. I'd thought it up as a way to tease myself, but it turned out to be quite accurate. It was murky and the walls bled with leaks. It felt as if despair had been banished to that space. One insignificant window hovered at the top of the wall opposite the stairs. Below the window was a large wash basin for cleaning dishes. We had to lug the water down to the basement from a well outside. We stored dishes and food in some cupboards with glass doors. I stored fresh food and baked goods in a pierced-tin closet to keep bugs away. The extra buffet and icebox sat against another wall. People in Labellum actually had iceboxes that they filled with large chunks of ice from the Mississippi during the winter and stored in such a way that the ice lasted through much of summer. The stove and oven sat next to the stairs. We did much of the work on a large wood table in the middle of the room and a small dough box with an unfinished wood top for chopping.

While Mrs. Schwab worked on the dishes, I would dust off the tablecloth and fold it. Then I would sweep, moving from the dining room to the parlor and other commonly used areas while ignoring the glares coming from the knickknacks. In the parlor's main seating area around the fireplace, I swept each day around and under a green sofa with clawlike feet. The seat of the sofa curved up into the arms, which rounded over and under, making the entire piece look like a menacing leer, the white tassels of a large doily throw its teeth. Next, I'd move toward an adjacent blue love seat that had two chair backs but a fused seat, like conjoined twins connected at the hip.

Mismatched wooden chairs were placed sporadically around the room, and I had to move them all around every time I swept. I'd move one and then turn and another would confront me, and then another, and another. One with ghostly hands drifting up, like smoke, one with two green bug-eyed pads on the back, and one with three overlapped leaves for a seat. Another had thick layered waves that resembled muscles I'd seen in books but not those of a human—some other creature. The muscles of a chair?

I would polish everything, and I mean everything, even the doorknobs. I'd clean the lamps' black residue from the walls, and I'd clean John's ashtrays. He smoked cigarettes—never cigars like my father. Even when others smoked cigars, he favored cigarettes, but he mostly smoked when he worked and never at the table.

About the time I would reach the end of the hall, Mrs. Schwab would rise from the basement and trudge up the stairs, open the doors on the second floor, put our chamber in order, flip the mattress, and make the bed. She also polished fixtures, dusted, and cleaned out the chamber pot. Then she'd dump John's shaving water and wipe down the wash basin in our room. Finally, she'd refill the jug so we could wash our hands and faces throughout the day and before bed. Mrs. Schwab did these chores daily and dusted the empty rooms once a week. On the days she wasn't with me, I would do those chores alone. Those were the worst hours for me, alone with those empty rooms and the people who weren't in them.

Other chores depended on the day. On Mondays, when Mrs.

Schwab returned from our chamber, we would both go to the basement for laundry. Boil, wring, scrub, wring, soak, wring, and hang. The process took all of Monday and usually some of Tuesday. When we'd finished more than we could carry, we'd gather the wet linens and take them outside to hang. Whenever we rose up from beneath the ground holding baskets of wet clothes, I imagined us as captives released after years of undeserved confinement to a cell. Of course, when we went back, I couldn't help but imagine that our captors had immediately accused us of some other crime for which we were being forced back underground. I wasn't used to laundering, and afterward my arms and hands would ache from the scrubbing, so much some days that they'd quiver all through dinner and I feared I might drop the pitcher of water on John.

Tuesdays we ironed, starched, and mended. We would also start baking food to last the entire week, which meant we had to plan all meals in advance. We finished baking on Wednesdays. Then we'd beat the rugs and scrub the floors. Every time we scrubbed, I wondered, who scuffed all these floors? Doing the floors drained me of energy, but I enjoyed the freedom from the basement.

Thursdays, John would bathe at 5:30 a.m., before work, and I would bathe after he left. I had to lug buckets of water from the well down into the basement to heat on the range and then haul them back up to the tub. Of course, I would fill the tub with only an inch or so of warm water, and then we used a sponge to draw the warm liquid over our bodies. Whenever I bathed, I wondered what it would look like if the raven-footed tub could really take flight and if it could, whether or not it would do so with me still in it? My hair was so long that it took all day to dry by the fire, so I washed it very rarely, using perfumed soaps made from animal fat and lemons. Afterward, I cleaned the tub and brushed my teeth with a horsehair toothbrush and bicarbonate of soda. I would have liked to save our bathing day for when Mrs. Schwab could assist with the water, but I needed her too much for the other chores, and there just wasn't enough time on those days for bathing.

I dreaded Thursdays when I had to face the house alone. I would
spend at least an hour fiddling with self-cinching and skirt-clasping
tools as I tried to dress myself, but usually I still couldn't do it quite
right. Worse, when I prepared breakfast and cleaned the dishes in
the basement, there were constant noises above and around me,
as if something lurked there. I told myself that what I heard in
the basement had to be a scurrying mouse or another critter, but
I couldn't speculate what the thumping and clacking from above
could be unless it was the furniture moving around of its own
accord—scuffing the floors, no doubt.

Although I despised the basement, other areas of the house
were just as disturbing. I constantly sensed a presence when I was
alone, especially in the parlor. Whenever I would clean mirrors in
there, I'd see a flash or a blur in the reflection. I'd spin around and
search among the clusters of tables and chairs, the web of bric-a-
brac that could easily conceal a tiny trickster. I'd eye the grouping
in the left corner, the china cabinet on the wall with the curved
sides and glass doors like eyes. Or I'd peer at the middle cluster
with the game table and gangly treelike figurines, a lopsided vase
practically dripping off the table. Or I'd study another cluster of
seats surrounding the window-box garden. The cabinet for gar-
dening supplies lingered nearby. Its appendages swirled, too. Could
the inky sliver I'd see out of the corner of my eye have been one
of those winding arms?

Thankfully, I didn't lose all my sanity on Thursdays because,
when I didn't have wet hair, our driver and stable hand, Mr. Samuel
Buck, would take me into town to make calls and weekly purchases.
I ordered many things by catalog, even groceries, but I still had to
visit the milkman, the egg man, the butcher, and a provisionary
for apples, butter, potatoes, and the like. The first time I visited
the little town, I expected to see long drooping trees and a jungle
of foliage overwhelming chipped and worn buildings. To my surprise, Labellum actually appeared to be clean and kempt, with little
white shops and bushy trees lined up in neat little rows. I could

see grassy hills in the distance. The trees were mostly oak, the type with rounded tops. Little patches of forest were interspersed throughout the valley but cleared from the town center.

Labellum's original inhabitants situated the town on a criss-crossed grid, with narrow alleys. The white buildings were square, with flat fronts and angled roofs. Almost every structure looked alike, with two windows on the upstairs floor and two more flanking a single door. I'd thought people avoided painting buildings white for fear that they'd show filth, but everything here looked cleaned and pressed. Perhaps this little town had discovered the secret to being rid of things like dirt.

Fridays were lonely, too, but I had to labor only on chores I hadn't completed during the week. I had fewer chores than women in the past because factory production made it possible to buy ready-made clothing, and food preparation and storage was easier. My mother used to badger me to be grateful that I didn't have to spin my own thread or grind coffee without a hand-cranked grinder—not that she'd ever ground coffee in her life. I usually had a lot of extra time on Fridays, so I set it aside to receive callers, but in such a small town, calls were infrequent. I'd spend much of Friday mending mindlessly, reading, or just dreaming of faraway places and occasionally jerking around to see if a noise behind me had in fact been made by a living creature skulking among the figurines.

Or I faced my correspondence:

*Dear Emeline,*

*My darling child, your father would be so proud. Thanks to the Dorrs, your sisters and I are not living in the desperate conditions we feared. Now family, they have offered an extraordinary amount of kindness, resources, and connections that will allow us to prosper. Mrs. Dorr introduced several well-bred young ladies to your brother, and she is sure she knows a young man who will show an interest in Florence.*

*Emeline, your husband has given you and your family so much more than we could ever expect in our situation. He could have married a woman of much higher worth and standing, but he chose you. Do not risk disappointing him. We wouldn't want to lose all that we have been blessed with again. Sometimes marriage can be difficult. You will not always be happy or comfortable, but you must always remember what your husband sacrificed for you.*

*With all the love in the heavens,*
*Your Mother*

Unfortunately, I had little options for distraction. I never settled on any accomplishments. I didn't paint or etch wood or play the pianoforte. I'd never found meaning in such things. I tried making crafts from seashells, but they never came out right, and my floral arrangements were deplorable. Thankfully, society considered reading an acceptable way for a woman to improve herself. Even if society did not approve of the literary subjects I chose.

I developed a talent for locating and consuming writing deemed unsuitable for a young lady, such as Dickens, *Wuthering Heights*, sensations like *The Woman in White*, by Wilkie Collins, and various science and medical texts. Although I found the house distasteful, the library brimmed with books I had never heard of, and John brought even more, many of them professional volumes I inquisitively thumbed through in his absence. When we first arrived, John had said he wouldn't work Saturdays and Sundays, but he did. I spent those days bored and anxious. It didn't take me long to go through all his books, but they were mostly about law, which I found a terrible read. Nothing made sense in law books. Still, there were some masculine finds—Henry David Thoreau's *Walden* and *Civil Disobedience*, Thomas Carlyle's *The French Revolution, A History*, and Charles Darwin's *On the Origin of Species*.

When John did stay home, he would spend the day working in the library. I wish I could say his presence was a comfort to me, but it often made things worse, specifically because when he was home he insisted we close all the doors. Light still filled the rooms we were in, but there was something about traveling through dark halls and the knowledge that darkness hid behind every door.

Sundays we attended services. John had once mentioned committing Sundays to a leisure activity like cycling or tennis. I internally leapt at the idea, but he never brought it up again, always having too much work and not a moment to spare, not even to play a game or tell me something about himself. So I focused on improving myself, hopefully to his liking. Or I read.

The redundancy was dreadful. No task accomplished was really an accomplishment. I cleaned things that would just get dirty again. I baked things that we consumed. Nothing had lasting value; I had to redo everything, over and over. Perhaps I might have felt a sense of purpose if the drudgery had ended with a smile on his face, but every day began and concluded the same way. John would emerge from the library unaware that my cheer was in spite of my efforts, the tedium, and how depressed it all made me.

"How was your day?" I would ask.

"Hmm?" He would say, refusing to look away from his read.

"Did your day go well?"

He might stab a bit of food with his fork, hold it up to his mouth, and pause for a moment. "I like it."

"John, I asked you how your day went?"

"What?" he would ask. "Oh—um—fine."

# Five

*March 1901*

John, Mr. Marcellus Rippring, and Dr. Walter Bradbridge reclined in the parlor, which was dimly lit by lamps and glowing remnants of a fire. Thick cigar smoke billowed above their heads, but John puffed a cigarette. They were celebrating some success story that had brought the three of them together. They toasted one another and occasionally roared with laughter.

This was the first time I'd met anyone John worked with. Dr. Walter Bradbridge was son of Dr. Benedict Bradbridge, one of the most important clients Mr. Coddington's office represented. John had informed me that Mrs. Margaret Bradbridge, wife to the senior physician and mother to the younger, determined a lady's place in Labellum, so it was of great importance that I make a good impression on any Bradbridge I might meet. Walter Bradbridge looked young for a physician. He had a gentle disposition and a round face with puffy red cheeks. I observed him as I entered the parlor to bring them refreshments. He reclined in a high-backed chair and chatted cheerfully.

I knew I shouldn't listen to their conversation, but I had an overwhelming desire to know what all the excitement was about.

How I longed to hear something interesting after spending so much time alone. How I longed to be spoken to. I took my time as I brought them coffee, filled their whiskies and brandies, and served desserts.

"You were impressive today." John raised his glass to the young doctor.

"Thank you," Walter said. "You as well. I'm glad you came and not Mr. Coddington."

"You didn't panic. Others have not had the strength."

Walter chuckled. "I suppose it helped that my father had repeated over and over and over that the day I stumbled upon this to contact the authorities and my lawyer without question."

I placed a tray on the side table. It was filled with liquors, coffee, peppermint cakes, and a crystal bowl of candied plums. I'd purchased the cakes for my own callers, but it seemed that John's parents didn't know as many people in Labellum as I had anticipated so I didn't have a day of introduction. Further, Mr. Coddington and his wife didn't seem to care to send letters of introduction. I felt quite ill toward John's employer, who had yet to introduce himself and who worked John as if he were some sort of load-bearing animal.

John continued. "We knew it would happen sooner or later."

Marcellus lurched forward, snatched a candied plum and popped it into his mouth. He slouched to the side, and his knobby shoulders looked lopsided. Marcellus worked as a detective for the Labellum Police Department. It seemed odd for such a small department to have its own detective when the rest of its staff consisted of only a sheriff, a deputy, and one or two patrolmen, all of whom worked out of the local jailhouse. As he chewed noisily, his open mouth exposed plum and saliva. He was tall and slender, and all the angles of his body seemed sharp. I half-expected his elbows to slice through the chair.

The most bizarre thing about Marcellus, however, was his wife, Mrs. Ida Rippring, who was as high-society as they come. John's mother had told me she could have as much control over Labellum's society as she wanted. So why had she chosen to marry Marcellus? We were invited to dine with the Ripprings that weekend. Perhaps I would discover their secrets.

Marcellus swallowed the mushy remnants of the candied plum. "I didn't think you had it in you, Walter."

"What do you mean?" John tipped his glass toward the young doctor. "Walter, I think you showed some real backbone today." John laughed and took another sip of brandy.

I placed the bowl of sugar cubes on the table and motioned to Marcellus to see if he wanted more whiskey.

He grunted and extended his glass, keeping his attention on the men. "When that girl started screaming and screeching, you turned white!"

I pulled back at the mention of screaming, and whiskey dripped down his knuckles and onto the rug. John's laugh trailed off uncomfortably. Marcellus transferred the glass to his other hand and shook the right, sprinkling liquor about the room and onto me. A drop landed on my cheek, just under my eye. I scrambled to fetch a cloth from the tray. I peeked at John, fearing he would be upset, but he wasn't looking at me. Walter's body had stiffened, and he stared at Marcellus.

I dabbed Marcellus' hands with the cloth. "My apologies."

He didn't respond.

Finally, Walter adjusted in his seat. "Empathy is a necessary skill in the field of medicine. I can't shut it off."

"Says who?" Marcellus asked as I moved from his hand to the floor. "Your father doesn't practice that way."

Another pause.

"I assure you it's an important quality in my profession, no matter how my father practices."

"Not in mine." Marcellus snickered.

John cleared his throat and repositioned himself. "It must have been difficult, but you did the right thing."

Walter glared at Marcellus for a moment longer and then faced my husband. "Honestly, John, I'm not sure if this is something to celebrate. I understand the legal issues and want to see these people removed from society, but I personally feel it's unacceptable to hold physicians accountable for doing their jobs. Physicians shouldn't be charged for aiding a patient as long as they report it. We take an oath to preserve life."

"Your oath doesn't cover criminals," Marcellus said and coughed a wet cough.

"Actually, it does."

John smothered his cigarette in a nearby ashtray. "Mr. Coddington knows that, but it is the law. When doctors are held accountable for reporting, arrests increase significantly."

"I'm not all that sure if I would do it again," Walter mumbled.

Marcellus gulped his liquor. "Ha!"

John shifted his eyes to Marcellus and then to Walter. "I'll mention it to Mr. Coddington, but you know he doesn't think highly of my opinion."

I picked up the tray.

"How *did* you find yourself in such a situation in the first place, Walter?" Marcellus asked.

I meandered toward the door.

"She sent her driver."

"Did he just blurt it out?"

I stopped to reposition a goblin-like statuette, stalling.

"What else would he have done?"

I started toward the door again.

"I can't believe how sloppy these people are when things go wrong," Marcellus scoffed.

"If your daughter was bleeding and screaming, I'm sure you'd be a bit sloppy yourself."

I stopped with my back to the group of men. They paused, too, until John cleared his throat. I walked out and flattened myself against the wall outside, listening.

"I don't have any children," Marcellus said.

"Neither do I, but I assure you, you would do the same," Walter said.

"Walter, you're just going to have to grow a stronger backbone."

"I think I should be going," Walter said.

I left the hallway. Obviously, Walter had helped Marcellus apprehend someone and John had been called to be present as his lawyer, but screaming, bleeding, refusing treatment? They wouldn't celebrate such a horror. Good people wouldn't, but I didn't know if these people were good people. I didn't know if John was a good person.

# Six

*March 1901*

**M**y nerves twitched. John had made it clear in the past month or so, most recently during the ride over, that it was imperative that I dazzle the people we were to dine with that evening. The invitation suggested a casual dinner, but in the Rippring dining room, I eyed the intricately designed silver and chargers from Italy and wondered if I had underdressed. I imagined the dinnerware's owners would cringe at our bug bowls and salamander silverware. Ida's dining room gleamed with gilded crown molding, a large mirror in an intricately etched frame, and a sparkling chandelier.

Meanwhile, the dining room waiting for me at the house sat like a dark cave, a narrow hole full of bugs and bats posing as spoons and tea cups. The hanging gas lamp was no chandelier, and there were no mirrors or large paintings of landscapes, only maroon wallpaper and dark wood wainscoting. I could see it in my head transforming into a real cave with teeth and a long rectangular table for a tongue, hungry.

"Ma'am?" The butler held out a bottle of Port.

"Do you have sherry?"

"Of course."

I removed my gloves and placed them on my lap.

Margaret and Dr. Walter Bradbridge also made it to dinner, although the senior physician did not.

"Walter, have you entertained any fine ladies as of late?" Ida asked.

"Um—well—I—"

Margaret interrupted to answer for him. "Oh, no, there are very few ladies worth courting here."

"Yes, very few. Perhaps a trip to the city could help?" Ida handled her crystal goblet with slender fingers.

"What a wonderful suggestion." Margaret beamed.

Walter's face tightened. "Thank you, Mother." He sighed and turned to the hostess. "Ida, I appreciate your interest, but I want to focus on my work."

She eyed him. "Oh, yes, ambitions. If I might be so bold, I have to disagree with this impulse to start a practice. You have one here. No need to find another. It will be all yours someday. You are a fine physician. Now find a wife."

Margaret nodded eagerly.

"I wouldn't call it an impulse, but thank you for the advice."

"You aren't keeping anything to yourself now, are you?" Ida asked.

"Nothing of the sort." He unfolded his napkin with his eyes down.

"Hmm." Ida sipped her wine.

The servants placed finger bowls in front of us. I gently dipped my hands. Marcellus sloshed perfumed water onto the lace tablecloth.

"Emeline?" Ida turned her focus to me. "What do you think of the committee?"

"I'm joining." I jumped at the opportunity to please. "Margaret told me you've played an important role in making the committee a success."

She didn't respond. I feared everyone saw through me.

The servants entered in a procession and clinked bowls of rich cream soup in front of us.

"How did you come to live in Labellum?" I asked.

"We moved here for my husband's sake." Ida eyed him, but he didn't look up. "For his work."

"Really—"

"I'll make it easy on you, dear." Ida gave a tiny grin, revealing two large front teeth. "He does not need to work. When we wed, he insisted he continue. It gives him some sort of satisfaction, I suppose." Her smug demeanor turned weary.

Marcellus focused on his soup, his stringy hair hanging around his face.

"But why Labellum?" John asked. "I would think you would want to mingle with the highest society—if you don't mind me saying?" He lifted a spoonful of soup. "New York or Paris or something like that?"

Ida pursed her lips and lifted her chin at her husband, but he didn't offer an excuse. She hesitated. "Well, he—we wanted for fresh air."

I wondered what the real reason had been. It obviously had something to do with Marcellus. I wondered if some scandal had forced them into exile. I could sense how uncomfortable she had become, so I changed the subject. "What exactly does the church committee do?"

Ida lifted her glass and the butler quickly moved to pour more Port. "I created an event committee to organize balls and other events for the families of higher standing."

"That sounds entertaining."

"But that's not the committee you will be joining. Only the highest-class women in town are members."

"Oh."

"The church committee used to do little useless things around town, so I had Margaret spruce it up and now it funds my event committee."

"What did they do before?"

"Oh, nonsense activities to keep themselves busy, I suppose—taking food to families with newborns, knitting scarves just to give away."

John stirred his soup. "Walter, perhaps Ida would enjoy hearing about her husband's and your accomplishments in Murielle County."

Marcellus grumbled.

"Thank you, John," Walter said. "I'm certain the ladies hear enough of that day to day."

"Nonsense." Margaret pepped up. "His father was very impressed with his recent catch." She shifted in her seat to face him. "I've never seen him congratulate you in such a manner."

"How so?" Ida rolled her sleepy gaze toward him.

"I—" Walter tried.

Margaret continued. "I haven't seen your father that pleased since the day you agreed to join his practice—"

"It wasn't anything." Walter waved a hand and tried to hide his dimples. "We merely enjoyed a cigar together." His cheeks grew a little flush. "Besides, I'm sure our work with Mr. Coddington's firm is not appropriate for dinner conversation."

"Indeed," Ida said.

Margaret leaned forward. "Ida, I think it is our duty to inform Emeline of a certain individual." She tilted her head.

Ida nodded, sipping her wine.

"Pardon?" I asked.

"There is a despicable woman named Olivia Urswick you must do your best to avoid."

"Mother!" Walter's eyes shot open.

John froze with a spoonful of soup at his lips. Marcellus continued eating.

Margaret ignored her son's protest and dabbed her lips with a napkin. "She is a horrible, wretched woman, a spinster, posing for polite society."

"Oh, yes," Ida said. "She's not just a spinster, either."

John's eyebrows slanted and he slumped, clearly uncomfortable. I didn't want to upset our hostess, but this was not light or pleasant conversation.

"She had a child out of wedlock," Margaret exclaimed.

Oh, dear God, I thought.

Walter shook his head.

"Uh, I'm sure there are plenty of respectable women, though."

"Her father was a fool," Ida said.

Margaret continued. "He left everything to her despite the fact that she refused to marry, and her bastard child was a girl." She shook her head. "Not even a son to carry on the family name."

John cleared his throat. "Uh, Walter how did you—"

"Why did she not marry?" I asked without thinking. "I never heard of such a thing."

"You won't believe it, Emeline." Ida widened her eyes. "She refused him."

"Why would she do that?"

Margaret shook her head. "Stubborn. A stubborn mule of a woman. She willingly brought shame to herself and her family."

"Perhaps there is another suitor?"

"This was twenty years ago. Her daughter is grown. Fled this town and her family's shame. Olivia's in her late forties now. Trust me, she couldn't tempt any man with half a wit."

"Oh my."

John glared at me.

"All right, Mother, that's enough," Walter said.

"Her bastard child even considers her mother a wretched woman," Margaret said. "She doesn't even speak to her."

John stared at me for a moment longer and then stood. "Excuse me."

"Even more—" Margaret continued.

"That's it." Walter stood and threw his napkin down.

I felt a sudden urge to stop everything and take it all back. "No, wait." I put my hand out and accidentally hit my water goblet. "Oh!" I tried to stop it from falling, but then I hit my sherry glass and it smashed into Ida's goblets, knocking them over and breaking them. Glass shards flew, and red wine spattered all over Ida's face and bosom. The rest quickly ran off into her expensive, influential lap.

She screamed, jumped up, and raised her hands.

"Emeline!" John shouted.

"I'm sorry!"

"What happened?" Margaret shouted at me as she stood. She rushed to Ida and began blotting at the red streaking down the hostess' gown.

"Ida, I'm so, so sorry." I covered my mouth with my hands. "It was an accident."

She cringed at her gown and then shouted, "This dress is from Paris, France!" She scowled at me for a long moment and then stormed out of the room, red wine trailing her the entire way. Margaret chased after her.

Marcellus snorted a chuckle under his napkin. John and Walter stood speechless. John flushed with humiliation.

"It was an accident," I pleaded.

John and Walter sat slowly. Marcellus continued to snigger and eat while the rest of us waited without speaking.

Ida and Margaret never returned. Instead, the butler informed us the evening had come to a close. Marcellus didn't even say "good evening"—he just stood, dropped his napkin onto the table, and sauntered out. Walter stayed behind to wait for his mother, and John and I left surrounded by awkward uncertainty. John didn't say anything to me all the way back to the house. I wasn't sure if he was infuriated or just speechless.

It wasn't until we were undressing for the evening that he dropped onto the bed with his back to me and said, "I can't imagine anything going any worse."

I stopped undressing and turned to him. "I'm sorry."

He didn't respond.

"I'll apologize again tomorrow."

Still he said nothing.

"I'm sure she will understand. It was an accident."

He went to sleep without saying another word.

# Seven

*March 1901*

The next day I called on Margaret, hoping she would tell me Ida wasn't angry. Margaret seemed to like me, and I hoped she'd understand that it had been an accident. When I entered her parlor, she was dressed for walking, and fussing with her straw brimmed hat and gray-streaked hair.

"Oh, Margaret, I do apologize. I thought you were receiving calls today?"

"Emeline, yes, yes, but I've ordered an emergency meeting for the church committee." She stuffed a wrinkly hand into a leather glove.

"When would be a better time?"

"Dear girl." She gripped both my wrists. "You must come. What better orientation?" She moved toward the door, one hand still clutching me.

"Um—but—" She released me and I halted. "Um, sure." I didn't want to go, but it might give me the chance to apologize to Ida.

"Wonderful. Come along then."

I trailed her into her carriage. She commanded her driver to make haste. Then she popped her attention toward me. "So, my dear, what will you contribute to the committee?"

I had hardly settled into my seat. "Um—uh—actually, I haven't given it much thought yet." I rubbed my gloved hands over my skirt to smooth it. "How can I contribute? A donation or just my time?"

"Both."

"Oh." I mentally tallied up the allowance John had allotted me. "I'm sure I could offer more with my time."

"I agree."

"I suppose I could spare one Sunday a month."

"Splendid—to start."

When the carriage slowed to a stop, we stepped out, and I realized the driver had taken us to the back of the church house. I followed Margaret into a tiny stuffy room where about a dozen bustling women were hard at work quilting and knitting. Margaret motioned for me to follow her, and I obeyed. I eyed three women fussing with some papers and a cash box at the front of the room and realized Ida was among them. Panic fizzed up from my stomach and settled in my throat. "Good day, Ida," I croaked.

Ida turned and narrowed her eyes. "Emeline."

I felt like an injured rodent before a bird of prey. "How do you do?" She crossed her arms and pursed her lips.

"Emeline! What do you think?" Margaret asked.

"Uh...wonderful turnout for last minute."

"I disagree," Ida snarled.

"Excuse me just a moment." Margaret marched to the front of the room and faced the women, who promptly hushed their conversations. "Ladies, thank you for coming on short notice. You show far more dedication than those not here." She grimaced. "I assure you, if we work hard, we will have no problem remedying this shortage." She stepped aside.

I returned my attention to Ida and the women at the cash box glowering at me. Ida's back was to me. "Ida?" She didn't move, so I said it louder. "Pardon me, Ida?"

The glowering women didn't inform her of my attempts. I wanted to skulk away, but their glares entrapped me. I reached out and tapped Ida's shoulder like a child. "Pardon me, Ida?"

She slowly rotated.

I timidly looked away before forcing myself to meet her eyes. "I—I really would like to apologize again for last night. I hope I can make it up to you."

"I doubt it."

One of the other women smirked.

"It truly was an accident. I can speak to my husband about replacing your dress."

"You couldn't afford it." She turned back around.

My heart dropped. What else could I do? Was she going to turn all of Labellum against me? Would John be angry with me? I closed my eyes and willed myself not to cry. I opened my eyes and saw Margaret waving me over. Happy for a reason to flee, I accompanied her as she circled the room, occasionally stopping to scrutinize a stitch. "How are you and Mr. Dorr settling in?"

"Uh…it's coming along."

"How is Mr. Dorr after last night?"

I hesitated. "I'm not sure."

"I'm happy Mr. Coddington acquired someone as polite and professional as your husband. My husband and son were hesitant to accept new counsel."

I lowered my gaze for a second. "Margaret? I don't know what to do." I looked up and saw she had moved on without me. I shuffled to catch up. "Margaret?"

A plump woman entered and everyone looked at her.

"Mrs. Colt! How nice of you to join us." Margaret eyed her as she scuttled to a seat and quickly picked up a patch for one of the quilts. "I was beginning to think you had no sympathy for this committee." She turned back to me. "What was that, dear?"

"Um." I stared blankly for a moment. "Oh—uh, you said there was some hesitancy about my husband?"

She continued to circle the room. "My husband doubted such a young man could represent him or our son as effectively as Mr. Coddington. Of course, Mr. Coddington could have sent Mr. Dorr to any of his offices, but he brought him here specifically to handle *these* cases. My husband just needed some extra persuasion, and I think your husband's recent success with our son has done it."

"Oh." I tried to hide my confusion. John told me nothing of his cases. I had no idea why physicians required so much attention from a law firm. Then I remembered what I needed to ask Margaret. "Is there anything I can do about Ida?"

She stopped. "Well, Mrs. Swift, I've seen you work faster than that. Perhaps if you stopped yapping."

The woman complied, almost cowering.

I couldn't believe Margaret's disappointment. The women in St. Louis would never stand for it. Actually, women in St. Louis wouldn't join a profit-oriented quilting bee in the first place. Quilting bees were for socialization, comfort, and friendship. Church committees were for charity. Margaret and Ida obviously held power in this town, but why so much?

"What were you saying?" Margaret moved on.

I scrambled to keep up. The room seemed to grow stuffier with my effort. "Ida is furious with me. I tried to apologize."

She stopped and stood with her arms crossed, staring out at the sea of quilters. "I really don't know what to tell you, Emeline." She wasn't looking at me but at the volunteers.

"What is the emergency?" I asked.

"We didn't have enough material for the Saturday sale." She put her hands on her hips.

I scanned the room. "How many were you short by?"

Margaret leaned in close and whispered, "Emeline, I'll tell you a secret. We aren't short."

"Pardon?"

"We weren't short."

"You weren't?"

Her lips drew up and into a leer. "We only have this quilt sale once a year, and Ida and I wanted the most out of it."

I paused a moment. "How many events will it sponsor?"

"Not really sponsor, more like silent donation. It's all for the spring ball, a lavish event for the couples of the highest station."

"It's not a town event?"

"No, no. But Ida does allow the volunteers, so you and Mr. Dorr will be welcome."

"Do you ever raise money for…charity?"

"We are giving back to the community."

"Oh—of course."

She stood stiff, with her arms still crossed, and shook her head. "I cannot believe they all didn't show up."

"How many?"

"Five."

It still seemed to be an impressive turnout to me.

"Don't be fooled—" She paused and squinted at something across the room. "Excuse me." She stomped over and snatched a few pieces of material from a table and then marched to another woman. "Mrs. Doyle, did I not tell you to make sure all the expensive material went on the same quilts? If it is all mixed together, we can't charge more for the nicer ones."

Mrs. Doyle, a pretty woman with shiny chocolate hair, did not respond to Margaret the way the others did. She sat very still and gnawed at her cheek.

"Mrs. Doyle!" Margaret leaned forward and all took notice. "Have you gone deaf?"

The entire room slid into silence.

Mrs. Doyle faced Margaret. "No."

"Don't let it happen again." Margaret tossed the scraps on top of what Mrs. Doyle was working on.

Mrs. Doyle blinked but did not move. I closed my mouth, and the women in the room resumed their chatter.

Margaret returned. "Now that you are a member of this committee, I'm sending you on your first chore."

"Oh—um—"

"I'm going to have you call upon Mrs. Grace and a Mrs. Williams. They are two members who didn't show today."

"But I haven't been introduced—"

"They always accept new callers."

"I really don't feel that would be appropriate."

Margaret's smile faded. "You know you're in a bit of a mess with Ida."

"I apologized and even offered to pay for her dress."

"Oh, you couldn't pay for that dress."

I looked down.

"If you contribute, I might be able to convince her to give you a chance. I'm sure your husband would want you to make it up to Ida after that scene last night."

I glanced at Ida and swallowed. "Where do I go?"

Mrs. Bradbridge instructed her driver to a yellow Queen Anne. A butler answered the door, stiff and judgmental. He peered down at me over a large pointed nose.

"How do you do? Are the ladies at home?"

He motioned for me to enter. "Are you expected?"

I placed my card on the silver receiving tray. "I'm afraid not."

He scrutinized me for a moment longer and escorted me into an oversize yellow sitting room. He read my name from the card and stepped aside.

I crossed the threshold into the canary-colored room, its walls frosted with tiny etched flowers. The parlor was like a field in spring. I introduced myself and explained who I was to Mrs.

Francis Williams, her mother, Mrs. Ella Grace, and Francis' fifteen-year-old daughter, Annie. They welcomed me with rosy cheeks and an immediate request to use their first names. Ella poured the tea and I admired her honey-colored hair, which looked like a braided crown atop her head. She seemed too young to have a grown daughter and a granddaughter.

"You've come from Mrs. Bradbridge, haven't you?" Francis asked before I could explain. Francis had fair skin and sandy-colored hair. She looked similar to her mother but had a smaller nose that tipped up slightly at the end.

I blushed. "I'm afraid Mrs. Bradbridge subjected me to an impromptu initiation and assignment."

Ella chuckled. "Margaret is something of an abrupt woman."

"A wretched woman." Annie dropped three sugar cubes into her tea. Annie's features were a mixture of her mother's and grandmother's, but she had strawberry-blond hair.

"Annie." Francis' voice hardened. "That's enough sugar." She turned back to me. "You are not the first unannounced caller we've received."

"Oh."

"Sugar?" Francis removed the bowl from her daughter's reach.

"Thank you."

Annie held out a tray of tiny flawless cakes spiraling around a silky layer of a cream. "You must try one of my grandmother's tea cakes."

I took one from the tray and took a bite. The spongy pastry melted into the sweet cream, dissolving my defenses. "Um…Mrs. Bradbridge wanted me to convince you to attend the emergency meeting." Why disguise it now?

"Oh…Margaret." Ella sighed, still cheery, while Francis rolled her eyes. "Her little games may work on the younger women, but I'm no fool. Her count is sufficient."

I admired Ella's resolve, but she didn't have a husband who expected her to win Margaret and Ida's approval. "Um—uh—"

"Oh, you poor thing. She's gotten you as well." Ella flashed me a compassionate smile.

"Looks that way to me," Annie said.

I looked at Annie, and my stomach sank with humiliation—even a fifteen-year-old thought I was pathetic. I thought it, too. I didn't want to obey Margaret's commands, but I had to if I wanted to fix the whole mess with Ida and make it up to John.

"Well, I don't see why we can't make an appearance," Ella said.

My eyes shot back to Ella.

"Just for you, Emeline, to keep you on Mrs. Bradbridge's kinder side, although I cannot say it will last."

"Mother, we have good reason not to go. We need to make a stand."

"We can make a stand next time."

Francis closed her eyes and shook her head, just barely.

"Ugh." Annie slumped.

"Annie!" Francis barked.

I leaned forward. "Thank you so much."

"Still, we'll wait until the last moment," Ella said. "Our appearance needn't be long."

"That's fine. Thank you again, so much."

"It's our pleasure, Emeline. Have you met anyone other than the charming Mrs. Bradbridge?"

"I'm afraid I didn't have many letters of introduction."

Francis sighed heavily before she sipped her tea, clearly irritated, but I ignored her.

"We are well known. Perhaps we could send some letters of introduction on your behalf."

"That would be wonderful." I struggled not to lick my lips or reach for another cake. I considered Francis and how to regain her favor. "What does Mr. Williams do?"

Francis lifted her head. "He owns Williams' Logging Company."

"Logging?"

"The Mississippi is one of the country's finest trading routes.

They ship logs down the river and sell them to lumber yards. It's quite lucrative, I assure you."

"I imagine so."

"What does Mr. Dorr do?"

"He's a lawyer."

"I've heard such distasteful things about lawyers. Does he enjoy it?"

I hesitated, thrown by her statement and unsure of the answer to her question. "I believe so." I glanced at Annie, who delicately bit into her fourth tea cake. "Are you in school, Annie?"

"Of course."

"I'm sure you are very popular."

She shrugged. "With boys."

Francis' head snapped in her daughter's direction.

"Boys?" I teased. "You are far too young for boys."

Annie grimaced. "It so happens that I am quite old enough for boys."

"Oh—I didn't mean—"

"Emeline?" Francis grabbed my attention, obviously to apologize for her daughter. "Do you have children?"

"Uh, no."

"Then I highly doubt you know anything about what young ladies have to handle these days."

Annie grinned.

"Well, I have three sisters of all ages, not to mention I was her age once."

"Having sisters is not the same as having a daughter, and just because young men showed you little interest at her age does not mean my daughter wouldn't have any prospective suitors."

I drew back in surprise. "No—I—"

"I'll have you know, she not only has suitors, but we are expecting a proposal any day."

"Francis," Ella said under her breath.

I opened my mouth but couldn't think of what to say.

"Emeline," Ella stuttered and lifted her tea. "You said Mrs. Bradbridge recruited you unwillingly?"

I saw an opportunity to redirect Francis' disdain. "Oh my, yes. She practically forced me. I offered one Sunday a month, and she had the audacity to say that was good for a start." I tittered a little too loudly. "I tried to tell her I couldn't because I am terribly busy, but she is relentless."

"I'm surprised you are so busy without children," Francis snipped. "I have two young boys and a maturing daughter, and I volunteer twice a week. Imagine what I would do with your time."

"Well, um, the house is quite large, and with only one servant for only a few days a week…"

"This house is far larger than your own."

"What? I—" I stammered and then stopped. "Pardon me, but how do you know the size of my house?"

"It might be hard for you to believe, but other people have lived in that house, and people stepped foot in it before you graced our town with your presence."

Ella's eyes flashed toward Francis as if ordering her to stop, but Francis had locked onto me.

"*I have* been inside your house," Annie said, tilting her head and grinning.

My stomach tightened, and my face grew warm. I tried to remain calm. "Forgive me, Francis, if I said something to offend, but you have many servants, and I'm sure your mother and daughter—"

Francis' eyes bulged and she sat straighter in her seat. "I can say with great certainty, I do not enslave my mother and children."

I swallowed. "Um—well—I'm trying to adjust."

Ella came to my rescue. "A new wife faces many challenges."

"Actually, I do not remember having any difficulty." Francis kept her eyes on me. "I slipped into the role of wife and mother the way a princess slips into a little glass slipper."

I curled my toes in my boots.

"A brief period of adjustment is reasonable," Ella said.

"Is that so?" Francis' eyes were still fixed on me.

I opened my mouth to respond but couldn't think. I awkwardly held my face down and to the side, blinking rapidly to keep my eyes dry.

"Forgive me, Mother." Francis stood. "I will not attend the meeting, as I have other responsibilities far more important than submitting to some crabby old woman because someone else doesn't have the strength to refuse." She stalked out.

Annie snickered under her hand.

I touched my face, looked away, trying to hide my tears.

"Emeline?" Ella reached over. "Are you—?"

The butler entered with a woman and her daughter.

I had to get out without revealing my hot, wet face, my utter humiliation. With my head down, I stood and bowed quickly to the next two callers and then rushed out. I opened the door for myself, scuttled down the steps, and blubbered to Margaret's driver that he was to take me back to my surrey, not back to the committee.

I fled home. I wasn't going to return to Margaret to report my failure and give her and Ida even more kindling. I rushed to my chamber with their words chanting in my mind. I paced back and forth. I tried hard to push down the feelings of despair—down into the basement, where they belonged. I was homesick, a failure as a wife, married to a man who loathed me, and surrounded by horrible, cruel women.

And my father was dead. My papa was dead.

I collapsed to the floor and screamed. No one was home—no one ever was—so I cried, I bawled, I wailed. It was the first time I'd really let myself cry since he'd died. I may have shed tears before, but I'd always held back and reminded myself to be strong for my mother and sisters, who were in the next room or down the hall. I hadn't fully realized it, but I'd hauled it with me all this way like an anchor dredging behind me. This was the first time I'd let it all pour out. I unfettered. I screamed and cried and wailed as hard and as loud as I could. I shrieked until my throat buckled into a wet choke. I sat there allowing tears to stream down my face and drip. I lay on the wood floor letting droplets fall onto the panels. I stayed there awhile just sobbing.

I wondered what my father would say if he were here. I wondered what he would think of me.

Finally, I sniffed, wiped my cheeks, and rubbed my eyes. I pushed myself up onto all fours and stood in front of the mirror. I studied myself, eyes red and swollen, face flushed and streaked. A scene of a woman in a cascading gown was engraved into the frame of the mirror, the dress section stretching over the left bottom corner of the reflection. Her body twisted as she gazed back while drifting into a sweeping world of metallic wind and butterflies. I often sat in a wicker rocking chair by the window and imagined the white walls reflected in it as a cloud-covered sky above an ocean.

I dropped into my simple chair and stared out the window, swaying back and forth, my lower lip trembling. Something moved outside in some overgrowth. I watched it peek out, but it slipped back before I could see it. I looked at the trees. A bird landed on a branch and hopped around without apparent purpose or care. Then it flew away. It had no obligations in life other than the necessities. All it had to do was gather food, care for its young, and fly, fly free.

Sometimes while sitting there staring out the window, I imagined a place in my mind, a white room. A simple space coated in white paint. The white represented responsibility, obligation. It didn't require what responsibility and obligation required, but it had the same effect. It maintained the person in the room; it kept the person alive and well, along with everything and everyone that person cared for, but nothing the person held dear existed in the room. The person was alone. The person experienced no joy from bearing the weight of responsibility, earned no prize.

I imagined a particular person in the room—a woman, also clothed in white. This woman constantly faced a dilemma. She longed for freedom. She longed to be the bird.

Her open palms grazed the rutted expanse of the wall. She knew that something lay beyond—beyond the white. She could burst out into the world of grass, sky, and lavender, but she knew that if she broke through the barricade, everything she protected would crumble, suffocate, and wither behind her. Her own freedom would last only moments because she, too, couldn't survive without the white. Earth and water would smother her, and radiant light would slice through her like a blade.

I imagined her pressing with both hands, weighing freedom against existence and all that depended on her, but in the end she lightened her stance and stepped away. She always chose to stay, to fulfill her obligation.

The rustling in the thicket outside grew louder, as if something were waging battle in it. I blinked myself out of my imagination back into the white room where I sat. I needed to cook supper. I couldn't serve him like this. I had to collect myself. I had to be strong. I dabbed my eyes and told myself to be strong, be strong like I had all the other times. I tried, but I just wanted to fall apart. My fortitude was gone—in a puddle on the floor. It was as if, when I let go for that one moment, when I unfettered my anchor, the end of the chain slipped away and I lost it.

I was trying to keep my face from contorting and my eyes from bursting into tears when I noticed the rustling bushes again. What strange creature could throw such a tantrum? I envisioned a predator, like a wolf, but not the regular kind. I imagined it with matted fur and scarred skin, like charred red flesh. Its ears were square, as if someone had lopped the tops off. Its eyes were piercing, glowing.

What a strange thing for me to think of. I had never seen such a beast. Why would I imagine that? I studied the thicket. What if it were that wolf? What if my imaginary creature were real? What if it were down there rattling the bushes, devouring a victim. No, it wasn't real. It seemed so vivid, so real, though. Then I wondered if I pictured it clearly enough, could I make it appear?

I closed my eyes and pictured it again, and then I looked down at the bushes and froze. There, two yellow eyes stared back at me. The face and body were hidden, but the eyes were there. I shot up but turned away, hiding myself from my creature. It wasn't real. I had made it up. I was scaring myself. I cackled, unhinged. If I'd created it, I could just make it go away. If I looked, nothing would be there. I spun back around.

Yellow eyes. Yellow eyes glared up at me. I squeezed my eyes shut again. If I had made it appear, I could make it disappear. Or was it real and I'd tricked myself into thinking I'd done it? I looked again. Still there. It was no ordinary being; it knew that it was seeing me and that I was seeing it. It knew my secret, it knew my sin, and it was there to punish me. Had I imagined that? No. I turned away. Was it real? Was it truly real?

I whirled back—wait—gone. No eyes. What? I—did I?

I threw myself at the window, my hands and face slammed against the glass as I tried to see more. Nothing. I pushed away. I lifted my hand to my cheek and quickly dashed back to try to catch the beast at its cruel game of hide-and-seek. Nothing. Not even a group of flowers or yellow leaves. I must have been tired. I sat back down in the chair and looked out again—still nothing. I stood up. Supper. It had just been my imagination.

I put my back to the window. Then all the misery the creature had distracted me from came screaming back. Francis knew. Ida and Margaret knew. They could see it in me; they could see I was a failure. I absolutely hated this wretched house. It grew worse with every moment. The furniture taunted me. The walls closed in on me. The animated bric-a-brac and reptilian china snickered at me. All of it wanted me to know I was a failure. I couldn't even get my husband to speak to me, let alone love me. He'd given up the chance to have a worthy wife for what reason? He'd felt sorry for me, or his parents had made him? All because my father had died. My father was dead, I was alone, and I'd failed him.

I thought of the woman in the white room—she chose to sacrifice her freedom for the people who relied on her to survive, but how long could she possibly survive without freedom? How long could she last before choosing the alternative? How long could I? Damn the world and every sacrifice everyone wanted from me. I had made enough sacrifices. I couldn't keep my promise or make my father proud because he was dead.

*My dearest James,*

*Forgive me, James. I've given all I have to make this marriage work. Nothing could make this wretched existence tolerable. My husband is a cold, heartless man. He has made no effort to build affection between us. You said his quiet manner was better than an unpleasant disposition, but please believe me when I say this is worse.*

*Not only has he condemned this union, so has the place he chose for us to live. The house itself, I cannot endure. Every day in it I am filled with terror and a rigid ache deep in my heart. I never understood how a person could hurt just from being, until now. I cannot bear it.*

*My dearest brother, I dread asking any favor, but I must beseech you. Please. Please, save me. I know you can enlighten Mother, and if she cannot possibly care for me, I know you will. My dear, dear James, please come soon.*

*Yours, Emma*

# Eight

*April 1901*

The church in Labellum was modest and poorly ventilated. I imagined it would grow hot and stuffy when spring submitted to the wet heat of summer. It was a white wooden church with oak pews and scuffed floors. No varnish. If Ida and Margaret weren't in charge of the committee, the group could use its funds and time to make the church nicer, fix the windows so they could open, put some kind of finish on the pews, and give the pastor a decent place to preach from. He had nothing but a music stand donated from the schoolhouse, just for Sundays. Church volunteers had to promptly return it before Monday classes. Actually, the schoolhouse could have used some help, too. I had avoided Margaret since I failed her assignment, and she didn't seek me out either.

Pastor Tomas asked us to bow our heads so he could lead us in prayer. I could hear the rain beating the roof like falling pebbles. We had just finished singing a few hymns and were still standing. I decided not to join in Pastor Tomas' prayer but to make one of my own instead. I prayed that God could help free the committee from the grips of those two selfish women and let it be handed down to someone who would actually give back to the community.

I pleaded for James to come swiftly but safely, and I prayed that my family and society would forgive me. I begged forgiveness for my inability to honor my husband as God would surely want me to. I prayed for John—I prayed that my choice would lead him to marry a woman he truly loved and one who could serve him properly. I asked forgiveness for all my choices, all my sins.

I finished my prayer before Pastor Tomas had. He continued to ramble on in a flowery show of inspirational words louder and louder. I didn't join in but opened my eyes and indiscreetly scanned the parishioners. John held his head low and mouthed the words, his eyes squeezed shut.

There is something extremely painful about continuing to live a life you've secretly given up on. Every smile was a lie. Every moment alone in my mind was a moment spent waiting to escape. I had to keep my plans to abandon John a secret until James arrived, so I had to continue being the honorable wife. I had to continue cleaning, cooking, socializing, and attending church. Church was especially unpleasant.

I planned to tell John I wasn't feeling well after the service, and I knew he would believe me because keeping up my facade did seem to take a toll. My color had slowly grown pallid, dark circles formed under my eyes, and my entire face seemed to sag. I didn't mind. I could use the excuse to avoid Margaret and Ida. The women from the church committee always brought cookies and sweet tea. Everyone mingled after church, even John, but only because his colleagues were there. Church was where I finally met Mr. and Mrs. Lewis Coddington, but I hardly spoke to them otherwise. They didn't call on us, nor did we call on them. I'd been concerned about this once, but now, knowing I would be rid of this place and these people, I didn't care.

Pastor Tomas finished the prayer and began a hymn. I scanned the attendees and saw the Coddingtons singing a little louder than everyone else. From the way he peered down at everyone with glassy eyes, I gathered that Lewis Coddington considered himself superior. Martha Coddington was a boisterous, plump woman who didn't lift her chin to me or anyone the way her husband did.

I moved my eyes to the front, where Margaret and her husband Dr. Benedict Bradbridge sang stoically. The esteemed doctor towered over his wife. His white hair and beard reflected his many years of experience in the medical field. I had finally met the senior physician, but he hadn't spoken a word to me since John formally introduced us. He didn't seem to speak to anyone much. I had finally realized why Margaret could get away with anything in Labellum. No one would risk offending the only doctors in town by upsetting her. Their son, Walter, wasn't in church that day, but on other occasions I'd seen him worship humbly.

I had hoped church would give me the excuse to meet the famous Olivia Urswick, but she obviously didn't do things like most people and never attended services. She was becoming something of a legend in my mind.

I peeked at John to make sure he hadn't noticed my lack of attention to the hymnal, and then I glanced at the Ripprings. Marcellus always appeared to be distracted during church. He fidgeted throughout and mumbled the hymns. Ida looked tired, or bored perhaps, and oddly unbothered by her husband's constant squirming. I wondered why Ida had married Marcellus. He offered her nothing, he had the worst manners, and he was far from genteel. Perhaps love? I scrutinized his greasy hair and square chin. Perhaps he'd looked different when he was younger. The hymn ended, and everyone sat down.

Pastor Tomas delivered a lengthy oration on charity, occasionally pausing to shuffle his notes on the tiny schoolhouse music stand. It was about the importance of selflessness and sacrificing for others. He read from the book of John and described Jesus' many efforts to help the poor, sinners, and the undeserving. "There are many poor sinners in Labellum," Pastor Tomas said, "and it is up to those of higher learning and stature to save them."

I wondered who would actually heed his call.

I hoped these people would think of this sermon when John arrived at church alone, his wife having abandoned him. I hoped they would be sympathetic to his plight. I hoped the women would cook him meals and the men would extend invitations despite the embarrassment. He wouldn't have to endure much, though, as the failed woman would carry the full weight of dishonor. Perhaps they would glorify John for having married such a wretched person. I hoped the people of St. Louis knew this sermon and would forgive me. I knew very well the extent of the consequences I might endure. I would probably die an ostracized spinster like Miss Urswick. She managed. Why not I?

After the sermon, Mrs. Tomas played an eloquent tune on the piano, and Pastor Tomas called for attendees to come forward if they wished to be forgiven for their sins or recognized as Christians in front of the congregation. Then he bowed his head and everyone sang a hymn as people hesitantly stood and swayed uncomfortably down the aisle. I personally found the altar call unpleasant to behold and experience. Brave souls staggered to the front with eyes on their backs. They knelt and prayed in imaginary privacy. It was impolite to watch, and most people tried to ignore the scene or pretended like me. I tried to focus straight ahead and I sang the words to the hymn, but my eyes frequently darted toward the center-stage worshipers.

I felt a puff of air next to me. I glanced over and saw that John wasn't there. He was marching to the front. I stared at the back of his head, his slicked-back hair. He reached the altar. I glanced down at my hymnal but lifted my gaze back up without actually having found the words. I realized I had nothing to sing, looked down, and fumbled. By the time my eyes shot up, John had knelt next to another man in a brown suit. John bowed his head. Why was he up there? Was John a pure man—a man of God? Or was he up there because he was wicked—a sinner? He knelt for several minutes, humbled and defenseless in front of the Lord and his church. The song slowed, and John rose quickly and turned back. I was the first thing his dark eyes landed on. I blinked and dropped my eyes to the book. John glided back down the aisle and to his seat next to me. I stiffened, pretending it had never happened, pretending as everyone pretended. He pretended, too.

# Nine

*April 1901*

"Miss, you look awful white," Mrs. Schwab said. "Pale as this here linen." She lifted a damp mass from the bucket we used to rinse. She hauled it out and squeezed water from it and fed it into the wringer. Her sleeves were rolled up, and the muscles in her forearms flowed in waves as she cranked. She wore her dirty-blond hair slicked back in a tight knot.

"What is your meaning?" It had been weeks since I'd sent James the letter, and I had yet to receive a response. I was growing more desperate each day, cringing at this veneer life and the approaching anniversary of my father's death. Not to mention the wolf. I had seen it eyeing me from below my window, waiting to devour me, punish me, give me exactly what I deserved. I feared leaving the house. I feared staying in the house.

"You ain't ill?"

"No."

"When was the last time you went out into the sun?"

I snarled at her. "You say that as though the sun here is pleasant. I despise it."

"Forgive me, miss." She looked away.

I took the shirt she had just wrung and clipped it up with clothespins. James must have received my letter by now. Why would he not respond to inform me of his plans, to tell me when he would come, to soothe my anxiety? Perhaps he had to make arrangements. Persuading Mother might take time, as would preparations for my return. I had to be patient, but every second was excruciating.

"That why we hangin' the laundry down here? You scared the sun'll dirty up that pretty skin?"

I glowered and heaved up a basket of dried shirts and another of wet linens. She followed, seeing we had filled the room and needed to hang the rest upstairs. We maneuvered around shirts and sheets suspended from lines across the kitchen. We scaled the narrow staircase and went into the parlor.

"Ain't Mr. Dorr gonna be upset we drippin' water everywhere?" Mrs. Schwab clipped a shirt onto one of the many lines we'd strung up in the parlor earlier.

"No." He wouldn't notice. I clipped up a soggy pair of trousers and watched a puddle form on one of the parlor's heavy rugs. Beads of moisture would continue to drip for the next few hours. If he did notice, he'd probably blame Mrs. Schwab, but what could he do? He didn't care for her but couldn't dispose of her for lack of servants. She was more likely to drop dead from working while with child than get fired.

"In the light—I'm sure of it—you look sickly."

"It's the basement. I don't like it down there."

"Forgive me, miss, you seem prickled. Sure you don't want to take a rest? I can do the work today."

"No." I bent down and fumbled in the basket, mumbling. "I don't even have children. This should be easy."

She looked around. "I don't know, miss, it's a pretty big house, and you ain't got much help. My condition don't make me much of a worker. Shouldn't be long now, though. I'll be lighter soon." She squatted, balancing the globe between her legs. She hauled up another damp walking skirt, and I saw that she was near the bottom of her basket.

"It's the basement." I picked up the basket of dried linens. "I can't breathe down there. Continue without me. I'll be down after I put these away." As Mrs. Schwab waddled toward the basement stairs, I felt as if I had committed a crime and allowed an innocent to willingly brave my punishment.

I lingered in front of the stairwell, walked up a few steps, and curved right into the narrow space where I couldn't see the bottom or top floors and always felt encased in alabaster. My shoulders scrunched forward and the basket crowded my front. The walls seemed to press inward. I could see myself like bleached marble in a solid tomb, holding a basket of linens for all time. I refused to think of my father in a coffin. I quickened my step, wrestling with the thought: an eternity in a stairwell. I made it past the second corner, reached the landing, and saw black.

The hallway was dark. Mrs. Schwab was supposed to open the doors every morning when she cleaned our chamber, but they were closed. She wasn't especially skilled at following directions. I clenched my teeth at her carelessness. How could she forget such a thing? How could she walk down a dark hallway and not think of it? I didn't have a lamp. I couldn't see anything other than slivers of daylight from beneath each door.

I held the basket with my left hand and felt for the first door with my right hand. I hated that moment just before opening the door. I dreaded it, which is why I'd given Mrs. Schwab the task. When we'd first arrived, I made up little stories about each of the rooms, just something to entertain myself with, but they'd turned against me. With the first door, I always conjured up the image of a woman and a child—he seemed familiar. They were stiff and displeased with each other. The woman wore a plain white frock and appeared to be a caretaker of some sort. Her face glowed and her cheeks were flush. She combed the child's hair with force, preparing him for the end. His face remained still and his eyes closed. He had no breath. I rotated the doorknob, and the woman's eyes jerked toward the door.

I prepared myself to find them inside, staring at me, judging me for my choices. The imagined scenes seemed so real that I almost believed they would be there. I didn't believe in spirits or ghosts. I didn't believe the house was haunted. These were creations of my own. I had never actually seen them except for in my mind. Yet for some reason I kept expecting to find them there. I feared I might have brought them into reality, the way I had the wolf. I opened the door but failed to look in before the sharp sunlight blinded me. It stung my eyes and I snapped back, feeling the built-up heat radiate out. I forced myself to look into the room. Empty.

I moved to the next door on the left. This door instilled a completely different feeling in me. I envisioned a young girl, almost a woman. She had plastered pictures and posters on her walls the way young boys do. The room was a happy young room, yet she sat on the end of her mattress gaping at her hands. What had she done with them? She dropped something, and it clanked against the floor. I knew the sound, that of a small empty bottle, but I refused to think of it. I clasped the handle and she jolted. Overwhelming luminescence bleached out the scene. Little multicolored shades and black spots blinked in front of my face as the world re-formed in front of me. I looked in, but no one was there—nothing on the floor.

I stumbled a little as I continued and shifted the basket under my left arm so I could grab the doorknob of the next room across the hall on the right this time. A wall to this room shared a wall with my own. This room didn't frighten me as much as the others, for a little girl inhabited it. She skipped, giggled, hummed, and amused herself all day. She covered her head in pink and white frills and ribbons. I turned the knob and pushed, letting it slowly swing inward to reveal the room. The light filtered out in a glow rather than a horrendous assault. It saddened me; she was never there. I considered a dark brown stain in the middle of the wood floor. I didn't know what had caused it. Sometimes I saw her curled up on top of that spot, weeping.

I sighed in anticipation of the next room, my greatest horror. The door to this room was positioned too close to the perpendicular wall, so I'd initially assumed it was a linen closet. It wasn't until I'd opened it for the first time with the intention of storing some sheets and towels that I found a large room extending narrowly to the right, along the left wall of my room. It almost seemed disguised, hidden.

I stepped forward and clutched the doorknob. I shivered at the thought of what squatted behind that thin wood. I always felt this presence lurking. I knew the room was filled with sunlight, but in my head I saw only darkness. I saw a gangly inhuman creature enveloped in black. Its long limbs formed angles as it scuttled across the bare floor, knowing I was about to enter. It was sin. I wanted to cry, the fear was so immense. I couldn't banish the thought that it was really there, the thought that it would actually attack me, that it was my fault, that it had come from me—it existed only because of me. I felt the way I had when I'd created the wolf—when my father closed his eyes. I wanted to leave the door closed and ignore it, but I couldn't let my silly fears influence me so.

I prepared myself for the light. I didn't know how to prevent the sting other than to close my eyes and open the door quickly. I twisted the doorknob and extended my arms as the door moved inward. I flinched. The light should have been released, but I didn't see the red glow from behind my shut eyes. I slowly opened them, just a little at first, but saw nothing, absolutely nothing. I opened them completely and saw darkness.

I squealed and fell backward. My back and head slammed against the wall across from the dark room. Shirts and pants flopped out of the basket. How could it be dark?

"Mrs. Dorr? Are you all right?" I heard Mrs. Schwab pound up the basement stairs.

I sat up against the wall with clothing scattered around me. I stared into the dark hole feeling the presence creep out and hover over me, its gangly limbs stretching across my body. If it took me, what would I become?

"Miss?" She was at the bottom of the stairwell.

I had to force my words, and my voice cracked. "I—I'm fine."

"Do you need me?"

I tried to stand, but my corset straightened me like a board, and I couldn't wrench myself into a standing position. I reached for my chamber doorknob and pulled myself up. I bent one leg and then the other, my gaze fixed on the dark room, rapidly scanning for a glimmer of the beast. How could it be dark?

"Mrs. Dorr?"

"I..." I paused to gather my voice. "I'm fine!"

Her heavy steps drifted away.

I stood up and looked into the darkness. I had to face this. I hesitated and then slowly inched into the room. I could feel it watching me. I raised my hands in front of me, wondering if I might suddenly feel its ragged flesh. I squeezed my eyes shut and told myself it wasn't real. My steps were heavy. Darkness pounded in my ears. It felt as if the door had shut behind me. I staggered in an endless darkness that belonged to no place. I took another step and another until, with the tip of my left middle finger, I felt it. It was standing in front of the window. It was standing right in front of me.

I stopped. Oh, Lord. Oh, God. I was touching it. This was it. Now it had me. It had me. My heart pounded. I cringed and I waited. I waited for something, for pain, for an end. Had it happened? Nothing happened. It didn't move.

I eased my left hand slightly forward and felt the strange texture envelop it, soft—like velvet? I opened my eyes, grabbed it, and yanked. A sliver of light appeared. It took me a moment. Curtains.

# Ten

*April 1901*

"Emeline, how are you?" Margaret was calling.

"I am well. Please, sit." We were in the pink sitting room. The parlor rugs were wet from our most recent laundry day. John hadn't noticed the damp rugs for an entire month, but Margaret would. The sitting room was terribly fuchsia. It made me dizzy as though the room rose and fell in suffocating, pink waves. I gestured Margaret to a safe wooden chair, for there were many dangers in this room. Margaret, however, chose the pink and white striped hugging chair. I called it such because it appeared to be cushioned and welcoming, but the arms curved inward and the tall back rounded around you, creating the sensation of being unwillingly clasped from behind. Margaret removed her gloves and I bit my lip and clasped my hands to my chest, waiting for her reaction to this outlandish piece.

She glanced up as she pulled off the second glove. "Emeline?"

"Um—uh—no." I paused, lowered my hands. "No—I mean—yes, fine." I pulled my shoulders back and forced my good posture. Mrs. Schwab didn't work that day, and I'd failed to lace my corset properly. My spine felt weary while unsupported.

"Is this a bad time?" She looked at me sideways.

"I just—um—" I tried to think. "Sorry. About Mrs. Grace and Mrs. Williams."

"Hmm? Oh. Yes. Ella showed right as we dispersed. She didn't make a single stitch."

"Mrs. Grace stopped by?"

She waved a hand. "It's all right, dear. Honestly, I would have preferred she not show at all. I just sent you so you could fix things with Ida."

"Um—thank you."

"Not that it helped."

I poured her tea.

She took sugar but no cream. "That committee is full of fools, and it's only going to get worse if they put that dratted woman at the helm."

"Pardon?"

She sipped and then huffed. "They didn't tell you?"

I shook my head slowly.

"I expected them to pounce on you. Good, then I can tell you the truth before you hear their lies. Mrs. Grace is trying to steal the committee from me." She exhaled noisily. "That's why I sent you there. To test you, but I guess they knew that."

"I thought you sent me to help me with Ida?"

"Hmm." She sipped.

"I thought Mrs. Grace seemed…capable." I hid my grin by lifting my teacup.

Margaret thrust a finger at me. "Well, you're wrong. She will drive that committee into the ground"—she pointed down—"and you'll see. They'll come begging, begging me to come back. Not that they will go through with it."

"I thought Ida had final say."

She shrugged one shoulder. "There really isn't anything that says one way or the other."

I remembered my posture and thrust my bosom out.

"How is Mr. Dorr?"

"He's working."

"I imagine Mr. Coddington keeps him busy with the work he's doing."

"I don't understand why it calls for him to work at all hours."

"Well, it's sinful what's going on, is it not?"

"Um…I suppose." I didn't care enough to try to figure out what she meant.

"Your husband is only doing what he knows is just, and you have to support that." She jabbed her finger at me again.

"Course."

"You know, my husband and son both work at all hours, too."

"Oh."

She slurped.

The room pulsated with pink, as if it were a stomach preparing to digest. Nauseating. I was supposed to be talking. I didn't know what to say. What were we discussing? "I'm surprised your son isn't wed yet."

"Hmm." She peered over her teacup. "It's this town." She sighed. "My poor boy. I'm afraid I might have to go to some length to match him up." Margaret leaned forward, teacup in one hand, saucer in the other. "I must hurry before he settles for an under-privileged country girl. To be honest, I'm afraid he may already be at risk."

"Really?"

She sat up. "Ida suspects it, and I think she might be right."

"Who's the young lady?"

"I'm not sure, yet. He's said a few things—asked how I felt about a woman with this quality or that. And people have spotted him out at odd hours. When I ask, he says he had to see a patient, but his father doesn't know what he's going on about."

"Are you going to put a stop to it?"

"I just need to convince his father to send him to the city, where he can find a proper girl." She sipped. "Or find the little wretch."

"Has he asked his father to go to St. Louis?"

"Oh, he would never. He is reverent of his father, never questions him, never opposes him. He is loyal." She nodded firmly.

"Hmm. I thought he wanted to start his own practice."

She snorted. "He says that to others but hasn't said a word to his father. It's a silly notion, really, and he knows it."

I felt bad for Walter. He seemed to have a gentle disposition—not one for confrontation. His father probably ruled over him even more than Margaret did.

"How is that handmaid?" Margaret asked. "The one who refused her lying-in. Poorly raised." She shook her head.

"She manages."

"You must have tremendous patience. I hold my servants to the highest standards, and I make sure they perform to capacity. This little colored girl—one of the servants found her sleeping in the hay, so I heaved a bucket of slop on her. I guarantee she won't sleep when she should be working again. If she does, she'll starve—I'll toss her out like a ratty old dog."

"Hmm." I narrowed my eyes at her.

She surveyed the room again. "I know you didn't decorate, but I wouldn't be too put out."

I scanned the room cluttered with figurines, doilies, and an overcompensating pink prairie motif. "Did I say I felt put out?"

"No, but…" She shrugged.

I suppose I hadn't needed to. There were fat porcelain children, firefly lamps, butterfly vases, and candy dishes shaped like sheep. My eyes locked onto a cabinet with eyes for windows and ducks strewn across its belly. "I can see why the previous owner abandoned it all."

"The Nelsons didn't abandon this house."

I perked up. "You knew them?"

"Oh, yes."

"What happened to them?"

"Run out."

"Why?"

"The bank confiscated their estate. Probably why your husband got it for such a bargain."

"That is a sad story." I thought of the family leaving town, heads hanging low. The house, filled to the brim with their belongings, watching as they faded into the distance. The furniture had obviously grown bitter after their abandonment. "And his family—what of them?"

"I assure you they are not living in any circumstances as fine as the ones you've commandeered."

Could it have been the house? The house had swallowed them up.

"Emeline?"

"Pardon?"

"Are you happy with it?"

I spotted something out of the corner of my eye. "I—saw…"

She shook her head. "What's that, dear?"

"I'm not certain." I froze, dumbstruck, and inhaled deeply. "It was pink."

"Pardon?"

I looked up at her. "Pardon?"

"I asked if you and your husband were happy with the house?"

Had she not seen it? "Um—I…"

"Go on."

"My husband is a bit—um…shy."

"What do you mean?"

"Pardon?" I leaned forward and studied the chair.

"What do you mean when you say he is shy?"

"I—I don't know if he's enjoying it here…with me."

She scrunched her face.

I leaned back and touched my head. Why did I tell her that? She would tell everyone—I didn't care anymore. "I mean, I don't know if he enjoys being here." There it was again—a pink and white swirl. The chair—it was moving.

"Did he tell you that?"

I watched the chair. "No."

"No?"

The chair's candy-cane arms stretched out in front of Margaret. She didn't even flinch. My eyes darted from the chair to her and back again.

"He isn't happy around you?"

She didn't see it. Was it real? "I don't know."

It locked its thick arms around her. It was going to squeeze.

"Mar—" I wanted to warn her, but I couldn't.

She sipped her tea, undeterred. "He must be happy to see you after a hard day at work?"

It tightened around her waist.

I shook my head "no."

"Oh." She paused and put her teacup down, the chair moving with her. "Are things not well between you two?"

The striped arms tightened and tightened and tightened.

I tried not to look at the chair. I didn't know what to do. My eyes darted back and forth between her and the creature twisting around her like some pink and white striped python. How did she not feel it? "Uh—fine. He—he just—he's busy."

"If he isn't content at home, something is wrong."

I couldn't stop glancing down at the horrifying event happening before my eyes. I tried not to reveal the horror on my face.

She paused. "Emeline? Are you all right?"

I shook my head and wrenched my attention free. My bottom lip trembled.

"What are you looking at, child?" She searched around herself, oblivious to the violent struggle between human and chair.

"I'm sorry. I—I—" My heart pounded and my hands trembled.

She eyed me curiously. "I've overstayed my time. I should go." She stood with her gloves in hand, and the chair suddenly returned to its original shape. It had been squeezing the very life from her moments ago. How? She must have been near death, but there the chair sat, ordinary and motionless. I rose, confused, hunched forward, staring in wonder.

"Perhaps you need to make more of an effort to please your husband. The next time you call, we will discuss some specific things you can do." She eyed my stale tea cakes. "Perhaps a cook."

I lowered myself back onto the rosy sofa. How could this be? What did it mean? The chair had moved, attacked. What—

"Emeline!"

I looked up, wide-eyed, mouth open, perfect posture gone.

Margaret studied me. "Perhaps you should come see my husband."

My eyes wandered.

"You look pale."

# Eleven

*May 1901*

"John?"

"Hmm? Oh, um. Fine." John absently sifted through the mail.

We were eating breakfast, oatmeal and steak. I would have expected a remark on the odd pairing from anyone else, but not from John. I almost wished my mother were there to express concern over my black and blue dress accenting the dark circles under my eyes—at least she cared. It angered me, but I no longer cared what he thought of me. "Are things well at work?" I asked in a snide tone.

"Hmm. What?" He lifted his head.

"I said, are things well at work?"

"Oh—well." He returned to the mail. "I suppose."

"I am starting to think you prefer work to home."

"Hmm?" He picked up his steak knife and sawed at the charred meat.

"Do you enjoy work more than me?"

"Hmm?" He stuck a chunk into his mouth.

"John!"

He looked. "What?"

I shook my head. "Never mind."

He shrugged.

I sighed. "I'm trying to ask if you—sometimes it seems—do you prefer being at work, more than you...prefer being here—with me?"

"Hmm?" He didn't look up.

"Do you feel relaxed?"

"Huh?" He still didn't look up.

"I mean, are you relaxed when you come home?"

Finally he raised his head, aloof. "Pardon me?"

"Are you more relaxed at work?"

"Emeline, what are you talking about?"

I lowered my eyes and prodded my food. "I'm just wondering."

His eyes fell to the post. "About what?"

I wanted to scream but I restrained myself. "How...is...work?"

"I told you, fine."

"You've never really explained what you do at the firm."

"What's there to explain?"

"What do you do?"

He scratched his head, bewildered. "I'm a lawyer, Emeline."

I sighed and laid my head on the table. He didn't respond even though I kept it there for a minute before sitting back up. "I am interested in your cases. What do you do all day?"

"My cases?" he mumbled, stuffing food in his mouth. "I'd rather not."

I gave up.

When he finished his steak and two bites of oatmeal, he stood. "I have to go in for a while."

It was a Saturday, but I wasn't surprised.

"I shouldn't be long."

I stared at him.

He laid his napkin on the table and left. The front door clacked shut. I sat for a while, watching the dishes. Finally, I stood, gathered the plates and lowered them in the dumbwaiter. Then I descended into the basement. I removed the excess food, filled the basin, and scrubbed mindlessly, trying not to let the place drown me in anguish. It pounded on my emotions, my weaknesses, like crashing waves, but I remained as steady as jagged rocks sticking out of the sea.

I wandered in my head to distract myself. I pondered where I would go when James freed me from my marriage, but James still hadn't responded to my letter. What if he'd told Mother and she told him to ignore it? No, he would come anyway. He would fight for me. He promised.

I racked a clean dish and lathered the next. A loud thud made me jump. Then I heard noise from above, creaking sounds, as if someone were traipsing across the parlor. I let my head fall back and stared at the ceiling. It had to be John. I placed the wet dish on the stack, picked up my ivory lamp with the tall cylindrical glass cover and cautiously scaled the stairs. I always moved with wariness while in the house alone, for I feared disturbing something. At the top of the stairs, I looked down a dark hallway. I hadn't opened the doors, in case John returned quickly. If he'd been home, he would have left open the door to whichever room he was in. None were ajar.

"Jo—hn?" It felt like hollering underwater. I cleared my throat and took a breath. I was preparing to raise my voice when pounding on the second floor stopped me. I turned my eyes up and listened, too frightened to move. Was it John? Was it the beast?

A clanking noise came from the parlor. I saw the glow of the lamp on the doorknob, hesitated, heard clacking, and inched over. I grasped the knob, twisted it, and pushed the door open.

It opened to reveal that all the furniture in the parlor was moving, dancing. The winding appendages of the bizarre tables and chairs were actually twisting and twirling. The legs were flailing, and the statues and pictures were sashaying. I dropped the lamp, and the glass cylinder shattered on the floor. My disturbance did not halt the wooden beings' frenzy. I thrust my hands out. "Stop! Stop! You must stop!" The furniture continued to dance as if I didn't exist. I looked around at the chaos and tried to think of the appropriate action. I needed to stop this. John could return at any moment. "Stop!" I screamed as loud as I could to cut through the clanking and flailing. "Stop! Stop! Stop now!"

They refused to respond, and an unbearable sense of urgency rose within me from deep in my abdomen. I screamed and grabbed at the snaking extremities. I took hold of the leg of a chair and snapped it off. With the sound of the chair's limb breaking free, an unquenchable need to demolish these rebellious objects began to boil in my gut. I bunched my hands into tight little rocks and experienced my own detonation. I picked up a statuette and hurled it at the wall. I kicked over a table, and all the bric-a-brac crashed to the floor. I stomped down on the legs of the table I'd knocked over, breaking all but one off. I continued seeking out the most frail furnishings and tearing them limb from limb. The entire room fell into a hush. I seized a detached extremity and waved it in the air. "Do you see? Do you see what I can do to you?"

The room sat motionless, as if nothing had happened. Had it not? I scanned the parlor and saw the disarray that had resulted from my thrashing. My heart skipped. John would be home soon. I couldn't allow him to see it. What would he think? What a cruel and evil trick the furniture had played on me. Quickly, I ran about the room and turned chairs and tables upright and gathered the smashed pieces of bric-a-brac together. I scuttled and tripped on my skirt. I swiftly removed the broken table, dismembered pieces, and shattered porcelain and ran down the stairs to stow them with my melancholy in the basement.

As I set the rubble down in a corner, I heard thumping again. I dashed upstairs and into the parlor to find the furniture at it again, only this time instead of merely dancing, the pieces were running amok. The bastards knew I would be the one to suffer the consequences. They didn't speak it—they couldn't, being only furniture—but I knew they were calling out in an uproar, "Do you see? Do you see what *we* can do to *you*?"

I watched as one reached out and tipped over a potted plant, scattering soil everywhere.

"No!"

A twirling vine from a cabinet slid up the wall, lifted off a mirror and let it crash to the floor.

"You wretched things!" I scrambled to pick everything up. I moved from place to place standing tables up, positioning chairs to face the proper direction, and gathering shards of porcelain and glass. I picked up trinkets and statuettes and put them in their places. Every time I cleared something from the room, I returned to worse. Every time I put something right, I whirled around to find it all wrong again. "No, no, no."

Finally, I couldn't take anymore. I fell to my knees, covered my face with my hands and screamed. "Stop! Stop! I'm begging you—please stop!"

"Emeline?" A calm but curious voice broke through the insanity. Nothing around me was in motion. There was only me, a lifeless parlor, and John's voice. I opened my eyes, lifted my head and peeked through my hands to see his lanky form standing in the open doorway, his cheeks twitching and his eyes bulging. "What happened?" He sounded oddly concerned.

I looked up, stunned. I lowered my trembling hands from my face and clasped them at my chest. My mouth hung open but could not form syllables.

He stared.

"I—I tripped?"

"You tripped?"

I nodded ever so slightly.

He pointed. "You have blood on your face."

I lifted my hand to my left cheek and felt a wet slick but no pain. I noticed a slit in my sleeve that revealed a little blood-speckled flesh. "Uh—I—I cut myself."

John observed the room—furniture tipped over, chairs facing every direction, dirt strewn across the floor, little piles of broken porcelain and glass throughout. He may have suspected my dishonesty.

He bent down and picked up a rounded fragment of a vase.

My eyes darted to and fro in panic. I realized how I must have looked, on my knees in the middle of the room, panting, with a red smear across my face, a cut arm, surrounded by wreckage. "It was an accident."

He rubbed the broken porcelain with his thumb. "Well, I'll be in the library." He turned and walked out.

I looked over my shoulder at the destroyed parlor, everything limp and lifeless. "Damn furniture."

That evening, I sat in the parlor in my tea gown, a loose lounging gown that didn't require a corset or petticoats. John had decided to work in the parlor rather than his office, so I had to join him to make sure the furniture behaved. Their shadows flickered on the walls next to the garden. John sat in a brown armchair facing the empty fireplace. The chair I occupied felt like a wall between John and me. Its back rose high above my head and rounded forward. It provided a small amount of security in such an awful life—room.

I sat there and stared at the window garden with a book open on my lap. The garden was all I could bear in the parlor. There were ferns hung from the top of the window and flowers resting in jardinieres and some on stands. I had recently added the Ageratum alyssum. It was just a small white flower, but the name reminded me of the word *asylum*. I very much enjoyed the notion of a mad flower. At that moment, I wished I could crawl into the window-box jungle and build a little home there surrounded by insane flowers.

"I should let you know Mr. Coddington asked me to travel to St. Louis to meet some clients."

My heart leapt at the opportunity. "Oh?" I could see my family, plead with my mother, and never return. "When are we to leave?"

"In the next few days, but I'd prefer it if you stayed here."

A ball in my stomach sank like a rock. "What?"

He paused. "It is a real honor that he asked me. This is extremely important." His tone sounded troubled. "I cannot let anything potentially make me look bad."

He meant me.

"Besides, I think a trip might be too much excitement for you right now."

I held back sheer hysterics. "What? Why?"

"How have you been feeling lately?"

Why was he asking *me* questions? What was he playing at? "I've been well."

"You haven't felt ill?"

"No."

"When Margaret visited you recently...were you ill?"

I tensed. A couple weeks had gone by since Margaret's encounter with the chair and I had yet to hear any mention of it, so I had stopped worrying about it getting back to John.

"She told her husband you didn't seem well."

"She caught me at a bad time, and she hasn't visited as of late. If I were feeling poorly, I'm confident it would have passed by now."

"Well, she told him you acted strange."

"I'm fine." I failed to subdue my irritation. Silence screamed in my ears until he finally spoke again.

"Actually, you have been acting a bit peculiar."

"I'm quite well, thank you."

"She suggested you see Walter."

"I just told you I am not ill."

"Maybe not *ill*."

I twisted around in the chair and awkwardly perched myself on the arm to peer at him. "What are you suggesting?"

"She's concerned for your nerves. I'm concerned, too. Traveling will only make it worse."

I slowly returned to my proper sitting position and kept my voice calm. "I am well, and I would like to go to St. Louis and see my family."

"I've spoken with Walter. He's coming for a visit tomorrow."

I grasped my wedding ring with two fingers and pulled up hard, not to remove it but to break it off and possibly tear off a digit in the process.

"I cannot delay this trip, and I wouldn't feel right leaving you unattended if you are not well."

"You are not listening. I just told you I am not ill." I heard the tremble in my voice—did he?

"Walter's coming tomorrow and that's that."

I glared angrily into the garden. A treelike lamp whose limbs curled over and clutched a dewdrop of light cast a shiny glow on broad green leaves. What would Walter conclude? What if he said I was out of my wits? I wasn't. I really wasn't. It was the house. It was this place. It's not me, I told myself. It's not me! I screamed it in my head. It's not me! "It's not me!"

"What?"

Oh my. I'd said that out loud.

"Emeline?"

"Nothing—I." I gripped the book in my lap. "This book is all—it—it's interesting."

The shadows on the wall rose and fell. I looked at my garden again, but there was something strange, a dark spot that hadn't been there before. Something moved. I jumped up and gasped, and the book fell to the floor.

John ran to me. "What? What?" His hands were up, ready to act.

I wanted to cling to him, hide behind him, but I didn't. "There—there is something in the garden."

John picked up the tree lamp next to my chair and peered into the garden. As he moved things from side to side, I swayed from side to side with him.

"There's nothing there," he said.

"No. I saw it."

"You're seeing things."

"No, I am not. No. I saw it. There's something in there." My bottom lip shook.

"Perhaps you have a fever." He touched my forehead.

I flinched. He pulled his hand back. Did he know? He reached for my head again, and I ducked.

"I'm worried, Emeline. You should rest until Walter examines you. Don't worry about breakfast. Mrs. Schwab—"

"She doesn't work tomorrow."

"I'll pay her extra. Now come with me upstairs." He reached for my hand.

"No." I pulled away. "No. Take me to St. Louis. Take me to St. Louis. I want to see my family."

"Emeline." He stepped closer. "I can't take you anywhere like this."

I went to the other side of the chair and gripped its arm. "No."

"Emeline?"

The arm of the chair slithered beneath my grip. I screamed and leapt away.

John rushed toward me and grabbed me.

"No!"

He lifted me and cradled me in his arms.

"Please." I kicked and thrashed. "Please take me to St. Louis with you. Please."

"Do you really want your family to see you like this?"

"Yes, yes," I whimpered. I stopped kicking and submitted to him. I didn't want to be in the parlor anyway.

He carried me to the room and lowered me onto the bed. He pulled the bedspread over me even though I was still in my tea gown. I looked at the ceiling, letting tears slide down onto the pillow. The house had tricked me. I wasn't going anywhere.

# Twelve

*May 1901*

$\mathcal{D}$r. Walter Bradbridge leaned over me. I stared into his powder-blue eyes and tried to speak volumes to him without saying a word.

"It was good of you to keep her in bed, John."

He must not have heard my eyes.

John stood a few feet behind him, spying over his shoulder.

If he said I was mad, I didn't know what I would do. Then again, how could he not reach such a conclusion when I knew John had misconstrued the facts? It was up to me to sway him, but I was so distracted listening to them through the walls. The little girl was giggling and humming to the left, and I could sense that wicked being pacing behind the wall opposite the bed.

"Is she ill?" John paced behind Walter.

"I'm not ill," I said.

"She doesn't appear to be sick, but I'm afraid—well." He straightened and spoke to John in whispers.

John's blank expression grew concerned as he brought his hand under his chin.

He was telling him.

"What would bring this on?" John asked.

"She is still in mourning, which can take a toll, but there are a number of—"

"What?" I yelled, surprising myself with my outburst.

Both Walter and John jumped and looked at me.

Walter touched my hand. "It's nothing to fret yourself over."

He continued talking to John as if I couldn't hear. I wished they would speak up.

John folded his arms. "Can I leave her in this condition?"

"You shouldn't have to cancel. I know this is an important trip." He situated his instruments in a black leather satchel.

John sighed. "That's a relief."

"I want to go," I said.

"Emeline, I don't think that would be wise," Walter said.

"What condition?"

He shook his head. "Don't you worry yourself about that." He turned his back to me. "It might actually be best for her to be alone. The less stimulation the better."

John nodded, holding his chin with one hand and an elbow with the other.

"You'll need someone to check on her, though."

Sounds seeped through the walls like black blood—how could they not hear it? They were so loud they drowned out their words. I watched their mouths move, but their voices no longer resonated in my ears.

Walter set his bag on the table next to the bed, and abruptly my senses returned. He spoke to me in a tone meant for a child. "I believe we are all finished here."

My lips shook as I waited to be condemned with the diagnosis, but he said nothing more. He took hold of his bag and strode to the door. John followed. Would he not tell me? Was he to judge me to John and deny me my own sentencing? They left, and the door clacked shut.

I flung off the coverings and leapt from the bed. In nothing but my thin nightgown, I felt a slight chill as I tiptoed to the door. I put

my ear to it but heard nothing but my own heart thumping. I had
no choice. I turned the handle and gently opened the door a crack.

I heard John ask, "Another? When? Who?"

I peered through the crack. They were almost to the end of the
hall.

"I really can't say. She is a woman of some stature. I don't want
to risk saying. She seemed to hint at it, but I can't be sure."

"Did you inform Marcellus?"

"No. I'm not going to accuse anyone until I'm certain, especially
not to Marcellus. He would pounce like a rabid dog."

"I gather it's his line of work that makes him like that," John
said.

"The way he questions these women, it's invasive and cruel.
Most are young and scared, but by the time he's done, they're even
more damaged. He treats this like it's a damn witch hunt. I don't see
how the police department and the circuit judge would condone
such methods, especially when…well, never mind."

"Walter? It's just me. Client privilege."

"I'm not sure. It could just be a rumor, but I heard he left
Chicago because of his methods. Apparently, he went too far."

"Really? That can't be. How would he have gotten this position?"

"Mr. Coddington. They knew each other, and Mr. Coddington
has more than enough influence and connections to help Marcellus
acquire the position. I'm sure he thinks Marcellus' results are
worth looking over his past indiscrepancies. He always gets the
dying confession."

"What do you mean by 'too far'?"

"I don't know, something about forcing a signature, threatening
people into confessing. Wouldn't surprise me."

"That is serious. It can't be true." John continued, but they
began down the stairs. I crept out the door and scurried down the
hall like a sly feline. I slowed and stopped next to the room with
the keeper and the dead boy. Despite the closed door, in my mind
the woman rotated toward me and lifted her finger to her lips, and

I heard, "Shhh." I glanced in her direction and then focused on listening.

Walter continued, "Mr. Coddington assumes these people are petty criminals, but it's not that simple."

I could hear their voices become lower, and I crept after them. They had to discuss my diagnosis eventually, in John's library, certainly. I could hide just outside the door.

"I'd say something myself, but I'm afraid Mr. Coddington's opinion of me might make things worse," John said. "Have you spoken to your father about it?"

"No. He's a stubborn man. He would take my objection to how we handle it as my attempt to condone the crime. I can't stand it, but I can't do a thing about it." A pause. "Another topic, St. Louis."

"Oh. It will probably be another excuse for Mr. Coddington to berate me and it'll give my father the opportunity to do the same. I'll sit in on Mr. Coddington's cases and meet Mr. Hawtrey and the GOS board."

"Quite a respectable assignment."

"I know. I should be honored...and I am. I know how critical these visits are for Mr. Coddington."

They turned again, and I followed, carefully balancing my weight with each step. I expected the walls to move, but they remained still.

"You know this might be Mr. Coddington's way of showing his approval," Walter said.

"Does that mean I have finally earned a good report from your father?"

"I can't confirm it."

"Walter, you know you really helped me out with him."

"Having lived in the man's house, I understand how difficult he is to satisfy. I still haven't figured out how to convince him of my value."

"My father is the same way."

"I have to stick by his decisions even if I disagree."

"How's that?"

They rounded the final turn. Quiet but swift, I crept to the last corner. They were on the ground floor and inches from John's library.

Walter continued. "There's new information out there, new criteria to consider, new techniques, new tools. It's a new century, for God's sakes. He refuses to progress."

"That doesn't mean you can't."

"Not while it's his practice and not my own." Walter huffed. "If I tried, I'd regret it. He'd make sure of it."

"And what of your other dilemma? Would he hear of that?"

"Oh, no. No, no, no. I couldn't, not yet."

"But I thought you said—"

"My mother despises every woman in this town, and when it comes to such matters, he defers to her."

"I see."

Walter sighed. "If she knew, she'd—I honestly don't know what she'd do."

"That bad?"

"That bad."

Then I heard nothing more. They had gone into the library! Suddenly the walls contracted quick and hard. My heart leapt, and I jumped. I tried to regain my footing, tilted, and placed one foot in front of the other, but I couldn't maintain my balance and I tripped, losing my grip on the corner. I tumbled forward with a thud, a bump, another thud, and a final slap. I landed partially on the bottom step and partially on the floor. I let out a groan and looked up to see John and Walter standing stunned directly in front of me, hand gestures frozen in place. Perhaps they hadn't gone into the library. We all just stared at one another at first. Then the two men regained their composure and quickly dipped down to assist me. "Emeline, what happened?"

"Uh—I—" I stuttered as they lifted me off the floor, my nightgown disheveled.

"What are you doing?" John asked.

"Are you all right?" Walter asked.

"Um—forgive me." My eyes bounced to and fro. "I—I just—"

They each held an arm, and I whipped my head back and forth, pleading with each of them.

"I just wanted—" I hesitated.

"Emeline?" John said.

"We need to get her back upstairs," Walter said.

"What's wrong with me?" I shouted.

They stopped, stunned again. Walter hesitated. "You just need some rest, that's all. We should take you—"

"Please."

Walter released my arm and stepped in front of me, putting his hands out the way lion tamers do. "Calm down, Emeline. You have overextended yourself, that's all."

My eyes darted from Walter to John. "I am not hysterical." I reached out to Walter, desperate. "I'm not crazy. I'm not hysterical."

"No, Emeline. No one is saying that," Walter said, guiding my hand down. "You are going to be just fine. You need bed rest, no stimulation."

"Behavior like this isn't helping you either," John said.

"But—I—"

"Let's get you back upstairs." Walter extended his hand toward the stairs, and I submitted. I had been tamed.

They left me in the room again. I squeezed my eyelids shut. They opened to tears. Why did I care what they thought? I wouldn't be here much longer. I couldn't go with John to St. Louis, but James would come for me. He would come. The beast grinned at me from its dark room. James would come.

# Thirteen

*May 1901*

Walter had condemned me to bed rest, to prolonged motionlessness. He even insisted I not visit the outhouse but use the chamber pot at all times. I had hoped Mrs. Schwab could be my primary caretaker, but John unexpectedly decided her condition made her too delicate and unreliable so he dismissed her. Instead, I would endure a parade of mortification from Margaret, Ella, and Francis. I assumed he would add Ida, and my dignity would have no hope, but instead Walter had recommended Miss Olivia Urswick. I was thrilled. I might have been locked up, but when James arrived I would be free, and this was the woman who could reveal how to survive beyond the walls of obligation.

Perhaps I could have welcomed Walter's recommendation to rest if, after John left, the house's modesty hadn't deteriorated. I heard them scuffling behind closed doors. I detected scraping on the walls. I sensed the little girl skipping and twirling. I had expected such disturbances, but I had not expected beings elsewhere in the house to reach me in my room. The basement called for me to toil in its darkness. The furniture in the parlor twisted and coiled, cheering in my absence. The wolf stalked and waited for me just outside. Everything felt like a bright light stinging my eyes, but in my mind. I wondered how long until one of the furnishings would gain enough strength to open the door and seize what was left of my sanity.

I thought I could make out footsteps a few times and sat up stiff and stared at the doorknob. In the afternoon I heard the steps again, but not those of two feet. It sounded like several. A table? They were louder than the others I had heard and approached with definite intent. I shot up and drew the blanket to my chin. The doorknob jiggled. The door creaked and slowly swung open. They were really coming for me.

"Emeline?" Francis entered, Ella following.

I sighed and lowered the blanket, grateful to behold a human rather than a disgruntled love seat, but I was mortified to be seen in such a state by these two women.

"How are you?" Francis grinned.

I tried to hide my hair by pushing the tangles and waves behind my shoulders. I imagined how I looked in my disheveled night-gown, my hair hanging in tangles to my waist and my body loose without a corset.

The two women must have worn their finest afternoon toilettes for the occasion. Francis glowed in tangerine silk, and although it was customary for older women to wear darker shades and heavier fabrics, Ella wafted in canary-colored chiffon. "We'll be staying here for a few nights to make sure you have everything you need."

They'd been scheduled to arrive that morning. "I am aware."

The two women stood at the foot of the bed without removing their gloves or hats, which were spruced up with feather plumes and silk rosettes.

Francis maneuvered around the bed and handed me a white envelope. "I have your post."

"The post is for John, I'm sure," I said with a nasty inflection.

Francis responded in kind. "I can read, dear."

I placed the item in my lap.

"No one answered the door when we rang. Has your handmaid gone to town?"

"John didn't think it fit for Mrs. Schwab to continue working in her condition."

"Oh," Ella said. "Are you going to be all right without someone here at all times?"

"We cannot stay all the time," Francis said. "We have our own duties to tend to."

I clenched my teeth. "I'll be fine."

"You must be frazzled about the house?" Francis focused on something above my eyes, presumably my hair. "I don't see how it could be beneficial to your health to wallow in disarray."

"We will help you, Emeline," Ella said. "We won't let any dust settle."

I paused, allowing my indignation to fill the room.

Francis simpered. "There's nothing to be ashamed of—"

"Are you both well today?" I interrupted.

They looked puzzled.

"Yes," Ella said. "Are you feeling any better?"

"Do I not look well?" I feigned aloofness.

Francis crinkled her nose. "I hope you remember we are taking time away from our responsibilities and our families to help you."

I squinted.

Ella glared at her daughter, but Francis ignored her, so Ella softened her expression and looked back at me. "How do you think you will do in the evenings? We might not be able to return until late."

"I will be fine."

"We should go downstairs. Dr. Bradbridge said we mustn't overstimulate you," Francis said. "And that is obviously easy to do."

I bit my cheek. "Wonderful, because I have no desire to keep company with the likes of you."

"How dare you?" She took a step forward.

"Francis." Ella stepped in front of her.

Francis hesitated and abruptly spun and stamped out.

Ella stuttered. "Uh—don't worry about anything, Emeline. I'll fetch you something to eat." She followed her daughter out.

I lowered my eyes to the envelope Francis had handed me and saw the return address. It was from James.

I ripped open the envelope and yanked out the letter. I had been waiting since March, and it was now May. It's going to say he's on his way, I beamed inside my head. I rapidly unfolded the stationery and held it up, shaking with excitement:

*My dearest Emma,*

*Forgive me for taking so long to respond to your correspondence. A whirlwind lifted my world up and spun it into chaos after you left. I started working and moved into the boardinghouse but quickly realized I could afford my own apartment with a little encouragement from the Dorrs.*

Now I understood why he hadn't written. He was settling into things and he'd even found an apartment so he could take care of me.

*I would have stayed in the boardinghouse, but I needed a place to call my own because I won't be living alone much longer. I'm so excited Emma, I'm engaged to be married!*

I exhaled slowly. I squeezed the letter and continued.

*She is the most genteel and beautiful woman I have ever met. The Dorrs introduced us. You will love her, Emma, I promise you. She looks forward to meeting you.*

A feeling came over me, the same feeling a doll must experience when it's dropped on the stairs on Christmas morning and watches its beloved child run toward a puppy with a big red bow around its neck.

*As to your request, I'm sure you understand how difficult that would be for me, as I am so busy with a new job and already overwhelmed with wedding arrangements. Mother is so happy to have two of her children married. Of course, I am sure by the time you receive this letter you will have already overcome the difficulties of a new marriage.*

This must have been the feeling the doll experienced as the puppy ripped its left arm off.

*Mother and the three hens miss you dearly and are very proud of you. You should know they are very well cared for, thanks to you and the Dorrs. They boast of you often. You would be amazed to see how tall Ruth has grown. Lillian too is blooming and has been greatly improving her manners. Oh and how sophisticated Florence is becoming and popular too—thanks to the Dorrs.*

*I miss you ever so much and long to hear from you.*

*Sincerely Yours,*
*James*

I dropped the letter onto my lap. Warm droplets slid down my cheeks and fell onto the paper in little black splashes. Every moment, for months now, had been a moment of waiting—waiting to leave. I'd used up all the strength I had just to endure and only because I had the assurance I wouldn't have to maintain it. The only reason I'd made it as long as I had was that I used every ounce of my vigor, clinging to the idea that James would come for me. For the first time, I looked around the room and faced it as a permanent situation. No one was waiting for me. No one was planning for me. No one was coming. It was a white room, and I was trapped in it.

# Fourteen

*May 1901*

The moon was missing, and darkness crept into my room like an intruder and disguised the white walls. I stared into the black, waiting for something to happen. I intended to escape from the bed, but I didn't stir for a while. Each night, I would wait until Ella or Margaret retired for the evening and sneak out from beneath the covers and onto my feet. On the first night, I was desperate to move, but with each night thereafter, the simple acts of moving, standing, and walking were more and more like wading through mud. How many days of nothingness and nights of skulking had there been? I felt as if I had already spent an eternity trapped in this room.

Everyone refused to confirm my diagnosis, but hysteria or not, resting was certainly not a cure. The longer I rested, the more fatigued I felt. I awoke exhausted. I languished throughout the day. Rest was the only thing I was allowed to do. I wasn't even permitted books or pen and paper. If my visitors found any contraband, they seized it. All I had to read was James' letter, which, after rereading several times in search of some hidden meaning, I hurled across the room in a crumpled ball. With nothing to think of other than my prison and James, I submitted to sleep, abandoned the world, and found a fragile solace in the deep void of nothingness behind my eyes.

At night, a part of me wanted to stay in bed and never move, but my extremities were anxious, about to twitch if I didn't force them to carry out their purpose. I laughed at myself, pitiful. I owned no will. The only freedom I experienced came with the footsteps I stole in the night. I didn't enjoy them, though, because I took each step with trepidation for fear of waking the beings beneath or, worse, the monster in the empty room next to me.

I opened my eyes to the dark and waited for them to adjust. Finally, I raised the blanket and slid my lower limbs off the right side of the bed. They felt wobbly, like the stalk of a feeble flower. I placed my toes down first and lowered my feet cautiously. The wood felt cool beneath my feet despite the warmth in the air. I stood but didn't expect the heaviness of my body, and I had to lean against the mattress to steady myself.

The beast crept along the wall, mimicking my steps. It had no need to attack—I was right where they all wanted me. The people in the empty rooms down the hall were in their beds. The little boy was made up peacefully, prepared for his burial—his keeper's work complete. The young woman lay awake, staring with wide, glistening eyes at the tiny bottle on the floor. The little girl had sweet subtle dreams. As for the rest of the house, the furniture and decorations were at rest, but they were all well aware of my presence and the need to keep me in my place. Had that been their plan all along? The war had been won—they'd triumphed—and now I was their prisoner. The beast watched me constantly, followed me, ready to pounce if I revealed any strength of will.

I edged to my window. I twisted my hands around each other. My wedding ring pressed into the two adjacent fingers. I couldn't see anything outside. I stepped toward the center of the room. The silence was so intense that my ears hummed to fight it. The air was so still that my own existence was suspect. The house made no sound, but I knew it was awake. Each night when I repeated those steps back and forth across my chamber, I felt it growing tired of me.

What were they doing down there unsupervised? I studied the floorboards and gradually lowered myself. I positioned my hands flat on the floor, brought down my right ear, and listened. There was nothing but silence drumming in my ears. I tried to disregard the constant hum of quiet and listen, but a startling thud sounded from the wall opposite the bed—the monster. I lifted my head but remained on all fours. I did not dare move.

I slowly rose, perceiving its stare through the wall. I concentrated in the direction of the thud as I shrank back to the bed, taking each step with caution. I lifted my limbs off the floor and buried them under the bedspread, which I promptly drew to my chin. I eyed the room. I wondered if anything was with me. It was so black that something could be lurking about and I wouldn't know. I wanted to light a lamp, but I didn't want to draw its attention.

I knew it had a plan for me.

They must have roused downstairs. I heard wood scuffing against wood. In my mind, I saw the furniture. I saw the leg of a table slide out from beneath it and drag its quadratic body out from its position. Then the other tables' legs started to move. The cabinets noticed and began twirling their slender appendages. The sofa, chairs, and tables all woke up and began to slink about the parlor. The bugs on the dishes in the dining room took flight, and the salamanders slithered off the spoons. The sitting room started to contract and digest everything inside it. I could feel the people down the hall, stirring in their rooms, scrutinizing me, judging. The beast scratched at the walls like a sinister man scratching a chalkboard long and hard without letting up.

It was too much.

The scratching stopped and a deep groan slowly rose up out of the house's gut—the dungeon. It started low with a rumble and grew louder and louder into an inhuman wailing that seeped through the cracks and crevices. I covered my ears and scrunched down. The beast started to beat the wall again, and the furniture wouldn't let up clacking and clanking below. There was so much noise. I squeezed my ears harder and closed my eyes. I didn't know how much longer I would last. How much longer could I last?

# Fifteen

*May 1901*

By the time I met Miss Urswick, I had spent several days in bed crying, cowering, and floundering in boredom. My other keepers came only once or twice a day, usually bringing me all my meals at once and instructing me to space them out. Then they left me alone. Francis, Ella, and Margaret always remained downstairs. No one offered to stay or attempted conversation. They repelled my questions and thoughts, warning me of the consequences of stress. Aside from our initial greeting, any time I asked a question or spoke at all, Margaret would "shhh" me. All I had to look forward to was Miss Urswick, but when Margaret learned that she was one of my sitters, she made every effort to take or delegate away her shifts. I was elated when I learned she couldn't stop the spinster from sitting with me for a night.

Miss Urswick had something I wanted: freedom. She was without a husband, without a brother, without a father, and she survived. I needed to know if I could survive outside this room. Could I do it alone? There had to be a way; I needed there to be a way.

By the time we met, my nerves were so rattled by the presences—
I was so desperate—that I struggled not to burst into tears and beg
her to reveal her secrets. "I've looked forward to meeting you," I
said.

Her eyes turned quizzical. "Have you?"

"Yes."

"Call me Olivia." Her voice rasped, and little wiry kinks of red
hair stuck out of her bun and the little curls haloing her forehead.
"Has resting done you any good?"

"I'm afraid not."

"I'd gather sleeping all the time would be awfully tiresome."
There was something about her—proper enough but not quite
right.

"It has the opposite effect."

"Why do you keep lying there then?"

"Um—" I hesitated until an uncomfortable feeling seeped into
the space between us. It thickened the air. I tried to think of something to say—what could I say? What could I ask her? All I wanted
to know was how she did it. How did she survive? How could I
go about it gracefully? I felt anxious and impatient. I had to say
something to rid us of this silence. "Why did you never marry?" I
was stunned by my own words.

Her smile dropped and her lips pinched together.

"I mean—I'm curious how you manage on your own?"

"I do fine."

"Forgive me—I meant without a husband?"

She raised her voice. "I do fine."

"Forgive me, I mean how do you…"

"What?"

"Um—how do you survive?"

She didn't move or speak.

I swallowed and waited.

She just stared.

I started to panic. This wasn't polite or subtle. "Um—I'm

asking for personal reasons." I lowered my head. "I'm—not doing very well."

She squinted. "I have a small garden, goats, some chickens."

"That doesn't sound like it would be enough."

"Everything doesn't have to be machine-made and purchased from factories."

"How could you not marry?"

"What is it to you?"

"I'm not trying to offend you."

She spoke carefully. "I am not one to be under the whim of a man."

I perked up and leaned forward. "But—your parents, society—they must have pushed?"

"My parents died. I don't give a holler about society."

"You must have thought you couldn't survive."

"Special clause in the will—I inherited." She lifted her chin.

I smiled at the thought and then frowned. She had money. That's how she did it. I had no money. There was nothing to inherit. She didn't have a family to care for. She had all the right circumstances.

"You aren't happy?"

I gestured at myself, confined to my bed and a chamber pot.

"Suppose not." She paused. "I'm surprised you're not with child yet."

"Oh—uh—we've only just wed." The truth was, we had only been with each other the one time.

"Most don't even wait on that."

"Pardon?"

"You know many are with child prior to that."

"My mother always said God only blessed married people with children."

"Excuse me?"

I jolted.

"Do you really think I don't know you already know all my business?"

"No."

She grunted. "And if you do know, why are you trying to get a rise out of me?"

"I'm not. I apologize." I put my hands up. "I didn't think."

"You know, though."

I nodded, sheepishly.

"That was real clever—Margaret fighting tooth and nail to keep me away when you two are actually toying with me."

"No." I shook my head. "I'm just curious."

"About what?"

"I—I don't know."

She raised her voice. "If you want to know something, don't try to wring it out of me by poking me with a twig. Use your hands and squeeze."

"What?"

"What do you want?"

"I—I just wanted to know how you did it."

"Did what?" She was angry now. "Lose my child's respect?"

"No!"

"What game are you playing?"

"None."

"You have no right to my business."

"I'm not trying—"

"No." She stood quickly. "I'm not staying here if this is how I'm going to be treated." She stomped to the door and slammed it behind her.

"Wait. I'm sorry. Please don't leave me alone. Please! Please!" I listened to her clomp down the hall and down the stairs. There was a long silence and finally the slam of the door. I was alone. It would be dark soon, and I was alone—alone with the house.

It was another night with no moon, just utter darkness, and this night it was only me and the house. There were no shadows; the white house had become black. I lay awake for most of the night. Finally, I drifted off but roused quickly when I heard sadness in a dream. I realized the sound was the little girl's crying. I turned my head toward the wall her room shared with mine, then to the beast's wall across from my bed.

I became aware. For some reason, the wicked presence decided it would no longer tolerate me. I could feel it lowering its antlike body between bent limbs, hairy arms outstretched. Its energy, its rage built. I could see it in my head. As it let the feeling boil in its abdomen, it crouched and nearly disappeared in the shadows of the empty room. I wondered for a moment if it had gone, if it slept. But it sprang up and released every ounce of its frustration at the wall. My vision fell back into my room. Pounding. Pounding. Then I heard scraping sounds, as if a rat had been trapped with a snake. It was coming for me.

Screams like light burst into my mind, and I was momentarily disoriented. When I found my way back, the scratching was louder, and I knew I couldn't remain within my chamber any longer. I thrust off the covers, felt my feet hit the floor, and flew toward the door. I took the doorknob in my hand. I sensed the house's unrelenting hunger for me. I gripped the knob and hesitated, fearful that the beast would do the same at its door in the next room. I feared that if I made a sound, something would snatch me up, but I couldn't flee silently. I couldn't move with caution, not when it was trying to get me.

The scratching gave way to banging. The wife within me told me not to go. I wouldn't be able to live beyond the white walls— nothing I cared for would survive. Loud thuds sounded. I had to stay. I was supposed to get better. My family needed my marriage. I had to be a good wife. Pounding. Scratching. James wasn't coming. I couldn't abandon my obligations without help. I should be loyal. Banging. I had to honor my father and mother and everything that depended on me and my marriage. I couldn't do it on my own. I needed the Dorrs to take care of them. I had to maintain the walls.

James had abandoned me. Pounding. I had no choice. I had no one. Pounding. I had to stay. I must stay. Pounding. I had to stay. You have stay. You have to stay. You have to stay.

I screamed, "I will not stay!"

I stepped back and yanked the door open. When I saw the flash of the empty corridor, I ran. My feet slapped against the wood floors. The people in the rooms whipped their heads around as I blazed by. They kept their eyes on me, twisting their necks just beyond what was natural. I quickened my step to escape the hall and ended up in the stairwell.

The moment I fell into the cave of steps, the walls moved in. Wailing sounded as they narrowed toward me. I tripped and fumbled. Before, I'd never been sure if I truly heard the house creak and moan, but now, as if it knew my urgency, it left nothing to my imagination. I slammed against the wall where the stairwell curled left. I sensed something reaching out for me as I hit each step. At the final corner, my right foot reached too far, and I felt my heel hit two or three steps in a row as my left leg bent under. I put my hands out as I fell forward and hit the floor at the bottom of the stairs. I heard the clawing and scraping sounds of oddly shaped feet thrashing down the second-floor hallway. The beast had broken out and was coming for me. There was no time for either pain or grace. I pushed myself up and began a sprint.

My feet bound down the hall, and all the rooms in the house lunged at me. Ella and Francis must have opened the doors. As I dashed past, I caught glimpses of things inside the dining room and the library, alive. I rounded the corner and rushed down the hall to the front doors. As I pulled them open, I spotted the furniture in the parlor clanking, leaping, and reaching toward me. I burst outside and did not waste time shutting the door behind me. I ran as fast as I could into the woods beyond the house. I could hear the house call after me in my head, screaming: *You must stay! You must stay!* But I ran. I ran.

I flew into the woods and tore through fallen branches and

brush, but then I felt something clawing at my nightgown. I had completely forgotten the wolf stalking outside the house, waiting for this moment. It knew what I had done, knew I deserved to be ripped apart, and some part of me wanted it—wanted to be held accountable—but every other part of my being screamed to run, just run. I shrieked. I didn't look. I just tugged and yanked until my gown ripped.

I heard crinkling and the sounds of flailing as it rushed after me in the thicket.

I ran and I ran. The scrambling behind me faded away, but I kept running. Branches scraped my arms. I scrambled over bushes and through unknown vegetation creeping up from the forest floor. I ran long after the call of the house faded into the distance. I did not care about my health. I did not allow my feminine weakness to have its say. I didn't care about my lack of clothing or my bare feet. The chill air did not sway me. I heard leaves crackle and twigs snap, but I didn't feel them beneath my feet.

Finally, I slowed. It must have been close to morning because a haze of light filled the forest, revealing a white mist. As I moved farther and farther from the house, the trees spread and gave me room to move. The air felt cool and thick. The green faded as I moved into the fog. I kept on and on until suddenly I stumbled onto a beach. It was the banks of the Mississippi. The river was blanketed with the thick vapor, which formed a wall so high I could not see the end and so thick I could barely see where the water began. It was salvation, freedom.

I collapsed onto the sandy bank and lay there. I had escaped. I had escaped the house—the room. I had escaped my marriage. I was free. What should I do? I could do whatever I wanted. I could do anything. I could take the steamboat to St. Louis. I could live in a boardinghouse. I could go back to school and become a nurse. I wouldn't go to my brother or my mother. I'd disappear—be missing for a while. I could do it on my own, without James. He would regret abandoning me. When I reappeared, I would have made something of myself. I'd be able to provide for them, and they wouldn't shame me or think me a failure.

I sat up and folded my legs under my filthy nightgown. I leaned back, and my hands sank into the moist earth around me. If I didn't tell them about my escape, they might assume I'd perished. I hoped they'd mourn me. I hoped they'd lament. What if they realized I'd run away? Would they just discard me, disgraced by my failings? Would they ever accept me again? Would I ever see my sisters or mother or James again? Abandonment was reprehensible. Anyone who knew I'd deserted my husband would not want anything to do with me. Out of everyone, I was least concerned about John. He would probably shrug off the entire experience and remarry someone of worth.

I would need to explain myself to the men on the steamboat. I ran my fingertips over the fine soil. I regarded myself. My white nightgown with ruffles and ribbons was torn and streaked with muck. I shifted my gaze from my grubby garments and exposed flesh to my sullied and abraded feet. They were caked with sludge and blood. I had been treading through branches and rocks. My feet didn't hurt, though. How would I explain my appearance? I could claim I had been assaulted. Perhaps if I told the men on the boat that the attackers had stolen everything I had and I needed to get to my home in St. Louis, they would take pity on me.

I should have been panicked. I should have realized I had to go back. But I was calm. I was at peace. I could have been in heaven, and I might have thought I was if I had been fully dressed and my feet hadn't begun to throb. Still, I was enraptured, sitting in ethereal wisps on the banks of the Mississippi, free from the house, the creatures in it, my obligation, and my marriage—that white room. The sheet of vapor would lift soon, but it would still be a while before the boat came along. I decided to fill the time by basking in my freedom.

My reverie was interrupted by a horrific noise that slashed through my calm. I jolted and whirled around to the forest behind me, my heart thumping. I saw nothing but fingers of fog dipping in and out of the trees. Was it the house? No, the house was different. I began to fear for my safety. I was vulnerable, a woman alone, not to mention without clothing. I heard it again: a high-pitched wail. It sounded like the ragged edge of broken glass. It was a woman's cry.

My first thought was to find someone, a man to assist me, but that wasn't an option. I was on my own. Without resolving to move, I stood and headed into the gauzy veil. The howling continued, drawing me closer to its source. I stepped carefully with my arms outstretched, fondling the mist to avoid running into a tree. Sifting through the murky white was like walking through a wall. All I could see were the outlines of the trees. I tottered on, with bushes and twigs scraping at my ankles.

I stopped when a groan sounded, like a blow to the stomach, not ten feet from me. I couldn't make out anything. I squinted and bobbed my head as if I could peer around the dense mass. I proceeded slowly and saw a figure on the ground. As I approached, it sharpened into the form of a person. I scanned the area for danger—an attacker, an animal, the wolf? There was nothing but this person. I was afraid to speak. "Mi—iss?"

She gasped and lifted herself onto her elbows. "Are—are you a ghost?"

"No—no. Forgive me." I must have appeared as an eerie shape. I moved closer. "I heard your cries."

"I—I'm," she said between short breaths.

As I moved closer, we became visible to each other. I saw a scraggly thing with an oversize swelling where her stomach should have been. She was with child. "Mrs. Schwab?"

"Mrs. Dorr?" She was so surprised that she momentarily forgot her pain. "What—what are you—" She shrieked.

I winced. "Are you injured?"

"No." She pulled her lips back and clenched her teeth. "It's coming."

"What?"

"The child. It's coming!"

"What should I do?"

She shuddered, unable to respond. Pieces of her normally pinned-back hair were glued to her face with sweat. In a small desperate voice, she whispered, "Help me."

I tried to think—did I know what to do? I had read so many books—the nursing courses. Nothing came close. My mother had taught me home medicine, but this hadn't been among the lessons. I had aided Mother when she was expecting my younger sisters, but I was not allowed in the room during the final moments. I remembered her cries, though.

Mrs. Schwab pointed between her limbs. "I need—wait for the baby."

"What?"

There were lectures, lectures, the voices of my mother and college professors coursing through my head. "Remember, Emeline, this is important—if your child is bleeding, stop it right away—class, laudanum helps with severe pain, but morphine is better—the state of Missouri has outlawed midwifery—when a woman is with child, she must be seen by a physician—at this school, when it's serious you contact a physician—Emeline, if you are ever unsure, send for a physician—you'll need a physician—send for a physician."

I staggered around her and fell to my knees. I looked. A bulbous mass stretched the delicate flesh between her limbs. "Oh, Lord!" I shouted. "You need a physician!"

"No!"

"What's happening?" I asked.

"Can you see a head?"

I looked back and then away again. "I don't know."

"Well, what do you see?"

"Something. Maybe it's a head. You need a physician."

"I need to push!" she screamed.

"What do I do?"

"Push the skin away so the head can pass."

"What?"

"It's the baby's head, but it ain't comin'. Please."

I reached out and gently pressed.

"Forcefully."

I jerked back. "No, I can't."

"Push the skin back until you see the head."

I swallowed and pressed harder. I clenched my teeth and pushed. The skin popped back, and Mrs. Schwab screamed. A fully formed head had emerged, and blood trickled from a tear in Mrs. Schwab's skin. "Oh, my Lord. I'm so sorry. I'm so sorry."

"Is the head out?"

"Yes."

Mrs. Schwab exhaled and relaxed. "Thank heavens." Then her breath grew rapid again and she attempted to expel the rest of the child from her body. "It's not coming." She exhaled loudly and let her body go limp. "Mrs. Dorr, I beg you," she panted, "help."

"How?"

"Pull."

"Pull what?" I shouted.

"The shoulders."

"There aren't any." My hands shook.

She curled up, gritted her teeth, and forced out words. "Find them."

"I don't—"

"Inside."

"What?"

"Please." She groaned.

With the head out, her flesh was loose. I reached out. I pressed in, and warm sodden flesh enveloped my hands. My fingers could feel the baby. "I think I have it."

"Puuullll!" She screamed and bore down once again.

I could feel the force behind the baby as I pulled, and then the entire thing slipped out. My heart raced and my body trembled. I laughed and wheezed with relief.

Mrs. Schwab exhaled and slumped down for a moment.

I regarded the baby, its face scrunched up. It was so incredibly small.

Mrs. Schwab gathered whatever strength she had left and reached out.

I moved forward on my knees and handed her baby to her.

She cleaned the baby's face and nose with her wrapper dress. The baby started to howl. Pink flowed to its face and body, and Mrs. Schwab chuckled and cried.

"Is it all right?" I asked.

"She's a girl."

I observed something attached to the red, screaming child, a line from its stomach leading back into Mrs. Schwab. "What is that?"

She remained beatific. "It's normal."

I observed her and her baby, both aglow. I couldn't help but remark, "She's amazing."

"Yes." Mrs. Schwab gazed at the child.

"Is she supposed to be that small?"

"They're always this small."

"Always?"

"Yes."

We sat gaping for a long time until Mrs. Schwab finally spoke. "We need to clean. The fluids are dirty."

Despite my new understanding of why birthing is considered a miracle and not a massacre, I realized the horror once again. Blood had doused Mrs. Schwab's entire lower body and the child. My arms and front were sticky from it, too.

She pointed to a pail. "I brought that for water."

"You were fetching water at this hour?"

"No. I knew it was time. Done it plenty. Mr. Schwab left for the fields already. Figured it best I not frighten my chillin. Thought I could do it alone."

I widened my eyes. I couldn't imagine the courage. "Uh, I'll go." I stood and scooped up the pale.

"Mrs. Dorr?"

I stopped.

"You done more than I can thank you for."

I smiled shyly at the compliment. "I'll be only a moment."

I rushed to my beach by the river. The fog had lifted, leaving frail traces of mist here and there. I dipped myself into the frigid Mississippi, submitting to the sharp chill in the current. I scrubbed the blood off my skin. I rinsed off what I could from my nightgown, but it faded into a salmon color. The blood felt slick between my fingers. I didn't know why I didn't feel ill. My sisters always grew nauseated at the sight of blood.

I returned to Mrs. Schwab. I placed the bucket of water next to her and then spotted a knife in her hand. I didn't have time to react.

She held it against the line coming from the infant's belly and quickly pulled.

I gasped and covered my mouth.

She didn't respond to my horror. "How is it you came upon me?"

"What are you doing?" I shouted.

She tied the remaining line into a knot. "It doesn't hurt. A midwife would do the same." She ripped a piece from her clothing, dipped it in the pail of water, and started to clean the baby. "How is it you out here?"

"Are you certain that didn't hurt?"

"Yes."

I caught my breath and gulped. "I just went for a walk."

"Miss?"

"I was out here walking." It wasn't the most believable explanation. "I do that some mornings."

She pressed her lips together. "Without dressin'?"

"It's difficult to dress without a handmaid, Mrs. Schwab." I tried not to sound too much like her mistress.

She returned her focus to her baby and spoke no further on the topic.

"What now?" I asked.

"I need to get home."

"Can you stand?"

"Only one way to—" She balanced the baby and pushed herself up.

I put my hands out as if to catch her. "Let me help."

She stood and then dropped her weight onto my shoulder.

"How far do you live?"

"Not far." She pointed to the left. "That way." We hobbled in that direction, with Mrs. Schwab's weight on me.

"Were you scared doing this alone?"

"Not until you came up, and I thought you were about to do whatever it is ghosts be a-doin' in the woods."

I chuckled a little.

"I wasn't too scared, but it ain't like I ever done that without a midwife before. Didn't have a choice, though."

"I was terrified."

"No. You were amazin'."

I smiled bashfully.

After walking quite some distance, we approached a shanty with a small grimy window in front. The broad planks that made up the structure were deteriorating. It tilted slightly, like it might topple over. There were scattered pieces of wood and a hatchet near the door. The sight troubled me.

"Thank you again." She swayed toward the door.

"Would you mind if I called upon you?" I don't know why I said it, guilt perhaps, but I continued. "This afternoon?"

She furrowed her brow, confused.

"To check on you."

She nodded and quietly slipped inside.

I turned around and began to pick my way back into the woods. I thought about what had happened with Mrs. Schwab. I replayed it again and again in my mind. I had never encountered anything like it, not in reality or in my imagination. I had actually helped her and her child. I had helped someone. My actions made a difference for someone. It mattered. I stopped trudging through the leaves and realized I didn't know where to go. I could still catch the steamboat, but I suddenly had this unshakable urge to see to Lottie Schwab's wellbeing as if she were my own flesh.

Then, the fog cleared and the veil of possibility dissipated like a dream. I couldn't run off and start from scratch, and if I did, I would never be accepted by my family or anyone else I knew in St. Louis. My mother would lose not only the money I sent her from my allowance but also the financial support and connections the Dorrs provided directly. Not to mention that I'd saddle her with the shame of having a daughter who ran away from her husband. It would be too much to bear on top of everything else my family had endured. I couldn't do that to them. I thought about my father looking down on me, disappointed.

I shuffled and tiptoed through the brush, attempting to shield my feet from further damage. The expanse of the woods was shorter than I'd thought. I moved some tree limbs aside and saw the house. I imagined it would snicker at me as I crawled back like a slave incapable of surviving without her master. It held its tongue, though. It looked down at me with silent indignation—and awe. I stepped onto the groomed lawn and knew I was returning to bondage, to my agonizing existence, but I felt different. I'd broken down the white walls, and I had survived. Although I might have decided to go back to the house, back to the room, the walls had been broken down, and I had no intention of putting them back up. I didn't care about any of that anymore.

I passed through the doors I had left open after bursting out that morning. I thought of a disappointed parent opening the door for an ill-behaved child, but I didn't cower. Nearly naked and covered in dirt and blood, I entered with my head up, a rebellious child without fear of her punishment. Nothing tittered or taunted as I passed. I sensed contempt, but the narrow stairwell didn't dare close in on me that morning. The people in the rooms watched, bewildered, as I passed. They recognized the change in me. I had broken down the walls of my prison and I was free to do as I pleased. Even the beast sat in silence in the middle of its dark room. Its eyes followed me as I marched past, opened my door, and entered.

# Sixteen

## May 1901

"Emeline!" Francis shouted.

"Yes?" I turned to face her while buttoning my sleeve.

"Why are you out of bed?"

I had on a black skirt with white embroidered swirls at the bottom and had just finished doing up the black buttons on a high-collared white shirtwaist with matching black swirls on the cuffs. I'd decided this day was as good as any to start transitioning from black mourning garb to second mourning shades like whites and purples. I pinned on a matching hat swathed in black silk with a gathered crown and feather. "I have some business to tend to."

"You can't!" Francis shouted.

"Not in your condition," Ella agreed.

"Do I not look well?"

They paused.

"Actually, you look much better," Ella said.

"No!" Francis shrieked. "You are not supposed to do anything strenuous without Dr. Bradbridge's consent."

"Call upon him if you must, but my business cannot wait." I stepped around them.

"What business could you possibly have?"

I tilted my head and pressed my lips together. I didn't care about Francis anymore. I had reached the end of my rope, and when I'd cut myself loose, I survived the fall.

"Your driver isn't here. You can't go anywhere."

"I plan to walk…for my health."

"No, Emeline, I cannot allow this." Francis shifted toward Ella. "Mother?"

"Perhaps some fresh air will do her good if she feels up to it."

Francis turned to her mother, cocked her head, and widened her eyes.

I went for the door, but Francis leapt in front of me. I moved back and forth to get around her, but she bobbed and weaved. I pushed past her and our shoulders collided.

"No!" Francis reached out and pulled my shirtwaist from my skirt.

"Francis!" Her mother cried.

"Get off of me." I wrenched away from her, but she clung to my blouse until it ripped. I stopped and saw an inch-long tear along the tail of my shirt. I shot my eyes back up.

Ella covered her mouth with her hand, her eyes wide.

"Don't ever touch me again." I stormed out before Francis could regain her momentum. I glided down the hall enjoying the clunk-clunk of my boots and the rustle of my petticoats. I'd actually missed them. I tried to ignore the shooting pain from my raw feet, laced up tightly in high-heel boots. I was quickly distracted, however, because with each door I passed someone called out:

"Where do you think you're going?"

"You'll be sent off for this!"

"Come back here!"

I continued without a pause. The stairwell had little time to respond to my swift appearance and departure like a gust of wind. The downstairs rooms stuck to glaring, the furniture standing proud and defiant. Before the white walls knew it, I was off once again.

I walked around the side of the house, peered back to make sure Ella and Francis weren't watching, and vanished into the woods. Although I wanted to be swift, I held up my skirt and watched where I stepped so I wouldn't ruin my dress. Traversing the woods fully clothed and corseted proved to be more challenging than doing it naked and barefoot had. My feet ached dreadfully now. I felt like a child taking a secret path to a place only she knew about.

As I drew near my destination, I heard squealing and giggling—the sounds of playing children. For a moment I thought the little girl had escaped the house, too. Then I saw a redheaded girl dart off, and I saw several more children scattered around the shanty. I stopped when I saw a little naked boy standing next to a bucket of water. An older girl dunked a rag into the bucket and soaped him up. The sandy-haired boy, perhaps nine or so, spotted me. The rest quickly became aware of my presence. The older girl, perhaps sixteen or seventeen, approached me with a confidence the other children lacked. I knew she was Mrs. Schwab's daughter by her fair, freckled skin, but unlike her mother, her hair shimmered bright amber in the sun.

"Are you lost, ma'am?"

"I'm here to see Mrs. Schwab."

She cocked her head and squinted. "Are you Mrs. Dorr?"

"Yes."

She grinned. "I didn't think you'd actually come."

"She is your mother?"

"Yep. She told us 'bout you." She skipped to the shanty and opened the door. "Go ahead, miss. She's awake."

The poor state of the shanty exterior did no justice to the squalor inside. The one-room shelter had two tiny windows that only allowed a miniscule amount of light to enter. There was nothing in the place other than a wood-burning stove in the corner, a small table without the company of chairs, and several areas made up as beds. All the children must have been outside. Mrs. Schwab and her baby reclined on a mattress in the corner. I wanted to cry. How could anyone live like this? How could anyone raise children here, let alone as many as she was raising?

I knelt beside her and immediately feared ruining my dress, but I didn't want to insult her, so I grinned and peeked at the little bundle in her arms. "How is she?"

"She's doin' well." Mrs. Schwab had tied her hair back into something of a bird's nest. "Didn't think you were really fixin' on comin'."

I smiled, shrugged. "Have you named her?"

"Not yet."

"How are you doing?"

"The bleedin' stopped, so I ain't ganna need a doctor."

"Are you sure? Perhaps you should see one anyway."

"No."

"Why?"

"Ain't got money for that."

"I think this might be worth the sacrifice."

She repositioned herself. "Look around, Mrs. Dorr. Does it look like I got anything to sacrifice?"

I looked down in embarrassment. "I didn't—"

"Did you see the chillin outside?"

"Yes. Your daughter was very kind."

"I got six. Just added one more this mornin'."

I wrung my hands, my lace gloves scuffing my skin. Guilt riddled my insides.

"They sleep in shifts—they hunt for squirrels to eat 'cuz I can't buy 'em food."

"I'm sor—"

"I lost my job recently"—she paused—"as you might recall, and I ain't got money for nothin', and I sure ain't got none for no fancy doctor."

I stopped fidgeting.

Her lips relaxed and she hesitated. "Forgive me. Um…" She repositioned the baby and sighed. "I'm sorry. I get like this after. I shouldn't talk to you that way. You done so much for me."

"No. I didn't do anything. You did all the hard work. I didn't even know what I was doing."

"But you did. You brung my baby into the world."

"Only because of your instruction."

"You picked it up like a natural."

I shook my head.

"I don't want to offend, but I ain't never seen a woman of your station do anything like that—like…"

"Yes?"

"You were like a midwife. Others would have ran or fainted."

"Well, I—I used to be interested in nursing. I volunteered, took a few courses in college, but nothing like that."

"Is that so?"

"I'm going to get you your position back. Mr. Dorr won't be able to find anyone else, and you aren't in a delicate condition anymore."

Her expression lifted. "Thank you." She looked down at her baby then back up. "You learned nursin'? Does that mean you know cures for when you get a puny feelin' in your belly—or what have you?"

"What?"

"You know, when your stomach gets riley and begins a-burnin'?"

"Dyspepsia?"

"That there's the one."

"Subnitrate of bismuth."

"Mighty expensive?"

"I have some. I know how to make it."

"Wooo," she hooted. "That there's some useful know-how."

"Which of your children—?"

"Not them."

"Oh."

"Mrs. Dorr, you've done such a service for me and you didn't have to. Most wouldn't have. I shouldn't ask for more, but would you do that for someone else?"

"Do what? Deliver a baby?"

"No, no." She waved a hand. "They got the stomach pains."

"Oh. Oh. I don't know."

"You done it for me."

"That was an urgent situation."

"But this is urgent, too."

"A stomachache?"

"They got more than just a stomachache."

"They?"

"Chillin. They've been ill for weeks."

"With what?"

"A friend of mine, his wife passed two months back, and he's been left to care for their four chillin all by himself."

"Oh my." I put my hand over my mouth.

"The little ones are bedridden, and Mr. Whitmay, my friend, he don't know how to care for 'em."

"I can't even imagine, but—"

"He's just terrified he's ganna lose his babies, too. And he might if they ain't cared for."

"Mrs. Schwab?"

"Round a week ago I told 'em I'd try to find some way to help and had thought of nothin' until I see you know stuff. If you took a look at 'em, you could figure out what medicine is fittin'."

I thought about it. If John, Walter, or, God forbid, Margaret ever found out, they would use the information to send me to a sanatorium or an asylum. "I could get into trouble for doing something like that."

"You could get into a heap of trouble runnin' around in your underthin's, too."

My mouth fell open.

She sighed. "Please. They desperate." She leaned forward. "No one will ever know, and it'll just be this one time."

I breathed deep. Could I? The family was in need. With Ida and Margaret ridding this town of charity, they'd never find help elsewhere. Besides, I didn't care about being a proper and good wife anymore. No one would ever know about it anyway. What kind of Christian would I be if I didn't help? It was just this one time.

When I returned to the house, I saw a carriage in the drive. Had Ella and Francis waited for me? I pushed back the last few branches and the carriage came into view. It was worse. I gently opened the front door, knowing that Margaret was waiting inside. I could not believe Francis had run to her own enemy to keep me down. I entered the foyer and heard voices from the parlor.

"Her behavior is deplorable, absolutely outrageous," Margaret said.

"Her condition may have worsened." The second voice was Walter's.

"May have? No, it's obvious. She knew very well she needed to be seen by you before leaving bed. She isn't the type to be disobedient."

I scrunched my face.

"She intentionally disregarded your instruction. She is obviously unstable."

"This condition is unpredictable," Walter said.

"Her mind is clearly deteriorating. You must inform her husband. Take action. Your father would."

He sighed. "I think we should refrain from making conclusions until I examine her."

"Nonsense! Tell your father."

"I don't think that's necessary."

"Why aren't you taking this seriously? You didn't even have her try the water cure."

The water cure was treatment for hysteria. "I knew it," I whispered to myself. They thought me mad.

"Sometimes those things only make the situation worse."

Margaret huffed. "That's only if there is a misdiagnosis."

"Misdiagnoses are common when doctors conclude with haste or when they listen to unfounded advice."

"Well! Pardon me."

"Mother, I didn't—"

"Why do you insist on tormenting me? You don't listen to me. You won't tell me anything."

"Not again. I am not courting anyone. It's all in your head. Ida's gossip."

"Ida is not a gossip."

"I am courting no one. I have neither the time nor the inclination."

"We'll see."

They stopped talking, so I entered the parlor and feigned surprise.

"Emeline." Walter said. He and his mother stood.

"Margaret, Walter." I removed my lace gloves.

They sat back down on the sofa facing the fireplace. "We didn't hear you come in," Margaret said.

I stood in front of them.

"You seem well," Walter said.

"Yes, I—"

"You shouldn't be out of bed without a physician's permission," Margaret interrupted.

Walter shifted toward his mother and blinked. "Thank you." He returned his eyes to me. "You could overstrain yourself."

I met Margaret's yellow-green eyes. "I appreciate your concern, but as I told Mrs. Williams, I wouldn't have left if I was at all concerned for my health." I folded my hands and lowered my chin. "Walter, you suggested I rest. I understood that to mean, once rested, I could return to my life."

"I can see you have regained color and your strength, but I'm not so sure you should return to your duties so soon."

"I disagree, and if the diagnosis was what I assume it must have been, too much leisure can also become a problem."

Walter rubbed his chin considering my opinion.

"Emeline!" Margaret shouted. "I am concerned you are worse."

"Then it's too bad you are not my physician."

Her eyes bulged and her mouth fell open.

Walter curled his lips in, holding back a sly smile, no doubt. "I suppose—in moderation. If you experience any stress, I trust you will return to bed rest and send for me."

"Of course." I glanced at Margaret, who appeared to be silently boiling over.

"Very well, we should be off." Walter rose and eyed his mother, who stamped up and out.

After the door clacked shut, I slumped into a chair and exhaled.

I went to the library and skimmed the titles on the shelves until I reached the medical texts. John had them for his work with physicians. I felt unexpectedly exhilarated about the idea of visiting the family. I picked out a few books, took them to the gothic desk, and sat in the imperious seat, the lofty back lingering high above me. When I sat in it, I understood why the previous owner had chosen it. I felt like a queen—no, a bearded king! I smiled at the thought, and then I started with a lean volume, skimming the table of contents and flipping to relevant sections. I had learned enough about medicine and Latin in college to understand what I read, but I did intermittently require a medical dictionary.

I pored over all kinds of cures and remedies for dyspepsia and other stomach conditions until I reached stomach cancer and felt nauseated. Father. I lowered my gaze slowly and noticed a colored piece of paper under the book. I could tell from the form of date and address that it was a personal letter. I slid the leather-bound book aside and saw the word *wife*. I thought of James. Without even checking the signature, for fear it would reveal otherwise, I yanked the paper out from beneath my book and tore through the words:

*Dear John,*

    *I am fully aware of the difficulties of marriage, and I assure you they are quite normal. These qualms will pass. You are a man now and have responsibilities, obligations. It is your duty to take care of your family, not only for your own honor and that of your new wife, but also that of the Dorr name. I fully expect you to put all your energy into making this marriage successful.*

    *As to your second query, I am disappointed with your lack of confidence in me and my decision. Mr. Coddington is a well-educated and successful lawyer. His mentorship will take you far in your career. Being a lawyer has nothing to do with values, beliefs, or morality. Leave that to your wife. Your job is to work hard, harder than you've ever worked before, and without complaint. I will not grant any more attention to these concerns. I will not hear of them, not from your lips nor your pen.*

    *Your mother misses you.*

*Sincerely,*
*Richard Dorr*

Disappointment and a glimmer of heartache felt heavy in my chest. How could I have ever thought John Dorr might care for me? I permitted the heartbreak to hold me for only a moment, and then I reminded myself that I didn't care. I resisted the pain and retreated to the books.

After reading until I could no longer, I found a large satchel. I went to the medicine chest and recalled from class the necessities of a nurse's kit. I packed a thermometer, petroleum jelly, a measuring cup, absorbent cotton, sticky plaster, bandages of muslin, spirits of ammonia, subnitrate of bismuth, a pain reliever called Hoffman's anodyne, and a stronger pain reliever called laudanum, made from a small amount of opium diluted in alcohol and usually used as a cough suppressant. Next, I went to the sewing materials kept in the sitting room and grabbed thread, needles, and pins.

I'd once read that oil of cloves and tallow melted in rose water to soften skin were essential for a nurse's kit, so I mixed them up.

I lay in bed that night with tingles all over. The house was alive with noise and movement, but it didn't trouble me. I planned for the following day. I predicted the problems I might encounter. I considered what to say if I saw anyone I knew. So much thrill and thought occupied my mind, but I slipped into slumber without effort.

# Seventeen

## May 1901

I cinched and tugged into my dark-violet walking skirt with decorative machine stitching. It had a matching jacket that narrowed at the waist where the skirt and jacket met and widened at the top, revealing my white-lace shirtwaist underneath. I pulled on my gloves and pinned in my violet hat with bunched netting along the brim. Along the hall, the stairwell, and the main hall, the house sat silent, suspicious. I turned the corner and discovered why.

John situated himself as Mr. Buck carried in his suitcase and set it next to the coat rack. John hung up his morning jacket and saw me. "Emeline? What are you…"

I stood frozen at the end of the hall. "Um—I'm fine."

"Pardon?"

"I mean—Dr. Bradbridge said I'm fine."

"Oh."

"I'm back to my regular routine." I tried to smile reassuringly.

He stared for a moment. His overall appearance seemed somewhat more cheerful than usual, down to his brown and white checked vest and trousers. "I didn't expect such a swift recovery." His eyes dropped and then rose again to scrutinize my appearance.

He brought his fingertips to his lips and gestured a little with the same hand as he said, "You do look…well." He grinned.

"Um, thank you." He actually seemed happy to see me, but I couldn't believe it after reading that letter.

He took a step toward me. "Are you leaving?"

"I'm to call on Mrs. Grace and Mrs. Williams…to thank them for sitting with me."

He ran his fingers through his hair. "And Margaret?"

"Of…course."

"Good." He licked his lips, shoved his hands in his pockets, and an odd grin stretched across his face.

Neither of us moved for a moment. I heard a bird chirping outside. Why was he just standing there smiling at me?

"Um, I should be going." I hesitated on my first step but then took long strides until I reached him. The sound of my boots clacking sounded awkwardly loud. He didn't move, so I maneuvered around him. "Pardon me."

His expression dropped as I squeezed by.

I reached the door.

"I think the rest did you good," he said. "You seem…different."

I stopped and looked back with my eyebrows raised. He was the one acting different.

"Hope you won't be long. I'd like to hear about your week," he called as I walked out.

I didn't look back. "It was fairly dull, thank you."

I instructed Mr. Buck to take me to the general store and told him to wait. I entered the store, where I usually ordered bulk items for delivery. I roamed for a few minutes, trying to overlook the owner's wife, Mrs. Landry, who eyed me while sucking her bottom lip. If I waited long enough, Mr. Buck would step off the surrey and find a diversion. Moments passed, I went to the entrance and peeked out. Mr. Buck had crouched down and was trying to lure some pigeons to his outstretched hand. I glanced back at Mrs. Landry, who watched me without modesty, her chin sticking out like a little fist.

"Good day." I quickly stepped out.

I coursed by the succession of square buildings, avoiding the looks of passersby. Recalling the instructions Mrs. Schwab had given me, I counted to the fifth break between the buildings and slowed, scanned for curious eyes, and made my descent into the alley. It was narrow and dirtier than the regular street but nothing like the alleyways I had glimpsed in St. Louis.

Several colored women and a few men loitering outside shot me suspicious glares. I approached the third wooden staircase on the left. I gripped the rail but then removed my hand, fearful that the chipped alabaster might flake onto my glove. I held up my skirt and scaled the staircase. I knocked.

No answer.

"Is anyone there?"

No answer.

"I—I am here to help."

Nothing.

I sighed and ambled down the steps and stood at the bottom for a moment. I reached into my bag and pulled out the instructions. I started counting the tenements to make sure I was at the right one.

"Ay!"

I turned to see a dark woman holding a baby.

"You lost?"

"Uh…Um, yes. Could you help me?"

"Maybe."

"Well, I'm looking for the Whitmays' place."

"Who's you?" She gave me a once-over.

"Um, I—I am a friend." I struggled. "A friend of mine told me—um, I know medicine and things of that sort."

"You sure 'bout dat?" She eyed me one more time, long and hard. "They aint's got no money."

"I'm not charging."

The next thing I knew she was banging on the door of the upstairs apartment. "Ay! You chillin get yo' butts on out here for this lady!" she hollered. "She done come on all the way out here from who knows how far! Get on out here!"

I looked around, awkwardly.

"Dat'll do it." She hobbled back down the stairs, her baby undisturbed on her hip.

I heard something while I waited. I stepped closer to the door and distinguished the sound of footsteps and then the jiggle of the knob. I stepped back and the door opened just enough to reveal a small colored boy staring out with one pallid eye.

"Good morning. My name is Mrs....uh..." Oh, no. I couldn't tell him my real name. Staring blankly at this little boy, I quickly thought of how the colored folks had chosen new names after the war, like Freeman, to declare themselves free men. I needed something like that. I needed to quickly formulate a new name and identity just as they had. "Freeman." I couldn't think of anything else. "Mrs. Freeman."

The boy cocked his head, eyes squinting.

"Um, Mrs. Schwab sent me because I know a little medicine."

He blinked.

"May I come in?"

He shuffled away from the open door. I pushed it open, entered, and shut it behind me. The little boy, maybe only seven years of age, joined four children who were sleeping in a pile of blankets. The group of children ranged in ages from around five to ten or eleven. Droplets of sweat covered their skin, but they appeared to be shivering. One girl, older than the boy, opened her eyes and watched me. The boy couldn't have been any older than nine or ten. The whites of his eyes burned against his dark skin, moist like soil.

"Is your father at home?"

The boy shook his head.

"I'm going to take a look at you now."

He didn't object.

"Does your tummy hurt?"

He shook his head.

I put a thermometer in his mouth. "Does your head hurt?"

He nodded. His sister sat up, and her frazzled hair held in a lifted position. Another child woke and watched as I examined the other two.

"Does it hurt anywhere else?"

The boy pointed to his throat. His sister nodded in agreement. I took out the thermometer. He had a fever. They were obviously ill but it wasn't dyspepsia. I looked around the small tenement. I knew of several things I could do for them, but I hadn't brought the right supplies. I decided to open the windows to air out the room with the mild spring breeze, scented with white prairie clovers. It smelt like new beginnings. Then I placed wet rags on their heads.

"Stay this way until I return. I'm going to come right back."

They stared blank faced at me, and I hoped I hadn't made a liar out of myself.

Mr. Buck held my hand as I stepped up into the surrey. "I thought you needed to go to market, ma'am."

"I had other errands as well. I don't need you to accompany me at all times, Mr. Buck."

"Forgive me, miss." He circled around to the other side, stepped up, and positioned himself in the driver's seat.

"Take me back to the house. I need to fetch something and then we must return."

He turned around and put his arm on the back of the seat. He cocked his head, clearly wondering whether I was serious. I thought of telling him I had forgotten funds to pay the market account, but instead I glared. He sheepishly turned back around and did as was told.

During the ride back to the house, I tried to think of what I might say to John. He would consider it foolish for me to visit town twice in one day. He would disregard any excuse and insist I wait. I couldn't let those children wait. By the time the house had come into view, I still hadn't thought of a legitimate excuse. Perhaps I could get in and out without his noticing that I'd returned at all. I stepped off. "I'll be right back. Stay here. I don't want to disturb Mr. Dorr."

I quietly crept to the front door, holding my skirt to hush the swishing. I twisted the knob as gently as possible. The door slipped from its place, and the house grew giddy at the opportunity to sabotage me. I slowed my breathing, stepped inside, and moved the door silently back into place. I faced a dark hallway, every door shut, just the way he liked it. I could see a dim illumination at the end of the hall. I'd never closed the doors after Ella had opened them, so John had actually gone from room to room closing them after I left. There was a small glow coming from around the corner. I knew it originated from the library—what other room would he be in?

I did not dare light a lamp or a candle but tried to feel my way by gently sliding my fingertips along the right wall. I felt the rippled texture of the wallpaper. Then I smelled the pungent scent of cigarette smoke, the cigarette probably sitting forgotten, burning away in the ashtray. I attempted to will the house not to make a sound.

I curved left with the hallway and spotted the library, the last door on the right. Sunlight escaped the room and spilled onto the first step of the stairs. I held my skirt high and clutched it tight with my left hand. I stepped lightly to prevent my boots from making a clacking sound. I couldn't make a mistake. There was nowhere to hide and no excuse at hand. If I made the slightest noise, he could poke his head out and see me creeping.

When I approached the library, I flattened myself against the wall. I leaned my head closer, carefully, without allowing the brim or feather of my hat to show. I listened, hoping he was engrossed in his work, perhaps with his back to the door, but I heard nothing, not a scribble or a shuffle. Usually I would have to battle for his attention, but I knew on this one occasion that he would be glad to raise his eyes just in time to catch my attempt to dash. Then I realized I couldn't dash—the sounds of my shoes and my skirt would alert him. Yet if I moved slowly, he would surely see me. I had no alternative, and I couldn't remain there any longer with my heart racing.

I moved, and against my better judgment, I dashed. I cringed at the quick click-clack of my heels, followed by the whoosh of my petticoats. It was far louder than I had predicted. I pulled my skirt high in front of me to prevent it from swaying back into the doorway. I stood like stone after my leap, my eyes closed. I hoped I wouldn't open them and see him, hands on hips, about to ask what in tarnation I was doing. I slowly opened my eyes, the corners of my lips still curled in suspense. He wasn't there. I exhaled, slowly and quietly. Sin to Moses! He must have assumed it was just the house, breathing the way it did. I could see him in my mind sitting at his desk and being too wrapped up in whatever he was doing to actually check.

I continued my pursuit, stepping gingerly. I knew the house would attempt to inform John of my scheme. I'd evaded his eyes, but I didn't know if I could evade his ears. The sound of creaking floorboards on the steps above might be more obvious than the sliver of color he'd thought he saw pass his door. I stepped slowly and carefully, wincing with every creak and groan. I made it to the stair's first right turn without hearing any noise from below. Then I slipped into the narrow space between the two turns where you couldn't see the top or bottom of the stairs. Darkness filled the space. I couldn't see the step in front of me.

The stairwell had not attempted to assault me since my experience with Mrs. Schwab, but now it knew I was vulnerable. The darkness prevented me from seeing it, but I could feel the pallid walls narrowing. My stomach wrenched. I couldn't keep away the thoughts of being stuck in the walls, eternally bound within the darkened white—buried, unable to move. I quickened my step, risking a ruckus.

A part of me wanted to fall to my knees and give up, beg the walls to spare me, but the thought of the children broke through my fears. The memory of the depression and horror I'd experienced while trapped in my white room followed, and a fury burned inside my chest. I stopped fumbling for steps and stood still as the walls inched closer. I clenched my hands and opened my eyes. In the darkness, without speaking, without making a sound, I stretched my arms out, felt the solid mass beneath my palms and pushed. In my mind, I screamed with all the strength of my entire being without making one real sound.

The walls gave way and my arms stretched as far as they could. All was calm. I took in a long deep breath and exhaled. I smiled with satisfaction and continued my trek up the staircase. I reached the landing and dropped my head in relief. Suddenly, my eyes refocused, confused by the light, and standing before me was John. I froze. My lips parted, eyes unblinking. John had been upstairs the entire time, not in the library.

"Emeline?"

"Yes?"

"What are you doing?"

I had no idea.

"Are you all right?" He held up the light to see my face.

"Yes." I shrank away from the brightness.

"Where's your lamp?"

"Um." My eyes bounced back and forth.

"You're back then?"

"Yes. What?" I could only react. "No."

"No?"

"No—I mean I'm back now, but I'm leaving."

"Pardon?"

"I forgot something."

"What?"

"I forgot something for Mrs. Grace."

"What did you forget?"

"Um, a donation for the church committee."

"I thought dues were collected at the beginning of the month?"

"They are." My arms and shoulders relaxed out of their caught stance. "This is a different donation, for a special case."

"What case?"

"Uh—children."

"Children?"

"Needy children."

He squinted. "Do you have enough left in your allowance?"

"Of course."

He looked me over. "Why are you fumbling around without a lamp?"

"Uh, I must have forgotten." My smile felt taut. "In a rush."

"Hmm. Well, you'd better be off if you're going to be back in time to make supper."

"Of course," I said, giddy and compliant, shocked by his consent. I hopped out of his way as he passed me.

"Wait." He halted and my heart fell. "Here." He handed me the snake-handle lamp and started down the stairs. "I couldn't stand the thought of you slipping."

"Thank you." Why was he being so nice, so trusting? He left and I felt a little dizzy but pushed the feeling aside because I still had things to do. I went to the linen chest and packed several items into a bag. Afterward, I rushed down the stairs, no longer terrified to make a sound, and barreled down to the basement for a thin cut of beef, some barley, and a few dried vegetables. I moved too quickly for the dungeon's sadness to settle. I went back up and passed the library without acknowledging John.

Mr. Buck, now surely suspicious because of the amount of time I'd spent in the house, took me back to town. He returned me to the general store, and once again I entered and waited for his subsequent distraction. I paid no attention to Mrs. Landry and quickly left, feeling absolutely rushed and concerned that my running about town again, this time carrying two stuffed bags, would certainly end in someone spotting me. I quickly made my way down the alley and knocked on the door of the little tenement. The small dark boy opened the door again, just a little, saw that it was me, and allowed me to enter.

I set my bags down and opened the larger one, pulling out fresh linens to give to the children. They took the sheets, and two older children got to work laying them out. The younger ones pulled the material to their faces, inspecting the superior fabric. I asked the boy to gather water in a bowl and gave him a rag. The children took turns cleaning themselves and one another. Slowly, their skin transformed from the appearance of fresh soil to that of wet ebony rocks. After they were clean, I slathered a mixture of turpentine on the outside of their throats and chests to ease the congestion.

I was in a terrible rush, given that I had to clean a little apartment in the same time that a brief social call takes. I started to sweat as I swept, dusted, wiped down surfaces with a damp cloth and organized what little clutter existed in the tiny space. Meanwhile, I boiled the meat in some water to create a beef tea and added the barley and dried vegetables. They sipped the warm brew, and I instructed them to inhale the steam deeply.

"I must go now, but you need to do your best to keep yourselves clean, and once you are better, help your father keep this house in order just as I have done today."

Their white eyes darted toward the door and I spun around. A burly colored man stood in the doorway, his eyes tight with anger. Moist dirt covered his leathery skin and collected in little beads. He dropped a heavy bag that clunked when it hit the ground. "Who are you?"

Blood rushed to my cheeks and my heart raced. I stood. "I—I—"

"What are you doing with my children?"

I put my hands out. "Mr. Whitmay, I—I'm trying to help."

"We don't need no help."

"No—your children—" I motioned toward them.

"We don't need any help. Get out!"

He stepped close to me, and I stepped back closer to the children. "Who are you? Why did you come here? Why did you come into my home—why? Did you come to steal my babies?"

"Please, sir—Mrs. Schwab sent me."

He lowered his shoulders, but his threatening scowl remained. "How'd you get in here?"

"A lady from downstairs knocked for me. I'm not charging anything." I gestured toward the children again without removing my eyes from the bear in front of me. "I only wanted to help."

I felt the small, soft hand of the little boy slip into mine. Mr. Whitmay widened his eyes at his son and then his eyes fluttered at the sight of his clean home. His children were clean and so was their bedding, and they all had soup, which cooled as they waited for their father's response. His eyes turned on me. "They...look betta."

"I don't think they are very ill."

"They've been like this for weeks." He gestured with his large hand.

"Sometimes sickness will linger without cleanliness, food, liquid, and rest."

"I don't have the time. I don't know how. I don't know how she—" He shuddered and his eyes glistened. Men were not taught how to care for children or illness or themselves. He'd probably neglected the cleaning duties since the day his wife had passed because he didn't know how to go about them.

"It's all right." I reached out to touch his hand, giant and moist. He flinched and pulled back. I knew it was unacceptable for a colored man to touch a white woman, but I didn't care about those things anymore—society, rules. He was just a man. Besides, I couldn't help but try to comfort him. "You're doing fine, and you'll learn. Your children can help, too."

He rubbed the back of his neck, his eyes darting back and forth.

"If they don't get better, tell Mrs. Schwab. I'll come back if you need me." I picked up my bags and passed him to get to the open door. I peeked over my shoulder to see him wrapping his muscular arms around his children before I left.

Mrs. Schwab breathed in the scent of the stew, her eyes closed. "Pork?"

I nodded.

She buried two fingers in the heap of moist meat, boiled potatoes, and rehydrated vegetables. She pulled out a hunk and put it in her mouth, closing her eyes again. She lay on her side on the mattress with her baby asleep next to her. The house was as it had been the other day, lacking children but filled with evidence that they had been crowded there not long before.

She sucked her fingers, one by one. "You can call me Lottie. It ain't proper, but I think we past that, don't you?"

I nodded. "You can call me Emeline if you wish."

"I won't when others are around."

I looked away. "Thank you."

She rubbed her baby's head and touched her little nose. "You want to hold her?" She shifted to sit up and pass her swaddled babe to me.

"Can I?" I took her in my arms and regarded the little thing lightly bundled in a thin cloth, so small and pink.

"Hope you don't mind…I already used your name." She set down the bowl of stew and slowly caressed the head of her sleeping daughter. "Emma."

I looked up at Lottie, blinked rapidly, and then lowered my eyes to Emma. An astonished smile grew across my face.

"I wanted sometin'—sometin' to remind her—and me…to be grateful."

We sat staring at Emma and avoiding each other's eyes for a few moments until Lottie spoke. "I'll return to my duties next week."

"No, that's not necessary." I handed her child back. "You need time."

"No, I need money." She rocked the babe ever so slightly. "My husband is workin' as hard as he can, and it ain't enough. We now got seven chillin to feed."

I looked around the shanty and imagined what Lottie's life must be like—hunger, the constant struggle.

Lottie looked at her baby. "She's ganna hate me."

I stroked the baby's head. "What do you mean?"

"For havin' her." She lifted wet eyes. "For bringin' her to this wretched world."

I shook my head slowly, somewhat confused.

"They all ganna hate me."

"Why do you say that?"

"As soon as they realize…Already started with Lucy."

"It's not your fault. What could you have done?"

Her chin quivered as she closed her eyes and pinched her lips together.

"You couldn't have done anything differently."

"I coulda tried harder to stop it…end it."

"What?"

"I—I knew I was expectin'…before quickenin'." She lowered her voice. "Coulda ended it."

"No." I put my hand on hers. "You couldn't have."

"You never heard of a—abortion?"

"You mean murder your unborn child?"

Tears dripped from her eyes. "It ain't murder before quickenin', before it's got a soul."

"You did the right thing."

"I hear of ways to do it yourself. People doin' it behind closed doors."

"I don't think you could have done that."

"That's what I thought, but—" She took one of Emma's little

hands between her thumb and forefinger. "My chillin will suffer for her. She will suffer. They already eat half what they should. My husband and I ain't hardly eat at all."

Lottie was oddly thin for having just had a child. I stared at one of the water-stained walls and realized what she already knew. The boys—the gems of her family—would darken in the sun and become rough and broken from labor. They would die young, their bodies breaking. The girls—if lucky—would become servants or go to the city to work in the factories. Eventually they, too, would mourn the suffering their many children would endure, having no ability to provide enough food, shelter, or promise of better days. How could the world allow this fate to befall anyone, children? How could society look down on people like Lottie? How could I have looked down on her—on people like her? I turned my gaze from the wall to this desperate woman, and everything I had ever known changed. I changed.

She held the baby tight and her tears fell. "I was too selfish to let her go," she said.

# Eighteen

*June 1901*

After that day, my life continued on as it had before the bed rest. It was as if I had never helped Lottie or the Whitmay children. I cooked. I cleaned. I sat at the table to eat. I didn't speak with John. I dealt with the house. I tried to sleep. I woke up. I cleaned. I didn't do it because I cared or wanted to please. I did it to keep away any lingering suspicions regarding my "condition." No one knew it, but I didn't care about any of it anymore. I had broken down the walls. It was my secret. It felt liberating. It felt like power. But if it was power, I didn't know what to do with it.

It was less than two weeks later when Lottie returned to work. I had to persuade John to reinstate her, but it wasn't too difficult. On her second Monday back, I became fully aware of how much I valued her company, even more so than her work. Still, I welcomed her helping hands, especially with laundry, even though I could do the task now without aching for days afterward. My arms had grown tight and shapely over the past few months. First we scrubbed with a washboard and soap, and then we rinsed and rinsed again. Between steps, we put each piece of clothing through a hand-cranked wringer. Scrub. Wring. Dunk. Wring. Dunk. Wring.

We did that over and over for hours, but real conversation eased the task and the occasional pangs.

"Do you enjoy being married?" I asked.

Lottie shrugged. "Sure."

I took a shirt to the washboard and used my palms to push it down with force against the rippled aluminum. I was positioned on a stool in front of it. "Your husband is never…"

"Never what?" She cranked the wringer.

"Um, well, bothersome?"

"Well, sure, he's bothersome."

"But you still like being married?"

"Sure."

"Why? What do you like about it?"

She crinkled her nose. "Well…he's bothersome, but he's also wonderful."

"Did you marry for love?" I stopped scrubbing.

"Sure did."

I started scrubbing again. "I didn't."

"You don't love Mr. Dorr?"

"I don't think so."

"How can you not know?"

I shrugged and plopped the sodden shirt into her pile.

"Well, how do you feel about him?" She fed the shirt into the wringer.

I shrugged and removed the last article of clothing from the boiling water with the tongs.

"Don't you find him pleasin' to look at?"

I dunked the fabric into the sudsy bucket. I tried to ignore the burning where the soap crystals had rubbed my skin raw.

"He ain't ugly."

"No, he's certainly not. I find him attractive, but…"

Lottie stopped and leaned against the center table.

"He's so—he's so indifferent toward me."

"Indiffent?"

"Indifferent."

"That's what I said."

"I don't think he finds *me* pleasing to look at. He doesn't care about me. He doesn't care about anything." I paused and wiped my forehead with my forearm. "Except for Mr. Coddington and his firm."

"Well, he married ya. Gotta mean sometin'."

"I don't think he married me because he had affection for me, not anymore."

"You got money?"

"No, I didn't."

"Hmm." Lottie huffed.

"What?"

"But he still married ya."

"I think his parents had more to do with it than he did." I had more to do with it.

"Why you think that?"

I handed her the shirt. "It's complicated." I never would have asked if I'd thought they'd force him. I still felt foolish when I remembered begging. How did I ever think he had affection for me? It was the funeral—the things he said, how he helped me. He had come to see *me* the day my father died. I thought he wanted me.

"Hmm." She pushed herself off the table and took the shirt to the wringer.

I sat for a moment while she cranked, rolling my hands around to loosen my wrists. "Your parents didn't mind you marrying for love?"

"Only had one parent. Never knew my pa."

"What happened to him?"

She continued wringing. "Don't know."

"You never asked?"

"Never got a answer."

"What about your mother?"

She paused and then continued wringing. "She don't like Mr. Schwab."

"Why?"

"He wadn't high-class enough for her." She cranked harder. "She said I knew how to read and how to write and I should marry a man who'd take care of me. She didn't gather. No man can take care of me the way Mr. Schwab does."

That explained why Lottie sometimes used proper English. She was literate. Her mother had wanted her to speak properly—to marry up. She'd probably fallen back into slang after she decided not to.

She pitched a shirt onto the heap next to the rinsing bucket and took the next pile of clothing to the boiling water.

I stood and groaned a little as my back loosened. I went to the crank. "Switch?"

"Course, ma'am." Whenever she used a pointed "ma'am," I realized I had forgotten my place as well as her own.

Lottie took the stool and moved it to the rinsing pale, where she plopped herself down and began swishing. "Why is your Mr. Dorr so in—diff—er—ent?"

"Indifferent."

"What I said."

"He hardly speaks to me. I don't think he has any affection for me at all."

"I don't know, I seen him lookin' at you pretty pleased on occasion."

"No you have not."

"Have too. Besides, how could he show no affection when you married?" She handed me a shirt.

I put it in the wringer and pushed my weight into the crank. The water dribbled out into a bucket. "He just doesn't. It's as though I live with a stranger." I paused. "And, I found a letter."

"From a girl?"

"No. From his father. It referred to complaints about me."

"That don't sound too different from a marriage." She sniggered under her breath. "Anyway, I mean he's gotta show you some affection when you lay at night?"

I opened my mouth but didn't speak. I blushed.

"That there's natural rouge." She chuckled. "C'mon now. After what you did for me out there in the woods, ain't no shy left in a one of us."

I pressed my cool, wet hands to my hot cheeks. "Well, it didn't feel affectionate."

"Every time?"

"It was only the one time."

Lottie looked at me with a question all over her face.

"What?" I removed the shirt from the wringer.

"Nothing." She looked away, clearly lying.

"Mr. Coddington works him all day every day. He seems too tired. Is that not normal?"

"I dunno."

"Is it normal to not feel loved?"

"I suppose everyone's got a different normal. He married ya. He know what that means. He's gotta have some affection for you."

"I don't know. What does affection look like exactly?"

She shrugged.

"What does your husband do that makes you feel loved?"

"He kisses me."

"See—that." I pointed at her. "Kissing. We don't really do that."

"Y'all got married quick, right?"

"Very quick."

"Well, maybe he just busy, not used to it all. There is signs other than kissing, too."

"Like what?"

"Like paying extra attention to you. Staring, smiling a lot at ya, making excuses to be near you That's how I first knew Mr. Schwab had sometin' for me. He'd do nice things for you, too, try to go out of his way to make you like him back. Or at least that's how it was before we were married—those things ain't as obvious once you married. So maybe you skipped that part so it ain't so clear."

We paused, and I wondered why I cared. Why did I still have this desire for him to want me? I'd broken down the walls. I didn't have to care about him or care about why he didn't want me. It wasn't my obligation anymore. I had done everything right and he'd done nothing. If he wanted me, he needed to do something about it.

"I'm sorry, miss. I haven't the foggiest idea what else to tell ya."

I picked up a basket of wet clothes and grinned, roguish. "You know, it doesn't matter. I don't care anymore."

# Nineteen

*June 1901*

Wednesday. I scrubbed the floors: back and forth, back and forth, dunk, slosh, back and forth. I had let Lottie hurry home for her baby's midday feeding before a visit from Ella and Francis. The house didn't bother me as much on days when Lottie was there, even when she left for a short while. It still moaned and the furnishings still shifted when I wasn't looking, but I had begun to successfully ignore them. After I'd finished in the parlor and put everything back in its place, I walked to the bucket positioned left of the bay window. I bent over it and heard something, so I stopped and listened. After a moment, I heard more, Lottie's voice from outside. She wasn't alone. Perhaps groceries were being delivered? But she sounded distressed.

"No." Her voice was shrill. "We can't."

I stood straight and faced the open parlor door closest to the front doors. I listened as the voices grew closer.

I heard a man's voice. "Please. What else can we do?" Then I heard him groan. No, it was a third voice. "Please, Lottie," the first voice begged. I heard the door open and the voices barged into the house.

"Mrs. Dorr?" Lottie called.

I hadn't moved. I watched Lottie plod in, but she didn't see me right away. Two men shuffled in behind her. One was tall with freckled skin and peppered hair. A colored man leaned on him, covered in sweat. He held a wrapped hand close to his chest, the cloth deep crimson and moist. They spotted me standing stiff, eyes wide, brush dripping in hand, bucket next to my feet. No one said anything at first. We all just stood and stared.

"Mrs. Dorr, I am so sorry," Lottie said.

I didn't move or speak. I opened my mouth to ask a question, but nothing came out.

The peppered-haired man's eyes darted to Lottie and then back at me. "Forgive us, Mrs. Dorr," he said. "We didn't know what else to do."

"This is my husband," Lottie said. "Oliver Schwab."

Oliver motioned to the dripping man. "And this is Mr. Roy Turner."

Mr. Turner bobbed his head to greet me, but his grimace remained.

"He's slit his hand in the fields, and it keeps bleeding," Oliver said.

"I'm so sorry." Lottie shook her head. "My husband knows you helped me and the Whitmays. Mr. Turner can't go to a doctor."

I watched a drop of salty sweat fall from Mr. Turner's forehead and land on the freshly scrubbed floors.

"Forgive me, ma'am." He groaned. "I ain't got nowheres else to go. I needs my hand. I needs it to work."

I was still frozen there, shocked.

"Mrs. Dorr?" Lottie asked.

If anyone saw this—two men, two lower-class men, one colored, here while John was out—I'd have been institutionalized. "Quickly. Take them to the basement."

"Follow me," Lottie ordered.

We scrambled downstairs, and I instructed Lottie to fetch the supplies I had taken with me to the Whitmays. She moved swiftly, leaving me unaccompanied with the two men. A lump sat heavy in my stomach, like a ball of dough, and I couldn't think for a moment. Then I regained my composure. "Mr. Turner, I need to remove the cloth." I pointed as I quickly moved toward him, and he pulled back slightly and bumped up against the big cutting table in the center of the room. I didn't hesitate. I unraveled the damp garment. The scarlet color spread from the cloth and appeared brighter against my fair skin. Mr. Turner clenched his teeth as I removed the last pieces from the gnarled gash across the center of his left hand. I grabbed a bowl, handed it to Mr. Schwab, and pointed toward a bucket of fresh water I had fetched earlier for the floors. "Fill this with water."

I heard Lottie coming down the stairs. She delivered my satchel, and I removed several items. I gave Mr. Turner some laudanum for the pain. "Lottie, I need more light. Will you get a lamp?" She rushed up the stairs.

"Place the bowl here Mr. Schwab." I pointed, and he set it on the table. I dipped Mr. Turner's hand into the water. He tensed and cringed. The blood seeped out and expanded like a cloud as his wound gushed with greater intensity. I lifted his hand out and pressed hard on it with a towel. He slammed his other hand on the wood table and groaned through clenched teeth.

Alarmed, Oliver stepped closer. "Mrs. Dorr?"

"Forgive me, Mr. Turner." I bore down, and he struggled not to pull away. "It's to stop the bleeding." After a few minutes I released the pressure and lifted the cloth to see. The blood was no longer surging, so I cleaned off the dry blood bordering the wound. As I finished, Lottie returned with a lamp that had two women spouting from the staff and reaching up as if trying pry themselves from the porcelain.

"Hold it up to his hand." With the wound clean, I could see that it was worse than I'd thought. The gash was too deep. It wouldn't heal on its own. I grew warm and felt Lottie and her husband lingering over my shoulders. "I'm going to have to close it."

Mr. Turner clenched his teeth and nodded.

"It's going to hurt."

He nodded again, looking as if he might cry. I realized he was younger than I had thought, in his early twenties.

"Lottie, I need a bottle of strong spirits."

She started upstairs again.

"Something strong!" I called out.

She stopped halfway. "What, like blackstrap?"

"We don't have that. Just grab something, anything."

Lottie came back down and handed me a bottle of scotch, a substandard wedding gift from one of John's St. Louis friends. He wouldn't even notice it was gone. I handed it to Mr. Turner. "Drink this."

He did without question. From my satchel I took a book that described how to close a wound with needle and thread. It was just like mending, I told myself. I'm just mending—mending a glove.

Mr. Turner kept at the bottle, swallowing large gulps. I couldn't believe how easily the liquid flowed from the bottle to his mouth. Scotch wanted to be sipped. As Mr. Turner grew lethargic, he swayed back and forth against the table.

"Lottie, I can't do this with him standing. Clear the table." She and her husband removed a couple of bowls, some wooden spoons, and the tin of flour. "Mr. Schwab, lift him up."

Lottie nervously rubbed her right eyebrow, clearly realizing we were about to lay out a drunk and bloody field laborer on the same table we prepared food on. Oliver didn't hesitate. I poured water over Mr. Turner's wound again and put an antiseptic on it. The antiseptic should have stung, but Mr. Turner had slipped beyond minor sensations.

"What's that?" Lottie asked.

"It's to kill germs," I said.

"What are germs?"

"Germs—they make you sick."

"Really?"

"Oh, yes," Oliver said. "I heard 'bout 'em. They on everything, too. People get 'em off of telegraphs and from books and sich."

"No." Lottie clasped a hand to her chest, fingers splayed out.

"Yes, they be causin' a real scare."

"What is to be done about 'em?"

"I gather what she be doin'." Oliver pointed at me.

"They're all over, always have been," I said. "That's why you clean to prevent illness."

"Oh," Lottie said.

"I'm ready," I said.

Lottie handed me a needle with white thread tied to it. Mr. Turner had his eyes closed and appeared to be sleeping. He held the nearly empty bottle against his side. I took a long, deep breath and let it out. I positioned the needle against the side of the gash. Holding the skin taught, I pushed and felt the pop as the needle punctured the skin. Mr. Turner let out a dreadful cry and yanked his hand away as the rest of us winced. I heard the clink-clang of the bottle hitting the ground and the gurgle of draining liquid.

I held my hands up. "I'm sorry. I'm sorry."

Mr. Turner mumbled something angrily, and then followed it with submissive apologies.

"Mr. Schwab, I need you to hold him down."

Oliver refocused. He hesitantly placed a hand on Mr. Turner's chest and the other on his forearm.

I took the needle hanging by the white string from his hand. The needle slid stiffly through one side and then the other as I pushed forcefully and Mr. Turner howled.

"More spirits, Lottie!"

Lottie picked up the bottle. "He drank it all."

"Get more."

She hustled noisily up the stairs.

Her husband stood at the opposite side of the table. Neither of us spoke—waiting. Then he lifted his gaze. "Thank you."

I looked up.

"Most would have turned us away."

I nodded, accepting his gratitude and looked away. We stood silently until Lottie returned, but she stopped halfway down and leaned over the wooden banister.

"Where are the spirits?" I asked.

"When I went up I heard a knockin'. Mrs. Grace and Mrs. Williams are in the parlor."

I'd forgotten they were coming. I couldn't stop now. I had already begun to mend his hand, and we had already used an entire bottle of Scotch from John's liquor stores. I couldn't let him sober up and start over later. "Tell them I am in the middle of an important task and will not be able to see them. Send my regrets."

Lottie moved her lips and shook her hands as if repeating it in her head as she clomped up the steps.

"Wait," I whispered loudly.

She stopped.

"Get the spirits."

She hustled back up.

"Ple—please miss," Mr. Turner slurred. "Don' lemme put ya ow."

Rushed, I decided to test the spirits and laudanum again. This time I held the wound together and drove the needle through both sides at once. He wailed, and I gritted my teeth. Oliver jumped and covered Mr. Turner's mouth, muffling the sound. Mr. Turner's smothered curses were followed by stifled apologies.

Lottie returned.

"What?"

"They said they'd wait, and then they hear Mr. Turner's cry and I couldn't explain it. They think sometin' wrong."

I moved toward the stairs. "I'll just have to explain it to them myself."

"You can't." Lottie pointed at my dress.

I beheld the splattered blood all over my shirt and apron. I clenched my fists. "Lottie, you have to get rid of them."

"They won't go."

I looked back at Mr. Turner on the table. "Tell them I am coming, but it will be a few minutes....And get the spirits."

I pointed at Oliver. "Do not let him make a sound. We can't wait."

Oliver placed his hand over Mr. Turner's mouth, and I forced the needle in again, pulling the string to close the edges together. Mr. Turner grunted, heaved, and wailed. It sounded so loud, but we couldn't wait, so I did it again and again and again.

Lottie returned with the spirits.

"Can you hear that up there?"

"A little. More in the hallway." She handed the bottle to me, and I passed it to Oliver, who fed it to Mr. Turner.

"Go talk to them. Try to keep them from hearing the noise. Ask them questions, tell stories, anything."

"They'll think I'm mad."

"I don't care."

I signaled Oliver, and he put his hand back over the drunken Mr. Turner. I drove the needle in and cringed as cries escaped Oliver's hand. We continued this until Mr. Turner finally fainted, whether from the liquor or the pain I couldn't say.

About ten minutes later, Lottie plodded down the steps as I worked on the next-to-last stitch. My stiff lip and bulging eyes demanded a report.

"They told me to leave them be."

I shoved the needle in again. "I'm almost finished, but my dress is soiled. I need clean garments."

She nodded and ran back up.

I'd finished by the time Lottie reappeared with a suitable ensemble. I washed the blood off my hands.

"They're talking about your health," she said.

"Quick, help me." I swished around to find Oliver staring in shock.

"Oliver, turn around," Lottie said.

He obeyed.

I sighed in disbelief at my current situation.

"Sorry, miss." Lottie peeled off my shirtwaist and camisole and then my walking skirt. "What are you going to say?"

"I have no idea. I have to explain what I've been doing—what the noises were."

Lottie re-tightened my corset. She slipped the black skirt over my head because I couldn't step into it while wearing petticoats. She put a fresh camisole over my head and helped me into a clean shirtwaist with little black flowers on it and fastened my belt. "Go."

"I don't know what I'm going to say." I patted my head, making sure my hair was secure. "What would be so important that I would try to cancel a call?"

"I thought callers were supposed to willingly leave if the miss said she couldn't see them," Lottie said.

"It's my health. Everyone thinks they are excused from manners."

Lottie handed me a cloth. "Your brow, ma'am."

I dabbed the sweat away and fanned my face. It was the first time I'd realized how warm I was in spite of the constant temperature of the cool basement.

"You seem healthy to me," Oliver said. "You should tell 'em they ain't allowed to not have any manners no more."

"That's not a bad idea." I wiped my hands with the cloth. "Prepare some tea."

I hustled up the stairs but hesitated at the top. I realized I hadn't felt hopelessness in the basement that entire time. Then voices drew my attention, and I crept closer to the parlor.

Francis was snide. "I think we should notify Mr. Dorr and Dr. Bradbridge straightaway."

Ella lowered her voice. "While we're there, we should mention something about *our trip*."

"What?"

"We should tell people ahead of time. It will set in their minds, and they won't question anything later."

"I don't know. I'd prefer we not draw any attention to it at all."

"What will people say when we suddenly go away without reason?"

Francis sighed. "What if someone catches us in a lie?"

What in tarnation were they talking about? A lie? About a trip?

"They won't. We'll go over our stories together. It won't take much."

They stopped speaking and I waited, hoping to hear about this trip. Someone sighed.

"This is ridiculous. If I don't see that woman in here in five seconds, I'm going to—"

I swept into the parlor. "Ella. Francis."

They stood up from the green sofa. "Good day, Emeline. How are you feeling?" Francis accused more than asked.

"I'm well. And you?" I lowered myself into a chair, and they sat back down.

"We are very well, thank you."

"It seems I've missed some intriguing discussion."

"Uh—um…we were speaking of your servant girl." Francis tripped over her words.

"Oh?"

Then she snapped back to her usual self. "We've been here a good twenty minutes and haven't seen a spot of tea."

"Twenty minutes, you say?"

Ella looked down at her hands.

"She's brewing it now. I'm sorry you waited so long, but I believe Mrs. Schwab tried to inform you I was busy and unable to see you right away."

"You were aware of our visit, were you not?" Francis asked. "We informed you well ahead of time."

"Of course, and I would have sent word, but an urgent matter arose at the last possible moment."

"The polite thing would have been to inform us yourself so that we could be sure you were in good health instead of sending your handmaid." Francis used sharp and exaggerated gestures.

"It is acceptable decorum as far as I am aware."

"You were recently ill," Ella said. "We were concerned."

"We *are* concerned," Francis said. "Then we heard those strange noises."

"As you can see, I am well, and I have been well for several weeks now. Dr. Bradbridge confirmed it. You no longer need be concerned with my well-being. And those strange noises are exactly why I asked that you return another day."

"Pardon me?"

It came to me. "A horse of mine is injured. It is—"

"Those noises were not that of an injured horse, and they sounded far closer than your stables," Francis barked.

"I have a few windows open to keep the heat from building. Perhaps that is why you presumed to hear the noises closer. I do not appreciate having to defend my attempts to be dutiful, which, of anyone, I believe you would appreciate, Francis."

A thick vein throbbed in her forehead.

"Of course, Emeline," Ella said. "We are only interested in your well-being."

"Thank you. I understand your concern. I am only requesting you no longer use it to intrude."

"Emeline, I find your objection to our aid an insult," Francis said.

"I'm afraid I must insist, and I must also request you depart." I stood. "As I tried to inform you before, I am tending to an urgent matter."

Francis tried to object. "Wait—"

Ella touched her daughter's arm. "Come now, we should be on our way." She rose.

Francis hesitated a moment until her mother's nudging persuaded her to move for the door.

"Thank you for your time, Emeline," Ella said. "We're happy to see you doing so much better."

"I appreciate your understanding, Ella."

Francis snapped her head back but said nothing.

They walked out as Lottie brought in the tea from the opposite entrance. "That was like greased lightning. What happened?"

I shrugged and flashed a little grin. "They left."

We lugged Mr. Turner, half-asleep and half-drunk, to Lottie's. After dropping him onto a mattress, Oliver crouched to observe him and then looked at me. "Thank you, Mrs. Dorr, for this."

"I am just glad I could help." I moved to leave.

Lottie touched my shoulder to stop me. "Would you do it again?"

I turned. "Do what?"

"You know 'bout stuff not everyone know," she said.

"What do you mean?"

"Ever since that Coddington come to town, none of the poor folk been able to get any help with sickness and the like."

"I don't understand."

"You know…"

I raised my eyebrows.

"He finds people who ain't got a doctor's license. People 'round here used to help one another out of kindness and God and such. They helped with stuff ain't need no doctor for but stuff not everyone know 'bout. Like midwives, who knew things 'bout babies and helped with deliveries. Then that lawyer come down from the big ol' city and gave them people papers and threw big bug words at 'em until they stopped or left."

"Why?" I asked.

Oliver stood and walked to us.

Lottie gestured dramatically as she explained, circling her arms around and pointing. "He had the whole town talkin' how danger-ous it was havin' anyone other than a doctor fix 'em, say people been killin' people, say people been hackin' people up left and right in the city, and it wouldn't be long till they start hackin' on us too."

"Had they?"

She squeezed her lips into an uncertain pout and turned to Oliver.

Oliver folded his arms and clenched his shirt.

Lottie looked back at me. "We ain't too sure, but the town was so convinced, damn near forced all them kind folk to stop or leave, except for—one tried to fight 'em, at a courthouse."

The little shanty swelled with humidity and I shifted my weight.

"Matter a fact," Oliver said, "Mr. Nelson used to live in the house you in now."

"The man who lived in my house didn't charge anything?" I asked. "He went against Mr. Coddington?"

"Was a good man," Oliver said. "Most of the people who helped others with the little things were friends, family, and the like, but he helped anybody and knew city medicine."

Lottie waved at a fly buzzing around her head. "He and his wife delivered several of our chillin." She touched Oliver's arm with a doleful expression. "His family helped with lots a stuff."

"He said he wouldn't bow out to Mr. Coddington," Oliver said. "He was one of the few who knew some things, knew the law."

"And...what happened?"

Lottie sighed and her husband lowered his chin.

"He didn't know enough," Lottie said in a quiet voice.

"The costs were too much," Oliver said. "He lost his home to the bank, all the furnishin's. Everythin', gone. The whole town turned against him and his family, even people they helped. Mr. Coddington and the Bradbridges led the pack."

"Just when things couldn't get any worse, they did," Lottie said.

"When Mr. Coddington attacked Mr. Nelson, he stopped offerin' to help so easily," Oliver said. "Too afraid it would get him in more trouble. One of the people he refused was the brother of a girl that Mr. Nelson's eldest boy, Daniel, was tryin' to court."

Lottie stepped in. "When his father wouldn't, Daniel tried— didn't go so well."

I put my hands to my mouth. "What happened? Did the boy kill him?"

"No, but he got real sick," Oliver said. "But that wadn't what everyone heard."

Lottie continued for him. "Mr. Coddington and the Bradbridges ruined that poor family. We didn't know what to believe."

Oliver touched Lottie's arm. "That detective man, that docta, and that big ol' lawyer had everyone fooled, so they left." He sighed.

"Why would the Bradbridges do such a thing?"

"They the only doctors in town now," Lottie said. "Everyone gotta go to the Bradbridges or die."

"I can't believe the younger doctor, Walter Bradbridge, would do such a thing."

"He does whatever his father want him to. Like a dog," Lottie shook her head.

"So that's what John does for a living? He puts people in jail for that?"

"I hear you husband works on sometin' else." Oliver scratched the back of his head.

"What?"

He hesitated and looked down with one hand on his chin, clearly pondering how to word it. Lottie and I stood there waiting. The fly buzzed.

"What?" Lottie demanded.

He shook his head and leaned close and whispered into her ear. She dropped her eyes. "Oh."

"What?"

"Abortionists."

I shook my head. "What?"

"He takes people that do that to court." Lottie pursed her lips.

"Abortionists? Here?"

"Might be more common than you think," Lottie said, and I remembered what she'd told me. "Plus, some them folk travel."

Oliver scratched the back of his neck. "I think it takes a lot to find 'em and then take 'em to jail, and by then someone else is doing 'em. There's always someone, right?" He looked at his wife.

Lottie didn't respond.

"And my husband handles those cases?" I recalled conversations I'd overheard and felt a sense of relief. He wasn't a bad person. "Isn't that good?"

Lottie hesitated. "Sure. Suppose." She straightened her frame. "But that ain't no matter. What is, is you like Mr. Nelson." She gestured toward me. "You know things. You—you could help people who don't need a doctor but need the little stuff. I know I said I wouldn't ask after the Whitmays, but there's so many people needin' help and can't afford a Bradbridge for the small stuff. They charge a whole dollar just for showin' up."

"Uh…" I thought about it. I could help with minor problems. I knew enough from school, but would that be the right thing? Would that be dangerous? "I—no, no. They should be seen by someone who knows what they're doing. I can't."

"No, you can. Think of Mr. Turner and the Whitmays. You helped them. You helped them when no one else would."

"No, no." I lifted my hands. "I couldn't—I mean—well…I—no, I couldn't." I really couldn't have after what they'd told me about John and Mr. Coddington. "My husband?"

Lottie's hopeful expression fell.

"Forgive us, Mrs. Dorr." Oliver squeezed Lottie's shoulder. "We shouldn't have asked you. It's too much."

"Oliver, hish up." Lottie shifted her weight toward me. "Listen, these people can't afford no doctor, and with Mr. Coddington runnin' the show 'round here. Ain't no physician seein' no one without a price, not if they were dyin'."

I shook my head. "I—I—"

"And they have—people dyin' without help. Why you think Mrs. Whitmay dead?" Lottie said.

I glanced at Oliver. "I thought the untreated ailments were all minor?"

Lottie's voice lifted in frustration. "Sometimes the small stuff gets big when you can't afford to get fixed up."

"But if I—if I did that—just for people who really needed it—what would happen? What if someone found out? They'd think I'm crazy for sure. I could go to jail. What about my husband? Would he go to jail or send me there?"

They looked at each other, Lottie's hand to her chin.

"It would only be for emergencies." Lottie spoke slowly, reassuringly. "Only when people really need it. You already done that."

I thought for a moment. I wanted to help people. Helping the Whitmays and Mr. Turner had been rewarding. The experience with Lottie had changed my life. "But my husband?" No, I didn't care what he thought, I reminded myself.

"He ain't worryin' about these little things." She motioned toward the unconscious Mr. Turner. "He worryin' about the biguns. We're talkin' desperate people, and we talkin' stuff so small, nothin' like what them big bad abortion doctors doin'."

I glanced at Mr. Turner and wondered what would have happened if he hadn't gotten any help because he couldn't afford it. It would have been wrong not to help him or anyone else. I narrowed my eyes at Lottie. "Only emergencies."

She nodded.

"Only when there is absolutely no other option, when it's impossible to get professional help—and no one can know."

Lottie's lips curled into a mischievous leer. "We'll be crafty 'bout it."

# Twenty

*1899*
*Grantville College*
*Grantville, Missouri*

The infirmary superintendent, Mr. Schafer, scrutinized me through a pair of thin-rimmed spectacles.

I squirmed in front of his oversize desk as I filled out a volunteer form.

"Are you one of the nursing students?" he asked.

I lifted my gaze and shook my head. "No." My college courses consisted of etiquette and watercolor, the latter of which proved only a sad reminder of my lack of talent.

Mr. Schafer twitched his wiry mustache. "Usually those are the girls I get."

I signed the form and pushed it forward.

He slid the paper off his desk and snapped it vertical. "Hmm. Well, maybe we can find some use for you."

I clenched my hands under his desk.

"Come on then." He stood and gestured for me to do the same. He guided me to the infirmary, where there were tall windows on one side of the room. There were ten iron rolling beds, five on each side of the room. They had thin mattresses encased in crisp sheets.

"We have two on-call physicians and two nurses." Mr. Schafer strode down the middle of the room and I followed. The clacking of our shoes on the wood panels echoed a little, and a chemical smell pinched at the inside of my nostrils. "A part-time nurse and a full-time head nurse."

We entered a small room with filing cabinets, books, and papers stacked everywhere. The blinds on the slender window were closed. Note cards, an inkwell, and a cup of pencils cluttered the windowsill. Amid the mess, a pristine woman worked at her desk, tiny in comparison with Mr. Schafer's.

"This is our head nurse," Mr. Shafer said. "Miss Mary McKenzie, this is Miss Emeline Evans."

The nurse stood and circled the desk. "Good morning, Miss Evans. How lovely of you to volunteer." She wore a stiff white shirtwaist with billowy sleeves, a caramel-colored skirt, a full-length apron, and a little white cap. "What year are you?"

"She's not a nursing student," Mr. Schafer peered over the rim of his glasses.

I lowered my eyes and fought the urge to sprint out of the room.

"Is there anything she can do, or should I send her back?"

Miss McKenzie shifted. "I'm sure I could find something." Her voice sounded buoyant.

Mr. Schafer shrugged, turned on his heel, and left.

I relaxed a little.

Ms. McKenzie went to a filing cabinet across from her desk and slid open the top drawer. "Here's where you will find new-patient forms." She drove her hand in and removed a single sheet of paper and pointed to the top line. "And fill these out. Simple."

I nodded.

"And…" She looked around and jumped at the sight of a stack of papers on a table to the right of the filing cabinet. "Right now you can help me by folding these fliers and sticking them in some envelopes." She started removing books from the table, along with a stack of jostled newspapers with headlines that screamed "GERMS." She scooped them up and piled them on the corner of her desk. She grasped a chair and scraped it across the floor to a position in front of the table.

I seated myself, picked up a flier from the table, and skimmed it. "Grantville physicians will be at Merchants Hall on September 17th," it read. "One Day Only. All persons should be seen by a physician once a year."

Ms. McKenzie returned to her seat and scooted the chair close to her desk.

I watched her while I creased and pressed the fliers. I observed her ring finger—bare. My Aunt Cheryl once told me that the only well-off women who weren't married and worked were ugly, dumb, or otherwise defective. However, Miss McKenzie had a heart-shaped face with bright brown eyes, pronounced cheekbones, and pink lips.

Her eyes popped up, and I plunged back into my task.

"Are you interested in nursing?"

I fumbled with the envelope. "Uh—my dormitory chaperone suggested I volunteer somewhere." I shook my head and raised my shoulders. "I thought this seemed interesting."

"Hmm." She made a check in an open file in front of her. "Usually girls choose to do something for the spring festivities, or at least that's how it was when I was a student."

I shrugged. "I just wanted to do something different." The truth was I had thought college would be an escape from the expectation to dedicate my life to the pursuit of a husband. As it turned out, though, for girls college served as another opportunity to seek out suitors. My mother had constantly prodded me about it in her letters, and all my classes were just fancy training for future wives. I had come no closer to finding a suitor at Grantville College than I had at home, and I was agitated by the mere thought of it. I had wanted to escape and instead found myself surrounded by girls fluttering and tittering over social engagements and hairstyles, but the nursing students were different. They did not flutter or titter. They carried books and walked across campus quickly to be on time for classes that actually mattered.

"Do you like science?"

I shrugged. "I have not had the opportunity to form an opinion."

"Now is the time."

"What's it like being a nurse?"

"It's wonderful. It's not like it used to be when people despised women in medicine." She folded her arms and leaned back in her chair. "People respect women nurses now…as much as anyone can respect a working woman. Nursing schools want unmarried middle-class women, not men."

"Really?"

"And the pay is much higher than a secretary or telephone operator, enough to live."

"Do you live on your own?"

"I rent a room."

"Is it hard?"

"I have to be frugal. I don't get to enjoy every meal, but my landlady bakes me treats out of pity. I have enough entertainment with books from the library, and several of my friends from school live nearby. We meet for tea and card games, and we try to save enough money to attend the theater sometimes."

I smiled, dreamy at the thought of living so modestly, so independently.

"And I get to make people feel better, all day," she said.

"Is it difficult? Or…disturbing?"

She leaned forward. "School was difficult."

"You said you went here?"

"They only teach introductory courses here. You have to go to a hospital-based school before you can apply for a nursing license. It takes about three years, and the hours are grueling, but you get to have hands-on experience with patients. The nursing students provide almost all of the hospital labor, even in surgery."

"That's astounding. I didn't—"

"Ms. McKenzie!" A flustered woman I recognized as a teacher burst into the office. "Come quick."

Ms. McKenzie stood, and I raised my hands but hesitated, unsure what to do with them. She grabbed a clipboard and hustled to the filing cabinet, yanked out a sheet of paper, clipped it to the board, and thrust it at me. "Come on. First patient." She and the other woman rushed out.

I followed them into the main infirmary room with all the beds. I halted at the sight of a woman about my age writhing in pain. She lay on the first bed to the left with her foot propped on a stack of towels. Her shoes and stockings had been removed and her peach-colored skirt hiked up, revealing her white petticoats underneath. A piece of glass the size of a silver dollar stuck out from an open wound on the side of her right foot.

The teacher paced back and forth. "I don't think I can look. Blood makes me faint."

"Emeline, I need to call in the doctor for this." She motioned to the teacher. "Mrs. Simon, come with me, please." She touched the frantic teacher on the back and directed her toward the door. "I'll be right back, Emeline." As she passed me, she whispered, "Try to distract her."

I swallowed and inched toward the patient.

The bed's metal frame squeaked as she clenched it and shifted. She had a small round face and golden, curly hair falling out of a tousled pompadour.

I studied her foot. The shard of glass had embedded itself near her heel. Blood and dirt were caked along the side and bottom of her foot, but the wound wasn't gushing. It glistened. I realized it didn't bother me to look at it.

I lowered myself into a chair. "I didn't get your name."

"Lucille...Mills," she said as she crinkled her face.

I wrote it down. "I'm Emeline Evans."

She grimaced.

"What happened?"

"My friends and I were having a picnic, and I took my boots off to feel the grass.…We were being foolish, playing around, and I just stepped on it."

I blinked and widened my eyes, surprised that she had taken her shoes off in public. Intrigued and kind of in awe, I wanted to ask her more, but I realized discussing how she'd done it wasn't doing much to distract her. "How long have you been at Grantville?"

"Huh?" She glanced over and gulped. "Oh, um…my first year."

"Me, too. Well, second trimester."

Her eyebrows dipped.

"What are you taking?"

Lucille focused on her foot. "Home finances, child education."

"Do you have Mrs. Kratz?"

She dipped her head with a swallow.

"Did she tell your class about her husband's hair dilemma?"

She shifted her eyes in my direction. "Yes."

"And the cream that turned his scalp yellow?"

"Yes." She giggled and loosened her grip on the bed. "She's not too modest, is she?"

I shook my head. "Do you think she tells everyone about it or just her students?"

Ms. McKenzie returned, her skirts shuffling. She slowed and relaxed at the sound of our tee-hees.

I shifted to face her. "Ms. McKenzie, have you ever heard of a balding remedy that turns the scalp yellow?"

She held back a mischievous smile. "So you're taking Mrs. Kratz then?"

Lucille roared and I doubled over. Lucille even bounced her foot, but after a quick "ouch," she propped herself up on her elbows and continued laughing. Her tears were gone and her cheeks flushed.

"Well, you got this one to pep up." Miss McKenzie propped her hand on her hip. "I think you'd make a fine nurse after all."

# Twenty-One

*July 1901*
*Labellum, Missouri*

Lottie's craftiness consisted of a scheme in which she acted as the source of contact and connected families in need with me. Then I stole about town under my ridiculous pseudonym, "Mrs. Freeman." Lottie insisted on my continued use of the name because it led people to expect someone different, not because she thought it absolutely hilarious. We crossed the "emergencies only" line immediately and never looked back.

To arrange time to see these people, I had to neglect some responsibilities and rush through other duties, such as calls. The mattresses weren't always flipped, and the mirrors acquired a little dust, but John wouldn't notice anything. He wouldn't realize it if I stopped cleaning altogether. He wouldn't notice if I served cooked toad.

During that first truly blistering-hot month of summer, I saw several women and children who were exhausted from the heat in the fields. I brought them water to drink, fed them sugary pastries and apples, and gave them damp rags to place on the backs of their necks. I mixed up an aloe jelly for their sunburns and gave them two old parasols for shade while they worked.

There was a malnourished elderly woman, her lips endlessly chapped, plagued by head lice. I soaked her hair in kerosene oil and wrapped it up like that. I told her to keep the cloth on for a full night and day, and soak again at least three times to kill the lice and their nits. After a full day, the lice died and she thoroughly washed her hair using soaps I provided. I also gave her petroleum jelly for her lips and recommended she eat eggs and milk daily to keep the skin healthy.

Lottie helped with a few calls involving a first-time mother frantic over her newborn's colic. Lottie instructed the mother to feed more often for shorter periods of time and avoid cow's milk. Lottie and I took turns visiting her and watching the baby so the exhausted mother could sleep or run errands. Lottie said I must always keep the baby moving gently with rocking and swaying, never bouncing. After my first deafening visit riddled with panic, I offered to do Lottie's chores so she could take more shifts.

After seeing a few people, I realized those who couldn't afford doctors didn't need the advice of a professional for things no worse than minor burns and shallow cuts, which were certainly not worth the expense. My experience from volunteering and knowledge of home remedies were more than sufficient to solve most ailments. I planned to refer to John's medical texts if I came across conditions or symptoms I wasn't familiar with, but many didn't need medical assistance at all. I found myself a teacher on several calls, providing—ironically enough—lessons in home care. Many people were still poorly informed regarding germs. Much of what I saw could be solved with proper nutrition, diet, and a clean household.

The Whitmays' dilemmas stemmed from a lack of knowledge after the loss of Mrs. Whitmay, whose role, as a mother, was to tend to matters of health and hygiene. After our first meeting, I continued to look after the Whitmay children's health, and Mr. Whitmay developed a profound trust in me. Thus when he discovered his daughter injured, he had Lottie send for me. I rushed over, and Mr. Whitmay hurried me in and pointed me toward his eldest daughter, Wendy.

The tenement felt like a hothouse, but Wendy had a blanket over her. I knelt beside her and she sat up. I tried to touch her arm reassuringly, but she pulled away. Mr. Whitmay removed the blanket. Wendy looked off blank-faced, as if she weren't aware of the slick blood between her legs. Bright red streaked across the blanket but appeared like black smears on Wendy's dark skin. Much of it was dry, but some glistened. I searched all over her lower body but couldn't find anything.

When I learned she had woken that way and just turned twelve, I exhaled and smiled gingerly. I explained what happens to girls when they get older and to women every month. Mothers often waited until bleeding occurred before explaining it to their daughters. When it had first happened to me, I thought I was dying. I told her she was becoming a woman. This was pleasing to little Wendy, who must have thought she was dying, too.

The expression on Mr. Whitmay's face suggested he hadn't even thought of it. Women often kept their monthly bleeding hidden, so Mr. Whitmay probably didn't know enough to recognize it. It was only natural to panic when his daughter appeared inexplicably blood-smeared one morning.

People apologized for requesting the illegal assistance, but it wasn't necessary. Each time my knowledge went to good use, *I* was of good use. For the first time, I was not making choices for the sake of my family, my husband, or my station. I acted of my own free will. My problems were still there, but my secret, the use of my own will made the façade tolerable. I was happy. I was actually happy. It made me think of that white room. This would be the part where the woman stood on the other side and breathed in the fresh air. She knew it couldn't last forever—eventually, everything would collapse and there would be no more air—but she didn't care. She just breathed.

# Twenty-Two

*August 1901*

$\mathcal{I}$ pulled out my chair and sat at the dining room table for breakfast—coffee, milk, fresh berries, and flapjacks with butter and syrup. I had been craving flapjacks like our old servant Kathy used to make, and I woke up early Saturday morning so I could get started on them. Just the right amount of sunlight from outside brightened the dining room's maroon wallpaper and created a cheery atmosphere. Even the reptile flatware seemed in good spirits. I felt cheery as well, transitioning into lighter mourning clothes. I rushed the transition a little because women wore lighter colors in summer and I didn't want to stand out more than necessary. John sat at the head of the table eating with a book to his left. I wrote in a notebook to my right, trying to organize my thoughts. With my extra responsibilities, I found myself struggling to keep track of my daily duties.

Oh, yes, I remembered now. I wrote, "Ella and Francis—make amends…?" I couldn't have these women constantly watching me, waiting for a fit of hysteria. I had managed to soothe Margaret's disapproval by spending an entire call expressing compliments and gratitude, but Ella and Francis would not be so easily pleased. Nevertheless, they had avoided me since I forced them out of my house, so maybe I didn't have to fake friendliness. I certainly didn't want to be friends, at least not with Francis, who—

"Emeline?"

I lifted my head.

John stared with raised eyebrows.

"Yes?"

"Did you not hear me?"

I locked onto his dark eyes. "I'm listening."

"Well, I—" He turned those eyes down. "How have you been feeling?"

"I am well...still."

"I am pleased to hear it."

I went back to making notes. "I wish everyone would stop with this health nonsense," I said under my breath.

"Pardon?"

I scratched notes as I spoke. "I'm sick and tired of people constantly prying when I wasn't ill to begin with."

"I find it interesting you would question a physician."

I made a few more marks on the paper.

"Let us speak of something else," he said.

"Whatever you like." Inside I scoffed at the idea of having a conversation.

"Have you gotten all settled in the house?"

I looked at him, baffled. We had been there nearly eight months. "Yes."

"That was silly." He squeezed his eyes shut and shook his head. "Of course you are." He took a bite of food.

I returned to my task.

"What are you writing?"

I clung to my line of thought. "Um...notes."

"Notes about what?"

I sighed. "Things I need to do."

"Oh."

I thought of a few books I should sneak out of John's library.

"You never used to take notes."

I recalled a text that described symptoms and attached conditions to them. What was it called?

"Emeline?"

"What?" I snipped.

"Do you have a lot planned for the day?"

I sighed, put my pencil down, and lifted my gaze. "A bit."

"Ah."

I picked the pencil back up.

"Do you expect to be busy all day?"

I spoke through my teeth. "Quite likely."

"Oh." He pushed a piece of flapjack around in syrup with his fork.

I returned to my task. I couldn't recall the title, but it had a blue spine and—

"I was hoping we could take a walk…"

Blue and—

"For your health."

My head shot up.

John still pushed his food around.

"Thank you, but as I said earlier, I'm fine."

He glanced up quickly and then back down. "No—I know. Of course." He stabbed the little bit of flapjack and popped it into his mouth.

I returned to my thought. Blue and—

"Tomorrow?"

"John, I am fine."

"No—I…"

"No?" I shook my head.

"No—I mean—that's not what I meant."

What was he doing? Trying to make conversation? Suggesting an outing? Since when did he want to do anything with me?

He sipped his coffee and shook his head. "Another day."

I lowered my head, keeping my eyes on him in case he decided to suddenly burst out again. He didn't.

It was too hot for the house to bother me much on Tuesday. Everything swelled and groaned in the wet heat. The air in the basement was thick and damp but still relatively cool, so I actually lingered over putting away dishes. Lottie had gone home to feed her baby, so I was surprised to hear her pounding down the steps, back so soon.

She rushed down, panting in a panic.

"What is it?"

She bent over, put her hands on her knees and huffed and puffed.

"Are you all right?"

She took a breath. "We got a problem."

"What is it?"

"A woman," she panted, "at my house—frantic—her husband has some horrible sickness."

"What?"

She huffed again.

"What's wrong with him?"

She shook her head. "No idea."

"You didn't ask?"

"She so frantic she just kept hollerin', 'Get someone over there, now, now, now!'"

"Then I should go." I dried my hands and started toward the stairs.

Still breathing heavily, she put out her hand. "There's a problem."

"What?"

She took a deep breath. "Their place is across the street from Mr. Coddington's office."

"What?"

She nodded.

"Why can't they go to your house?"

She shook her head. "She say he refusin' to leave. I gather he's hurtin' that much."

"I must go then, but I can't leave the carriage across the street without Mr. Dorr or his associates noticing. Even parking down the block and slinking past is risky. His office has windows. Anyone could see."

She took a final deep breath to end her panting. "I have an idea."

"Do tell."

"I read this detective book once. The bad guy aimed to go to a place when he knew the detective waitin' for him to go there, but he tricked him by goin' to the detective where he hidin' and tell him he knew he there."

"You read detective novels?"

"Yes, my favorite is some English feller Sir...sometin' Doyle."

"Sir Arthur Conan Doyle?"

"That the one! He got a 'Sir' in fronta his name 'cuz he's so good."

I clamped my lips together to hide my smile.

"That's what you should do. Go on and tell Mr. Dorr you there."

"Lottie, that's the opposite of what we want."

"He won't be suspectin' nothin'. Who in dere right mind would go on and tell someone they there right before doin' sometin' they ain't supposed to do?"

"A crazy person."

"Exactly." She pointed at me. "He won't think you up to nothin', 'cuz it's mad to go greet him first."

"Lottie, that's genius."

Mr. Buck drove us to town immediately. John's office was on one of the streets with lots of businesses. It was a white building with a gray roof and two front windows. I had never visited him and wasn't sure if it was acceptable. Mr. Buck helped me out of the surrey, and then he helped Lottie. As soon as I walked away, Lottie was to tell Mr. Buck she needed to get something from the house across the street and go there while I set up the diversion.

I entered the office, and two men sitting at oak desks positioned opposite each other immediately stopped their work and eyed me.

"Good day," I said.

No response.

"I'm here to see my husband, Mr. Dorr?"

One of the young men stood and disappeared into the back.

The other one eyed me suspiciously. "One moment, ma'am," he said flatly and returned to his work.

John came out of a back room and approached with his head tilted and brow furrowed.

"Good day." I beamed. "I was in town and thought I would come by." I handed him a small basket with some bread, jam, and dried fruit.

"How thoughtful." He took the basket. He smiled a little but his eyes questioned. "You've never come by before."

"I suppose not."

He held his eyes on me, licked his lips, and smiled.

I felt obvious. "Well, I should be on my way."

He blinked and dropped his smile. "All right."

I left, feeling all eyes on me. I shut the door, sighed, and started back toward the surrey.

"Wait," I heard, followed by the sound of the office door shutting.

Caught, I froze and slowly turned around. He glided to me in his regal way.

"Yes?"

John reached out gleefully and slipped his hand into mine. "Thank you."

"Oh." I looked down and felt his skin, warm and smooth. "You are welcome."

I met his eyes and felt strange looking directly at him. His eyes—they were dark—dark brown.

He leaned forward a little as if to kiss me.

Surprised, I flinched.

He pulled back, hesitated, and dropped my hand. "I guess I should…" He motioned back toward the offices.

I watched unblinking as he returned to the office. Had he tried to kiss me? What was going on? No he couldn't have—for one thing we were in public. Still, he had been oddly interested in me since returning from St. Louis. That strange conversation at breakfast. He seemed different, as if he wanted to be…affectionate? Or was it me? I'd changed. Maybe he was reacting to that change? I sighed. All that time I'd tried so hard and nothing. Now that I wasn't trying…I laughed to myself. No, it couldn't be. Well, even if he was trying to kiss me, I didn't care. After all my unrequited efforts to build affection between us, I wasn't going to just submit to his wants now. I could hardly believe it after not receiving the slightest hint of affection from him for so long, but a part of me hoped he did want me because I wasn't going to give him anything. I hoped he would feel what I had felt, rejected. I exhaled, pushed it from my mind, and made my way back to the surrey.

Mr. Buck offered his hand to help me up, but I stopped.

"Where's Mrs. Schwab?"

"Um. She said she needed something from that house." He pointed across the street. "She said she'd be only a moment."

"What? What kind of negligent person handles personal matters while in town with her mistress? I must fetch her at once."

"No, ma'am. Please let me."

"Mr. Buck, when I need your assistance, I will ask for it." Poor Mr. Buck probably didn't like me very much. "Wait here."

He stepped out of my way, and I quickly stalked up to the house and banged on the door.

When Lottie opened the door, she was holding her hand to her mouth and nose. I quickly stepped in and she closed the door. It was as if I had entered another world—a dark, muggy, dirty, and cramped world that stank of mold and warm ale.

Lottie squinted. "Go as planned?"

"Apparently not in here. What happened? Are we too late?"

"You ain't goin' to believe me."

It was then that I heard the woman yelling and ranting, practically screaming. I rushed toward the flustered thing. She fluttered around a large man at a table drinking a hefty mug of beer and devouring a huge mound of meat and potatoes. When she saw me, she turned her ranting in my direction. "Do you see this? Do you see what he's like? There's something wrong with him. Don't you smell it? It's horrible. He's disgusting. He's sick. He's terribly, terribly ill. You have to help him. You have to help me."

"I'm fine, woman. Leave me be." He spit out little bits of food as he spoke. He was sweaty and hairy everywhere except for the top of his head. He spilled beer down his chin. Then a noise came from beneath him, followed by a stench.

I covered my nose and mouth. Lottie covered her face, too, but she shook with laughter.

"You see! You see! It's like this all the time. All the time. He stinks. He stinks horribly. There's something wrong with him! There's something terribly, terribly wrong. He's dying, I tell you! He must be rotting from the inside out!" She couldn't have served as a model of cleanliness herself, but I could tell that under different circumstances, people would have considered her quite the beauty. She had blond tresses falling out of her loosely pinned mass, a little face, and a prim nose. Unlike her husband, she had a beautiful figure. I wondered if this was an arranged marriage gone sour or some sort of love affair that had taken a turn for the worse. Either way, she obviously felt dissatisfied with what she had ended up with. "Fix him!" she screeched. "Please help me! Cure him of this evil!" She paced violently, hands flailing.

I thought back to a book I had recently ordered called *Advanced Home Remedies and Nursing for Your Family*. I'd skimmed a few sections about some of these symptoms, thinking I wouldn't have any use for such things. Who would contact me concerning body odor? Next time, I'd make sure to read the entire book.

Lottie fought a wry grin. "Can we do sometin'?"

I closed my eyes, attempting to remember. Flatulence, I recalled, was related to diet but had more to do with the habit of swallowing too much air. I considered the man devouring his meal and sucking down a dark brew while fending off his wife. The body odor was obviously a hygienic issue. I could do nothing for baldness, not without turning his scalp yellow.

"You're sick! You're disgusting!"

"Ma'am, ma'am." I stepped closer. "Your husband's stench can be fixed through some changes in habit."

The woman clung to her disheveled frock. "Please! Please!"

"He needs to take regular baths and not wear the same clothing day in and day out."

"That's right, woman. You need to do some launderin'!" he yelled through a mouthful.

"Also, his diet could be healthier, fewer heavy foods. But more importantly, he needs to eat smaller bites and be wary of swallowing air along with it."

"What?" He shoved a mound into his mouth. "Dis woma eh ouwa har mind."

His wife flew at him. "Quiet, you. You are sick! I told you! You be eatin' all this garbage! You been eating us outta house and home. You need to take a bath. You're disgusting!"

"Ma'am, ma'am." I held my hands up.

She flailed back around.

"It might help to ask nicely." I used a graceful hand gesture to suggest the simplicity of kindness. "Also, you can encourage this by joining him."

"What?"

If she bathed regularly, which she needed to do, he might be more inclined to stay clean as well. "You should join him." I nodded. "In bathing."

"What?" Lottie chimed in.

A strange look crossed the woman's face, her mouth open and her lips pulled back.

Her husband stood, gulped down the rest of his beer, and slammed his mug down. "I'll do it." He wiped his mouth with his arm, snatched his wife's wrist, and gave her a big sloppy kiss. "Let us bathe!" He stomped out, dragging her behind him.

We stood motionless in shock.

"What just happened? Where are they going?"

"I suppose to the Mississippi," Lottie said, giggling.

"What?"

Lottie started laughing hysterically before folding over and grabbing her sides.

My eyes moved back and forth as I put it all together. "I didn't mean bathe with each other. I meant..." I grinned, shook my head, and started to chuckle.

# Twenty-Three

$\mathcal{M}$r. and Mrs. Hughmen lived in a small upstairs tenement located in an alley, like the Whitmays. I ambled, reading the scribbled directions written in my notebook and stopping occasionally to search for the correct address. When I located it, I walked up the white-painted steps and knocked on the door. Before I could rap twice, a petite white woman with frazzled hair opened the door.

Her tired eyes scanned my appearance. My attire didn't suit my task. I had on a half-mourning toilette of mauve silk with black details on the bodice and a straw hat with an upswept split brim and silk flowers.

She lifted her eyes and aligned them with mine. "You are Mrs. Freeman?"

She had expected someone else—everyone did. "Yes. I am."

At this, her judgment and alarm vanished. "Please, please come, come in." She opened the door and without delay pointed to a man face up on a mattress in the front corner of the room. Two more mattresses were rolled up and tied against an adjacent wall. The apartment had a little stove and a kitchen area to the right, with a worn table and two chairs. There were no rooms other than the main one, and all their clothing and other belongings must have been stuffed into two unfinished wooden trunks. The walls melted with water stains.

I walked over to the man but struggled to kneel. My corset and layered petticoats made the task difficult. I nearly collapsed on top of him but managed to lean over instead. From his frame, I could tell that he had once been a strong man but had withered and become frail.

He opened his eyes. "Miss? Are you in the right place?"

"Oh." I'd thought he was asleep. "Good day Mr. Hughmen. I'm Mrs. Freeman."

He chuckled. "Is that so?" Droplets of moisture collected in his greasy hair and full beard. His dark complexion and black hair suggested he was Italian, but he lacked the accent. Perhaps his family had immigrated a few generations back. "Call me Larry and my wife there is Ethel. You'll have to forgive my manners." He began twitching and rubbing his hands back and forth all over his body. He sweated profusely but also shivered, clutching a blanket. "Haven't got the stomach for 'em—manners."

"He hasn't eaten in days, and he's grown so weak," Ethel said, the sound of pleading in her voice. She stood only a foot or so away, hands clenched.

Hadn't eaten in days—my heart jumped—like Father.

"She exaggerates." Larry sniggered, wet and raspy. "She's just frilly."

I smiled.

"You don't laugh?" Larry asked.

"I do."

"Then you can stay."

He wore only a nightshirt, and I was nervous about examining a man's exposed body. The men I had examined were always fully clothed and not in such poor condition.

I reached toward his arms but then pulled back. "May I?"

"If you can." He tried to quell his tremors, without success. "I'm a bit of a fighter."

I had to pry away his hands to see his chest and belly.

"Don't forget I'm a married man." He snickered.

His flesh had torn in places where he had rubbed and clawed too much.

"Forgive me." I tried not to appear embarrassed. I couldn't imagine Miss McKenzie embarrassed. I examined his skin closely but found no rash, and I combed through his hair and beard but found no lice. I felt his head, hot and moist. "How long has he had a fever?"

"Not long." Ethel's hands were clenched at her bosom.

"Get some cool rags. We'll try and bring it down."

"There's more." Ethel walked over and flung off the blanket that covered everything below his waist.

"Oh." I turned my head away. The lower limbs were considered an extremely private area so much so people avoided saying the word "leg" out loud.

"Now, woman, let the girl get to know me first." Larry chuckled and started to hack.

"Look. Look." She gestured.

I cautiously peeked back to see Larry's swollen legs.

Larry tried to sit up to see. "Like hairy white sausages, eh?"

I tried to think. I tried to put together the symptoms, but this was completely unfamiliar.

Ethel placed a moist cloth on her husband's head. I rose and she followed. I was surprised to spot a small boy in a corner. I hadn't noticed him before. He was perhaps seven. He stared at me, and I stared back.

Ethel stepped forward. "He's Jacob."

I regained my focus. "I'm sorry."

"Why? What is it?"

"I don't know."

"But, you—you know medicine."

"I know some things, but—"

I stepped away from Larry and lowered my voice. "I don't

know what's happening to him. And it's serious. I can't—he needs a physician."

"You don't have to go off and hide just to flatter me," Larry called out and laughed again.

I looked over my shoulder then looked back. "Did you give him spirits?"

"He doesn't drink. That's just Larry." She made a face. "We can't pay for a doctor."

"I know, but you have no choice."

"No one will come without money."

"I don't know what else to do."

Her eyes darted back and forth.

"A loan perhaps," I said.

She lowered her chin and brought her fingers to her lips.

"Do you have any means of getting one?" I squeezed the handle of my bag and curled my toes in my shoes.

"Maybe. I'll try."

"All right." I hesitated. "Have you kept the boy away?"

Her eyes shifted to the right. "Mostly."

"Keep them separated, and keep your distance as much as possible. Keep things clean."

"Pardon?"

"It will keep you healthy."

I returned to Larry. "We're going to get you a physician. Your condition is beyond what I know. I can provide a laudanum tincture but not much else."

"Don't be silly, missy. I don't need no docta. I'll get along just fine."

"Larry, shhh," Ethel said.

"Mr. Hughmen, I think it's best we just get you a physician."

"I said call me Larry. No sense in being formal after you've seen the harry sausages!" He chuckled.

His wife smiled and shrugged.

I swallowed my laughter, shook my head. "Just contact me when you make the appointment. I want to be here when the physician comes."

"Can *you* be here?" she asked.

I looked around. "We'll have to find a way for me to hide."

# Twenty-Four

*August 1901*

"Did you have a good day?" John asked.

I focused on my work, stitching my mauve skirt. I suspected I had ripped it when I knelt next to Larry Hughmen. "Productive. Yours?"

We were sitting in the parlor. A Gustav Mahler symphony sounded lightly from the phonograph. John actually sat on the green sofa with me this evening. He had been positioning himself closer to me in the parlor each night since that day outside his office.

"Quite good. Thank you."

The flickering flames of the lamps cast the furniture's shadows on the walls. They danced frantically, trying to disturb me. I paid no attention. The furniture lamented its failed attempts to torment me. My power to ignore and overcome it grew stronger every day. The stairwell almost expanded when I passed through now, afraid to challenge my newfound strength. The people in the rooms were drifting into a deep slumber; I saw their penetrating eyes less and less.

The beast was still there. Although I had succeeded on many occasions in ignoring it, too, it did not grow tired of trying to disturb me. It was a repercussion that would never cease to torment. I sensed it sitting in the middle of that dark room next to mine, glaring at the wall between us. Since I had moved the curtains in there, a stream of light would hit the floor just behind where the beast sat. Sunlight and moonlight would drift across the floor, forcing the beast to flee angrily from its spot time and time again.

I saw the wolf's glowing eyes outside my window at night. I saw bushes rustle during the day. It still paced and patrolled the house. It eyed me every time I left. I sensed no emotion from it, no anger like I did with the house and the beast, just a duty, an obligation to tend to. For some time, I thought I had the upper hand because it didn't attack when I left the house. Yet it remained, watching, waiting to hold me accountable.

Although I wanted to, I couldn't be certain that the house was truly buckling under my will. Was it plotting instead, waiting for the right time to strike? Would I fall? Like a dictator in some faraway country, I ruled an unsteady kingdom. A well-timed uprising could bring me down.

As I slid the needle into my hem, I wondered if I should stop wearing my corset on medical visits. It would certainly help with the stairs and bending over and so many movements. I remembered Miss McKenzie saying some nurses she knew went without corsets and petticoats for such reasons.

"… especially after I found out it was Mr. Hawtrey."

I snapped back to attention, wondering how long John had been talking. Why was he talking? I had stopped trying to make conversation with him a while back, and I had gotten used to not paying him any attention at all, but lately he had this urge to make conversation. I could only guess at how to respond. "Indeed."

"I'm going to be their guide to Labellum all week. I should be fine after spending so much time with them in St. Louis."

My complacent response must have sufficed. "Oh?"

"Yes, I told Mrs. Hawtrey all about you. She's looking forward to making your acquaintance."

"Me as well." I hadn't the slightest idea who he was talking about.

"Since then, Mr. Coddington has really begun to take a liking to me."

"Splendid." Why was he still talking?

"I have been so focused on work and pleasing him ever since we arrived here. I'm not sure if you noticed. I should probably apologize for being quite preoccupied."

Out of spite, I refused to respond. I poked the needle into the skirt again and pulled the long string of thread through.

"I thought we should hold a dinner for them," he said.

I stopped. "Pardon?"

He slid closer to me on the sofa and closed his book. "A dinner...for the Hawtreys."

I was surprised. John hadn't shown any interest in socialization after the mess I made at the Ripprings. "For how many?"

"In addition to the Hawtreys—well, let's see—Dr. and Mrs. Bradbridge, Walter, of course, Mr. and Mrs. Coddington, the Ripprings. Oh, and Mr. and Mrs. Williams and Mrs. Grace."

It was like my own personal firing squad. "I'm not sure if they'll be able to make it."

"Who?"

"The Williamses and Mrs. Grace." I had decided to put off making amends permanently, no longer feeling obligated to be friendly.

"Why not?" He had to reach farther for his tea after having scooted closer to me.

"Mrs. Williams has just been busy."

"We'll still invite them. The Ripprings probably won't make it either."

Thank the Lord.

"Oh, I can't forget Miss Urswick." He reached again to put his tea back down.

"Hmm." I remembered how Miss Urswick angrily abandoned

me. Neither of us had attempted to speak afterward, so I suspected she wouldn't attend either. I lifted my skirt and scrutinized the obviousness of the mend. I thought of Mr. Turner's dark hand spliced with white thread.

"Will you be able to cook for that many people?"

Oh. I had forgotten all about the cooking. Wait, John wasn't asking if I would fancy a night of entertainment. He was informing me I would be hosting a dinner party for ten or more guests. I felt irked for a moment but then I realized I could use this. "I'll have to hire another servant for the evening."

His eyes were stuck on me as if he hadn't taken them off the entire time. "It is really important that this goes well. You let me know whatever you need to ensure it does. I know there will be extra expenses. I am finally making a good impression, and I can't allow anything to spoil that."

"How would your impression be ruined at a dinner party?"

"If it doesn't go well, they might make some decisions about me professionally."

"That isn't very fair." I reached for my tea.

"It doesn't matter. If they think the food, conversation, servants or anything isn't perfect, they will think of it as a reflection of what could go wrong professionally."

I brought down the cup and let the bittersweet taste sit on my tongue for a moment before swallowing. "That's silly." I put my tea down.

"Emeline?" He reached out and touched my arm. "Trust me."

I looked at his hand. "All right."

"That means nothing like what happened at the Ripprings."

I stiffened. "That was an accident."

"Everything has to be perfect."

I narrowed my eyes at him and wondered if he noticed I wasn't acknowledging these little gestures of affection. I wondered if it bothered him. I hoped he longed for me to touch him back just as I had. I hoped every time I didn't, it made him crave it even more.

"Oh. Did you move that bottle of scotch we got for a wedding present? I'd like to offer it to the men before the dinner, but I didn't see it in the liquor cabinet."

I inhaled, remembering the bottle slipping from Mr. Turner's drunken grip and pouring onto the basement floor. "I thought it wasn't good."

"I don't care for it myself, but it's a very fine bottle."

My heart raced. "I'll search for it in the morning."

The missing scotch was an omen—this dinner could go bad quickly because John's professional image relied on dutiful service of the wife, not him, and I was faking it. I could fool John, but a houseful of Labellum's finest scrutinizers? The house had been hungry for something to hold against me, and this would be a prime occasion. It made me wonder how long I could survive beyond the white.

A sharp twinge of pain shot through my finger. "Ouch." I had pricked myself with the needle. I observed the spot of blood and then looked up at John, who hadn't noticed. I quietly put my finger in my mouth. The shadows danced faster and shook.

# Twenty-Five

*August 1901*

$\mathcal{E}$thel Hughmen sighed in relief when I told her I could embellish her pay and cover the doctor's fee if she served at our dinner party. Dr. Benedict Bradbridge required a deposit to make a first-time appointment, but the bank had refused Ethel a loan. Her mistress had agreed to provide her an advance but at an interest rate Ethel could never repay. First-time appointments had to be scheduled at least a week in advance, so I gave her enough medicine to ease her husband's pain and itching until the doctor could provide something stronger.

When I returned to the surrey, Lottie handed me a piece of paper with instructions on it and said a woman had requested I visit her alone. While I was visiting the Hughmens, Lottie had gone to speak with a couple of the people who gave her information when someone needed my assistance. We had Mr. Buck take us to the butcher, where Lottie went in to continue our errands, but I slipped away to find the house, which was nearby. I didn't have to walk far, but when I arrived at the middle-class home, I stopped to double-check the instructions, written in Lottie's curly hand. It said I was at the right place. It didn't make sense. The numbers matched. I was feeling invincible at that moment and decided to approach and ask if anyone had called for a Mrs. Freeman. I scaled the small steps and rapped on the door. I waited a minute or so until it opened.

Mrs. Josephine Doyle, a woman from the committee, opened the door. "Mrs. Dorr?"

I stiffened and my breath caught in my throat. "Uh, good day, Mrs. Doyle." I didn't know what to do next. I almost certainly had come to the wrong house and couldn't ask if she had requested a Mrs. Freeman. I'd had no idea that she was accepting calls on this day and had no excuse for standing there, stiff and strange, on her doorstep.

She scratched her left arm through her long-sleeve dress. "How can I help you, Mrs. Dorr?"

"I'm sorry. I—" Half of my body wanted to run. "I—did you call—um…"

"Pardon?" She reached under her high collar to scratch the back of her neck. Her face was flushed, her mouth open and her eyes fluttering.

"I'm not sure if today is…" I watched her hand jump to her hip to scratch and realized that her eyes were pink. "Mrs. Doyle, are you all right?"

Her cheeks grew a deep red, and her lips trembled into a frown. "I—I don't know. I'm—I—" A tear streamed down her cheek.

"May I come in?"

She moved aside so I could step in and shut the door behind me.

She burst into tears and covered her face with her hands. I took her into a tight embrace. I could feel her tears moisten my shoulder. "Mrs. Doyle, what has happened?"

She pulled away and scratched all over rapidly. "I'm having…a problem." Her face scrunched up and her frown deepened as she uttered a deep frustrated cry. "I don't know."

I couldn't reveal myself, not yet, not when it was a women this close to the committee. This could still have been some kind of amazing coincidence. "Why haven't you called a physician?" I held out my hands as if to catch her.

She shrank to the floor and landed in a kneeling position. "I've been itching and itching, and I can't stop it. I don't understand. I don't understand."

I crouched down. "I should call Dr. Bradbridge."

"No!"

"Why?"

She panted. "I—I—" She started hyperventilating.

"Mrs. Doyle?" I forced eye contact. "I want you to take a deep breath, as big as you can."

She inhaled deeply and then choked and coughed, her dark chocolate-colored hair unfurling.

"Again."

She struggled to fill her lungs and wheezed. It wasn't working.

"Mrs. Doyle, forgive me, we need to remove your corset. Are your servants at home?"

She shook her head. Her face puffed up and grew bright red. She wasn't suffocating, but she was certainly panicking.

"Your husband?"

She shook her head. Like me, she was recently married and without children.

Florence had once calmly and carefully removed my shirtwaist and corset after I fainted from a heated moment with my mother. Florence had been extremely respectful, removing only enough to reveal my back rather than expose my entire body to the open air. I decided that the same respect would be appropriate for Mrs. Doyle. I scooted to her back and quickly undid the line of buttons from her neck down. I opened her shirtwaist, loosened her laces, and pulled open the corset from the back. As I removed the clothing from her, I spotted a sea of little red bumps, like little blisters. From my book on advanced home remedies, I recognized them as hives.

"Breathe deeply." We sat on the floor for several minutes breathing together. When her breath returned to normal, I asked why she hadn't sent for someone.

"I did."

"Dr. Bradbridge?"

She shook her head and gulped.

"Why not?"

"I can't ever call on a Bradbridge again."

I shook my head. "Why?"

She lifted her head. She was breathing hard but no longer hyperventilating. "I quit the committee. I told Margaret to shove off, and I quit."

"Really?"

"That woman is a slave driver."

"Really?" I was questioning not Margaret's character but the idea of Mrs. Doyle yelling at her.

"When she and Ida started these committees, the townswomen thought they'd be fun, but that witch screams and pushes us till our fingers bleed. Then she keeps on pushing." She paused and then continued in a lower voice. "And all so she and her little friends can be the social queens of Labellum."

"Did you say that to her?"

"Something to that effect."

"What did she say?"

"She said I was a piss-poor quilter..." She still had to focus to breathe. "Humiliated me in front of the entire group and told me"—another deep breath—"if I didn't like it to get out."

"What did you say?"

"I stormed out. Said I quit, shove off!"

"You should have—" I stopped. I couldn't imagine doing as much as she had.

"A few other women were nodding." She perked up. "You know, a lot have stopped attending."

"Really?"

"You know Mrs. Grace and Mrs. Williams? They stopped going. Plus a few others. We're thinking about—I don't know…"

"Yes?"

"Overthrowing her majesty."

"How?"

"We are hoping to get the committee women to come together and call for a vote. If the majority agreed, then what could she do?"

"Margaret said something about this. I think…she might be afraid."

"Is that so?" she wheezed and slapped her hand on the floor. "Well then, you see I can't call on a Bradbridge after that."

"Are you sure? Dr. Walter Bradbridge seems…" I hesitated.

"I don't know." She shook her head. "He doesn't know whether to be a doctor or a Bradbridge."

At that I realized she had pretty much fully recuperated from her fit, but I still needed to handle the rash. "Where else do you have hives?"

"You know what they are?"

"I do."

"I thought it must be poison oak, but I had a tincture from when Mr. Doyle had it last month, and it didn't work." She looked down and then back up. "Have you had this before?"

"No. I'm just…" I smiled gravely. "I'm Mrs. Freeman."

She laughed. "I thought *I* was in trouble."

# Twenty-Six

*September, 1901*

"How did you get here?" I asked when Lottie appeared at my door on one of the days she and her husband were scheduled to work as field laborers.

"One of the gals that works with us had a friend lookin' for Mrs. Freeman. He gave her this." She handed me an envelope.

I started to open it.

"It had money for a driver, so I used it to get here and now I gotta get back."

"Money?" The type of people who contacted me weren't the type to have money to pay for a driver.

She shrugged. "Ain't got a clue. The letter say use the money and get to the address quick. My friend say it's about a lady ganna lose a baby."

"Oh."

"I can't go. I gotta get back and I used all that money to get here."

"No, it's all right. Mr. Buck is in the stables. I'll have him take you back, and I'll visit this woman straight away. After our encounter, I've been reading about these things." I ran around the house and grabbed my bag and several books with sections on the growing field of gynecology and obstetrics and then had Mr. Buck return Lottie and take me to the designated location. I told him Lottie had found a possible servant for the dinner party. The dinner was a wonderful excuse for all kinds of abnormal behavior although I could tell Mr. Buck was growing tired of my suspicious destinations.

I skimmed through the books on the way, reading the most important passages. One of the books explained that to prevent perversion physicians didn't look while they examined a woman or assisted in childbirth. The book had a drawing of a man on one knee. He appeared to be proposing marriage, except that the woman before him had her arms crossed and glowered at him because, instead of holding out a glistening ring, he had his hand up her skirts. How could they know what they were doing if they didn't look? I wished a midwife had written such a book, for it would have been far more useful. Midwives had once been the primary aide to childbirth, but licensed doctors had taken their place. I didn't know much about who was better, but I did know one thing: Midwives looked.

After a bumpy ride to the outskirts of Labellum, we arrived at what appeared to be an abandoned cabin. Mr. Buck's eyes and shoulders hinted at doubt. He had every reason to be suspicious, given that no proper lady would go to a servant for an interview. He jumped down from the driver's seat.

"Mr. Buck?"

"Yes, ma'am?" He clasped my hand as I stepped out.

"You can wait here."

"I should accompany you."

"I'll be fine on my own, thank you."

"But Mrs.—"

"Thank you, Mr. Buck."

He halted.

I walked to the house and knocked. No answer. I knocked again and waited. Still no answer. I waited longer this time.

I went to knock a third time but stopped myself. Instead I tested the knob to see if the door was locked. The door scraped the floor as it opened. Inside, a chair lay on its side and some leaves had built up in a corner of the dark room. I stepped in and the door sneaked back, catching on the floor halfway. The little shack had a couple of windows, but the shutters were closed. Light from the half-open door streaked across the room, and I lingered there holding my bag in front of me.

"Is anyone there?"

I heard a scuff and saw a strip of dim orange light glowing beneath a closed door. "Pardon me, is someone there?"

Then more shuffling, followed by silence. I heard steps behind the door.

My voice cracked as I tried to speak over the sound of my heart drumming in my ears. "U—um—I was told to come here, someone needed help."

The doorknob turned and the door opened. My heart pounded until the silhouette of a woman came into view and stopped.

"Forgive me—I knocked. Um…"

The woman didn't speak for a moment then leaned forward. "Emeline?"

"What?" Was it a trick? Who was it?

"Wha—what are you doing here?" she stammered. She picked up a lamp and squeezed through without opening the door all the way and closed it behind her. With the lamp in front of her, I could see her rosy cheeks, her blond hair.

"Ella?" I stepped back. "Why are you here?"

"Why are you here?"

Neither of us answered. We both stared.

Finally, without thinking, I reacted. "Are you waiting for someone, someone named Freeman?"

Her wide eyes moved from me to my bag. She crinkled her nose. "You? No—how?"

I exhaled in relief. "It's a long story."

"I don't know—"

The door behind Ella opened and Francis stepped out. "Is it her? Is she—" she jolted at the sight of me. "Emeline, um—uh…"

"It's all right," Ella said. "She's her."

"What?" Francis gave me a once-over. "No."

"I won't say anything if you don't."

Ella motioned to the room.

I wedged past Francis.

She stood stunned. "Wait—no—we can't trust her."

"She has just as much to lose as we do," Ella said.

Inside the room, Annie, Francis' daughter, lay on a bed, white, her reddish, blond hair damp from sweat. I maneuvered around to the side. I opened my bag, placed my handkerchief on an old night table, and lined up several tools. "Tell me what happened."

Annie saw me. "What is she doing here?"

Francis went to the other side of the bed and clasped Annie's hand. "She's the one who's going to help."

"What?" Annie was obviously in pain. Lottie had said the woman in need might lose a baby. Had her informant misunderstood?

"Francis?"

Francis twisted a handkerchief in her hands tighter and tighter as she spoke. "We couldn't do it here, so we went to the city. We had no choice. We took her to a physician—someone we knew, someone who could help her with her condition."

"Do what? I don't understand."

"Didn't someone tell you what this was about?"

"No, the message got mixed up. She said someone might lose a baby."

"Lose?" Francis shook her head. "No. She didn't *lose* it."

I blinked a few times then raised my eyes up at her. Was she saying…

"We had no choice. She's not married. If her father knew what she had done, he would cast her out—disown her. Society would taint her. No one would ever have her."

Annie started crying, and Francis held her daughter's hand up.

Annie's bottom lip curled and trembled a little with her sobs. "He said he—I thought he—he said..."

"I know, darling, I know." Francis caressed her hand. "He deceived you. He deceived all of us."

Suddenly, I understood why Francis had turned on me when I told Annie she was too young for boys—Francis had believed the boy intended to marry her daughter as well. I realized what Francis and Ella had been whispering about the day I stitched up Mr. Turner's hand. I didn't know how to respond other than to take out one of the books and flip through it to find the hazards of such procedures. The book had illustrations of tools and listed signs of injury and possible causes of death. I put my hand on Annie's shoulder. "I need to do some things to see what's wrong. It might hurt a little, but I'll be gentle."

Annie clenched her eyes shut and rolled her lips inward.

I moved a chair to the side of the bed. "Will you help move her?"

They did as asked while Annie used her elbows to position her lower body at the edge of the bed. Then I positioned her legs, and Francis helped Annie remove a cloth they had wrapped around her lower body to soak up the blood. The cloth wasn't soaked through, and she wasn't gushing when they removed it.

I cleaned her with a damp cloth and nervously checked to make sure there weren't any tears or cuts in the outer flesh. "Bring the light close." I read from the book and looked at her, comparing situations. I needed to be as thorough as I possibly could, but I couldn't see anything. I remembered the picture of the man with his hand up the woman's skirt. "I have to use my hands," I told Francis, wanting her consent.

"Have you done this before?" Francis bundled her handkerchief in one hand and went to bite a nail but pulled it away before she could.

"I delivered Mrs. Schwab's baby. I took classes on nursing and volunteered at an infirmary, but no, I have never done *this* before."

The women stared at me, their faces stiff and their mouths bowed.

"Do you want me to try or not?"

Francis hesitated, nodded, and bit that nail after all.

I rolled up my sleeves and Annie tensed as I felt inside. I tried to find any cuts, but all I could identify was the slick texture of blood. I used my fingers to press on the sides. She would have reacted if I touched a cut. "Does anything hurt?" I asked.

"Not there," she said through her teeth.

"Try to relax."

"Breathe," Francis whispered.

"Where does it hurt?"

She grasped the area just below her stomach.

The problem was deeper inside. I removed my hand, which was saturated with blood. Ella dunked a bowl into a pail and brought it over. I dipped my hands into it and scrubbed them. After drying them, I checked a few other things, noting her temperature and her heart rhythm.

"Well?" Francis asked.

"I can't see or feel any cuts or abrasions." I gently touched Annie's hand. "Annie, you can lie back down." I made my way toward the door while Francis helped Annie to move back. Then Ella and Francis followed. I whispered so Annie wouldn't hear. "She does have a fever."

"What does that mean?" Francis asked.

I hated having to say it again. "I don't know."

"But—"

"I don't know. Her pain is deeper, which might be normal, but I don't know for sure. I can only tend to minor issues. This is anything but minor."

"Then what good are you?" Francis threw her hands up.

I looked down and my cheeks burned.

Ella glared at her daughter before her eyes softened and shifted from Francis to me. "What can we do?"

"If she has an infection, she could become septic and…it could be fatal."

Francis cringed, covered her face, and turned away.

"If it gets worse, you'll have to take her to a physician."

"What?" Francis turned back. "We can't. You know we can't."

"You should have taken her to one in the first place."

"We did!" Francis shouted.

"Obviously not a good one."

"You don't know that." Francis pointed at me. "You don't know anything. You're not a doctor."

"No, I'm not." I folded my arms.

Francis stepped closer to me. "You know we can't take her to anyone and you of all people know why. We took her to St. Louis in the first place to avoid the risk of Mr. Coddington's firm finding out."

I didn't like Francis and I despised her decision, but did she deserve jail? Did Annie or Ella?

Francis leaned in and kept her voice low, her hands clenched. "The boy pretended to love her. He promised to marry her. She didn't know any better. She shouldn't suffer because somebody deceived her." She stepped back, placed her hand against her breastbone, and shook her head. "No, no. If we have to go to a doctor, I'm reporting you."

I widened my eyes and dug my fingernails into my palms.

"Francis." Ella's voice rose.

"No one can know. We'll be on the street or in jail." Francis reached out and grabbed my hand. "Just do something." Her voice quavered. She gripped my hand tighter. "We won't say anything if you help us. Please, just help us."

I pulled my hand away. "How?"

"The doctor in St. Louis. He'll know what to do. Just help her until he arrives."

"She needs to see someone soon."

"We'll send a wire."

I gave Annie something for the pain and did what I could to lower her fever and stop the bleeding. As I started to leave, Francis stopped me. "Emeline, we had to do this. She would lose everything if we didn't."

I stared coldly at her without responding. I didn't say anything. I just left.

# Twenty-Seven

*September 1901*

The next day I received a letter from St. Louis—from James. I stared at it. Part of me wanted to throw it out. Another part of me knew that I wouldn't do that and that I might as well just read it. I ripped the envelope, pulled out the paper and unfolded it.

*My Dearest Emeline,*

*It pains me not to hear from you. Did you receive my last letter? I am excited to tell you Mother is wildly planning my wedding for next spring. I hope to see you there more than anyone else.*

*These past months of separation have weighed on me. I miss you. Without you, all adventure and excitement have vanished. I think of our explorations and intrigues often. We were wonderful detectives. I miss those days.*

*The three hens miss you as well. They go on and on about you all the time. Mother raves about you to everyone she sees. We all miss you. She and the girls are doing well in our uncle's house and saving for a small apartment or cottage home. I was concerned Mother would be treated like second class, but they have become one big family.*

*Having not heard from you, I'm growing concerned about your
situation. Please write me. Inform me of your well-being.*

*Yours Always,*
*James Evans*

I clenched the letter and enjoyed the crinkling sound. I yanked
open a drawer in my writing desk and ripped out a sheet of paper,
slapped it down, and grabbed the pen and ink.

*Dear James,*

*Forgive my lack of correspondence. I have been busy living an
inscrutable unwanted existence. Forgive me for daring to request you
fulfill your word. How foolish of me. I find it convenient you now
suffer but showed no concern for my sufferings when I beseeched you.
Soon you shall suffer more knowing that your lack of compassion has
driven me to....*

I stopped. I wanted James to suffer. I wanted him to hurt as
much as I had, but I wasn't going to mail such a letter. Besides,
if I sent a letter like that, he might come to Labellum. I didn't
even know what I would do if he came to take me back now. I
didn't even know if I'd want to go with him anymore. I decided to
postpone my response until after the dinner party and take some
time to think about what I should write.

# Twenty-Eight

*September 1901*

Two days passed without a response to the urgent wire Francis and Ella had sent. Lottie had her husband check for one daily. I checked on Annie daily, and she wasn't getting better. Early on the third morning, Lottie told me they had received a response and it was at her house.

When we reached Lottie's home, I spotted a young man outside with Lucy. Lucy sat atop a barrel, and the man leaned against a wall of the shanty. He wore brown trousers and a loose plain shirt. No jacket. No waistcoat. No tie. He pushed off the wall when he saw us, and Lucy jumped down from the barrel.

"Mrs. Dorr?" he said.

"Yes?"

"This is Daniel Nelson," Lottie said.

I knew the name, but from where? Then I remembered. "Nelson as in the Nelsons who used to live here?"

"I'm pleased to finally meet you." He pushed his dark hair from his left eyebrow and stuck out his hand to shake.

I glanced at his hand. It wasn't the usual etiquette to shake hands or was it in this situation? I wasn't sure of the usual etiquette or if I cared. I took his hand in mine.

"I hear you live in my old house....Funny." He didn't release my hand right away but continued shaking it as he spoke.

"Funny?"

"Seeing that you've picked up right where my family left off.... Maybe it's the house."

I narrowed my eyes at him, dropped his hand.

"He's here for Annie," Lottie said.

I folded my arms. "Pardon me?"

"Annie," she said.

"My father received a wire from Mrs. Williams." He pulled a sheet of folded tan paper from his pocket.

"Your father? Your father did that?"

"Yes." His eyes were steady.

I shifted my weight.

"Will you take me to Miss Williams?"

I lifted my chin. "Our letter requested instructions or medicines. You don't need to see her to do that."

"I think it'd be best if I examine her myself."

"Why would I let you do that?"

"I am a physician."

"You?" I blinked and gave him a once over. "You're too young to be a physician."

"I started young."

"We can trust him," Lottie said.

I hesitated. "My driver hasn't returned."

"I have a buggy," he said.

Daniel gripped the reins and paid close attention to the horse. I stared at him until he shifted in his seat. "Is there something you want to say to me?"

"I heard stories."

He returned his focus to the road. "What did you hear?"

I raised my voice over the grinding of the buggy's wheels on the dirt road and recounted a shortened version of what Margaret and Lottie had told me.

When I finished, he nodded. "Some of that is true."

I waited, but he didn't elaborate. "What happened after you left Labellum?"

He kept his eyes on the road. "My father opened a practice in St. Louis."

"But it's illegal?"

"What do you mean?"

"Practicing medicine without a license."

"We are licensed. Always were."

"Wait—I thought...then why were you run out of town?"

"We encouraged people without licenses to help one another with simple remedies. We offered cheap and even free medicine, encouraged midwives, and you can't forget about those stories you heard."

"When—why did your father start doing...abortions?"

"When you don't always follow the rules, you get requests like that."

"I suppose, but that doesn't mean you have to do it."

"If it was the lesser of two evils?"

"It never is."

"I guess that depends on who you talk to."

I thought about things I had done, my father, the time with the dog—foaming at the mouth, strings of drool flying from its lips.

"We only do it when there is a life at stake."

"But—" I stopped myself.

"Yes?"

"But you put her life at stake."

"And if we left her in her condition, she would never be able to live a respectable life. Her father would disown her. Mrs. Williams would either have to risk her child alone on the streets or abandon her own life to take care of Annie on the streets."

I raised my voice. "But she could die."

"I won't let her die." He glanced at me. "Sometimes doing the wrong thing is better than doing nothing...but I think you already know that."

When we arrived, Daniel jumped down and entered the home without knocking or hesitating as I'd done the first time I showed up. I followed him but by the time I got into the room, Francis was thanking him over and over.

"Please." He motioned for us to step out. "Mrs. Williams, you can remain." He shut the door, and the light disappeared.

Ella left the lamp in the room, but the open front door allowed some light into the empty room. We stood just outside the door.

"How is she?" I asked.

Ella refused to pry her eyes from the door. "I think her fever may have gone down a little." She clenched her hands so hard that her knuckles were white.

"Is she still bleeding?"

"A little."

We stood there silent. I could hear Daniel, a low mumble behind the door, and then Francis, responding with one- or two-word answers. Ella's face was taut. I fidgeted, wanting to say something, anything. I wanted to take her mind away from this or just fill the silence and calm my stomach. Nothing came to me. Eventually, I started to pace, but Ella just stood near the door, her hands clenched together in front of her.

Finally, Daniel and Francis walked out. "There was a small laceration," Daniel said. "It didn't even need a stitch. It appears to be healing, but I treated her for infection."

"What does that mean?" Ella asked.

"She is going to be fine. I've given Mrs. Williams instructions on how to continue."

"The fever?" I asked.

"It's breaking. It's good that you were here for them, Mrs. Dorr. Your instructions saved Annie from some unnecessary pain and helped break the fever, I'm sure."

Francis and Ella sighed simultaneously. "Thank you."

"You can take her home if you wish. You can tell people she caught something on your trip."

Ella took his hand. "Dr. Nelson, thank you. Thank you so much."

"I'm glad to have helped. I'll be in town for a few more days in case anything else happens."

And that was that. Simple. In less than twenty minutes, he had fixed everything, and we were back in the buggy returning to Lottie's. I felt useless, pointless. What was I doing? I slumped. "It was good you came." I sighed. "I couldn't help them."

"That's why there are physicians." He gripped the reins.

"It's unfortunate that's not the case for everyone."

He glanced over.

I continued. "There aren't doctors for everyone, for the poor or for Mrs. Williams' daughter."

He kept his eyes forward. "I'm right here. I'm their doctor."

"Yes, but there isn't one of you everywhere."

"There's more than you think. Not all doctors are like the Bradbridges."

"Still."

"There are also people like you."

I shook my head. "I couldn't help Annie. I can't help everyone."

"But you help some."

I watched the greens and browns of the landscape pass. I help some, I thought. It made me feel a little better but not much. "Do you have somewhere to stay?" I asked.

"I'll be staying with Mrs. Schwab."

I pondered that. "I don't believe there's room."

He chuckled. "That's all right. I don't want anyone to know I'm in town. Plus, I grew up playing with her children. I haven't seen Lucy in years."

"Are you two close?"

He smirked at me. "She is the girl in the stories."

"What? What girl?"

"The girl whose brother was ill."

"Lottie never—"

"It wasn't Lucy's brother. It was her friend and Mrs. Schwab never knew."

"What really happened?"

"His family could not afford a physician. I had assisted my father before and thought I knew what I was doing." He paused. "I was wrong."

"Yes?" A bump in the road made my voice rise.

"The medicine I took from my father was the wrong kind. The boy had a bad reaction."

"Did he…die?"

"No. We told my father and he knew what to do."

"So it was all rumors?"

"Not exactly."

"Do tell."

"With all the commotion and panic, the news spread to Mr. Coddington, who used it to his advantage. My father's fight was over, and it was my fault."

I swallowed. "You only did what you thought was right."

"The night we left, my mother and sister were asleep on the steamboat, and I tried to apologize to my father. That was the night he told me he was going to make me a physician. He said, 'I should have known you'd do something like this. You've got the heart of a doctor. When you knew someone needed help, you didn't hesitate.'"

"You did it for Lucy." My lips curled up slyly.

He blushed. "Sometimes doing the wrong thing is better than doing nothing at all."

# Twenty-Nine

*1892*
*Forest Park*
*St. Louis, Missouri*

Sunday strolls were my favorite. After church, my entire family would visit a nearby park. It was the only time my sisters, brother, and I could run around and play in our Sunday best. My mother and father walked or chatted nearby arm in arm as we played tag, Marco Polo, and make-believe games. One particular Sunday close to fall, that time of year when the leaves start to turn but it's not quite cold yet, we could hear a few small chirps from nearby birds and a dog barking in the distance. It felt special because there were very few people in the park and my mother had packed a picnic basket with chipped beef, cheese, a loaf of sourdough bread, and apple dumplings.

James was twelve, so I must have been around fourteen. Florence was eight, Lillian four, and Ruth hadn't even been born. Lillian was the baby back then, hardly even a playmate. I remember James and I getting fed up with her when she didn't play our games properly. On this day in the park, James and I were becoming infuriated with her. We had been attempting a game of hide-and-seek, and she kept giving away our location.

"Here! Here! Here! We're over here!" Lillian shouted from behind a short stone wall lining one of the park paths.

"Lillian!" I shouted.

Then Florence jumped around the wall. "I caught you! I caught you!"

"Nuh-uh," James said.

"Not fair," I said with hands on hips. "You cheated."

"Did not."

"Did too. Lillian showed you. That's cheating."

"No it's not. I caught you."

"No, you have to do it again," I whined.

"No, I caught you. It's your turn."

"You're still it," I said. "Now take Lillian with you so she doesn't give us away."

"No. No fair!"

"Papa!"

My mother and father had sat down at a bench and must have been telling each other jokes because Mama kept throwing her head back, all cheeks and teeth.

My father called out cheerily, "Girls...and James, play nice."

I folded my arms and cocked my head at Florence with the kind of triumphant look only a big sister can give.

"Fine, but I get two turns next." She snatched Lillian's hand and stomped off with her.

James and I watched Florence and Lillian plop down in the grass. Florence covered Lillian's eyes, shut her own, and counted out loud. "One,...two,..."

James and I scurried toward a grove.

"... nine,...ten,...eleven,..."

"No, wait, over here." I grabbed James' wrist and pulled him behind a thick-trunked tree with peeling bark.

"... thirteen,...fourteen,..."

Although the tree was behind Florence and Lillian, we could see Mama and Papa from where we hid. My father gestured big and spoke softly to my mother, who tee-heed and giggled. I didn't know it at the time, but they were still a young couple, their bodies still full of energy and their minds still fantasizing about the future. I remembered watching them and thinking I wanted that someday. Then my father stopped talking and stared at something. He said something and then said it louder and stood up. My mother shot up to stand next to him.

That's when Florence screamed.

James and I darted around the tree to see a tawny dog galloping toward our sisters. It snarled and barked, drool dripping from its mouth in long white streams and its black eyes crazed.

"Run! Run!" my father shouted and sprinted toward my sisters.

Florence ran, but little Lillian didn't move.

"Lilly!" my mother screeched. Her hands were on her cheeks, and she was white with fear.

My father reached Lillian just as the dog did. My father slid down and threw his body over her and then gave the dog a quick kick across the jaw. He scooped Lillian up and started to run with her.

Unfazed, the dog shook, snarled, and started after them.

"Run!" My father shouted as he ran toward James and me.

The dog leapt and snatched my father by the back of his jacket, sending him flying back and Lillian tumbling forward. She rolled to a stop just in front of us, and James and I yanked her up and avoided the snarling dog and my grunting father wrestling with it.

He dodged its snapping jaws repeatedly and swung around it while rising to one knee in an attempt to escape. It lunged for him, but he dodged it and slid back down on the ground.

"Papa!" I screamed.

The dog veered toward the three of us and started at a gallop. Its teeth clomped as it barked.

My father quickly grabbed it by the hindquarters and dragged it away from us. It turned on him, and he tried kicking it away again and again, but it kept coming at him.

Again he got behind it, only this time instead of trying to flee, he lunged onto the beast, wrapped his right arm under the neck and his left arm on top, pinned the animal and jerked his arms down and back, causing a great big snap. The snarling dog went limp, and my father fell on top of it. He panted there for a moment before finally rolling over and gasping for breath.

The three of us ran to him. He saw us and moved away from the dog just in time to catch all three of us in one big hug. A moment later, Florence was on top of us and my mother just behind her.

"Did it bite you? Did it bite you?" she demanded, frantic.

"No." He breathed heavily, still hugging us. He stood and squeezed my mother hard while we hugged his legs. "I'm fine. I'm fine."

She clung to him. "I was so scared. Oh my God, Charles."

"I'm all right. The children are all right."

That night Mama and Papa let us all sleep in the same room, so we all cuddled up together, two to a bed. We wondered and whispered about the unknown until my father came in and sat on the bed Lillian and James shared.

"Are you girls all right?" He patted my brother's arm. "James, I know you're a tough lad."

James brightened a little.

"I'm tough, too," I said and squeezed Florence around the waist.

"Of course you are." He smiled gingerly and lowered his gaze. "Lilly?"

James spoke up. "She doesn't understand why you hurt the dog." We all stared.

"It could have killed you." He stroked Lillian's hair. "It wanted to hurt us, all of us."

"Why did it want to hurt us?" I asked.

"It was rabid. It had a disease. It didn't know what it was doing."

"It didn't know it wanted to hurt us?"

"Something like that."

I knew Papa had saved us, but it seemed wrong to feel so happy when the dog's neck had been cracked and it lay dead. "I still don't understand—"

"Thou shall not kill," Florence said in a soft voice.

We all looked at her and then at our father. She'd summed it up.

"Oh. I see." He sighed. "Girls—and James—I'm really proud of you for recognizing the contradiction in what happened today. God commanded us not to kill, but sometimes we have to choose to do something that seems wrong in order to do something right. I had to kill that dog if I was going to keep all of you safe."

"So we can break the commandments?" James asked.

"If there is something that is extremely important like a life at stake, then yes, you can break a commandment. You can't break a commandment just because you feel like it."

"And we won't go to hell?" I asked.

"You won't go to hell if you break a commandment for something of the utmost importance. It has to be something so important that you would risk anything for it, even if that means risking your own standing with God."

"Then how do we know we won't go to hell?"

"Do you think I'm going to hell for what I did today?"

We all shook our heads.

"If it is the right thing, so right you can break a commandment, then you'll know it. I didn't doubt for one second whether or not to kill that dog. I was going to protect you no matter what." He grazed Lillian's cheek with his thumb. "Besides, the disease that dog had would kill it anyway. It might not have looked it, but the animal was suffering, in pain. It was good to end it."

I'm not sure if any of us blinked, imagining it happening all over again.

"Does that make sense?" he asked.

"I think so," James said.

Lillian nodded.

"Yes," Florence said.

My father lifted his chin to me to acknowledge me, his face serene. "Emeline, does that make sense?"

I hesitated and then nodded.

# Thirty

𝒯he next request I received was from a woman whose symptoms suggested pregnancy, and Lottie was able to accompany me this time. As we approached a small house in a poor congested area on the outskirts of town, Lottie told me what she knew. "I never actually spoke to her. She heard about you through different people who knew me and gave me the message." She pointed. "This one." Lottie knocked on the door. The house was a run-down little thing, but in better shape than some of the others I had seen.

Understanding Lottie's dilemma and having seen Annie's less than a week ago, I didn't want to tell a poor woman she was pregnant. I couldn't imagine the news being anything other than bad, as the woman would either already have too many mouths to feed or be so thin and unhealthy that pregnancy would likely be a death sentence. Death was a risk with pregnancy even with the healthiest of women. Even upper-class women with the finest physicians were at risk of dying during childbirth.

"Come in," a male voice responded. The husband?

Inside, I could tell that whoever lived there wasn't of high standing but was still aware of the finer things in life and had attempted to acquire some of them. She had furnishings, poor-quality and well-worn but furniture at least. She had a grandfather clock, a writing desk, and a china cabinet, although it was empty. Maybe that meant the couple would do fine with a child. I didn't see any other children. We stood there waiting for someone to greet us.

"Anyone there?" Lottie called out.

"Yes," a man's voice said, and he appeared from an adjoining room. It was a young man in a fine suit. It was Dr. Walter Bradbridge.

"Walter?"

"Emeline?"

Silence. Stunned silence.

"What are you doing here?" he asked.

"I, uh, must ask you the same," I said.

"I—no," he fumbled, taken aback. He refocused. "Why are you here?" He eyed Lottie and then my bag.

I feared my inability to answer would prove my guilt. "I—I—uh…"

"It's my fault, sir," Lottie said. "I recommended a friend to serve at Mrs. Dorr's dinner party, and I coulda swore this was her house. Forgive us for intrudin' on *whatever* business you have here." She said it in an odd way, with a suggestive tone.

"Oh." I gasped a little and covered my mouth as if assuming a scandal. "We should leave." We turned toward the door.

"No, no." He reached out and took a step forward.

We halted and slowly turned around.

"This is Mrs. Crawford's home. She let me borrow it for the day."

"Oh," Lottie said.

"Forgive me—um—Mrs. Dorr, I can explain."

We stared at him.

"We've become aware of a colored woman practicing illegal medicine for the poor and others around town."

"No!" Lottie slapped her hand to her chest, overacting.

I cleared my throat.

Walter continued. "Mrs. Crawford lent me her home so I might lure this practitioner here. We really weren't sure it would work. All we had was someone who claimed to have known someone who knew a relative who used her. We sent a distress call through that line."

"Oh my." I could hardly feign shock, on account of my rapidly pounding heart and fear of his seeing it. "Well, we really should leave you in case this woman shows up."

"Yes, yes, you are right." He opened the door for us. "I'll make sure to let Mrs. Crawford know you stopped by, Miss…?"

Lottie waved a hand. "No need, got my houses mixed up is all."

"Forgive me again for the confusion."

"Not at all," I said.

As soon as the door shut behind us, Lottie and I exhaled and looked at each other.

"Do you know Mrs. Crawford?"

"Conniving rat of a woman," she said.

"Was that excuse due to another award-winning detective novel?"

She grinned. "That was all me."

"Your knack for intrigue is extraordinary."

"It comes to me naturally."

After we walked away from the house, I realized something. "Wait."

She halted. "What?"

"They know about me."

Lottie shook her head. "They don't know it's you."

"But they're trying to find me. If I coincidently show up at another fake call, they're going to figure it out. And if they realize you're involved at all…"

"What should we do?"

"I don't know. We need to be extremely careful. He said, 'We know of a person.'"

"Uh-huh."

"Who is 'we'?"

"Probably his ma and pa."

"We don't know that. It could be something to do with Mr. Coddington's practice. It could be Mr. Rippring or my husband."

She brought her hand to her chin. "I ain't got a clue."

I didn't know either. I tried to think. How could I find out who had put Walter up to this? "Well, someone else has to be involved. Dr. Bradbridge has to return to that person at some point to report what happened. He will probably go right after he has given up here."

"What? No," Lottie squeaked. "We jus' barely got away."

"Come on, it will be like your detective books. We have to. It's the only way to know who is behind it, and we can come up with distractions or a patsy or something—false clues."

Lottie threw up her hands. "What's the point? It won't stop 'em."

"Lottie, where's that adventurous spirit?"

"It's cowerin'!"

"We have to know."

Her cheeks puffed up as she blew out air. "How?"

I scanned the area. "His carriage isn't here. He obviously walked. We can follow."

She sighed. "If we get caught, I'm blamin' you."

I grinned.

I told Mr. Buck to meet us at the general store because we were near Hill and North Main streets. Lottie and I crouched behind a wall of unkempt honeysuckle bushes. All the berries had fallen off and lay shriveled on the ground around our feet. There we waited for Walter to give up on the fictional Mrs. Freeman. It was late afternoon when he stepped out.

"Look," I whispered. "There he is." I peered through a little opening I had made in the honeysuckle. Walter left the run-down house holding his briefcase. At the road, he looked right and then left before taking a sharp turn back in the opposite direction. He rushed along the side of the house and around to the back near our lookout. We crouched lower. I stiffened, thinking he'd see us, but he passed by.

I felt a rush of relief and then an urge to follow, but I waited until he had walked far enough that our rustling would not be noticed. "Let's go." We took off in his direction. I held my heavy skirt and petticoats up but still felt the occasional snag.

"Miss, be careful. Your dress," Lottie said trailing behind me.

We caught up with him. "Slow down." I put my hand out behind me, and Lottie stopped. "We can't let him hear us," I whispered. I stopped behind a tree. Lottie bent over to catch her breath. We watched Walter cross from behind the houses into an alley.

"Where's he goin'?" Lottie whispered loudly with her hands on her knees.

I shook my head. "A shorter route?"

"Seems peculiar to me."

We peered down the alley and watched him make a right.

"Come on."

We rushed into the alley and approached the turn. I peered around the corner. He hurried as if he had somewhere to be, someone to meet. "He has to be going to whoever is behind this. Why else take this sly route?" I motioned for Lottie to follow as I watched Walter round another building. "Let's go."

We trotted down the path. "Why is he going through these back alleys?"

"How should I know?" Lottie panted but kept up. I breathed heavily but felt surprisingly energized.

We continued to follow him, turning here and there.

Lottie snorted impatiently. "If he was fixin' on goin' all the way across town, why didn't he bring a carriage?"

At one point we were behind some businesses and I could see in between the buildings. "That's Main Street."

"Huh?"

"We are close to South Main."

"There ain't nothin' over there but a few old houses. We should get back anyway. Start dinner."

"Shhh." I waved my hand. "We'll think of something."

"We have some leftover roast from—"

"There he goes," I said over my shoulder. "Walk quickly but casually. We're about to get back into town."

We skulked down the alley toward Main Street.

"Then you can boil some of the dried squash"—she stumbled on her words as she scrambled—"and serve the last of my brown betty for dessert."

We were near the bend in Main Street, which became South Main. The general store, the Bradbridges, and Mr. Coddington's office were at the other end. Where was he going?

Lottie followed, still breathing hard. "Maybe you should boil some potatas."

"Focus. We are about to turn onto Main. He's going to be right there, so be quiet or he will spot us."

Lottie nodded.

I took a breath, turned the final corner, and attempted to stroll about twenty or thirty feet behind Walter until he reached a road crossing just before the houses, but then he stopped.

We stopped.

"Quick." Lottie whirled around and took my hand to bring me with her. She shoved me in front of her. We weren't the only people on the street, and maybe Walter wouldn't notice me, with Lottie blocking the view. My heart pounded, and I wondered if Walter would recognize Lottie's silhouette from behind and run in our direction.

"Stop. Stop," Lottie said. "He's gone."

We turned around. "Where did he go? Hurry."

We trotted as casually as possible down the street, passing strangers who eyed us curiously. "I don't see him." We approached another road crossing, but I didn't see him anywhere.

"There he is."

"Where?"

Lottie pointed to an old house with blue trim and peaked layered roofs just over the canal bridge. Walter entered the house and disappeared from sight.

I lifted my hand. "What? Who—who lives there?"

She didn't respond.

"Lottie?"

"Miss Urswick," she said.

"Why would he go there?"

She turned her palms up and shrugged. "I don't know."

"Are they acquainted?"

She shook her head. "I don't know."

We started back in the other direction.

"Does this mean Miss Urswick is trying to find Mrs. Freeman?"

Lottie's eyes moved back and forth but she didn't respond.

I wondered what possible reason he could have for going to Olivia Urswick. "Maybe she's ill."

"That woman wouldn't call on a doctor, let alone a Bradbridge, if she was about to die. She hates the Bradbridges."

"Either he is visiting a patient or someone who hired a spy. But why? Why would she care?"

"Didn't you say she wasn't too pleased with you that one time."

"But whoever is looking doesn't know it's me."

Lottie shrugged again. "We gotta go. Your husband's dinner will be late, then he ganna be suspicious, and I had enough of all that today." She sighed. "All this stressin' don't do nothin' kindly for me."

"He won't notice." I looked over my shoulder at Olivia Urswick's house and wondered what she knew as we started back toward the market where Mr. Buck waited with the surrey.

# Thirty-One

*September 1901*

$\mathcal{I}$t had taken more than two weeks for Dr. Benedict Bradbridge to schedule a house call with Larry and Ethel Hughmen for one o'clock on a Thursday. I arrived a half-hour early. The heat grew by the hour, and the unventilated apartment felt like a hothouse. It smelled of sweat and mold. I checked on Larry, who was asleep, and Ethel went about straightening up.

My eyes moved to the boy playing in the corner, his frail body hunched over, with clumps of hair hanging down. Jacob played an imaginary game with imaginary things. I had seen poor children substitute toys with a variety of objects such as rocks and twigs but never with nothing. He reached out into the air and stuck out his thumb and forefinger to grab what appeared to be a tiny invisible man. He moved the imaginary man around, his eyebrows furrowed. The bit of nothing between his fingers threatened something. Still holding the imaginary man in one hand, he reached out with the other and grabbed something else that wasn't there. This time, he stuck out his thumb and forefinger in the opposite direction. He moved the imaginary man toward the other imaginary thing and then yanked it away. I believe it was supposed to be a horse or another animal, but he didn't make any noises to go along with the movements. I had tried to talk to him once but he didn't acknowledge me. I wasn't even sure if he could speak. He was so slight, so easy to miss, that if Ethel hadn't spoken of him, I might have concluded he was imaginary, too.

I refocused on Ethel, who gestured toward an empty cupboard the way someone does when presenting a beautiful object to a person of importance. "To hide." Ethel's tenement consisted of the one room. There was nowhere else to go.

"It's small." I stepped forward.

"Yes. Forgive me. I should have let you know so you didn't wear a full toilette."

"It's all right. I'm supposed to be making calls. If I didn't look presentable, someone would notice." I sighed. "Do you have a place to hide them?"

"I have a trunk."

"Can you help me?" I removed my hatpins and hat.

"Course. I've served as a handmaid for many fine women."

As she removed my clothing, I tried to ease the tension. "How have you been handling all of this?" She undid my skirt and untied my petticoats.

I started to undo my blouse's buttons. It would have to come off along with my corset if I were going to curl up enough to fit in the cupboard.

"It's been difficult," she said. "I've had opportunities to work longer hours, but I can't find someone to look after Jacob, and without my husband's income there are bills I can't—" she stopped and cleared her throat. "It's been difficult."

I watched Jacob in the corner. He was only seven or eight. "I'm sorry." The petticoats rustled as she lowered them to the ground. I lifted my arms, and Ethel lifted my corset cover off.

"Don't be. You're helping us."

She slowly undid the hooks and eyes of my corset. Free from the binding, the flesh of my stomach and hips expanded under my chemise. I felt the air on my spongy skin, and there was a tingling just at the surface. Ethel took my clothes and shoes to a trunk. She placed them inside, pushed down on the lid, and then heaved herself on top of it to squish it shut. Then we heard knocking. "Quick." Ethel jumped up, ran to me, and pushed me toward the kitchen cupboard.

I hunched down into it with nothing on but my lace- and ribbon-trimmed chemise, shin-length drawers, and silk stockings. I pulled the door closed just enough so a sliver of space remained. My heart thumped and my stomach tightened. I patted my hair, fearful of cobwebs.

An older man with white hair and a full beard stepped into the room and passed Ethel before she had the chance to welcome him. Wearing a dark suit, he stood tall with broad shoulders.

The heat closed in on me as I sat curled into a ball in the cupboard. I tried to push the discomfort aside by quietly fanning myself with my hand. It didn't work. I just prayed I wouldn't sweat. Ladies do not sweat.

Dr. Bradbridge walked to Larry, knelt on one knee, and began examining him. Ethel explained his weakness and lack of appetite, but Dr. Bradbridge hushed her with a quick flash of his palm and then swatted away Larry's scratching hands so he could put a stethoscope on his chest. The itching had become far worse, and Larry had scabs and scratch marks all over. Larry didn't seem as verbally inclined around the doctor as he was around me.

I wiped moisture from my hairline. I was sweating.

Ethel stood a few feet back from Dr. Bradbridge and occasionally glanced over at the cupboard with a distraught frown and soggy eyes. I wished she wouldn't look.

Dr. Bradbridge peered into Larry's eyes and scrutinized his skin, which had slowly become a grayish-yellow color. Larry groaned when the doctor positioned his hands below his rib cage and pressed down on both sides. Then Dr. Bradbridge lifted the sheets to scrutinize his swollen limbs even though Ethel hadn't told him about them.

Dr. Bradbridge sighed and started to pack up his equipment. Ethel looked toward the cupboard again. Dr. Bradbridge, still crouched next to Larry, turned to say something to her. He moved his eyes to locate what she was looking at and I stiffened, my heart pounding. Ethel removed her eyes from the cupboard. His brow furrowed, and he cocked his head. Did he see me? What if he caught me here in the cupboard of a patient's home—naked! Dr. Bradbridge stood up, looked a moment more, and finally returned his attention to Ethel. I released the breath I had been holding, and my heart fluttered so fast I could feel it in my fingertips.

"He is jaundiced and has a severe case of cirrhosis," Dr. Bradbridge said to Ethel, ignoring the patient.

"What? But—"

"His drinking has ruined his liver, and it's inflamed. He has fluid in his legs and stomach."

Ethel shook her head and held her hands up. "He doesn't drink."

"Miss, I know cirrhosis when I see it." He bent down and took his satchel in hand.

"But he doesn't—" She choked on her own voice.

"There is nothing I can do. Soon he will bleed into his stomach and throat. I cannot treat." He moved around her.

"What? No. You're a doctor. You must do something." Ethel scuttled back in front of him and blocked his way.

He rolled his eyes, and his face reverted to the emotionless mask. "There's nothing to be done."

My eyes flashed toward Larry, who was awake and aware, but the news hadn't brought fear to his face. He no longer scratched. He watched, motionless.

Ethel's eyes darted to and fro as if searching for a solution.

"My regards."

Ethel couldn't control herself. Her eyes had been glistening ever since Dr. Bradbridge first hushed her. Her body convulsed and tears streamed from her eyes. "Please. Please, try. I can pay. Please do something—anything. I'll pay."

I covered my mouth. Tears rolled down my cheeks, sweat down my forehead.

"Ma'am, you must contain yourself. There is nothing to be done." He tried to navigate around her again, but this time she grabbed his jacket with both hands and her legs buckled, but she refused to let go of him.

I pushed my head into the side of the cupboard to try to see Jacob, hoping he was still deep in his imagination, but I couldn't see him.

"Please, doctor. I'll do anything. I will be in your debt for the rest of my days. Please."

Dr. Bradbridge looked down at her. "My condolences." He pulled away, letting her release his jacket one hand at a time. She collapsed to the ground bawling. Dr. Bradbridge walked to the door, opened it, and left.

I quickly scrambled out of the cupboard and to Ethel, who was shriveled on the floor, her face dripping with tears and saliva. I got a glimpse of Jacob on his knees facing her. Confusion and fear riddled his face.

I fell next to Ethel and grasped her back. She slumped over and slid until her face fell to my lap. I could feel her tears soaking through as she cried harder. I laid my head on her back and considered Larry, who looked more concerned about her pain than about his own death sentence.

Ethel pulled back and shook her head as if to say no, but she couldn't find words. I pulled her close again. "I'm so sorry," I said. "I am so sorry."

"He wouldn't help us," she said in my lap, her voice muffled.

"I know." He should have done more. He hadn't even offered medicines like those I'd supplied Larry with, like those my father had had when he was sick. He should have had something more potent than what I had to alleviate the pain. He should have had... morphine, something.

Ethel gathered the strength to peel herself from me and crawl to her son. She lifted him and carried him to his father. Holding Jacob was what finally brought tears to Larry's eyes. I remained on my knees a few feet away, watching as they hugged and wept for a long time.

After Ethel calmed down, I retrieved my bag and pulled out the laudanum. Although made of opium, laudanum couldn't relieve his pain, and stronger tinctures were not available through a druggist. The country had grown fearful of opium's dangerous effects after newspapers warned that Chinese migrants spread opium abuse and addiction, so laws had been passed restricting its use to strange places in the cities called dens. Morphine was one of the strongest opium derivatives, but it was controlled by medical practitioners. I couldn't get it without Dr. Bradbridge. I gave Larry more than the usual amount of the opium mixture, no longer fearing the consequences of liberal dosing. Then I gave him some extracts made from dandelion root, a diuretic, hoping it might help dispel the liquid in his limbs, but I didn't know if it would work. I'd also brought some camphor liniment to ease itching. I gave them all to Ethel and told her how to administer them.

"I swear, Mrs. Dorr, he doesn't drink."

"I believe you."

She rolled the medicines out of her hand onto the floor next to Larry. "I'll get your things," she said between sobs and sniffles. She went to the trunk and pulled my clothes out. She occasionally whimpered as she helped me re-dress. What would she do without a husband? She wasn't just going to lose the man she loved. Without him, she and Jacob would not survive.

I clasped her arms and looked into her puffy eyes. "It's not over. I will do everything I can. If anything can be done, it will be done."

She nodded with her eyes down. I think she had placed all her hope in the real physician. I know I had.

# Thirty-Two

1900
*The Evans' Residence*
*St. Louis, Missouri*

My father screamed. He screamed! It sounded like a bull charging, tearing through walls, breaking glass, having been poked and prodded and stabbed into a frenzy. I had never heard my father outright scream before. I barreled up the stairs and raced down the hall only to be halted by the doctor at the door. "What happened?"

James made it a second later. "What's going on?"

Then my mother rushed up behind us. "What's wrong?"

Dr. Morris dried his hands with a cloth, but they were stained pink. "The tumor is out."

My father wailed.

"Then why is he screaming?" I asked.

"He's waking up from the chloroform, and the morphine I gave him hasn't taken effect, but it's all right. He won't be in any pain in a few minutes."

"But the surgery? He's supposed to be better," James said.

"The pain is from the surgery."

My father moaned again from behind the door.

"Did it not work?" my mother asked.

"We have to wait and see." He lowered his voice and locked eyes with my mother. "As I stated before, he will likely need more surgery and the chances are…"

"But why is he in so much pain from the surgery?" James demanded.

"He's going to be in a lot of pain now, and it may worsen. You'll have to give him regular doses of morphine." He looked back at my mother. "Mrs. Evans, I will explain how you can administer it yourself."

The sounds from the room quieted.

"Mrs. Evans, we should speak about what happens next," Dr. Morris said.

"Excuse me." I stepped around him and into my father's room. I shut the door with two clicks. There he lay without a shirt, his stomach bloated and red, black stitching digging deep into blue and purple skin in a jagged line across his stomach. "Father?"

"Sara?" He whispered my mother's name.

"It's Emeline. Mother's outside. Do you want me to get her?"

"No," he whispered. He appeared to be near sleep.

The wash basin still held brownish water that Dr. Morris had used to clean his instruments. He had cleared off the dressing table nearby to lay them out. A bottle of morphine and a syringe lay on the nightstand atop a folded white cloth. I inched to the side of the bed next to the cleared-off table. To think Dr. Morris had been in here—standing right here—cutting something out of my father.

"Emeline."

"Yes?"

"It hurts. God, it hurts."

I hesitated, shocked to hear him use the Lord's name. "The doctor said he gave you something."

"No. No. I can feel it. I can feel everything…inside."

"I'm going to get the doctor."

"Wait. Don't leave."

I darted back and took his hand. "I'm here. I'm here." I couldn't avoid staring at the stitched wound across his belly. I noticed wet blood along the seams, gleaming.

"I can't stand it." He moaned through clenched teeth as if he were holding up twice his weight. "I can't stand it."

"The doctor said—"

"Make it stop. God, make it stop."

I glanced at the morphine on the nightstand. I snatched up the bottle and quickly read the tiny printed instructions. Doctors were recommended to give a certain dosage and then a subsequent dosage if the first did not take effect within fifteen to twenty minutes. I took the syringe from the clean cloth. I inserted the needle, pulled the plunger and watched the liquid fill to the appropriate level. I pulled it out and pushed the plunger just a little to force air out. I remembered Miss McKenzie showing me how at the Grantville infirmary. I inserted the needle into his forearm and gently pushed the plunger.

"Thank you." He exhaled. "Thank you." He relaxed.

What did it feel like to feel your insides, to feel where they had been sliced and nipped and stretched and sewn back together? I knew that thick layers of fat and muscle and tissue sat between the skin and the stomach. Dr. Morris had had to cut through all of it to reach the tumor attached to the inner lining of my father's stomach. I cringed as I forced myself to imagine it, as if facing his agony could somehow take it all away. If I could take all of his pain and feel it for him, I would. I would take it all.

# Thirty-Three

October 1901
Labellum, Missouri

Before I knew it, it was the night before the dinner party. September had come and gone so quickly with all that had happened with Annie and the Hughmens and with Walter having almost discovered us. I sat in the parlor and meticulously double-checked everything because I had found myself confusing recipes with cures. John sat nearby reading, completely unperturbed about the approaching event. He had no reason to fret. Everything, from the preparation of the house and food to the conversation, relied on the wife. The hostess was responsible for keeping conversation light, away from politics, religion, and gossip. Some of our guests loved to gossip, but I needed to keep their manners to the highest standards for Mr. and Mrs. Hawtrey, who would not be used to such behavior at a dinner party.

I heard a knock at the door and for a moment actually thought time had sped up and the dinner guests were arriving. "What?" I stopped and looked at John.

"Was that a knock?" he asked.

I sighed and laughed. "I thought I imagined it."

"Who'd be calling at this hour?" He snapped his book closed and stood.

It was probably someone from Mr. Coddington's office with some urgent matter. I returned to my checklist of worries for the dinner party. I feared for Ethel. I couldn't imagine her having to be near Dr. Benedict Bradbridge after the way he treated her husband. I told her she didn't need to serve at the party—I would happily give her the money, but she insisted. Then Larry told me she needed it, to feel useful, and he wanted to spend some time alone with his son, so I acquiesced. After Dr. Bradbridge's visit, I read every book I could find on liver disease but found nothing on effective treatments. I visited every day to tend to Larry's bedsores and see if Ethel needed anything like help with cleaning or with watching Jacob.

"Emeline?" John said from the parlor's entrance.

I didn't look up. "Yes?"

"You have a visitor."

A wave of alarm hit my stomach and then rushed to my head. A patient? An emergency? What would I say to John? I stood, turned, and stopped. A young man with chestnut hair stood in the hallway. He wore a crisp gray suit with a striped tie stuffed under a matching waistcoat. A small woman hung on his arm. She had dark hair, nearly black under a crimson ostrich-plumed hat. She wore a cherry-red traveling suit, and her lips, although not painted, somehow matched.

"Good evening," he said cheerfully.

I didn't move. I could hardly breathe. My heart pounded and my lips shook. "James?"

"James? What are you doing here?"

He stepped into the parlor with the girl still hooked to his arm. "I thought it would be appropriate to visit so you could meet my wife." He beamed. "Mrs. Carmine Evans, this is Mr. and Mrs. John Dorr."

Carmine? Like her dress?

"Delighted." She had a small voice.

I looked incredulously from James to Carmine and back.

"Forgive me for not sending word," he said. "There wasn't enough time."

Still, I stared, bereft of speech. Why should he have informed me of his visit. He hadn't even informed me that he'd moved up his wedding. The letter had said spring.

"Well this is marvelous timing." John stepped over. "A time for celebration. We are having a dinner party tomorrow night with the best of Labellum society. You'll meet them all."

I didn't speak. Was my mouth open?

"We wouldn't want to impose."

"No, no, of course not. Emeline prepared a feast. There are plenty of spare rooms." John grinned at me and put his hand on James' back and they headed for the door. "Let me help you with your things."

I stood across from Carmine. She forced an uncomfortable smirk before twirling around and following them outside, leaving me standing there alone. I hesitated for a moment, exhaled, and walked to the open doorway. Outside, they hauled luggage off a buggy without a driver. Carmine stood on the landing at the top of the stairs outside the house. She acknowledged me with a dainty glance when I came up beside her. I folded my arms and studied her. She was young.

The men took in several bags, and Carmine and I followed. I kept my arms crossed.

"We can leave the rest for morning," James said before turning to me. "Well, dear sister, are you going to tell me how you are?"

I responded in monotone. "Well."

"Ah." His smile faded.

John furrowed his brow and rubbed the back of his neck as

he observed me with confusion. "She's exhausted, I'm sure. She's been planning for the party day and night for the last week."

"Is that right?" James asked.

"Oh, yes," John said. "She's amazing."

I eyed John.

"We're quite exhausted ourselves," James said.

"Let me show you to a room." John led James and Carmine away. I lingered behind.

"What a lovely home," Carmine said.

I glared at the back of her head.

"From outside it appears to be a two-story."

"The stairs are hidden away at the end of this hall," John said as we veered left.

"I see," James said.

"It has an interesting layout. An architectural wonder!"

"Indeed."

"I'll give you a full tour tomorrow."

"Splendid."

We scaled the narrow stairway like cattle herded through a death hall.

"Does this thing end?" James chuckled.

John hooted and Carmine attempted a polite laugh but produced an uncomfortable squeak. I held my breath.

We reached the top. "All right. We have four spare rooms," John said. "Our chamber is there at the end. You choose whichever you like."

James went to the first room on the left, the room where I had seen the young woman staring at her hands. "This will do."

At least he hadn't chosen the room with the beast, but why didn't he want to be close to our room?

John and James took the luggage inside and Carmine followed them. She stopped to examine herself in the mirror.

"This really is furnished for a single person. Carmine, perhaps you would be more comfortable in the room across the hall, or next door."

James responded for her. "We'll be fine. Don't forget we're newlyweds."

"Oh, yes. It doesn't seem possible"—I faked a smile and looked away—"as I've only just met her."

"Thank you again. Forgive us. I think we will go right to sleep."

"Of course." John said. "We should as well."

James shut the door.

John placed his hand on the small of my back and I jumped, but for once my jolt didn't frighten him away. "You must be so happy they are here."

I feigned delight.

We started down the hall, and a faint giggle sounded from their room.

# Thirty-Four

*October 1901*

The next day was hectic with cooking and cleaning. I had no opportunity to speak with James. I didn't want to hold a conversation with him anyway. Nor did I want to endure another one of John's tours. I felt bitter every time I stomped by the parlor and overheard them chattering. But I didn't have much time to dwell on it before guests were upon us.

Olivia was the last to arrive. I greeted her, and we both pretended nothing had happened between us, as if she had never stomped out of this house while I lay helpless, bedridden, begging her not to leave me. Then she and Walter introduced themselves as if having never met. Now I knew I had reason for suspicion. If she had been a patient, they wouldn't hide it. Or would they hide such a thing because Margaret disliked her so much?

After Olivia's arrival, everyone filed from the parlor to the dining room. John and I sat at opposite ends of the table, but John occasionally glanced up at me, a glimmer in his dark eyes. As we settled and continued conversations from the parlor, Lottie and Ethel entered to pour water and wine.

"How have you been, Olivia?" Margaret tilted her head.

Olivia lifted her gaze, raised her chin. "Splendid. Yourself?" Her words had an indistinct tone only a woman could detect.

"Very well—very well indeed."

Olivia lifted one of our emerald-like goblets. "Tell me, Margaret, are you still ruin—ahem—running the church committee?"

Margaret's simper fell. "Actually, I've taken a step back."

Olivia raised her glass toward Francis sitting at the middle of the table. "Oh my, yes. Mrs. Ella Grace took the position of president, didn't she?"

Ella had not attended that evening. Francis appeared to be a little taken back but smiled graciously. "My mother is very honored."

"How odd, Margaret. You say you decided to step away? I heard you were relieved."

Margaret's lips pressed into a hard smile, but her eyes scowled. "That is too bad."

"I never saw you there, *Mrs.* Urswick."

Olivia ignored the jab at her unmarried status. "Margaret, we've been acquainted for years. You use my last name in polite company as if I'm royalty."

"Forgive me, *Olivia*, you know it's just so difficult to remember your...situation."

Walter's eyes darted back and forth between his mother, perched next to him, and Olivia, sitting across from him. Dr. Benedict Bradbridge rambled on in his own conversation, unaware of the covert acts of war taking place next to him. Other people in the room, however, had fallen silent as their nerves tingled in the direction of tension. Even John broke eye contact with Benedict to glance over. My eyes shot to Mr. Herbert Hawtrey and his tall, lean wife, Irene—the guests of honor who were sitting on either side of John. Herbert was a thin fellow with a large nose and long face. He was somehow involved with the Gynecological and Obstetrical Society, an organization critical to the Coddington firm. They couldn't have been as familiar with the battle as the guests who knew these women, but they had both started glancing away from Benedict's conversation and toward Olivia and Margaret.

At this time Lottie began placing bowls of tomato bisque in front of each of us, and I wondered if one of the two women would scald the other with hot soup. I had to stop them, but I felt like a lion tamer planning to force starving carnivores to use utensils.

"Olivia"—Margaret snapped her head toward her—"tell us, how is your family?"

Olivia's cheek twitched.

"How is your daughter?"

"I wasn't aware you had a daughter." John forced a pause into his conversation with Benedict. Then Benedict couldn't help but give his attention.

Had John really forgotten the conversation that had preceded the disaster at Ida Rippring's? Thank goodness the Ripprings hadn't attended. Ida and Margaret would have turned Olivia into the second course.

Margaret nodded gleefully. "Yes. Olivia has a grown daughter and grandchildren. They live far, far away. It's too bad they never visit."

Silence seeped in like a snake as everyone remembered that Olivia was a spinster. The sound of sipping and spoons scooping bisque filled the room.

Finally, Olivia turned to John. "Yes, I have a daughter."

"Um, uh," I stuttered, desperately seeking to change the subject but speaking before I had thought of something to say.

"Margaret, I heard you have an idea for a new benefit," Francis said.

"Oh, do tell us." Martha Coddington beamed.

Margaret's body shifted, and her eyes twinkled with delight. "Well, I had this idea for…"

Olivia rolled her eyes and drank her wine as Margaret went into the details of her plans.

I tipped my head gratefully at Francis.

As the courses continued, I listened to James talk about various lawyer issues with John, Benedict's ramblings about politics, and a wonderfully dull floral-arrangement discussion between Carmine and Martha. I had begun to believe the worst was over until I overheard a part of a conversation at the other end of the table when Herbert Hawtrey said, "...sin of the natural world!" I tried to hear more, but Margaret practically barked about her objections to the fact that the church committee was continuing quilt sales, as they had been her idea. Further, Martha and Carmine were kicking up a fuss over the hideous goggles required for riding in motor cars. I noticed Francis listening to Herbert with a hurt expression dressed up as a blank stare.

When Lottie and Ethel brought out the roast, John and I stood to help carve and serve while Lottie and Ethel assisted us. I quickly heaped large servings of boiled yellow squash and carrots on James' and Carmine's plates in order to make my way closer to the opposite end of the table so I could hear the discussion. I strained to listen and caught Olivia's addition. "No one's debating that it's wrong at a certain point," she said. "People are debating if there is a point where it should be acceptable—before quickening."

How did I know the word *quickening*?

I reached Walter just as he began to say, "There have been studies—"

Benedict's voice boomed across the table, "Dr. Johnson of the OGS called this a crusade against abortion, but it should have been a crusade against midwives."

I froze with my arm outstretched holding the serving spoon full of vegetables.

"These women know the laws, but they are immoral." He held a closed fist on the table. Why was he yelling?

"It's not just the midwives, though. Physicians are performing these operations, too," Walter said just before taking a bite of food, unfazed by his father's outburst. His calm reaction seemed to persuade everyone to settle back into their seats.

I too unfroze and dumped the mound of food onto Irene's plate. As I continued, John stared at me as he carved the meat, his eyes screaming for me to make it stop.

I sped up, maneuvering around Lottie as she dished out boiled potatoes. I scooped and served as quickly as I could while also thinking up a way to redirect the conversation. "Herbert, what do you think of Mr. Roosevelt taking the office?" The president had been assassinated at the beginning of the month, and the vice president, Theodore Roosevelt, was about to take the oath.

Herbert acted as if he had not heard me. "And those doctors are ruining the good name of the professionals."

"That is, obviously, why prosecution is just as important against the doctors," John's employer, Lewis Coddington said.

"I disagree." Herbert bit off a mouthful of bread but continued. "The physicians performing these surgeries are practically forced by the midwives." He stopped talking to chew but grunted to inform us he had more to say. He swallowed. "If the physician doesn't do it, the midwife might murder a woman trying. Some of these poor ones try to do it themselves with coat hangers and such."

I dropped the serving spoon, and it clacked onto the table before I scrambled to retrieve it. No one seemed to notice except for John.

Herbert continued, "What choice does that give a doctor?"

"I couldn't agree more," Walter said.

"I couldn't disagree more," Benedict said before gulping his brandy.

Olivia held up her glass to drink. "I certainly don't agree with coat hangers, but I think midwives are well trained. They've handled these situations for centuries. Most of us here were brought into this world by a midwife."

"You actually approve of abortion?" Margaret swirled her wine.

"What's the latest fashion in St. Louis?" I tried.

"You must have misheard me, Margaret. I said *midwives*. I approve of midwifery."

Margaret rolled her eyes.

Having been ignored once again, I finished serving and slipped back to my seat.

"There might be a few midwives who know what they are doing," Walter said to Olivia, "but without proper licensing and standards, how does a woman know who she can trust?"

Olivia responded to Walter without the same inflection she had used with his mother. "In my day, midwives focused on bringing life into this world, not taking it away."

"Well, things were obviously different in your day, weren't they?" Margaret said.

Walter glared at his mother for a moment and then answered Olivia. "It's hard to say what has and hasn't gone on behind closed doors or in the past, but this is a new century, and we are progressing toward an era of enlightenment, where the people who practice medicine are held accountable for the well-being of their patients."

Margaret's eyes darted back and forth between Walter and Olivia.

"Forgive me," interrupted Richard Williams, Francis' husband. He cleaned his hands on his napkin. "I am not as familiar with this topic. Did someone say these women are killing people?"

Francis shot a worried glance at me.

"These midwives and illegal nurses have no formal training, no licenses," Walter said. "Without any accountability, there's no guarantee they know what they are doing, and even though their intentions are usually good, they can kill people. We know of at least one woman operating in Labellum right now."

I gulped my sherry.

Then Benedict barked, "It's the abortionists that are out there causing sepsis, perforating the uterus!"

Sin to Moses! This was bad. John glared at me as he abandoned the meat and returned to his seat, but I pretended not to see him. I observed James, who sat wide-eyed, and then I regarded the rest of our guests, most of whom appeared to be intrigued rather than offended.

"These women just need to be reminded of their moral obligation," Martha said before taking a bite.

"That's why it's important to rid rural areas of midwives and abortionists and the women who encourage them," Lewis added.

"I can't understand what kind of woman would let herself befall such a circumstance in the first place," Irene said.

"I'd guess women of low class, prostitutes. Am I right?" Richard asked.

Francis closed her eyes and held her breath.

"Anyone attend a symphony recently?" I asked desperately. "The ballet?"

"The midwives are the ones more like prostitutes," Lewis said while studying one of our peculiar spoons with repugnance. "They are the ones being paid to sell their souls."

I felt nauseated.

"What happens to them?" Francis asked.

I turned toward her, surprised to hear her elegant voice.

"I know the midwife and accomplices are arrested," she said, "but what happens to the women who have the procedure?"

Richard eyed her quizzically.

"Well, first we send investigators, like Mr. Rippring, to question the woman, midwife, and any accomplices." Lewis sawed at his meat. "They are all arrested and tried, including the woman who had the procedure, unless she doesn't survive. To be honest, the entire process is much easier when they die."

Francis fluttered her eyes, fussed with her napkin, and subtly controlled her breathing.

"Why's that?" Richard hadn't taken a single bite of food during the conversation.

Walter kept his eyes on his plate. "The best way to get a conviction is to acquire a dying confession."

"We usually discover these midwives when something has gone

wrong and they are forced to take the woman to a real physician," Lewis explained. "All physicians know if they do not report the woman, they will be arrested, too."

"What's a dying confession?" Richard asked.

"Before the victim dies, she admits to the abortion and whoever is responsible," Lewis said. "That confession can be used in court like a testimony even if she's dead."

"It is the only exception to the hearsay rule," John added but still glared at me.

"You know, it's not just abortionists in these rural areas. People are abusing themselves left and right," Benedict said, lifting his brandy. "I had this patient recently who drank himself to death."

Ethel froze halfway through filling James' water glass. I dug my nails into my palms and broke skin. I looked at Ethel and tried to apologize with my eyes.

"I agree. I don't see why these people deserve treatment when they usually cause the problem," Herbert said.

"Exactly. That's why I didn't give him anything for the pain. He got himself in that mess, he should deal with the consequences."

The ball of Ethel's chin quivered. She filled the glass the rest of the way, pivoted casually, and slipped out.

Anger overwhelmed me. "You refused to treat?" My voice was louder than I had intended.

Everyone turned toward me. Then they looked back to Benedict for his reply.

He kept eating. "He was too far gone."

"But you didn't give him anything for the pain?"

"Darling, I think this is a little out of your depth," John said, squinting and forcing a smile.

I glared an audacious challenge at him and looked back at Benedict. "It is atrocious to refuse to end a human being's torment, no matter what."

Our guests shifted their gazes from me to Benedict.

He didn't appear to be offended or alarmed, but his eyes focused on me, and I had to fight the urge to shrink away. "Physicians are not blessed with unlimited supplies. The day you have to decide to waste them on a man who destroyed his own body, then you can tell me how to treat."

I wanted to tell him I had. I wanted to tell him I'd helped the patient he failed. I wanted to scream that I understood the importance of ending someone's pain far better than he ever could. I wanted to tell him what a despicable human being he was, but I couldn't. From everyone's silence, I knew I had already taken it too far. Margaret shook her head just slightly, just enough for me to see. John gripped his silverware. I'd expected the house to find a way to spoil the evening, but it didn't need to do a thing. I spoiled it all on my own.

After our guests left, Lottie, Ethel, and I descended into the basement and worked by lamplight.

Ethel handed me a dish to dry.

"Are you all right?" I asked.

She continued washing and kept her head down. "Did any of your guests notice?"

"No," I shook my head. "Dr. Bradbridge didn't even notice."

"That was bigwig cruelty at its finest," Lottie said angrily as she put items in their places with rough shoves and loud clunks.

"I'm not sure he did it intentionally." I placed the dry dish on a stack and took the next one from Ethel.

"How's that?" Ethel asked.

"I don't think he realized he was speaking about someone in the room. I don't think he recognized you."

Ethel stopped washing. "It felt like punishment."

"Don't think that."

"At least he didn't make a racket like that old bat Bradbridge," Lottie said.

"Sin to Moses!" I said. "When those two started at each other I thought I might faint."

"Since when do you dine with Olivia Urswick?" Lottie asked. "Ain't she the one huntin' us down?"

My eyebrows went up. "John invited her."

"Did the doctor say something about treating her?" Ethel asked.

"No, but with the way Margaret reacted to Olivia, I wonder if Walter might treat her in secret....But did you see the way he got all stiff during that fight?"

Ethel pursed her lips and nodded.

The dishes clacked as I stacked them, and I wondered why Lottie seemed quieter than usual.

"Emeline?" Ethel stopped washing and shuffled around. She kept her eyes down and used her finger to trace a circle on her wet palm. "I heard what you said."

"Said?"

"To Dr. Bradbridge."

"Oh."

"Thank you."

I smiled sheepishly.

She returned to the dishes. "It was a night fit for a loon. You are lucky nobody snapped."

"Well, I kind of did."

She grinned over her shoulder.

"I still can't believe they started talking about abortions at a formal dinner." I chuckled uncomfortably, feeling as if I shouldn't have brought it up just then.

Ethel exhaled. "My heart almost stopped."

"I just hope no one thinks ill of John," I said.

"All of them said things they shouldn't at a dinner table," Ethel said.

Lottie cleaned quickly and quietly. Too quietly for Lottie.

"Lottie? Are you all right?"

"Fine."

"Are you sure?"

"Said I was fine."

"I only ask because usually you have more input."

She raised her voice and spoke through clenched teeth. "I'm fine."

Ethel handed me a slippery dish.

"Been a long night," she said.

"Are you sure?"

"Yes!"

"Lottie?"

"Been a long night, and I just wanna finish these big toad dishes and be on my way."

"I'm sorry, it's just—"

She put down a bowl, whirled around, and slammed her hand down on the prepping table. "How can I help you, ma'am?"

My dish dripped onto the floor.

Ethel tried, "We just thought—"

"So ya'll talkin' 'bout me?"

"No—not at all," I said.

Ethel shook her head.

Lottie scowled at us as if she had unveiled a plot against her. "It ain't none of your business, and I don't want to talk about none of this."

"Maybe we could help," I said.

"I ain't never said I wanted any of your help." She stepped away from me, closed a jar, moved the empty bowl, and bumped a silver tray. It fell to the floor with a loud clatter.

We all cringed.

Lottie threw her hands up and covered her face.

I walked to her and reached out to touch her arm. "Lottie?"

She ripped her hands from her face and pushed my hand away. "Well, ain't you got some gall? You know, you ain't no different. You just another big toad." She pushed past me and charged up the stairs.

Ethel and I didn't know what was wrong with Lottie and couldn't do anything about it until morning, so we finished cleaning, and I instructed Mr. Buck where to take her. Back inside, I rounded the corner and there John stood. I jumped and fumbled to keep the cylinder of my lamp from crashing to the ground. He anchored himself in the hallway, legs parted and arms crossed. "Why did you talk to Dr. Bradbridge that way?"

I lowered my eyes.

"You very well may have ruined me. Do you know that?" He waited for a reply, but I couldn't form words, and a tingle crept up the back of my spine and scaled my neck. "Do you care?"

"I care." I feared facing his eyes.

"You didn't even try tonight."

"What?" I raised my voice. "I tried everything to keep those people from ripping each other apart."

He raised his voice louder. "Everything was fine until you started questioning the ethics of one of the most esteemed physicians in Murielle County and my foremost client."

"Nothing was fine up until that point, and how could I not after what he did? How could you not think the worst of him?"

"My opinion does not matter when it comes to Dr. Bradbridge's practices, and your opinion least of all. You don't know anything about medicine or his patients."

"I—"

"Quiet." He stepped closer and forced words from behind his clenched teeth. "What made you think you could speak to him—to anyone—like that?"

"I—I don't know what to say. I tried."

He hovered over me, silent. "You'll apologize."

"But?"

"You will apologize."

"Yes."

He stood a moment longer and sighed. "I'm sorry.... Everything was really lovely." He walked back to the library and shut the door, and I watched the light disappear with him.

# Thirty-Five

*October 1901*

I woke up intent on seeing Lottie and making amends for the previous night, but when I left the house, I found James sitting like a toad on the front steps. I edged down until I was one step behind him.

He looked back and smiled. "I've been looking for you."

"Outside?"

"Whenever I can't find you, I just go outside and there you are."

"Not this time."

"You're here now, aren't you?" He grinned.

I didn't. "Where's Carmine?"

"Inside. What do you think of her?"

"She's young."

"I thought women wanted to marry young." He stopped grinning as he realized who he was talking to. "Well, most anyway."

I narrowed my eyes at him and clomped toward the surrey.

"Why are you avoiding me?"

"I don't know what you mean."

"You've barley spoken to me or Carmine since we got here."

I turned back. "You didn't even tell me about the wedding."

"There wasn't enough time. Besides, you don't reply to letters anymore."

"I was upset."

"I apologize. We came here right after."

"Another decision you should have informed me of."

His brow furrowed. "You begged me. Your letter made it sound like you were dying. Now you're angry I came?"

I gripped my parasol and beaded drawstring purse at my sides. "Are you that dense?"

He grimaced and shook his head slightly.

"I was miserable." I waved my hand and my purse swung around. "You didn't do anything."

He used one hand to push himself to his feet. "If you were so opposed to getting married, you should have said no."

"No? No! Say no to our mother? To you? To our sisters? How could I? Our family needed this, remember?"

"That's not my fault."

I pointed at him with my parasol. "But you convinced me it would be all right."

He threw his hands up. "I thought it would be."

"You said you'd come get me."

"I'm here, aren't I?"

"You're a liar."

"What was I supposed to do?" He took a few steps toward me. "Help you abandon your husband? Help you destroy your life? Help you financially maroon our family?"

"You should have been here for me."

"You didn't even give it a chance." His voice grew louder. "You were here for a few months before you decided to give up."

"I tried." My effort to hold back tears caused a pain at the back of my throat. "You have no idea how hard I tried."

"You needed to give it more time."

"I needed my brother."

He tilted his head wryly. "And here I am."

I shook my head and rolled my eyes.

"So what do you want to do?"

"I have to go." And I stomped away.

If Lottie was home, she'd instructed her children to lie about her whereabouts. Lucy wouldn't let me near the door. Lottie wasn't in the fields either. I couldn't even find her husband. I didn't understand what had happened, why she had gotten angry with me. She called me a big toad as if I had treated her like I was above her, but I hadn't acted that way since that day in the woods. I returned to the house frustrated with Lottie and angry with James. I stayed in my chamber all day until it was time to cook.

John worked late, so when we sat down for dinner, it was the first time the four of us had been together since the dinner party. The silence at the table screamed. John was angry with me, and I was angry with James. Carmine must have felt awkward, being the only one without a person to be cross with. I planned to spend the entire evening in silence, but for some reason this was the night John refused to shut his trap.

"You said your father is a politician?" he asked Carmine. "That must allow for some lively social events."

"Not usually."

"Are you interested in politics?"

"I was educated in home arts."

"Oh? What did you favor?" I could tell John was struggling, but I wasn't about to help.

"I do watercolor, love floral arrangements."

I rolled my eyes and they landed on James, who was glaring at me.

"Did you attend college?" John continued.

"No need. James and I were introduced prior."

"Your parents introduced us, actually," James said and shot me a smug look. "Your family has been so good to us."

I ignored him.

James took a drink of his water and cleared his throat. "Why do you keep the doors closed around here all the time?"

I shifted my eyes to him.

John finished chewing. "It's a little system I came up with so we always know where everyone is. If the door is open, someone is inside."

"Ingenious," James said, raising his eyebrows. "It's awful dark, though."

"Hmm, yes, Emeline doesn't like it much either."

"Emma loves nature. With the doors closed, it feels a bit like the world is shut out."

I lifted my eyes from my plate.

"But only when in the hallway," John said.

"True. But she probably spends a lot of time in the hallway."

"Pardon?" John chuckled.

"She cleans all the rooms and travels back and forth to the kitchen all day."

John tilted his head in thought.

"She's having to be in and out of that dark hall back and forth, always having to open and shut doors, light lamps. I imagine it's more than an inconvenience."

John considered me.

I didn't do anything as brash as nod, but I looked back.

"How is it you thought of all this?" he asked.

"All of what?" James popped a piece of bread in his mouth.

"What women do? It's a mystery to me."

James glanced at me, finished chewing. "Emma showed me the secrets of her world. She always made the ordinary quite magical."

Carmine watched him, clearly smitten.

John changed the subject. "What type of law are you interested in?"

"I'm not sure," James said. "Right now I'm learning about fiscal law."

"I would think you'd want to follow in your father's footsteps— criminal defense."

"I thought so, too, but I'm exploring right now. I imagine that is why you decided to work for Mr. Coddington. You probably plan to work with your father eventually."

John rubbed the back of his neck. "I'm not sure."

"Oh?"

"My father expects a certain quality in an attorney that I do not seem to possess."

James cut his roast, left over from the previous night.

"He couldn't teach me, so he sent me away—here."

"You didn't want to come here?"

"Not at all."

I took a bite of squash. I had never thought that John might have been here against his will, too.

"What quality did he want you to learn?"

"He implied it to be…indifference."

Inside, I scoffed. Wasn't that John's specialty?

"Actually, at one time I had hoped to mentor under your father. I sat in on a few of his cases. He was ingenious, caring—nothing like the way my father practices." John's eyes were down, a little smirk forming. "There was this one case…" John observed our wide eyes. "I'm sorry. Is it too soon?"

I shook my head with a jolt. "No."

He shifted his eyes to me, the corner of his mouth pulling upward. "Your father took on cases for good reasons, not because he knew he could win. The case that really impressed me involved a man who was in fact guilty. A driver—he stole from his employer—no question. Your father, though—he proved the man only stole to rescue the employer's son, who had gambled himself into debt with some disreputable characters."

"He still stole," James said. "How did Father get around that?"

"Ah, the worker was literate." John lifted a finger. "Your father tracked down a letter of hire from his employer stating that, as his driver, his number one duty was to ensure the well-being of his family while in his care, no matter what."

Carmine applauded. "Extraordinary."

"He took risks to help others." John lifted his glass to his lips. "He knew some sins deserve forgiveness."

I stared at John unblinking and then glanced at James, who smirked at me.

I woke up late and dressed. John had risen early and gone to the office. I stepped out of my chamber and blinked. Light flooded the hall. All the doors were open. I stood there baffled for a few moments. Finally, I pried myself out of my stance and ambled down the hall and downstairs in awe. All the doors were open on the bottom floor as well. I went to the open parlor and saw James reading the newspaper. The parlor even seemed brighter than usual, light haloing James in the chair. The furniture appeared normal, unthreatening. Nothing moved behind his back or teased me out of the corner of my eye. It was just furniture, bric-a-brac, and James.

I flopped into a chair across from him.

"Good morning." He lowered the paper onto his lap. "It's a wonderful bright day, isn't it?"

"Thank you."

"You're not angry anymore?"

"How could I be? You're such a little snake."

He pinched his lips together, clearly pleased with himself.

"I'm still mad about the wedding." I crossed my arms, a little teasing but still serious.

"Emma,...we rushed the date to have an excuse to come here."

"What?"

"At first, I thought I could just check on you at our wedding, but when you didn't answer my letters, I feared John wouldn't let you come. You made him sound so horrible."

"Carmine didn't mind?"

"Not when I explained the situation. She's been a little displeased to learn you weren't in the desperate situation I described."

"Why didn't you believe me the first time?"

"It was such a drastic decision. I thought you overreacted."

"Why?"

"It wouldn't have been the first time."

"What are you talking about?"

"College."

I shook my head without a clue as to what he meant.

"You called Father at his office begging to let you come home. You swore up and down the place was a prison and not worth any education. You even said the teachers were idiots and couldn't teach you where the back of your head was."

I recalled the sobbing conversation. "Oh."

"When I didn't hear back from you, I assumed the worst. I feared you were unable to write, so I just panicked."

"Oh, James." I shook my head. "I feel awful."

"What is it about him? He seems nice to me."

"I don't know if you can understand what it's like to be married to someone who doesn't hold the least bit of affection for you." I clasped my hands and kept my eyes down. "When I wrote you, it felt like I had no reason to be here. There was nothing to look forward to, nothing to enjoy, nothing to live for. It's different for you. You have a profession, a purpose. My life had no meaning."

"What about John?"

"He's not mean. He just..." I shook my head. "There's nothing there."

"You're sure about that?"

I thought about it. "I'm not sure."

"How can you not be sure?" He leaned forward and the newspaper crinkled in his hands.

"Sometimes I think he is trying, but then something happens and I don't know."

"What about the doors?"

"You did that."

"I only talked about it at dinner."

"What?"

"He opened the doors this morning."

I imagined John waking up and deciding to do it, slipping out of bed, and moving through the house opening every single door.

"Seems like he's trying something."

The anger I held for John softened. A part of me wished we did love each other as I had thought we would. I lifted my eyes to James.

He was smiling.

I shook my head and disregarded the ridiculous notions of love. "I just don't know."

"Well then, my dear sister, what would you like to do?"

I shrugged.

"We're to leave soon. Should we prepare to take you with us?"

I ran a finger over the pearls on my wedding ring.

"Are you afraid of him?"

I kept my eyes on the ring as I shook my head. "Of John? No."

"Do you want to leave?"

"I don't know."

He folded the paper and uncrossed his legs. "You don't know?"

"I don't know."

All the little statutes in the parlor watched me.

"Is he treating you better?"

I lifted my shoulders.

"You've grown attached to the house?"

The furniture shifted and I gave him a wide-eyed stare. "No."

"Well, what then?"

I sighed. "I don't want to hurt him."

He smiled.

"I've lived with him. I'm married to him. It hasn't been bliss, but it has been different lately. He seems different."

"You seemed certain when you wrote that letter."

I sighed. "There's more to it now. There is something here, something I do here that I don't know if I want to give up."

"What do you do that you couldn't do elsewhere?"

"It's difficult to explain."

"I think my intellect can handle it."

"No…it can't."

He squinted at me. "What did you get yourself into?"

"Nothing. I'm just…I'm just not sure. You're right. It's a risky decision. I need some time to think about it."

"I thought you were desperate?"

"I'm not so sure what I feel."

"Emma. I won't be able to come back here again for a long while. If you want to leave Labellum, you need to decide before I go."

Everything in the parlor flung its attention at me.

I thought about what I had discovered about myself from Lottie and from the people of Labellum. I thought about whether it was all worth staying with John. Could it even last? How long until my white room collapsed without me in it? How long before my freedom would destroy everything I cared about? I couldn't possibly continue traipsing around town as Mrs. Freeman when I was really the "doctor-lawyer's wife." I would eventually be caught, ruin John, ruin myself, and be sent to an asylum. All the people I had helped might find themselves in trouble, too. Or I could leave with James and be free from it all, and I'd be the only one hurt, the only one shamed.

I breathed deeply. "I'll go." It was the right decision for everyone. It was for the best. My gaze lowered to the floor, to the rugs with little golden embroidered swirls.

"You know he loves you, right?"

My eyes shot up. "What?"

# Thirty-Six

*October 1901*

Larry's skin looked yellow and soggy like ground mustard. Large gaping wounds tunneled deep into the muscle on the undersides of his thighs and one of his arms. I used a warm, damp rag on the red, black, and yellowed tissue, gently dabbing away the foulest-smelling excretions.

My patient groaned and clenched his teeth with each touch.

Ethel watched, empty and exhausted. I don't believe she had eaten much lately. I hadn't noticed during the party, but her clothes hung loose. I tried to not think of what would become of her and her child when her husband died. What would have happened to my family if I hadn't married John Dorr? What would happen to them if I left him?

I pulled the rag off the wound under Larry's arm and sat back on my heels. Larry was going to die. The only thing we could do was relieve his pain, but the medicine I had wasn't any match for his infected wounds and rotting liver. I needed something stronger. I needed something only a doctor could provide.

"Ethel? I think we should talk to somebody about getting help."

"Who?" Tears welled up. "Dr. Bradbridge told that story to my mistress, and I had almost gotten a loan from her to help him. She's so angry she's thinking of firing me."

Ethel could hardly survive with a job, but if she lost it...What could I do to help her then? I finished cleaning Larry's wounds, picked up my supplies and approached Ethel. "I've done all I can."

She nodded and fiddled with her handkerchief.

I went for the door and stopped, noticing Jacob in the corner playing with the nothing he had.

I looked back at Ethel. "I promise, I'll figure something out."

I entered the canary-colored parlor and found Francis and Ella on the sofa just as they'd been the first time I called on them. They looked just as perfect as they had then—perfect dresses, beautiful posture, sipping their tea simultaneously.

I sat across from them clenching my hands. "There is a man, and he is ill—" A servant came in and I stopped, but then I realized that under the right circumstances what I needed to ask would not be inappropriate at all, so I started again. "He's in pain and his family is quite poor. They need supplies, and I thought maybe the church committee could do something for him."

"The committee doesn't do that," Francis said.

"With Margaret gone, the committee is free to return to charity work."

"What did you have in mind?" Ella picked up her saucer and teacup from the table.

"This man—he is dying."

"Has the physician seen him?"

"The senior Dr. Bradbridge has already seen him and said there is nothing he can do, but he is suffering, and his wife has no money."

"They don't have friends or family who will help?" Ella asked before sipping.

"No family, and no one else will help because Dr. Bradbridge told everyone in town that the man is a drunk, not to mention the fear everyone has of the Bradbridges and Mr. Coddington."

"Oh dear." Ella brought her fingers to her lips. The teacup rattled on the saucer in her other hand.

"Did Dr. Bradbridge give him something for the pain?" Francis scooted forward in her seat.

"He refused."

"What?" Ella said.

"Oh," Francis tilted her head. "Is this the man Dr. Bradbridge talked about last Saturday? I knew you must have treated him."

"Yes."

"What does he suffer from?" Ella asked.

I stood up and started pacing in front of them as I listed the problems I could not fix. "He has a damaged liver and jaundice. He is plagued by a constant itch, his limbs are swollen, his skin yellow, and now he has three large bedsores. His wife, Mrs. Hughmen, is exhausted and malnourished. She is also trying to care for a son."

"There's a child?" Ella said.

I stopped pacing and dropped into my seat. "Yes."

Ella set her tea down. "How can we help?"

I jumped back up and handed Ella a calling card with the Hughmens' address written on the back. "Call an emergency meeting, ask the women what they can contribute: money, clean sheets, food, children's clothes, or time to watch her child and husband or clean and cook for them. Or if they know of a job possibility."

"Does she not work?"

"Her employment is in jeopardy after her mistress heard the rumor that Mr. Hughmen is a drunk from one of the Bradbridges."

"Sakes alive." Francis shook her head.

"If anyone has heard anything about drinking, tell them it's not true." I turned to leave.

"Where are you going now?" Ella asked.

I turned back. "I'm going to speak with Margaret."

"Why?" Francis asked.

"I'm hoping I can persuade her to speak to her husband regarding certain medicines."

"Oh, I don't know, Emeline," Ella said.

"Margaret probably has even less sympathy for this man than her husband," Francis added.

"I don't see any other possible solution."

"Perhaps you should ask Olivia." Ella lifted her chin.

"Pardon?"

Francis squinted at her mother and then her eyes popped open. "Yes, you should."

"Why?"

"I'm afraid I cannot say," Ella said. "But I think she may be inclined to assist you."

They didn't know my past with Olivia Urswick, but I told them I'd consider it.

I went to Margaret's house next. She invited me to sit and then scowled at me as her servants brought tea and peppermint cakes.

"I wanted to thank you for attending our little engagement."

"Pleasure."

"I also wanted to apologize for my behavior."

"Oh?"

"Yes. I was disrespectful, and it was not my place. I hope you and your husband will forgive me."

She simpered and sank out of her tense posture. "Of course, dear. You just got away from yourself, didn't you?"

"Yes." I squeezed my gloved hands.

"It's too bad Miss Urswick can't be counted upon to remedy the damage from her actions."

I couldn't believe her. She was the one who had attacked first and in such an obvious manner that even her own son had looked furious with her behavior. "I also am here to ask for your guidance."

"Perhaps you should consider more bed rest."

I ignored her. "The church committee is trying to help a man who is dying."

"The committee doesn't do charity."

"They do now."

She raised her chin. "I knew that committee wouldn't last long without me."

"I have just come from Mrs. Grace. She's calling an emergency meeting."

"And?"

"The committee can only do so much. They cannot relieve the man of his horrendous agony."

"He needs to be seen by my husband, not by committee women."

"The church committee can't get anything like medicine." I placed my teacup and saucer on the table. "But you can."

Margaret squinted with her left eye.

"Perhaps you could ask your son to donate something."

"If they need medicine, they need to pay to be seen by my husband or son."

"You won't even try?"

"My husband would never." She turned her nose up.

"Then take it."

"Bite your words." She rose from her seat a little.

"I could tell you exactly what he needs. Please."

She straightened and stood. "How dare you?" Her teeth could crack walnuts. "What kind of little weasel are you?"

I stood, too. "How can you have no sympathy? Are you really that ugly inside?"

Her eyes widened and her lips snarled. She stalked from the seating area, and I stomped after her. She stopped at the parlor threshold and thrust a pointed finger toward the door. "You need to leave, immediately."

I brushed past her and out the front door. I scuttled down her steps and panicked as I walked away. How could I help Larry now? Ella and Francis had suggested Olivia, but why? Why would she ever help me? Was it because of how much she hated Margaret? I still didn't know if Olivia was the one hunting me with Walter. If I asked her and they were scheming together, she'd turn me in. She had to be conspiring with him. Why else had he gone to her house that day? Why else would they have hidden that they knew each other in public? I remembered why we first met, how Walter had recommended she sit with me during my bed rest. That meant they knew each other before I had become Mrs. Freeman. I thought of following Walter to her house and the way they acted at the dinner party, how he'd scowled when his mother insulted her. Then I knew.

Olivia opened her own door. "Emeline?"

"May I come in?"

"Of course. I should thank you for an entertaining evening the other night."

I stepped in and stopped in the hallway. "I'm sorry I must be quick."

"Are you all right? You seem shaken."

"I've come from the Bradbridges'."

"Ah." She crossed her arms. "What is it?"

"There is a man—dying and in agony. Dr. Bradbridge refuses to give him medicine for the pain."

"Is this the man you defended at dinner?"

I sighed. "Yes."

She grinned. "What can I do?"

"He needs medicine to relieve the pain, and no one can acquire it without the aid of a physician."

"What do you expect me to do?"

I hesitated. "You can get the medicine."

She drew back, shaking her head.

"You can get Dr. Bradbridge's support."

"I don't know what you mean."

"Dr. Walter Bradbridge, I mean."

She stepped back.

"I know you know him."

She put her hand up. "I met him at your party."

"Walter recommended you to care for me when I was bedridden. He had to have known you, trusted you."

"Everyone knows the Bradbridges."

"Yes, but he didn't recommend just anyone. He recommended you."

She covered her mouth with her hand.

"I know if you ask, he will help us."

She lowered her hand and hesitated. "I suppose I've been caught."

My stomach tightened.

Her body relaxed, as if she were relieved. "I am not one to hide, but he actually cares what his father and witch of a mother think. Obviously, they don't think much of me."

My stomach leapt.

"Normally, I would never stand for such foolishness, but when you care for someone…"

"You can get the medicine?"

She shifted her weight. "His father's opinion means a lot to him. I don't know if he'll go against it."

"His father never has to know about his involvement. We just need the medicine. Will you try?"

"I'll try."

I rushed back to the Hughmens', but when I arrived, I found Ethel weeping at the top of the stairs.

I ran and knelt in front of her. "What is it?"

She motioned to the closed door.

I scrambled to the door expecting to find Larry Hughmen's mangled corpse, yellow and pink. I clasped the doorknob and heard commotion. Confused, I quickly turned the knob and pushed. I gasped. Nearly every single woman from the church committee was inside, cleaning, cooking, washing clothes. Larry had clean sheets and fresh blankets. He had been bathed, and a woman knelt next to him, cleaning his scratches, while another applied fresh bandages to his bedsores. One woman stirred something in a pot on the stove. Another struggled with Jacob, trying to put a shirt on him but unable to pry his hands from a very real little toy horse.

Francis noticed me standing in the doorway and came over with her hands outstretched. "Isn't it amazing?"

"I—"

"Mrs. Hughmen"—Francis took Ethel's hands—"come get something to eat."

"Thank you." Ethel wiped away her tears.

Ella glided to me.

"This is a miracle," I said.

"We have all planned shifts and will help the Hughmens as long as they need us."

"Really?"

Francis returned. "And there's more."

"More?"

"This is an urgent need in Labellum."

"What is?"

"People like the Hughmens," Ella said. "After seeing this family and after learning what you do, we decided we want to help you—the committee, that is."

"But I thought—Mr. Coddington and the physicians—"

"They are arresting people who practice medicine without a license. We can't perform medicine, but we can still help those who are ill along with their families. We'll offer aid, cooking, cleaning, education on homecare and hygiene, and whatever else we can. We can do this within the law. Mr. Coddington can't scare off a committee, not when we know we are within our rights."

"I—I feel faint." I staggered, and Ella and Francis grabbed my arms.

"Is she all right?" a male voice asked from the open doorway.

"She's just a little surprised," Ella said.

I regained my composure and saw Walter wearing a dark suit and vest. He carried a leather case, and Olivia stood next to him. He immediately spotted Larry and walked to him with his professional gait as the women moved away. Ethel rose and moved with the others. Walter knelt next to Larry, studied his eyes and felt his heartbeat.

Larry whispered something.

"What?" Walter leaned over and listened. His serious expression suddenly changed and his composure gave way to laughter.

We stood silently as Walter inspected Larry. Finally, Walter lifted his head and spotted Ethel. I imagined he knew who she was because of her puffy eyes. He stood and approached her. "My deepest apologies. My father's diagnosis was accurate."

Ethel's eyes glistened.

He put a hand on her shoulder. "I will do everything in my power to make sure he is comfortable."

"You mean pain medicine?"

"Of course."

She threw her arms around him and buried her face in his chest, and Walter hugged her back.

While Walter gave Larry morphine and examined Ethel and Jacob, Ella landed on Olivia like a hawk and told her about the plans they had for the committee and how she and Walter could help.

As Walter started to leave, I stopped him. "Thank you so much, thank you," I said.

"I am happy to do it."

"But your father?"

"I'm not my father, but I'd appreciate it if this is kept quiet."

"Of course, of course." I feared saying more in case he suspected me, but I hoped the committee was enough of a disguise. Any of the members could have been Mrs. Freeman now. "You have done so much, but could I possibly ask one last thing?"

"Go on."

I moved in close to him so no one would hear. "Your father said the only cause of this condition is drinking. The accusation is so shameful for Mrs. Hughmen and her family. She's about to lose her employment. I know it is a horrible thing to ask, but could you possibly—lie to her?"

He pulled back. "No need to lie."

"Pardon?"

"Drinking isn't the only cause of liver disease." Walter didn't whisper.

"What?" Ethel cried out, clenching her skirts.

Walter straightened and spoke to her directly. "And drinking oneself to cirrhosis isn't an easy task to hide from a wife and child. If you never saw your husband drink, I highly doubt that was the cause."

Ethel staggered to him, grabbed his hands and put them to her face. "Thank you, thank you, thank you."

He took her hands in his. "Contact me if you need anything else, anything at all."

"Thank you, doctor. Thank you."

He and Olivia left together as they had arrived, and no one said a word about it.

I stayed for a while to help and sit with Larry. Eventually, everyone quieted down and Ethel and Jacob fell asleep next to him. He was awake, though, and on his thin lips was the slightest of smiles.

"How do you feel?" I asked.

"Ha. I'm dying."

"If I could—"

"I don't mind." He gazed at his sleeping wife and child, Jacob clutching his tiny horse. "I don't want to leave them, but at least I know they'll be taken care of."

I held back my tears and refused to think of my father. "We'll make sure of it."

"I know."

"The committee is amazing."

He motioned for me to lean in closer. "I hear you told that old docta what's what. That's what I call amazin'."

I chuckled, slightly embarrassed.

"Finally, you laugh."

I gave in and giggled.

"Thank you for what you've done for my family. These women may have made the difference, but you told them how to get here."

My eyes watered.

"Don't get moist over me." He moved his eyes to Ethel. "I'll be fine. They'll be fine."

# Thirty-Seven

*October 1901*

$\mathcal{I}$ cried all the way home. I was happy, sad, grateful, mournful, relieved, and in misery over everything Larry and my father had experienced and everything they wouldn't. Toward the end of my journey, however, my tears gave way to rejoicing as I thought of what the committee was going to do for the town. By the time I arrived home, I was giddy. Then I saw Lottie sitting on my front steps. I hopped off the surrey and ran to her.

She jolted, thrown by my glee.

"Lottie, you will not believe what happened. I asked Francis and Ella to help Ethel. They got the entire church committee over there cleaning and cooking." I was practically jumping, my hands flailing. "And Olivia Urswick!"

Lottie's eyes widened.

"She got Walter over there. He gave Larry medicines and told everyone that drinking didn't cause the disease."

"How?"

"Well, they're kind of—you know—courting?"

Lottie looked flabbergasted.

My exhilaration vanished as I remembered our argument. "Uh. I'm sorry. I'm just so happy."

She waved her hand.

"I apologize for the other night."

She shook her head. "It was me."

"But you never came back."

Lottie shifted her weight back and forth from one foot to the other. "I'm in trouble."

"What's wrong?"

"I'm with child."

"What?"

She crossed her arms and turned her back to me. "I can't have another. I shouldn't a had the last one."

"I—I'm…" I reached for her hand.

She pulled back and then looked up at the sky. I wasn't sure if she was talking to me or to God. "I have no money for food. I can't pay for 'em, I can't watch 'em. I don't have enough love. My body don't have a thing left." After having so many, Lottie had every reason to fear she wouldn't survive another. She spun around and grabbed my arms. "Emeline, I need you to get rid of it."

"What?" I pulled away.

"Get rid of it."

"No."

She covered her trembling lips.

"I won't do that. I can't do that."

"Why not?"

"You heard everything at that dinner. You know what could happen."

"Women do it all the time."

"I don't even know how to."

"Please."

"Lottie, women die when physicians do that. Think of Annie."

"She turned out fine. I know women who survive doin' it themselves."

"Then do it yourself."

"Believe me, I tried. I tried hot drinks, hot baths, violent exercise." She slapped her hands to her sides. "I jumped off a chair. I tried to roll down stairs, but nothin'. I know women have done it with an instrument, but I can't. I—I'm too—"

"Lottie, please. Don't ask this of me."

"Emeline." She grabbed my arms again. "I know they say it ain't right by God, but some say if it's before it starts moving, before it's alive…" She breathed hard, pushing the air out of her lungs forcefully. "I know it ain't right by law, but if I don't get rid of it, even if I live through it again, I ain't ganna be able to care for it or the rest of my babies. How is that right by anythin'?" She released me.

I thought of what Daniel had said about a life at stake. My father had said I would know whether it would or wouldn't be a sin, but I didn't know.

She put her hands together in praying fashion. Her face scrunched and her eyebrows dipped. "Please do this. Please. For my babies. For me. If you won't help me, I'll find someone who will. I'll risk it." She fell to her knees. "Please. Please, Emeline." She folded over and sobbed into her hands.

I clasped my hands over my mouth. She was my dearest friend. Ever since I found her in the woods, I wanted to help her, rescue her. She had helped me so much. I owed her so much. Could I really stand by and watch her go through a pregnancy that would surely kill her? Could I really say no when she might go to some hack who would do who knows what to her? It was a horrible, terrible thing, but doing nothing would be worse. I took a deep breath, and picked Lottie up off the ground.

I didn't say much at dinner that night. I was too nervous to fake conversation. What I was about to do was far worse than what I had been doing. It would ruin John if anyone found out I was providing medical care to the poor, but performing an abortion? I didn't even know if I could.

After dinner, James and Carmine retired to the parlor, and John asked me to join him in the library. I hoped he didn't notice that anything was out of place. I had spent the afternoon researching medical texts and his court records and testimonies, learning everything I could—how people had done it, the risks, what would happen afterward, everything.

John sat behind his gothic desk, and I sat in one of the chairs on the opposite side.

"What did you do today?"

I feigned confusion.

"Did you see Margaret Bradbridge?"

My heart jumped and my stomach tightened. "I made a few calls."

"Did you apologize?"

"Of course."

"Don't lie to me."

I was afraid to look at him, but I did. "I apologized."

"Dr. Bradbridge received an impromptu visit from his wife today."

My heart felt like a panicked critter trying to escape.

"Did you ask her to steal medicine from him?"

I opened my mouth, but nothing came out.

"Well, did you?"

"Um—I—"

"Why?"

I fiddled with my wedding ring.

"Was it for you?"

"No. No! It was for a man."

"What?" He shot out of his chair.

I stood. "No. I mean," I stuttered, "the church committee was helping a man. He was in severe pain, so Ella sent the committee to do whatever they could to help."

"What?"

"He's suffering."

"He should be seen by a physician."

"Dr. Bradbridge refused!"

"What?"

"He saw Dr. Bradbridge and he refused to treat him."

"Are you talking about that man? The man you argued about? The very subject you were to apologize for?"

"Well—I—"

"You agreed you'd apologize for your behavior, but instead you tried to make Margaret steal from her husband—my client? What possessed you to think—"

"You don't understand."

"I don't care!"

"John?"

"No." He pointed at me. "You—"

I lowered my eyes.

"You are lucky the Bradbridges are sympathetic to your affliction."

"Affliction?"

"I'm worried about you."

My mouth hung open.

"Dr. Bradbridge wants me to send you away."

"Please, John." I clasped my hands like Lottie had a few hours earlier. "I'm not insane."

"I want to believe that."

"I thought Mrs. Bradbridge would be sympathetic."

"And steal?"

"No. I asked her to talk to her son and request he donate some, but she wouldn't."

"So you went to stealing?"

"No—I just." I couldn't defend doing what I'd done. "I just wanted to help someone."

"And you trust your own opinion more than Dr. Bradbridge's?" He folded his arms. "If he didn't offer it, then it wasn't necessary."

"He didn't offer it because he thinks he has the right to judge and punish. He assumed the man was a drunk."

His jaw tightened. "Who is this person?"

"Mr. Hughmen isn't a drunk."

"Stop." He put out a hand. "I don't know what the committee is doing, but what you are doing is not acceptable." John stood and walked around his desk, and I shifted to face him. He took my left hand in his and ran a finger over my wedding ring. He squeezed my hand and caught my eyes with his. "I don't like people telling me to send you away."

I remembered what James had said. Did John really love me? I had wanted so much for him to love me, for me to love him, but we'd been stilted for so long. For so long, I'd thought that I was willing to love him and that he was the one who didn't love me. His demeanor toward me had changed over the last several months, but I was so determined to punish him that I refused to see love, and now that I knew it was there, a part of me ached for it.

"Do you understand why you were wrong?"

I choked on my whisper. "Yes." Did I even deserve his love after having betrayed him this way? What would all this do to him if he ever found me out or if I left him?

"You won't do anything like this again?"

I stared at the floor and breathed out my lie. "I won't."

# Thirty-Eight

*October 1901*

John went to work in the morning and I feigned my way through conversation with James and Carmine during breakfast, unable to concentrate. I spent the rest of the morning doing chores I couldn't skip as my belly burned with nervous energy. Around noon, I excused myself to go to town and went to my chamber to change into something suitable for errands.

I chose a loose-fitting white chiffon dress with half-sleeves and lace details on the bosom. A ribbon wrapped around the waist provided the hourglass figure, but it could be adjusted, which meant I could wear it without a corset. I wanted to go without the corset so that I could have full mobility. The dress was only for appearances, and I was sure I could get away without the corset if I saw anyone for a brief moment. Then I picked through my wardrobe and chose a simple gray shirtwaist without lace or embroidery, a black skirt, and an old apron, which I packed into a large black bag along with various tools I had prepared. I stopped at the sight of my reflection in the mirror adorned with the design of the metallic woman and the wind. I realized I had started wearing all white. I had transitioned into the last phase of mourning. Did that mean

I was letting him go? Would it all just disappear like mist? Could I allow that? I couldn't think of it then. I refocused, left the house, and rushed through the woods toward Lottie's.

Lottie had sent all her children out, so when I arrived the little home was quiet and bare, very different from the dwelling I had once stumbled upon, with little ones running and hooting outside. When she let me in, we didn't speak. I moved past her to her stove, where I put on a pot of water to boil. I quickly changed out of my white dress and gave it to Lottie, who hung it so it wouldn't wrinkle. I put on the working skirt and shirtwaist and went to the corner where Lottie had prepared as clean an area as possible. She had laid out a washed but old blanket and set up a wooden box with a clean cloth over it, where I lined up the instruments I had brought. They were mostly makeshift versions of the surgical tools I had seen in college and read about in John's books, but I had some real ones, too. "Where is your husband?" I asked.

"The fields." She watched the water.

"Is it possible he will return?"

"No, and even so—he knows."

"Oh." I stared at the pot with her, wondering if she knew that a watched pot never boils and if that was her intention. I took the apron out of my bag, and Lottie tied it on me. Little bubbles appeared at the bottom of the pot. The fire in my stomach radiated to my face. I had to remind myself to breathe. Lottie could die, I thought. I could kill her. I was going to end a life. No—I closed my eyes and told myself it wasn't alive yet, not before quickening, not before quickening, not before quickening. When the bubbles streamed to the surface, I took the pot off and placed it near the bed we'd prepared. I got down on my knees. "You have to lie down."

Lottie hesitated, arms crossed, standing near the stove. She stepped forward, stood on the blanket, waited a moment and then lowered herself to the bed. She quivered a little. I analyzed her position. "This will not do."

"What?"

"Do you have something you can put under you—to prop yourself up?"

She stood back up and fetched a rolled-up blanket.

"Are you certain no one will come?"

"Yes." She placed the rolled-up blanket on the mattress.

"I need light. I need to open the windows. If anyone came by…"

She shook her head. "Ain't no reason anyone ganna come here." She went to the window above where we were working and opened the shade.

"What about your children? There's no chance they'll return early?"

She sat in front of me. "Made certain of it."

"You are positive?"

She raised her voice. "I said I am."

"All right." I picked up a long tiny tube.

"What's that?"

"It's a catheter."

"What's it do?"

"I'm not going to use it for what it's meant for."

I placed it into the boiling water to sterilize it.

"Now what are you doing?"

"Remember the germs?"

She nodded.

"I'm killing them."

"Oh."

I pulled the catheter out. "Are you ready?"

Her eyes met mine.

"Lie back and don't look down here."

"Why?"

"I don't want you to move." I also didn't want her to see blood.

I positioned her legs so that they opened the hole in her drawers. I used a pair of forceps I had fashioned from kitchen tongs. Lottie made a noise of discomfort. "Did I hurt you?"

"No, keep goin'."

I took out a curette, a long instrument with a curved tip—another tool I had fashioned, this one from a metal coat hanger. I remembered the way they'd talked about it at the dinner and then pushed it from my mind. I was helping my friend. She needed this. I dipped it into the boiling water. If I inserted it too far, I could puncture the uterine wall and she would die. I slid the catheter into her, using it as a guide. I read how a catheter could be used in this manner from testimony in John's records. Everything I did was blind. Even with forceps, I didn't have a visual advantage. I removed the curette from the water and cooled it.

A professional would use the curette to scrape the inside of the uterus, but I wasn't a doctor. Even physicians accidentally injured women in the process, so I planned to use it another way described in John's records. Several women were not injured when the midwives used a curette-like instrument to agitate the womb, which forced a miscarriage and mimicked natural loss.

I inserted it. Lottie made a noise and jerked a little. I went rigid.

"I didn't mean to move."

"It's all right." I told myself to breathe.

"Keep goin'." She swung her arm up and over her eyes.

Breathe. I removed the curette. My heart began to beat rapidly when I saw a little red on the curette. I wasn't sure if this meant I had succeeded or failed.

I took some cotton balls with a smaller pair of tongs and dipped them in the water. I cleaned her as best I could and packed her with cotton, with the catheter still in. The second purpose of the catheter was to act as a further irritant. I was to leave it in to make sure the process completed. She made sounds of discomfort, but I kept going.

"Wrap this around you." I handed her a towel.

"Is it done?"

"Yes."

She tried to sit up.

I thrust out my hand. "No, stay down."

She stopped and lowered herself again.

I scooted to her side so she could see my face. "The catheter is still in. Tomorrow at this time, take it out. You should rest for the next couple of days. You will feel pain and bleed as..." I stopped.

She nodded.

I cleaned my instruments and packed them in a dry cloth in my bag. I removed some pills from my satchel and put them on the box and pushed it closer to Lottie. "Take these quinine pills every three hours and walk around a little, then straight back to bed."

She gulped.

"Send Oliver if anything goes wrong."

There was a small smear of blood on my apron. I took it off, balled it up, and put it with the other rags we'd used. "Could you get rid of this for me when you throw out the rest?"

She nodded.

I changed out of the work clothes, rolled them into a bundle, and packed them into my bag. I changed back into my dress, fussed with the buttons going up the back and the neck. "I would stay, but I have to go before John returns."

"I'm sorry," she said.

I formed a comforting smile. "No need."

I trudged through the woods at a brisk pace. It was late, nearly evening, and I still had to prepare dinner. Twigs and foliage crunched beneath my feet. Listening to it, I noticed something. There was more crunching than my steps could take credit for. I stopped, and so did all the noise. I tried to quiet my breath and listen, but a humming in my head drowned out sound. I felt my heart flutter. Something snapped nearby. My heart pounded, and I spun around but didn't see any movement. Was there something out there? My mind raced and I thought of the house, the wolf. Was it back? Or was it real? Was this what it had been waiting for? No matter how much good I'd attempted, I'd known this was coming. I deserved to be punished.

I quickened my step. I prayed in my head for it to be nothing, a small animal, a squirrel. The crunching behind my footsteps sounded again and quickened. I ran without thinking, and I heard the sounds of running behind me, too. I envisioned the gnarly, matted wolf nearing my ankles.

It snatched me—by the arm. By the arm? I screamed and tugged, but I was held in one place. He took my other arm and shook me. "Emeline!"

I stopped, breathing rapidly. I was trapped in his furious eyes. "John?"

"I saw you." His sleeves were rolled up to the middle of his upper arms. He wasn't wearing a jacket. He hadn't been taking a stroll. "I saw what you were doing." He squeezed.

"What?"

He released me and reached down, snatching the bag with my incriminating tools. "Mr. Buck told me what you've been doing— poor excuses, mysterious places, and that you went into the woods. I saw everything!"

I shook my head. "No—what you saw—"

"Quiet." He pointed at me with the hand holding the bag. He regarded it and then launched it into the woods. I heard it land far away. He held his finger close to my lips. "I don't want to hear you say another word. Don't."

I obeyed.

He took me by the wrist. "I have put up with this long enough." He jerked me and I almost fell forward, but he pulled me up and onward. I tripped over my dress and muddied it as he pulled me behind him. "You've made a fool of me."

I wanted to beg. I wanted to plead.

"Right under my nose."

I couldn't think, and I couldn't do or say anything.

"How could you do this? How?" John pushed away the last tree branches, which scraped at my arms as he dragged me. I saw the house waiting for us—laughing.

# Thirty-Nine

## 1900
### *St. Louis, Missouri*

A few days after learning that John had agreed to marry me, I saw him on the street in St. Louis. I was so confused at the time, grateful yet terrified because it meant moving to Labellum. Mother had asked me to run to the bakery for tea cakes because of the callers coming to congratulate us on the betrothal. It was still early morning when I strolled out of the bakery with a box of cinnamon-raisin cake, lifted my gaze, and saw him across the way in a brown suit, his waistcoat visible under the unbuttoned jacket. I knew it was him right away because of his body's angled structure, his pale face, and his dark slicked-back hair.

I saw him immediately because of the way he'd left the brick building, down and across the street from me. He slammed the door open hard and stalked out with long, powerful strides. His presence stopped me. He took several steps onto the walk, halted, put both hands on his hips and stood for a moment. Then he dropped his hands, turned and took a step back toward the building, stopped, and turned again.

It would have been perfectly acceptable for me to approach him, given that we were betrothed, but I hadn't dared. Although

I would never have characterized him as a violent man, he was suddenly intimidating. He paced, stopped, rubbed the back of his neck, and started pacing again. He acted as if he were arguing with someone in his head. A few times he pulled out his handkerchief to wipe his face in one full circle. He ran his hands through his hair, touched his face and let out a long hard gust of air like a halted train. I was far enough away that he didn't feel me staring at him. Still, I stepped to the side of the walk and pretended to fiddle with my box. I could make out his hardened brow and stern jaw line.

I wondered what could have made him so upset. On the building he had come from, there was a small sign above the door, and I tried to read the lettering. I could make out only one word, printed larger than the rest: *Law*. It had to have been his father's law firm.

As I watched him pace in front of the building, I tried to imagine loving him. He wasn't a robust man, but he was beautiful in his strange way, with his dark eyes, high cheekbones, long legs, and full stride. It couldn't be hard to love a man who looked like that. Finally, he stopped and moved toward the door. I thought he'd stomp back inside, but instead he kicked the building. He stepped back, hopping in pain. I giggled to myself. He took several big breaths, unclenched his fists, and buttoned his jacket. Finally, he lowered his shoulders and calmly walked back inside.

I wondered if he got angry often. I wondered if he would get angry with me. I told myself I would never do anything to make him angry. I would forget my own fears and wants. I would do it for my family, for my father. I would serve John, care for him, and make our home his sanctuary. I would make him fall absolutely in love with me.

# Forty

October 1901
Labellum, Missouri

John swung open the door and the house heaved. Without lighting a lamp, he pulled me behind him. He yanked me down the dark hall and marched us up the stairs. All the doors were shut again. Where was James? Without a lamp, I couldn't see anything. I felt John pulling me up each step and heard feet scuffling. I felt my feet hitting the risers and tried to keep my legs from buckling. I felt him drag me around the first right. How was he able to see? My boots clacked and scraped with each step. He pulled me through the isolated portion of the staircase. I wondered if the walls might close in on me, seeing an opportunity to encase me in darkness, but they let us pass.

We reached the top of the stairs and he yanked me down the hallway. I couldn't see with my eyes, but I knew the corridor in my mind. The people in the rooms watched through their doors. The woman who prepared the deceased boy turned from the vanity and gasped at the shocking scene. The young woman's head shot up, distracted from her own personal horror. The little girl watched from her hiding spot in the corner.

We stopped. John fumbled with the door handle, and I turned my head in the direction of the beast's room. I saw only black, could hear my breath as if time had slowed down. For all I knew, the beast could have been standing two feet from me, or inches from my nose. John opened our chamber door, light flashed across the beast's closed door, and John yanked me by the wrist and swung me in front of him into our chamber. I stumbled into the middle of the room. The lamps were lit. I rubbed my eyes. I heard him step in and shut the door.

He stood in front of the door, his eyes accusing. The beast crept close to the wall to listen to us. The little girl hushed her cries. John paced, stopped and lifted his finger, but instead of scolding, he shook his head. His slicked-back hair had fallen out of place. He paced again and stopped in front of his dressing table. He leaned over, put his hands down, and lowered his head, his body rigid—full of angles. "How could you have done this?"

I held my hands up, palms down. They shook. "I—I'm—"

His eyes hit me and I stepped back.

"What?" He clenched his hands into fists. "What do you have to say for yourself?"

My lips parted, waiting for something, anything—another lie, another excuse—but nothing came out.

"I am disgusted." His bottom lip curled up as the corners of his mouth dropped. "Why?"

"I—I—"

He stepped toward me.

I stepped back. His eyes locked on mine, and I feared looking away. "I wanted to help."

"What the hell are you talking about?" Jaw clenched, teeth flashing.

"I—I've been—she needed me to—"

He grimaced. "You're a—a—an abortionist?"

I shook my head, but I couldn't deny it.

"A murderer."

I stopped and looked up at him wide-eyed.

He stepped forward. "Why?"

I stepped back and put my hands up. "She—she was afraid—"

"No." He brought his hands up and turned away. "I don't want to hear this."

I felt the beast press against the wall, leering.

"How long?"

"Never—never before." I shook my head. "Nothing like this."

He whirled around. "What?"

"I've never done that before."

"But you've done other things?"

"I help people who are sick." I glanced at him and then lowered my eyes to the floor.

His voice became calm, rational. "You—are you—" He lifted his eyes with his head down. "Are you that woman? Mrs. Free—"

"Yes."

"You are what I am trying to stop."

I avoided his eyes.

"You may have killed her—you are ruining me."

"I know."

"You know? Of course you know!" He laughed bitterly. "You are guilty. So what should I do?"

I shook. "I don't know."

He came at me with force. "Do you know what I have done for you? Everything I have done and you do this?"

I backed up and bumped against my vanity, against the beast's wall.

"I have given everything for you."

A tear streamed down my face.

"This is how you repay me?"

I shook my head.

"I have given everything for this household. I have suffered—for this?" His brow glistened with sweat.

I squinted and felt a blaze in my chest.

"You really are crazy!" He pointed.

I balled my hands into fists.

He leaned over me and put his face close to mine. I recoiled as he shouted, "I have done everything for you!" His voice sounded shrill, as if he were crying, too. He stepped away and turned his back to me.

I remained against my vanity, eyes clenched shut, my breath heavy.

He paced and, in a much lower voice, began to rant. "I've done everything I was supposed to. And you! Nothing. No affection. No loyalty. Nothing." He stopped by his dressing table, paused and snatched a metal tray holding his cuff links and other items and hurled it against the wall. The crack, bang, and prattle of little metal objects hitting the floor startled the beast.

I'd spoiled everything? I hadn't tried? I'd given nothing? No. I stepped away from the vanity. I grit my teeth. My nails dug into my palms. The sound of my voice was shrill and wet. "I...have... given...everything!"

John stopped pacing and cast his blazing eyes at me.

"I have put everything I have into this. You—" I pointed at him and took a step forward. "You are the one who has given nothing."

His mouth fell open.

My voice trembled. "You provide for me? I take care of this cussed place." I waved my hands and looked around at the insulted house that encased us. "I cook. I clean. And I hate this place. I hate this damned house! And I especially hate you"—I pointed—"because you brought me here. You have done nothing but bring me misery." I put my hands to my head, recalling my frustration. "Whatever I have become is your doing—you made me this way." Now I paced. "All I do is try—try to be a good wife—try to be perfect—perfect for you—and inspire the slightest sliver of affection between us, but you—you are a walking, breathing corpse! I have driven myself absolutely and completely mad for you. I was ready to leave. I was ready to run away, go back to St. Louis, and be a spinster rather than be your wife. The only thing that kept me here was helping those people."

He stepped back.

I stepped forward. "And what I did for those people—for Lottie and for everyone else—"

"You—"

"Let me finish!" I screeched.

He stopped.

"Everything I have done was to help people, and I did it so I wouldn't go absolutely piss-pot loony in this cursed, awful place with you."

The monster stepped back from the wall, limbs tucked in close, fearing something would burst through and snatch it up. The little girl perked up in her corner, the people in the rooms down the hall stared in awe, and the furniture below cowered.

John looked shocked for a moment, but his face quickly returned to fury. He clenched his fists and turned red. "I don't try?" He pointed to himself. "I don't have affection for you?"

I realized I had said too much, pushed him too far. Would he turn me in? Take me to the authorities? An asylum? He took those long, powerful strides in my direction, and I backed up until I bumped into the wall. He grabbed me by the arm, pulled me toward him, and held me inches from his face. He sighed, closed his eyes, and lowered his voice to a whisper. "Do you not understand how much I care for you?"

I trembled. "I—"

Before I could speak, his lips were against mine. His hand slid up my neck and into my hair. Then he pulled away and dropped his head. "I'm sorry." He took his hands away from my body and placed them on the wall behind me.

I took deep breaths. I tried to catch his eyes with mine, but he hid them from me. My lips quivered, wanting to say something, anything. I brought my hand up to touch his face, hesitated. He really loved me. Then I imagined kissing him—how he'd feel if I did, how I'd feel—so I did. I kissed him.

Surprised, his eyes shot open, but I didn't stop. He wrapped his arms around me tight and pressed his lips and body against me. I think I heard the little girl giggle. It may have been me.

We rose as if to go somewhere but lost our footing and fell against the wall together. The beast jumped in surprise. The mirror depicting the woman on the beach fell off the wall and broke on the floor. I heard a crack and the cling-cling and crackle of glass shattering, but I didn't care.

We stumbled to the bedstead and fell onto the bed, but John stood back up and began unbuttoning his shirt. I reached back and unbuttoned my dress, starting with the high collar. John removed his shirt and began helping me undo the buttons I could not reach. When I felt the cool air on my skin, I remembered I wasn't wearing a corset or a corset cover. At the sight of my bare flesh, John exhaled from his gut, abandoned the buttons, and lifted me farther onto the bed. He got onto his knees over me, lifted my petticoats and dress to my waist, and bundled them between us. He stopped and locked his dark brown eyes on mine, and for the briefest of moments I saw into him and felt him see into me, and in that moment we understood each other completely. Then he slid his hands into my hair and kissed me. I felt his hot skin on my hands, and he slid his down my back under my dress. Exhilaration flowed up and over me, followed by a sensation I did not know. I let go of something then. I didn't know what, but I had never felt so out of control, so liberated. Free.

John buttoned up his shirt. I repositioned my dress and tightened the ribbon around my waist, and John helped with the buttons on the high collar. Then we sat next to each other, not speaking.

I felt oddly shy. "What now?"

"I don't know." He chuckled.

We sat there for a minute or so, silent.

"I thought you didn't like me."

He touched my cheek. "I've loved you for a very long time."

"You never showed it."

He took his hand away. "I was confused."

"I don't understand."

He lowered his eyes and fiddled with his clothes. "I didn't exactly want to get married."

I stared at him. "Do tell."

"I had feelings for you, but with your family's loss…" All of a sudden my parents arranged it. They didn't ask me. They informed me." John's eyes dropped down. "I liked you, but I wasn't ready to marry anyone. I didn't even know you. I didn't even know who I was yet. When we got here, I tried to be a husband, but everything felt so awkward and then I felt too stressed with work and pressured by my father to think of romance. Things were so awful at the firm. Lewis Coddington hated me when we first got here. I ruined everything I touched. Eventually, I was certain I couldn't do anything right. I couldn't be the lawyer my father wanted or the husband that you needed."

"I'm sorry."

"It's not your fault."

"No. It was my fault." I brought my hand to my throat.

"What do you mean?"

"I asked your parents to arrange it." We locked eyes and I gulped.

"What? But you've never shown any interest in me."

"I know." I lowered my eyes. "I—I asked because I wanted to help my family, but I was interested in you. You're so—every girl was, but I didn't think you were within reach. That's why I didn't show it before."

We didn't say anything.

"I wasn't within reach so you decided to ask my parents to make me?" He laughed and I giggled at how ridiculous that sounded. Then we were quiet again.

"I'm sorry you had to marry me," I said.

"I'm sorry you had to marry me." He squeezed my hand.

"I thought I had failed you."

"No. You're wonderful."

"Even after what I did?" I took my hand away.

He hesitated. "You said I drove you to that?"

"There were many things."

He rubbed the back of his neck.

"I did what I did today because Lott—Mrs. Schwab needed my help. It was the only thing to do."

"Are you joking?"

I looked up.

"You didn't have any idea what you were doing. She's probably going to die. That's what always happens."

"That's not true—not in your cases—"

John crinkled his nose. "You read my notes?"

"I—just—"

"Emeline, are you absolutely insane? Don't you understand? You might be a murderer. You could be arrested. You are going to be committed."

"Mrs. Schwab can't care for her children as it is. If she had another, it would die or kill her!"

"You don't know that!"

"She's my friend. I had to help."

He stood over me. "I'm your husband. You should have thought. You should have done what was right."

I stood. "I did."

"Emeline, I need to know that you will never do anything like this ever again. If you were to get caught—I should be taking you to the authorities."

I blinked rapidly and looked away.

"Promise me you will never do this kind of thing again?"

I was supposed to give in, like I always did.

"Will you promise me?"

I was supposed to submit.

"Emeline?"

"No."

He drew back. "What?"

"If you really cared for me, you'd listen to why I can't."

"If you really cared for me, you wouldn't risk everything I have worked for."

"I care for people in a way you can't even comprehend."

"No, Emeline. You're not a doctor! You don't know what you're doing." He pointed.

I pointed to myself. "I help when physicians won't."

He squinted and then widened his eyes. "That man, the one you and Dr. Bradbridge argued—you were playing nurse with him, weren't you?"

"I was doing what a physician refused to do."

"And he died!"

I gasped, brought my hand to my chest. "What?"

"You didn't help him. He died today."

"He died?"

"Did you kill him?"

"How could you—no." Tears rolled down my cheeks, slipped under my chin. "No one could prevent it."

"So you knew it was unnecessary to get involved with such a mess."

"I treated his pain and helped his wife. I would never do anything to hurt anyone."

"What about our servant?"

"You don't understand."

"Obviously, you don't understand." He marched to the door and opened it. "I don't know what I'm going to do. You're insane. You're absolutely mad!" He slammed the door behind him.

I spent the next hour pacing, going over everything in my head. It was dark now. I thought about letting myself go insane so John would curse himself for what he had said. I thought about punishing him. I could keep doing things behind his back. I could get caught. I was so furious.

The beast rustled, writhing in pleasure.

What now? Should I stay now that I knew how John really felt, or should I flee with James? If I stayed, would anything change?

The beast snickered.

Would the house fade away or would it take me over?

It started scratching the walls. I could hear it reach to the top and slowly claw down to the floor.

I shook with anger. Should I talk to him? Should I insist— should I—?

Scratching.

Should I argue? How could I stop helping people? I couldn't. I needed it. They needed it. It was the only thing keeping me sane. It was the only reason I had survived.

The beast cackled as it bobbed up and down. It returned to its scratching and noise-making.

I gritted my teeth. I couldn't think with that noise, the rebellion. I couldn't continue to live this way. I refused.

The evil creature scratched wildly and banged itself against the walls. It wanted to push me to the brink. It sensed weakness and wanted to strike.

I had to do something about John. I wanted to scream. The beast. The noise. The constant poking and prodding at my nerves. Scratching, banging, and scratching. I could hear the paint peeling under its talons. The scratching grew frantic, and I realized it had finally decided to tear through the wall to get to me. I couldn't stand it.

I bellowed a curdling war cry and threw myself at the wall. "Quiet! Quiet! I hate you. No more," I screamed as I pounded and scratched the wall. "How do you like the noise? Huh? How do you like it? Silence. Be quiet, damn you!" It stood back and cackled. I threw myself at the wall again. "Get out. I demand you get out of my house!" I stopped, teeth clenched. My lips curled. I looked at the door and then back at the wall. It saw my intention and stopped laughing. "You stupid beast, you think I can't get to you." I stomped to the door. I could sense it back up in fear. "Unlike you, I can use a doorknob!"

I threw my door open followed by the beasts door. I burst into its dark room and slammed the door behind me. I stood there in darkness and screamed with all my might and all my power. "Here I am. You want to take over? Do it. Try. I will rip *you* to shreds. Do something! I don't care what I've done, I don't deserve this. I don't deserve you!" My throat hurt from the anger behind my threats, and my fingernails dug into my palms. I raised my voice again. "You are nothing. You aren't real. You're a punishment. I created you, and I don't need you anymore. I don't want it! I don't want to be punished anymore! I don't need you. Get out of my house. Get out of my life. Get out! Get out! Get out!"

The door opened and light cut through the darkness in the empty room, no beast to be seen. Gone. Quiet. I turned around, my arms folded, teeth clenched.

"What is the matter with you?" John asked.

"Is that convenient for you?"

"What?"

"To conclude I am mad any time you wish?"

He shook his head. "No—I—" He paused. "You're acting crazy."

"Am I?"

"Yes." He motioned his hands toward me.

I pointed. "If I am acting crazy, it is only in reaction to your lunacy."

His eyes widened. He shook his head once. "Listen, Mr. Schwab is downstairs and—"

"What? Oh no." I moved quickly, bumping John as I passed.

"Emeline, wait." He followed.

# Forty-One

*October 1901*

"Emeline, stop!"

I no longer cared. I rushed down the stairs and through the hall. I scanned the library and the parlor for Oliver as John called out behind me, but I ignored him. I ran to the front door and ripped it open. I saw the back of Oliver's head, his scraggly peppered hair.

He turned around, revealing heavy eyes and a frown on his weather-worn face. "Forgive me. I had to come."

John appeared behind me.

"Is she all right?" I intentionally took up all the space in the doorway, forcing John to stay behind me.

"No." Oliver's expression grew uncertain and worried as John bobbed about behind me.

I spun around to collect my kit, but John stood in my way.

"Emeline, you can't."

I circumvented him and went to the sitting room, where I had stashed supplies. They were in a brown satchel, but I didn't need everything, so I dumped the contents onto the floor and began repacking the satchel, since John had thrown my normal bag into the forest. John stood at the door watching me scatter and pack what he would surely term incriminating evidence.

"Emeline, you have to stop!"

"What's going on?" I heard James ask.

"Emeline!"

I weaved around the pink sofa and the little tables and shoved past him into the hallway, where James stood.

John followed me out, sidestepped me, and grabbed my arm.

Oliver and James watched in bewilderment.

"Let me pass, John."

"Emma, what's happened?" James asked.

"No. I won't let you do this." John's grip caused pain to shoot through my bones.

"What's happening? Are you leaving him?" James shouted, and I felt a rock in my stomach.

John's face dropped, and he looked at me with hurt and questioning eyes that tore into me.

I knew what I needed to do to have a perfect marriage, the marriage I was beginning to truly want. I knew I had to stop, but I couldn't. I wouldn't. I tried to wrench my arm away. "John, I mean it. Move!"

He grasped tighter. "No. I won't budge, Emeline. I won't."

"Please."

"John." James rushed to us. "Let her go and we can talk this over."

"I won't move. I won't let you do this."

"John, if you don't let me go, Mr. Schwab will have to take her to the Bradbridges and everyone will know what I did."

John jerked his head back.

Oliver's mouth fell open.

James' eyes bobbed back and forth, his hands raised. "What did you do?"

John looked over his shoulder at Oliver, who gave a confirming nod. Finally, he loosened his grip and hesitantly stepped out of the way. I hustled out the door, with James trailing behind. "Emeline? What are you—"

"James, stay here. I'll explain later."

"But—"

Oliver kept pace as we flew past Carmine, who stood near James' rented buggy and watched agape as we marched into the forest.

We trekked through the darkness, Oliver leading the way through branches and brush. I heard footsteps behind us.

"Emeline, stop."

"Oliver, keep going," I shouted.

John trailed us. "Stop. Emeline, I'm begging you. Do you have any idea what will happen to you when you're caught?"

I saw a little lit square in the darkness, the shanty's window.

John ran up and stepped in front of me, forcing me to stop. "Emeline, I'll lose you, too."

I hesitated. "If you don't want to lose me, then stop trying to get in my way." I walked around him.

Oliver and I entered the poorly lit shanty, and John followed. He stopped ranting, and I had to look over my shoulder to see if he was still there. He observed the one-room shack filled with children, cowering and crying, the baby squealing in Lucy's arms, and Lottie wailing in the corner. I went straight to her. When John's eyes finally took in her state, he stopped in the middle of the room. She had only a sheet over her, stained between her legs with blood. Bloody smears and footprints of various sizes surrounded her. Her undone hair was stuck to her face with sweat, and her skin had gone clammy. She was curled up and clutching her stomach.

"Emeline, what have you done?" John said.

"Hold this up." I gave Oliver one of the blood-smeared sheets so that the children couldn't see what was happening.

"Hold this." I held up the sheet, prompting John.

He didn't move. He just stared at her with a dazed look.

"John!"

He shook his head and blinked rapidly.

"Hold this."

He swayed forward and took the corner, still staring at Lottie.

I peeled the sopping nightgown up and removed the sodden cotton. A gush of blood and tissue followed. I found the catheter and removed it.

John turned pallid and looked away. Oliver stared blankly.

One of Lottie's children, a young boy, maybe five, tugged on John's trousers. "You ganna make her stop hurtin'?"

"Go sit back down," Oliver ordered.

Lottie's head felt hot. I pulled some things from my satchel for the fever and the pain.

"Emeline, you have to take her to a physician," John said.

"You know what will happen if we do."

John lowered his eyes.

"Walter," I said.

"What?"

"He won't turn us in." I returned my medicines to my satchel, and that was when I noticed the blood all over me, the brightest shade of red on my white dress.

"But—"

"He helped us with Mr. Hughmen. He might help again."

"No. He reports people like you." He and Oliver still held up the sheet.

"We have no choice. Besides, I know something that may sway his decision."

"What?"

I stood. "Put the sheet over her and pick her up."

John hovered.

"Come on."

The two men draped the sheet over her waist and lifted. She moaned, and her face twisted. Oliver swung one of her arms behind his head and heaved her into his arms.

I noticed the baby's squealing again and the other children weeping. Blood dripped from the sheet.

"It'll be all right," Oliver grunted to his children as he carried her to the door.

"We'll take her to our house," John said.

Oliver ordered Lucy to watch the children, and we rushed into the woods.

Halfway, Oliver slowed down, and John offered to carry Lottie the rest of the way. As Oliver transferred Lottie into his arms, blood smeared John's white shirt, his forearms, and his rolled-up sleeves. He swept her up. He had offered to take her. He had offered to bear her weight and be stained with her blood despite his class and his disapproval of what was happening. Had something changed in him? I remembered when I'd first entered Lottie's home. I had felt overwhelmed by guilt for the way I and every person of my stature had thought about her and people like her, for taking them for granted. After that, I changed. Had John changed, too?

We saw dots of light in the bedroom and parlor windows of the house. We sped up a little when we cleared the woods. John scaled the steps with Lottie in his arms, and I passed him to open the door. John took Lottie into the hall. Our fumbling and shouted directions were louder than they had been in the woods.

James ran to us. "What's happened?"

Carmine appeared. "Dear Lord." She covered her mouth.

I saw my hands and dress slathered in slick scarlet. Blood was smeared all over John's and Oliver's clothes, too. Everything below Lottie's waist was sopping. The door, the hallway, the parlor door and some of the parlor furniture bore red streaks and handprints in a matter of moments.

John handed a pillow embroidered with a creeping design to Oliver to put under Lottie's head. I braced myself, expecting the parlor to respond. It sat dead, lifeless, just wood, porcelain, and stitching.

"I'm going to get Walter." John marched out of the parlor.

I ran after him and stepped between him and the door. "No. I need to go."

"You won't be able to explain this."

"I will. Trust me. I have to go."

His eyes moved back and forth. "I can't let you—"

"John!"

We locked eyes.

"Trust me. I know how to convince him."

"Fine. Come on." He started again.

"Wait."

He whirled back. "What?"

"James will take me."

"No. You need me there."

"No. I know how to convince him, but I can't have you there."

His eyes widened.

"Stay here and help Lottie."

He tilted his head.

"Please."

He turned without responding and went to the parlor, his fists clenched.

"Emeline." James stepped forward, Carmine grasping his arm. "What is happening? What have you done?"

"James, I have to get Walter. I need you to take me."

"Who? What?"

"A doctor."

"Oh, thank God." He put a hand on his head.

"I have to convince him to help us illegally."

"What?"

Carmine stood unblinking.

"James, please, just take me or I'll kill myself trying to get there on my own." I moved for the door.

James slipped out from under Carmine and thrust an arm across my chest. "You can't let anyone see you like that."

I looked down at the blood on my dress. I took John's black thigh-length jacket from the hanger. "Carmine."

Finally, she blinked and jolted out of her incredulous stare.

"Help them." I motioned to Lottie and Oliver.

"Um...all right."

We barreled down the road in James' rented buggy, bouncing and jolting with every rock and bump.

"Emeline, what in tarnation is going on?" James yelled over the sound of the wheels.

"It's complicated." I gripped the seat as we jolted.

"What happened to that woman? Why are you involved?"

"I—I did it."

"Did what?"

"You don't know what it's been like here for me, James. You don't know..."

"What?"

"I've been helping people who are ill, like a nurse."

He glanced at me and then looked back at the dark road.

"I've been treating people who are ill—people who can't afford a physician."

"Are you mad?"

I sighed. "I've been hearing that a lot."

"What about that woman?"

"She needed a dangerous procedure. I think"—I had to yell over the roaring hooves—"I think I made a mistake."

"Why?"

"She couldn't afford a doctor. It was the right thing."

"No. What's wrong with her? What did you do?"

I gripped the seat harder.

"Emeline?"

"An abortion."

"What?"

I yelled over the rumbling wheels. "I gave her an abortion!"

James regarded me, eyes wide, and then turned back to the road without saying another word.

When we stopped, I hopped out and James stayed. I ran to Walter's door and knocked loudly.

Walter opened his door. His shirt and vest were wrinkled as if he had been lounging.

"Emeline? I mean Mrs. Dorr?" He looked past me at James in the buggy. "Is everything all right?"

I shook my head and opened the jacket, revealing my blood-soaked clothes.

He gasped and jerked his head back.

"I'm Mrs. Freeman, and I've done something terrible." I felt like I might vomit.

His mouth hung open.

"And if you tell anyone, I'm going to tell everyone about you and Olivia."

His eyes shot open, but he didn't move.

I trembled. "Please. She could die."

He hesitated a minute before finally forming words. "I'll get my bag." He disappeared for a few minutes and returned with a black satchel. We stepped into the buggy, and James took us back to the house as I confessed everything. James drove with a horrified expression as I went into the details of the abortion.

When we returned to the house, Walter quickly walked into the parlor and didn't reappear for fifteen minutes. We all stood in the hallway trying to listen to the mumbled voices over our thumping hearts. I was hot and had removed John's jacket. When Walter came out, we gathered close as he whispered. "The baby is gone."

"Did I injure her?"

Walter scowled. "What you did was damn foolish."

I felt my cheeks flush and a twinge in the back of my throat.

"There is too much blood for me to say. I wouldn't be surprised if you mutilated her beyond repair. I should—"

"Don't chastise her," John said and my breath caught in my throat. He continued. "This woman has more children than I could count. If she had one more—she feared for her life. Emeline saw no other choice."

Walter's brow furrowed. "That is not the point, John, and I do believe *you* should know that better than anyone."

Oliver stepped forward. "Is she going to survive?"

Walter shifted. "I gave her something for the pain, but she has lost a lot of blood. I can't guarantee anything."

My stomach tightened into a twisted fist.

"John—" Walter stepped closer to him. "You understand the seriousness of this?"

John stood tall and lifted his chin. "Yes."

They didn't take their eyes off each other until Walter moved. "Excuse me." He walked out and slammed the door behind him.

I expected John to go after him and stop him, but he didn't move. We couldn't just let him leave. I sprinted to the door and scrambled halfway down the steps before I stopped and saw the blockade before me.

Lewis Coddington and the Bradbridges approached the house, followed by several patrolmen in black thigh-length overcoats and flat-topped derbies. Each clung to a wooden truncheon. Walter went straight to a tall slender man in a black suit with lopsided shoulders and a massive square jaw. It was Marcellus Rippring, the investigator who had once spoken of interrogating screaming women and refusing treatment in the parlor where Lottie now lay. They greeted each other and Marcellus' eyes shifted to me. "Mrs. Dorr, shall we go back inside?"

I stood paralyzed as Marcellus snatched my arm and escorted me back inside, where John and James still stood in the hallway.

"Marcellus!" John's eyes bulged.

Marcellus moved me forward, allowing Lewis Coddington, Dr. Benedict Bradbridge, Margaret, Walter, and three patrolmen to file into the foyer. Marcellus and the patrolmen positioned themselves in a circle around us, standing with their hands and clubs at their sides.

Lewis shook Walter's hand. "I'm proud of you, Walter, for doing the right thing and contacting the authorities and your counsel about this very serious matter." He shot John a glare.

"Thank you for coming," Walter said.

I shook my head at Walter. "How?"

"I had a guest when you came to my house. I informed her of the situation when I went for my bag."

"Was it Olivia?" I asked under my breath so only Walter would hear.

"I had no choice." Walter tugged at his collar and flashed a remorseful glance at John. "If I hadn't called, we'd both be held accountable."

"What is this really about?" I asked Walter in a low voice. "Honesty or how you look to your father?"

Margaret scowled at me, her hands on her hips. "How dare you speak to him that way?"

I pleaded with Walter. "You saw Mr. Hughmen. You know I help people. I do good."

"That, Emeline"—he pointed toward the parlor—"is not good."

Lewis and Benedict joined the circle of authority surrounding us.

James swayed back and forth, his right arm wrapped around his torso and his left hand over his mouth.

Lewis stepped closer to John. "Of all the people. All this time we've been searching for this 'illegal nurse' and the entire time it's been your wife." He pointed at me.

A vein pulsed at Benedict's temple. "You of all people know this is condoning murder," Benedict said in that deep, proud voice.

John swallowed.

Lewis stood tall. "If you cooperate, you won't be charged—just her."

"You should be grateful," Margaret said from her position outside the circle of men.

"Who are we taking in?" a patrolman asked.

"We need to get the dying confession." Marcellus jerked his head to the side to crack his neck. "We're going to need to speak with all of you in private." He nodded in the direction of the parlor. "Starting with the victim."

A patrolman marched into the parlor, his heavy boots clunking, and returned with Oliver and Carmine. Carmine went for James, but another patrolman cut her off and another grabbed Oliver.

The first patrolman went back into the parlor with Walter at his heel. "Wait. She needs a doctor present. Her condition is too unstable."

Marcellus nodded, and Walter went in before shutting the doors.

Lewis took John by the arm. "We need to talk."

"This way." John led Lewis and Benedict down the hall toward the library.

"John!" I cried.

"Mrs. Dorr?" Marcellus hovered over me. "Where can we speak in private?"

I looked at John.

His face stiffened, but he nodded.

I took a breath and guided Marcellus down the hallway.

Margaret stepped out. "Watch out for that one. Your wife knew she was trash from the moment she saw her."

I glared at her and then continued to the dining room. I watched John sit at his desk in the library just before Benedict shut the door.

We entered the dining room, and Marcellus closed the door with a snap. He sat at the head of the table, and I took the seat to his right—the same places where John and I sat for meals. The blood on my hands had dried and was flaking between my fingers. I wondered if John would cooperate and give me up. He should have. I'd destroyed his life, our reputations, and my family's good name, and it looked very much like I was a murderer and my best friend the victim. Would any of this have happened if my father had lived? Would it be different if I had kept my promise?

Marcellus slammed his pointy elbow down on the dining room table, slanted his shoulders, and lurched forward. "Dr. Bradbridge informs me"—he rolled his jaw around—"you're a bit mad."

I imagined the house smirking at me.

He stood up from his chair and pushed closer to me. He towered over me, his gray hair squiggling out of his scalp. "The term is *hysteria*, I believe."

"I am not crazy."

"Hmm. After everything you've done, you don't think something is wrong with you?"

I hesitated. "I am not crazy."

"Hysteria is an interesting disease."

I held my breath and shut my eyes.

"Do you know why it only afflicts women?"

I opened my eyes.

He turned his back to me. "How has your husband performed in your marriage?"

"Pardon me?"

"Your husband?" He spun back around. "How has he"—he leaned forward, breathing heavily—"performed?"

I avoided looking directly at him as he hovered inches from my face. "I don't know what you mean."

He straightened and started pacing. "Hysteria is linked to the female organs. The usual culprit is organ dysfunction…or dissatisfaction."

"What?"

"So, how has your husband performed?"

I realized what he was asking. I didn't respond.

He paced. "Another cause: The uterus detaches and wanders the body, tampers with the brain."

My lungs constricted and forced me to work to breathe. I sat up straighter and leaned back. Next to me—through the wall—I heard a muffled voice. The parlor was next to us. It was Lottie.

"Do you know how they treat hysteria?"

"The rest cure."

"Perhaps, when you were first diagnosed, you experienced such mild treatments." He fiddled with his fingers behind his back. "But for extreme cases like yours, they'll treat you *manually*." He peered down at me with hollow eyes. "Can you guess where they'll touch you?"

I cringed and recoiled. A sense of violation and disgust crept inside me.

He stood next to me, too close. "There's this device they connect to an electrical current. That's what they'll use to draw out your nervous tension. Or they remove the defective organs all together—a hysterectomy."

The pleading from the parlor sounded louder now, and I could tell it was Lottie moaning and cursing, fighting someone. I turned my head toward the wall, listening.

"But you're not just hysterical," Marcellus continued. "You're a criminal. Insane criminals don't have the same rights as others." His nostrils flared and his upper lip curled. "Do you know what they do with insane criminals?"

I wondered what they were doing to Lottie and whispered, "No."

He slammed his hand on the table, forcing my attention from the wall. "You won't get a trial. Your madness is the only evidence I need. They will stick you in a back ward where you'll be restrained and forgotten. If you fight, you'll be disabled."

I realized I was shaking.

"They drill into your skull." He stood over me and mimicked cranking something over my head.

I didn't move. The sound of my heart thudded in my ears.

"They take a knife and slice out a chunk of your brain." He drove an imaginary scalpel toward my head, gritted his teeth, and ripped the nonexistent blade back up. He held up his hand as if putting the conquest on display. I unwillingly imagined the tissue wiggling on the tip of his dagger.

He darted back around and faced me. "Your husband will cooperate with us. We have our dying confession. If you cooperate, confess, I'll send you to a women's prison instead of an asylum."

Would they really all give me up? Wouldn't that be for the best?

"I—"

A knock on the door interrupted me. Marcellus stomped over and opened it. I couldn't make out what the other man said, but Marcellus responded with frustration. "What? How hard—no, I have a better idea. Round them up."

The man left, and Marcellus turned back, folded his arms, and inhaled deeply through his nose, his lower jaw jutting out. "Stand up."

"Why?"

"I'm taking you into custody."

I stood. "But—"

"Move." He grabbed my arm, squeezing his thumb into my bicep, and yanked me into the hallway.

At the end of the hall, Lewis spoke to John in hushed tones. John rubbed the back of his neck, and his cheeks twitched as he listened intently.

Marcellus escorted me past John.

I craned my neck to keep my eyes on him, desperately seeking a glimmer, anything.

"Move!" Marcellus shouted.

I walked forward and saw Carmine grasping my brother's shirt while she wept encircled in his arms. A patrolman stood next to them at the front door. I tried to give James an apologetic look, but he focused on his wife.

I peered into the parlor at the two patrolmen circling Lottie like vultures. "Get her up!" one shouted.

Walter held his hands up. "If you move her…"

Marcellus dragged me out the front doors and down the steps as I scuffled and slipped. James and Carmine were marched out behind me.

Marcellus led me to a black carriage, pushed me in, and slammed the door shut. I scooted to the window and watched as James and Carmine clung to each other until the patrolman pried them apart. He escorted Carmine in my direction, and then they disappeared as they walked around the carriage. The door opened and Carmine stepped in and fell onto the seat next to me. She slumped over and wept on my shoulder. I wrapped my arms around her. She didn't deserve this. I turned back to the window, waiting for them to drag the others out. I felt the carriage bounce as one of the patrolman got on to drive. No one brought John or Lottie out. I didn't see Walter. What would they do to her?

# Forty-Two

*October 1901*

Carmine and I watched from the carriage as Marcellus and the patrolman who'd brought us here talked to the hefty Sheriff Robert Neal. Their faces were hardened, and then the sheriff raised a hand to his double chin. Finally, the men shook hands and the sheriff ordered a short, scruffy-looking deputy toward us. The deputy lumbered to the carriage and opened the door. "Get out." Puffed up, he looked pleased to talk down to two women of our station.

We stepped out, and he took us each by the arm. He marched us into the stone jailhouse, which opened into a room with two desks and filing cabinets and then split off into two separate rooms with cells. The deputy took us into the room to the left, which consisted of a hall and two cells. He opened the first cell door with a creak and shoved us from behind. We stumbled in, and he locked the door, doused the lamps, and lumbered out.

I looked around the cell. An empty bucket sat in the corner for excrement, and there weren't any chairs or beds, just cold, hard floor. A small table and a single chair sat outside the cell, as if placed there to torment us. I pressed my face against the bars, trying to peer down the hall and into the first room, but couldn't see anything. I tried to listen for when they brought James in but heard only footsteps and doors opening and closing. They would surely take the men to the separate room on the right of the jailhouse rather than give us the comfort of their company. After a while, I gave up and sat on the floor. Carmine had crumpled against the wall opposite me. Her head rested on her knees, buried under her unraveled tresses. We sat there for a long time, nothing but Carmine's sobs echoing in the air.

"Carmine?"

She moaned a little and sniffled. White moonlight from a tiny window streamed across her, making her dark hair look black as night.

"Carmine, I'm so sorry. I'm so sorry this is happening."

She wrapped her arms around her head. "Don't speak to me," she said between whimpers.

"You weren't involved. You're not going to be in trouble, I promise."

"Just leave me alone." She sniffed hard, and her curly unfurled hair bounced around her head.

"You have every right to hate me."

The stillness of the air thickened, and I could hear someone scuffing around in the front entrance. I pictured the deputy falling asleep at one of the desks.

"I do," Carmine said and lifted her head, revealing her streaked porcelain face. "I do hate you."

My cheeks flushed and I swallowed, surprised—hurt. I suddenly realized how much I didn't want my brother's wife to hate me, but I had earned her hatred. My mouth moved, but no words came out.

She glared a moment longer and dropped her head back down.

"I just want you to know I'm glad you married my brother. You make him happy."

She didn't respond.

"He didn't know about all of this. He never would have put you in such a position. He loves you."

Nothing.

"Hate me, but don't hate him for this."

"Please...don't speak to me."

I woke the next morning to the clank-clank of a wooden baton hitting the metal bars of our cell. The sound prodded at a throbbing headache I had from sleeping all night sitting up with my head hanging to the right. The left side of my neck was so stiff that I had to use my hands to push my head up.

"Hey, poodle." The stout deputy leered at Carmine, flashing black and brown teeth. "Let's go. Get up."

Carmine appeared to be as stiff as I was but even more disheveled. She got onto all fours and teetered up, stumbling a little.

I rubbed my face and felt the dried blood that still covered my hands and arms. I slowly started to stand, rubbing my left temple.

"Sit down, bitch," the deputy shouted.

I jolted, frozen in place.

"You're not going anywhere." His nostrils flared and his nose crinkled.

Carmine looked back at me, her eyes wide and her lips parted.

He grinned back at her. "Let's go, sweetheart."

She swallowed and moved toward the cell door. After she stepped out, he quickly relocked it, as if I might try to scramble out like a wild animal.

Carmine's breath quickened.

"Where are you taking her?" I asked.

"Ay!" He hit the cell bars with his baton.

I flinched.

He pointed at me with it and gritted his teeth. "Didn't I tell you to sit your ass down?"

I slid down the wall, terrified for Carmine.

"A pretty little thing like you would never be involved with a witch like that, would ya, honey?" He leaned in close to Carmine's face, and she squinted with the obvious effort it took to not recoil. "Somebody's"—he held the "s" too long—"daddy's here."

Carmine closed her eyes and exhaled. He bowed and motioned toward the exit as if for a queen. Carmine scurried out without looking back.

I sat and wondered if my father would have come for me. Then I realized that Carmine's father knew. What would he think? What would he think of James? Would he tell the Dorrs? They would tell my mother. My gut twisted into a hard knot. Everyone was going to know everything.

For a long time, I remained sitting for fear that the deputy would come back and yell at me again, but eventually I stood and paced. As the day went on, the heat and moisture grew in the cell, and flies buzzed in circles, occasionally landing on my bloody garments. I had been thinking all day about the expression that had been on my mother's face when my father died…the expression she would have when she learned what I was. I prayed that Carmine's father would help James but feared he would blame my brother. I wondered if John was with the Bradbridges or Lewis. He hadn't even lifted his eyes when Marcellus dragged me out. I would understand if he turned me in, but what about everyone else? No one deserved punishment other than me. Would John abandon my brother? What about Lottie? What had happened to her? Was she alive?

The deputy sauntered back in to check on me. He crossed his arms and leaned against the wall with his top lip crinkled as if he were offended by some awful stench.

"Could I have some water?" I asked.

"You don't deserve it." He stood there scowling at me for a minute. "You think you can get whatever you want 'cuz you a lady? You ain't no lady anymore. You ain't no better than a whore." He pushed off the wall with his foot and walked out.

I collapsed to the floor, overwhelmed with the heat and buzzing flies around my head. My mouth felt dry and my stomach ached for nourishment. Sweat dripped down my brow and moistened my back and under my arms. The blood had gone from a dry, crusty state to a deep brownish orange and I swore I could smell it, or was that my body's own stench? Eventually, I removed my boots, pulled off my stockings, and hiked up my dress to cool myself. I leaned against the wall and pressed my cheek against the rough but cool stone.

And that was how Ida and Margaret found me.

"Well, well." Margaret's raspy voice ripped me from an unsteady sleep.

I instantly coaxed my petticoats and dress down and jumped up. Ida peered in at me as if I were a rat.

"What's happened to Lottie? My brother?"

Margaret cocked her head at Ida. "She doesn't even ask about her husband."

"Please. Please just tell me. Are they all right?"

"No," Ida said. "They're not all right, thanks to you." She folded her arms. "Nevertheless, we've come to help you."

"Is that so?"

"I am a powerful woman and so is Margaret. I know we've had our squabbles, but I didn't realize the seriousness of your condition. Margaret witnessed it herself. We cannot assist you unless you admit you are not well. If you do, we will see to it you are treated and not punished for your actions."

"I am perfectly fine, thank you."

"Ha!" Ida snorted.

"There's no need to deny it," Margaret said, fluttering a lace fan. "We can help you. You won't go to prison if you're ill, but you have to admit it."

Why were they trying to get me into an asylum? Marcellus had told me what they would do to me there. "I will not claim madness when I am not at all mad."

Margaret shook her head. "I should have known. She's so out of her wits she can't even recall her hysterics. What I witnessed should be proof enough. She obviously manipulated Walter. She tried to lure him into sin." She fanned faster. "If my son is ruined because of your madness, I'll—"

What was she fretting about, I wondered. His reputation? She would have me locked up in an asylum to prevent rumors? I pursed my lips and stepped closer to the bars. "Your son doesn't need me to ruin the Bradbridge name."

"Don't bother me with your ravings." She waved her fan at me as if shooing a beggar.

"Don't you know?"

She simpered at me, unimpressed.

"Oh." I looked at Ida. "She doesn't know."

Ida narrowed her eyes and shifted her weight.

"Well, Ida, *you* should know."

She stared at me with her face pinched tight.

"What?" Margaret shot her eyes at Ida and back at me.

"Well, if you know everything about your son…" I cocked my head with a little shrug.

"Tell me."

"She doesn't know anything, Margaret," Ida snipped.

"I know plenty. I know who he is courting in secret."

Margaret's eyes widened.

"You know her." I raised an eyebrow.

"Who?" Margaret stepped forward and snapped her fan shut.

"You won't like it."

She hit the bars with the fan. "Damn it, who?"

I spoke slowly so she wouldn't miss a single syllable. "Miss Olivia…Urswick."

Margaret's left eye twitched. "You're lying. He wouldn't."

"Oh yes he would. Why else would he have recommended her to sit with me when I was bedridden? You remember that."

She shook her head without blinking. "I don't believe you."

"Who was with him last night? He failed to elaborate, didn't he? Who was the woman whom he asked to inform Ida's husband about me? Well, Ida? Surely, *you* know."

Ida glared at me without denying it.

Margaret clutched her stomach and shot Ida a wide-eyed look.

Ida snarled. "I'm going to see to it that you are thrown into a hole." She took Margaret's arm and pulled her a few inches away before Margaret stamped her heel and halted them.

Margaret wrangled her arm away and stepped up to the bars. Her face had turned purple and her eyes were blazing and watering at the same time. "You've ruined my son," she said in a deep seething whisper. "You ruined your own husband…and you killed that woman. You're a murderer, and you deserve to go to hell."

I couldn't blink, and my bottom lip trembled.

Finally, she whirled around and the two women marched out.

My hands fell from the bars. I swallowed and imagined Lottie's corpse, her belly swollen and her blood on the floor—just like my father's. I killed her. I had ruined everything and everyone I cared about. I thought of the white room. This was the part where the room collapses, just before the woman is smothered by her own desires. I deserved it, too. I deserved to be punished. I'd known for a long time. The house knew, the wolf and the beast were there to carry it out—they all knew it. I deserved hell.

# Forty-Three

"Mother?"

"Hmm?" She glanced up with sleepy eyes cradled by dark circles.

"Why don't you go to my room and get some sleep?"

She shook her head. "No. I want to stay with him." She gazed at my father, who snored lightly.

"He's asleep and he's fine. You want to be rested the next time he wakes up."

She had been up all night with him, and she spent half of it crying.

"Just take an hour," I said.

"I can sleep here." She shrugged.

"You'll strain your neck sleeping in that chair."

She bobbed her head.

"I'll let you know when he wakes up."

She sighed and stood up slowly, sewing in hand. "I won't be long." She hobbled out of the room, her skirts swishing.

I sighed, realizing how tired I was, too. The curtains blocked the daylight, and the room felt gloomy. I glanced down at my book, but the words blurred. I stared at the wall instead, losing myself in my own thoughts. I still wondered what my father had meant by asking me to make sacrifices. I planned to ask but only when he felt better.

Whenever he woke, a terrible pain tormented him, but he could sleep if given enough morphine, so when he stirred a little while later, I immediately grabbed the tiny bottle from the nightstand. "Father? I need to give you some medicine." Although Dr. Morris had shown Mother and James how to inject the morphine directly into the vein, the task usually fell to me. I was the only one who didn't squirm or recoil, and I was glad. It felt good to help in a way no one else could.

He blinked a few times and then opened his eyes wide. "Emeline?"

"I'm here. I'm going to give you some medicine."

"Still here?" He struggled to lift his head and look around the room. Bright red lines squiggled across the whites of his eyes.

"I'm here. Mother went for a nap."

He leaned back again. "I meant *I'm* still here."

I frowned and picked up the syringe.

"No." He held up his hand and stared at the ceiling.

"What's wrong?"

"It's unbearable." He shuddered. "The pain."

"I know. Let me give you this."

He waved and tried to raise his voice. "No." He wheezed a little.

"What can I do?"

"I don't want this. Not for you or your mother, the girls—"

"But the doctor said—"

His breathing was hard and raspy. He stifled his gags and coughs, trapping the soft barking sounds in his throat. His face crinkled as the effort tugged at the stitches in his abdomen. "I—I know I—" The gagging overpowered him, and I quickly gave him a brown- and red-stained cloth from the nightstand. He held it to his mouth and coughed. When he pulled it away, a sticky bright red blotch moistened it. "I'm dying."

"Father..." I put the syringe and morphine back on the

nightstand. "The doctor wouldn't have done surgery if he thought—"

He shook his head. "It's inevitable."

"You don't know that."

"The doctor told me. That's why I had the family come together."

"What? When?"

"Operations will keep me in this bed for a time, but I won't get out of it again, and I will die."

"No. Maybe he's wrong," I practically begged.

"Emeline,...I'm ready."

I put my hand on his. "Everything will be all right."

"Emeline, I want—I need you to help me."

"What do you mean?"

He looked up at me. "Help me."

"I'm trying to."

"No. Help me die."

I pulled my hands away.

He gagged hard and lifted the rag back up. He tried to wipe the blood from his lip but smeared it across his mouth and chin and looked back up at me. "All I do is suffer. Our family suffers. I want it to stop. You promised to take care of them. This is how."

"Please, let me get Mother." I moved to stand.

He grabbed my wrist. "This is how you are going to take care of our family. I'm going to die anyway. Your mother—God, I love her—but she won't stop trying. The longer you keep me alive, the more you spend on doctors and operations, the more my death is going to tear this family apart when I'm gone. You—Emeline—are already going to have to make sacrifices to take care of this family."

I shook my head. "I don't know what you mean by that."

"Lillian said something about you wanting to be a nurse."

I closed my eyes, ashamed. "No, it was silly."

He reached up and touched my cheek. "You would make a wonderful nurse. You are brilliant, but you aren't going to be able to chase dreams when I'm gone. I don't want you to have to forfeight such ambitions, but you can't take care of other people when I need you to take care of our family."

"I know. I will. I promise, but please don't ask me—"

"I'm ready."

"I can't." I wrapped my hands around my waist. "I'm so sorry, but I can't."

"Emeline. Help me."

I crinkled my face and a tear broke loose. "I can't."

"You can. You can for me."

I rolled my lips inward and another tear fell. "But Mother?"

"It's better for her—for them. I can't stand everyone watching me in agony. I can't stand the pain." He cringed. "Ending this now is the best thing for this family. It's the only thing I can do for our family now, but I can't do it on my own."

I shook my head. "It's a...sin."

"I need you to make this sacrifice with me." He smiled a little and gulped. "God will understand. I'll explain it to him myself."

My lips trembled.

"You remember the dog, don't you?"

I nodded.

"The dog was dying anyway, suffering."

I shuddered. I loved him so much. I took a breath and tried to speak, but it came out like a whisper. "I don't know how." Another tear fell, warm.

"The morphine."

I moved my eyes in the direction of the medicine and then back at him.

"I'll just fall asleep."

My bottom lip trembled and I wiped my eyes with the back of my hands.

"You can do it," he said. "You can do it for me."

I glanced at the bottle of morphine and blinked, wide-eyed.

His voice was steady, confident. "It won't hurt."

My hands trembled as I reached out and clasped the tiny bottle and syringe. My hands quivered so much that I couldn't get the needle into the bottle.

He reached out and clasped it with steady hands.

I used both my hands to slip the needle into the bottle while he held it. I pulled out three times the maximum dosage. I removed the syringe, stopped, and regarded him.

He nodded, smiling.

I tried to put the bottle back on the nightstand, but my hands trembled so much that it tipped and tumbled to the floor. I heard it clack and roll across the floorboards.

"It's all right," he said.

I didn't reach for it. I tied the rubber tubing around his arm and tapped until a blue vein bulged, as ready as he was. I swallowed and then stiffened myself from the inside out. I slid the needle in and fought not to shake. I took a breath, closed my eyes, and hesitated for a moment that lasted an eternity and passed faster than the blink of an eye. I pushed the plunger. When I opened my eyes, the last of the clear liquid entered his body, and I could not feel what I had done. I removed the syringe and the tubing and placed them on the nightstand.

"Thank you." He reached for me.

I hugged him hard.

"You are taking care of them. You are taking care of me."

I pulled back so I could see him. I wiped away the tears falling down my cheeks. Then I reached out and wiped one from my father's jaw.

He took my hand from his face. "I'm sorry. I'm sorry I asked this of you."

I reached for his hand and brought it to my cheek.

"I asked because you're strong. Things are going to be hard, but I know you will do whatever it takes to care for them. You will be strong."

I squeezed his hand. "I will. I vow it. I will."

He took in a deep breath and exhaled his words. "I...love you."

"I love you." I squeezed harder.

He stopped talking and just breathed while gazing at me. His face relaxed and his lips turned up peacefully. His breathing grew long and shallow and his eyes sank, heavy. He kept his eyes on me through slits. I desperately tried to think of something to say, anything. I wanted our last words to never end, but I couldn't think. Moments passed. He hadn't closed his eyes, but he clearly wasn't awake. I whimpered and held his hand to my cheek. I just held his hand and stared as his breath slowed and slowed until it stopped.

I stared at his lifeless body for a long time. Finally, I remembered to breathe. Blood was smeared on his lips and chin. I used the blood-smeared cloth to dab and swab it off as best I could and realized that his own blood was the last thing he'd tasted. I closed his eyes and stared at my hands.

I don't know how long it had been when I heard the swishing sound of my mother's skirts. If I saw her at the moment when she realized he was gone, I wouldn't be able to hide what I'd done, so I rushed out of the room. I passed her, my cheeks ablaze, but she didn't stop me. It would happen any minute; she would realize he had gone. James came out of his room, and I quickly squeezed his hand and asked him to sit with her so that someone would be there when it happened. I rushed away, expecting to hear her shriek at any moment. Everything inside me screamed to stay, but I couldn't. I could not stay. I would not stay. I wanted to flee. I wanted to run out of the house and down the street and never stop running. But I made it only halfway down the stairs before I heard her wail, the sound I had been dreading. I halted and turned back. I didn't have a choice. I had to be strong. I had to stay.

# Forty-Four

The next morning, Marcellus placed a tray with an ink well, a pen, and paper on the table outside my cell. "Are you ready to confess?"

Why had he waited until now? I must have looked ready to give up. I had taken my hair down after it collapsed into a heap on the side of my head. It now hung to my hips in distraught waves and half-curls. I had taken my shoes off, and my dress was stained and wrinkled.

"We know everything, Mrs. Dorr. We have Dr. Bradbridge, your husband, and the dying confession. It's up to you to see that no one else is held accountable."

My face felt greasy, and my eyes were sore and swollen from crying all night without any more tears to give. I stared through the bars exhausted, parched, and starved.

"If you don't want the innocent charged, tell me the same story they told me, exactly. I'm going to copy down your testimony, and you're going to sign a confession." He lowered himself into the chair, propped a leg on his knee, and dipped the pen to charge it.

I saw my white room in my mind. Had I broken out or was I still in it? If I had escaped, was this the part where I suffocated?

"Did you perform an abortion on Mrs. Schwab?"

I lifted my absent gaze and blinked, momentarily lost, breathing heavily. "What?"

"Did you perform an abortion on Mrs. Schwab?"

I couldn't escape it—all the white—without killing everyone in the process. I had thought on it all night, along with the promise I had failed to keep. Maybe I could still save those who survived me, my selfish escape from a white room. I could fight back and allow my actions to ruin everyone I cared about, or I could save them. I couldn't have freedom, but if I confessed, maybe they still could. I thought I'd broken my promise to my father, but maybe I could keep it in some small way. Maybe I could put the white walls back up—start making sacrifices.

"Mrs. Dorr?" He narrowed his eyes. "Your husband is cooperating, and I highly suggest you do the same."

"She was suffering." I mumbled.

"I don't care why you did it. I need to know how you did it."

"Pardon?" I glanced up. Why did walls have to be white? Why couldn't I paint them a different color?

"Explain the procedure."

I stared at the floor, feeling the cool stone under my bare feet. "Um—a curette." I realized I didn't feel the house anymore off in the woods grinning with blood-stained floors and teeth. I had really defeated it, my self-conjured prison traded for a stone floor and iron bars.

"No, Mrs. Dorr, explain it step by step."

"Pardon?"

He glared through the bars at me with impatience. "What did you do first?"

"Um…" Don't cry. "I boiled the instruments."

His pen scratched on the thin paper. "Go on."

"Then I…" I sighed. "I used a curette."

"You didn't ask the victim to lie down? She didn't remove her clothing? You didn't look at her?"

"Um—I—uh—yes, before I boiled the instruments."

"Then you should start with that, shouldn't you?"

A tear slipped down my cheek and splashed near my little toe. I quickly wiped the trail from my face.

"Mrs. Dorr, this is no time for emotional outbursts." He shifted and the chair creaked. "You have to explain everything in as much detail as possible."

"Why?"

He clenched his teeth. "Just do it."

I pressed my wedding ring deep into my skin.

"Then what?"

"I told you, I used the curette."

"Did you have her spread her legs?"

"What?" I didn't want to reveal these intimate details out loud, let alone to this disturbing man.

"You must not skip anything, Mrs. Dorr. Did you ask her to spread her legs?"

I felt exposed, naked. "I—um—I suppose. I'm not sure." More tears dripped.

"Start over."

"What?"

"From the beginning—start over. You are hysterical, not making any sense." He scratched something onto the paper. "Start from the beginning."

"Uh..." I wiped my face with the palm of my hand and felt dirt scrape across my cheek.

"Did you have her remove her clothing?"

"No?"

"Is that a question?"

"No."

"What did she have on?"

"Her drawers, a chemise. Underclothes."

"Anything else?"

"No."

"Was this your first abortion?"

I hesitated and nodded.

"Use words."

"I—um...yes."

"You have had no actual medical training and performed this procedure without consulting a physician? Is that correct? You have no understanding of these matters?"

"No, I do. In college I studied—"

"Do you have a license to perform medicine Mrs. Dorr? Yes or no."

"No."

"Dr. Walter Bradbridge didn't advise you?"

"No."

"Were you aware that you were likely to rupture the victim's uterine wall, damaging her internal organs?"

"Is that what happened? Is that how she died?"

"Answer."

"I knew, but I took precau—"

"And you still performed the procedure?"

"Yes, but you—"

"And Dr. Bradbridge was the one who warned you?"

"No. He didn't know anything."

"Was this Mrs. Schwab's first abortion?"

"What happened to her? No one will—"

"Answer the question!"

"Please just—"

"Mrs. Dorr! Was this Mrs. Schwab's first abortion?"

"Yes."

"How was her husband involved?"

"He wasn't."

"How was your husband involved?"

"He wasn't."

"How was he involved?" He repeated through clenched teeth.

I didn't answer. I wondered why he was pushing this. He said

John would testify against me. Did he think I'd accuse him because he'd turned me in? I wouldn't. I wasn't even angry with him.

He yelled. "Your husband—how was he involved?"

Why wasn't I angry with him, I wondered. Then it hit me like an avalanche: I care for him. No, I thought. This feeling was more than that. I think … I think I love him. I love him. I smiled, and Marcellus' face contorted in anger. I loved John, and I felt horrible for the way I had treated him, for forcing him to marry me, for having hated him when I really hated myself, for pushing him away when he tried to show he cared, for betraying him and putting him through all this when all the while *he* had sacrificed for me from the beginning. He didn't even want to be here. He loved me. I was going to keep my promise and sacrifice for what I loved, and I loved John Dorr.

"Mrs. Dorr!"

I stepped closer to the bars so I could glare straight into Marcellus' eyes, yellow against his moist skin. "He wasn't involved. Nobody was involved. It was only me."

"You're lying!"

My wedding ring clanked as I slapped my hand against the bars. "Are you deaf? I just told you. No one was involved."

He rose from his seat. "Mrs. Dorr, control yourself! Your husband has obviously known about your exploits and hidden them."

"No!" I yelled. "He found out the other night for the first time. He had no idea."

He stepped closer to me, an inch from the bars. "You need to calm yourself, Mrs. Dorr."

I breathed hard and pushed all my frustration into my fists.

"What about your brother and his wife?"

"No one, damn it!"

"Mrs. Dorr, if you do not calm yourself, I will take measures to ensure your cooperation."

I dug my nails into my palms to keep from screaming.

"Mrs. Dorr?"

I sighed. "No one knew anything. It was all me. I just wanted to help her."

He huffed. "You didn't."

I didn't wipe away the tears. I rolled my lips inward and tasted the salt. "I will tell you whatever you want, but only if you swear to me that no one else will be punished for what I did. It was me, all me. I'm guilty."

Just then someone shouted from the jail entrance, "How can you condone this?"

Marcellus jerked his attention away.

"It doesn't matter," a man's voice said, ragged and tired. "I have a writ for habeas corpus!"

"You know what happened! You know!" Another man bellowed.

Marcellus stood, quickly charged the pen, and pulled a folded piece of paper from the inside of his jacket. He shoved the pen and paper through the bars. "Sign it!"

I took them from him.

"Don't let her corrupt you." I recognized Margaret's voice coming from the front room.

"What's going on?" I asked.

"Sign it, Mrs. Dorr. Now!"

I unfolded the paper. The heading said "Coddington Offices of Law," and under it was a single typed paragraph: "I, Emeline Evans Dorr, confess to having knowingly committed a criminal act that could kill. I maliciously conducted an illegal abortion on Mrs. Lottie Schwab. My accomplices included Mr. John Dorr, Mr. Oliver Schwab, Dr. Walter Bradbridge, and Mr. and Mrs. James Evans."

"No." I shook my head. "I'm not signing this."

"We'll take out your accomplices. They won't be charged. Sign it now or we'll charge everyone. I will not offer this again."

I didn't know what to do.

I heard a voice that I was almost certain belonged to Lewis. "Step into that room, and I will see to it that you never work in the state of Missouri again!"

"You'll regret this for the rest of your life," Margaret shouted.

"Mother, move!" Was that Walter?

"That's it!" Marcellus unlocked the cell door, stepped inside, and locked the door behind him. He marched toward me, and I backed up against the cell wall.

Marcellus snatched the paper from me, grabbed my wrist, and whirled me around to face the wall. He smacked the paper on the stone and forced me to hold the pen to it. "Sign it!"

"No!"

"Sign it!" He squeezed my wrist, causing a sharp pain to shoot up my arm and panic to swirl in my head.

I spread my fingers and let the pen slip and clack to the floor.

"You wretched—"

"Release her this instant!" The ragged voice shouted from outside the cell.

I craned my neck and saw—dark eyes. "John?"

The stout deputy with rotting teeth trailed in behind him.

John pointed to the cell. "Open it."

The deputy's eyes darted from John to Marcellus, and the detective released me and stepped away.

I rubbed the skin on my wrist and stared at John in disbelief.

"I said open it," John demanded.

The deputy shoved the key into the lock.

I looked at Marcellus, wondering if he would lunge at me again.

"It's too late," he said. "She confessed."

John's body and face stiffened. "From the looks of it, she didn't sign anything, and she's not going to. Anything she said was obviously under duress."

Marcellus pointed down the hall. "I don't care what that dandy Bradbridge says or doesn't say." He swung his finger in my direction. "She is guilty."

"All you've got is hearsay!"

They stared at each other.

With two loud clacks, the deputy unlocked the cell and heaved it open.

John stepped forward and offered his hand.

"I thought you turned me in? I was sure you…"

His ungreased hair fell around his eyes. His white shirt billowed without a vest or jacket to hold it in place, and his sleeves were rolled up. He appeared to have not slept in days, yet he looked more striking and handsome than ever. "I wasn't about to leave you here," he said.

I reached out and felt his hand grip mine, and inside I rejoiced because I knew he wanted me. It happened so fast I didn't even think to grab my shoes. We dashed past the deputy, and Marcellus followed us down the narrow hall and into the front room with desks and cabinets.

Walter stood blank-faced next to the exit as his mother screamed at him. "How could you? How could you with that whore? Now you're a criminal, too? An abortionist?"

Sheriff Neal sat behind his desk, watching with a flabbergasted expression.

I watched with shock and confusion too. The last I'd seen Walter, he had finally made his parents proud by turning me in to the authorities.

Walter's jaw stiffened. "Mother, I have a right to love whomever I choose. I don't care what you think." He turned to his father, who was sitting in a chair at one of the desks. "Olivia and I are getting married. I'm starting my own practice, and I'm done waiting for you to think I'm ready."

His father focused his eyes elsewhere, but Margaret pounced. "You're not my son. You're no one. I don't ever want to see you again."

"Margaret!" The deep voice froze her. "That's enough." The senior doctor stood up and towered over her. "He's a grown man. He made his decision."

Margaret clenched her jaw and hesitated before finally turning and stomping out.

My lips twitched as I held back a smile. I couldn't believe what I'd just seen.

Benedict lifted his chin toward the hefty man at the desk. "Sheriff, can you hold this woman or not?"

My limbs stiffened as I expected to be hurled back into the cell.

Without getting up, the sheriff cocked his head toward Marcellus, as if searching for an answer.

Marcellus stood with his head forward of his lopsided shoulders. He grimaced and looked away from the sheriff.

Sheriff Neal threw up his hands. "He's got habeas corpus and we don't have a signed confession."

Benedict left casually, as if he hadn't cared about any of it, but Lewis approached us with his normally glossy eyes wide open and his placid face swollen with anger.

John squeezed my hand tighter and I trembled.

Lewis locked his knees and leaned forward as he snarled his words. "I'm serious, John. If you go through with this, I'm going to see to it that you are disbarred."

John smiled wryly. "If you put me on the stand, everything that man has done to my wife is going to be known."

"His methods are no different than any other detective's," the sheriff called from his chair, arms folded.

"Detectives are allowed to hold a woman down and force her to sign a confession?"

The sheriff uncrossed his arms, sat up straight, and squinted at Marcellus.

"I witnessed it myself and so did your man."

"Is that right?"

The deputy stood behind Marcellus, nodding.

John eyed Lewis. "You were well aware of his past in Chicago. What's going to happen to your cases when his *methods* are known? Everything will be thrown out." John looked back at the sheriff. "And what about you? Will you remain in your position after this?"

The sheriff pressed his lips into a thin, hard line, and Lewis' eye twitched.

Chicago, I thought. I remembered that. I remembered Walter

telling John about that, about Marcellus being dismissed in Chicago for going "too far," for…forcing confessions. I looked at Walter. He stood near the door, arms crossed, grinning.

Marcellus' chin jutted out, but he kept his eyes down and to the side.

Lewis swallowed hard and dropped his shoulders before finally backing away from us.

I stared at John, amazed by his gumption.

"Come with me." John pulled me out of the jail and into the daylight, which seemed brighter than normal. Walter followed us. We walked across the grass toward the road. The musty scents of the horses were oddly more splendid than I remembered. The colors—blue sky, white buildings, green grass—they were so vivid. Then I noticed the curious eyes and whispers of lingering pass-ersby who had undoubtedly spotted the Bradbridge, Rippring, and Coddington carriages outside the jailhouse. I didn't care that they watched us. I halted and forced John and Walter to stop. "What about James and the others?"

John flashed a superior grin. "We're lawyers." Then he gestured down and across the street.

I gasped and then laughed upon seeing James waiting for us in the driver's seat of his rented buggy.

"We kept them from taking Mr. Schwab too," John said. "They took you and Carmine for questioning, but they released her when we mentioned her father. I knew Sheriff Neal wouldn't risk hold-ing a politician's daughter without charging her."

"So her father isn't here? He doesn't know?" Hope swelled inside me. "I don't understand. How did you do this?"

John's brown eyes brightened. "Habeas corpus."

"What's that?"

"It's an official demand to release a prisoner who has been unlawfully detained without evidence."

"No evidence? But Walter—" I hesitantly glanced in his direction.

Walter stood tall next to John. "I don't condone what you did, Emeline, but I don't believe in watching people die either. That's why women like Mrs. Schwab end up butchered and why people like Mr. Hughmen rot in agony." He held his lips tight and his chin high. "And why people like you take such serious risks."

I stared at Walter's sad boyish face. I'd had no idea how much his understanding would mean to me.

He continued. "When I saw them mistreating Mrs. Schwab despite her condition, I remembered why I had once said I wouldn't call upon Marcellus Rippring again."

"But I thought you had already told him everything."

"No," John said. "Walter had *Olivia* fetch the authorities. He never actually told Marcellus anything. It took us a while to realize it ourselves, but Marcellus took you based on hearsay. They were only holding you for questioning. They had no evidence to charge you. That's why they were trying to get you to confess. The only way they could hold you without charging you is if they could claim you were insane."

It suddenly became clear why Margaret and Ida had pushed me to fall back on hysteria. Margaret's son had turned on her, and she wanted to blame it on a crazy woman and have Marcellus send me off to an asylum to prove it. But..."But I confessed, and what about what I did...to Lottie?" I lowered my eyes as they watered. "I killed her."

"What?"

"Margaret said..." I stopped.

John shook his head. "No. Lottie's at our house."

I looked from John to Walter in disbelief.

Walter nodded. "I wouldn't let them move her. Trust me, after the way she cursed at them, they tried."

"But..." My lips trembled and my skin tingled.

John grasped my upper arms and looked into my eyes. "They told you lies to get you to confess. Marcellus tried to physically force you to sign. That's how desperate he was. He went too far, and he has a history of that in Chicago. Anything he claims you said would be thrown out of court."

My bottom lip trembled, and chills fluttered through my body.

"Lottie is alive," John said. "She refused to testify. I refused to testify. Walter refused to testify. No one said anything against you. You didn't sign a confession. They have no evidence." John pressed his hands against my cheeks and kissed me quickly and then pulled back. "You're free."

I remembered to breathe, and my knees wobbled.

John smiled, took my hand again, and led me across the dirt road toward James and the buggy. I didn't even feel the stones and dirt beneath my bare feet.

We walked past the Bradbridge carriage, and on the other side Ida attempted to comfort a blathering Margaret. Walter stood taller but clearly noticed Margaret spotting us and breaking free of Ida. "You won't get away with this, you wretch," she screeched at me. "You've ruined my son. Walter, she's ruining you. She's ruined everything. That woman—"

John stopped and silenced her with a look. He pointed at me and I froze. "That woman risked everything she had, including her freedom, to help another human being, and I pray to God that I would have the courage to do the same."

# Forty-Five

*October 1901*

We all collapsed in the parlor, exhausted from having been awake for nearly forty-eight hours. I desperately wanted to speak to Lottie, but she hadn't wakened, still weak from losing so much blood. Lottie lay on a makeshift bed of blankets and cushions on the parlor floor because Walter said she shouldn't be moved to a bed. I refused to leave her, and Walter insisted he stay to tend to her, so we all remained in the parlor, lingering through the day and dozing on and off into the night. The house and the furniture sat quiet, lifeless. The only breathing came from the people resting within. After darkness fell, blue moonlight shone through the windows and onto our faces. I lay awake most of the time, sometimes enjoying the sweet comfort of John's arms wrapped around me and sometimes staring at Lottie. As I watched her, my heart both swelled with happiness and sank with guilt.

After drifting off for an hour or so, I woke and it was that time of the morning just before the sun rises and there's only a tiny glow on the horizon. I rose and lay in front of Lottie to observe her condition. She lay on her side and Oliver slept behind her. She breathed shallowly and looked better but pale, so I touched her to feel her temperature.

I hadn't expected her to open her eyes. She scanned the room and then looked back at me. "I didn't say anything," she whispered.

I whispered, too. "I know. Thank you."

"Everything all right?"

"Yes. Walter refused to testify."

She pursed her lips and blinked.

I motioned to where Olivia and Walter slept on the floor. After he'd announced his love for Olivia to his parents, we insisted on fetching her.

Lottie lifted herself a little to see and then blinked rapidly and looked back at me with an open stare. She lowered herself back down. "Am I all right?"

"I think so."

"I feel it, I think."

"I'm so sorry."

"I'd figure you'd find my feelin' betta a good thing." She grinned.

I gave her an apologetic frown.

"Don't—please. I shouldn't of asked you. I never thought all this would come of it."

"Me neither." I huffed, thinking of it all again.

"You did me a great kindness."

I shook my head. "I could have killed you. I thought I had killed you."

She stared off. "Those men act like you was the devil. They don't know nothin'."

"Don't they?"

She fixed her eyes on me. "No."

I pushed my hair back from my face and threw the long locks behind me. "Can I tell you something?"

"Course."

"I've never told anyone." A sense of dread crept up from my bowls and swelled in my head. She waited, unblinking. "I'm a murderer." The swelling in my head started to tingle and made me feel dizzy with shame. "I killed my father."

She didn't react. She didn't move.

"He had stomach cancer, and he asked me to do it, to end his suffering, and I killed him. He's dead because I killed him."

She didn't say anything, and I felt ashamed that everyone had done so much for me when I was a guilty, evil thing.

"You should probably sleep more," I said and pushed myself up off the floor.

"Emeline?"

I stopped on my hands and knees, expecting to be told the awful truth about myself.

"I don't know all about right and wrong, and I don't know about God or the devil, but what you did for me—I think you a godsend."

"No." Tears welled up and curdled my voice. "You almost died, Lottie. I shouldn't be doing this, not even the nursing. I—only physicians should. It's selfish. I'm selfish."

She raised her voice a little. "But the doctors don't." She stopped, realizing the volume of her voice, and whispered again. "You—you doin' sometin'. You helpin' people. You doin' good."

"I don't think I did good with you."

"I'm your best friend. It's different." She grinned, teasing, even now.

I couldn't help but laugh just a little.

"You don't care 'bout money or what anyone say. You help people who need helpin', and you helped your daddy, too—you helped him in the most unselfish way."

I shook my head.

"You could only hurt after helpin' him like that. You got nothin' but pain from it. That was all for him. You *sacrificed* your own self for him...and for me."

I thought about what she'd said and a tear slid down my nose and onto the floor.

"Helpin' someone when you gotta live with a terrible pain for doing it—that don't sound like a devil kind of thing. That might well be the kinda thing God forgive people for. If not, well, I'm sure your daddy talked to him for ya."

# Forty-Six

*1902*
*Labellum, Missouri*

The house was alive. Everyone was running around. It was one of those spring days when the sun seems light and the air is at just the right temperature. All the doors and windows were open, so the cool breeze came in and made my white chiffon dress flow behind me whenever I moved.

"What about this one?" Francis pointed to an end table with swirling appendages and decorations.

"Yes." I wrote it down in my little book.

"And this?" Annie held up the tree lamp that clutched the little dewdrop.

"Oh, yes." I wrote it down.

Francis stopped and eyed her mother, who was sitting on the green chair with the high back drinking tea and making notes. "Mother, how about you join us?"

She waved her hand. "Darling, presidents don't do such things. I am supervising."

"Seems you're relaxing to me," Annie said.

"And this?" Francis pointed at the chair Ella sat on.

"You know"—my eyes bounced from the muscle-bound chair and the conjoined love seat to the owl bowl and other figurines— "there's nothing I really need here."

Ella lifted her chin at Francis. "I'm not getting up."

"Oh yes you are." She playfully put her hands on her hips.

"Is that so?" Ella lifted her chin at me. "I'm going to buy this chair."

I smiled. "All right."

She beamed at Francis. "There. Now I can do whatever I please with it."

"I'll tell Oliver what's going." I glided out of the parlor, chuckling. The front door was open, and I could see Oliver, John, Walter, and Francis' husband, Richard. They were talking and leaning over some large papers. Oliver called out to one of his children running about the yard to be careful.

I stopped in the doorway. "Gentlemen, everything in the parlor can go."

John straightened, put a hand on his hip, and gave me a suspicious grin. "Really? I never would have guessed."

"Well, it is for a good cause."

"Darling, what do you think about widening the stairwell? It'll make it easier to get people and supplies up there."

"Now that's an idea," I said jauntily, twirled around, and stepped back into the parlor.

Ella still took notes in the chair while Annie teased her. I had feared that Annie's experience would alter her, but her gleeful and stately demeanor had returned, the only difference being a hint of maturity that can only come from experience.

"The men will be along in a moment," I said.

"All right," Francis and Ella sang simultaneously. Annie said it, too, but just slightly off.

I glided down the hall and passed the empty sitting room. The library remained mostly intact. We had already emptied the dining room, and whenever I saw it now, I laughed, imagining that the utensils and dishes had finally sprouted real limbs, wings, and other appendages and all they had used them for was to scurry off to the woods, where they had always longed to be. That was just in my imagination, though.

I stepped into the doorway and the eldest Schwab girl, Lucy, lifted her head from what she was writing at the end of the table. "Oh. I hope you don't mind. I borrowed it from your desk. I'm writing Daniel." She smiled shyly. "He asked me to keep him updated."

"Isn't he coming down for the auction?"

"Yes. But, I—I don't want to wait. I'll give it to him when he arrives."

"Use as much paper as you need."

She beamed and continued.

I continued to the stairs. The stairwell didn't move anymore, and it almost seemed a little wider. I could hear voices when I reached the landing. I stepped down the hall and peered into the rooms, whose doors were open wide. They had all been stripped of their furnishings except for the basic pieces like beds and nightstands.

As I swept past each room, I remembered the people who were once imprisoned within. After I'd confronted the beast—and my guilt—and after that night with Lottie, I never saw them again. When John and James brought me back from the city jail, the house was different—lifeless. It was as if none of it had ever happened. The inhabitants had just disappeared. I wasn't sure if it had happened after I confronted the beast, or while I sat in the city jail, or when I confessed my deepest sin to Lottie. Maybe it was everything.

Sometimes, I tried to picture them leaving. They would have stepped out of their rooms, wearing their best traveling suits and carrying luggage. They would have brightened and laughed cheerily, the dead boy not dead but free, the nurse's work finally complete. The young woman would have walked tall and confident with all her posters and dreams under her arms, the empty bottle of morphine long forgotten. The little girl would have skipped out, dolly in hand, her life ahead of her.

I came to the last room, the one that had housed the beast. The door was open, and I entered without trepidation. The women inside chatted and roamed around.

"There isn't anything in this one," Ethel said, holding Jacob in her arms.

"It's so strange. I thought it was a closet at first." Olivia cocked her head.

Lottie circled the room with her hand to her chin. "I like it. It's like a surprise."

"You want this one to be set up, too?" Ethel asked and set her son on the floor. He quickly scurried to a corner, pony in hand.

I imagined the layout in my head. "We should be able to put two or three in here."

"Sounds perfect." Ethel clapped her hands together.

"Those curtains are going." I pointed.

"We should measure for the beds," Olivia said.

"The measuring tape is in my room. I'll be right back." I patted Jacob on the shoulder on my way out.

I entered my chamber. Everything was still in there. I was fond of the furnishings in that room. John had even repaired the mirror that we had knocked off the wall. I still spent a lot of time there, imagining and dreaming, but my fantasies were different from the ones I'd used to have.

I took the measuring tape off John's dressing table and I heard a noise outside, a rustling. It reminded me of sounds I'd heard once before a long time ago. I walked to the open window and looked out. John, Oliver, and Richard were unraveling the banner. As they lifted it up, I could see that it read "Auction to benefit The Labellum Medical, Law, & Aid Society." John's eyes met mine, and his thumb popped up enthusiastically. I nodded, delighted. I lifted my eyes above the banner to the edge of the woods. I thought of the wolf. I thought of how it must have scampered off—yellow eyes, a turn, and a flash of a tail. I didn't really see it, though. It was only in my head. I didn't see anything like that anymore, and I was happy for it.

After the incident with Lottie, John and Walter had become the black sheep of their professions. It was all for the best, though, because not long after, Ella and the church committee had an idea about how to help the poor and ill-stricken. They suggested starting an organization that could pay small salaries to John and Walter for providing their services to people who could not afford medical or legal aid. We even recruited James and Carmine in St. Louis as well as the Nelsons to act as liaisons and help us work with similar organizations there.

We'd decided to put off having a family until I finished nursing school, so John and I offered the house to serve as headquarters and to accommodate those who needed extra care. We decided to auction off the furniture to earn money for the organization. Although certain people went to great lengths to ruin our reputations by exposing me as Mrs. Freeman, it turned out it only rallied support for the society. Even more so after the Labellum Police Department relieved Marcellus Rippring of his position and he and Ida left town. Rumors swirled that he had tortured me when I refused to name my clients. It seemed I was becoming something of a legend, and it was creating a lot of interest in the auction and our society. We even expected Dr. and Mrs. Bradbridge, who, after much negotiation, had recently met their son and Olivia for tea.

Thinking of it made me giddy, and I twirled around in my chamber, admiring all the white. I still sometimes thought of my white room. The white represented responsibility, obligation, and by being in that room, a woman clothed in white supported and maintained herself and everything she loved. Nevertheless, white is a pale thing like a canvas ready to be transformed into whatever the heart desires. She could paint it yellow or lavender or even paste up wallpaper. Walls are not permanent. If she felt like knocking one down, installing a window, or adding a door or two, she could feel free. She could even go outside for a while. Maybe she would invite someone in to help her or just for the pleasure of their company. She might as well make it the way she likes. It is, after all, her room.

# ACKNOWLEDGEMENTS

Nothing that I have done or continue to do as a writer and artist would be possible without my wondrous husband, soul mate, and best friend, Jonathan Carroll. You read copy. You give critique. You act out action scenes with me. You know the remedy for my writer's block. You let me cry to you about my characters. You indulge and even praise my psychotic artistic process. I could not write without you. I could not have written this book without you. You give me the strength to get through every step, and every day you sacrifice so that I can pursue my dreams, and for that I am eternally grateful and in awe of you.

I am so very grateful for the Churchill County Library and the Kings County Library. For years I visited these libraries on a weekly basis to retrieve books that helped me create *A White Room*. I couldn't have done it without either of them and their wonderful staff.

I want to express lots of love and gratitude to my supportive friends, family, and test-readers. This novel would not be what it is without you. Thank you Dr. Eileen Walsh, Christy Lattin, Rebecca Taylor, Kelly Cantley, and Barbara Carroll, who suffered through and helped shape initial drafts. I am so grateful for Dorothy Puder, Rene Lynn Miller, Gloria Werner, Laura D. Jones, Benjie Smith, and Barbara Mathews, who provided no-nonsense critique and helped refine the final manuscript. Thank you so much to Virtual Muse authors Lindy Gligorijevic, Steven M. Long, Steve Masover, Dan Berger, Kristina Eschmeyer, Kate Raphael, and Miranda Weingartner not only for your help and support with *A White Room* but also for making me a better writer overall. A special thanks to

Andrew Eddy for inviting me into VM, for your keen eye, and for helping me discover habeas corpus. And a big bear hug for the members of the Kings County Writer's Group.

I also want to express my gratitude to Allison McCabe and Daniel Lazar for their expert advice and encouragement, which helped me understand the industry, tailor my work, and, most importantly, have faith in *A White Room*.

I am incredibly grateful to all the talented and generous professionals who made this book beautiful inside and out. I am so appreciative of my cover designer, Jennifer Quinlan of Historical Editorial, Smith Publicity's Sarah Miniaci, Anita Bihovsky, and Kate Knapp, and The Editorial Department's wonderful staff who made the entire process easy and fun. Thank you Jane Ryder, Chris Fisher, Morgana Gallaway, and copy editor Doug Wagner, whose knowledge of word usage and bundt cake taught me a lot. I'm also thankful for the beautiful and artistic work of photographers Kim Lamb and Corey Ralston. Thank you all for your hard work, support, and patience with my many questions.

Finally, thank you to anyone and everyone who reads this book. Without you, the love and tears I pour into my work would never be known, would be for nothing. I write because I want to express the magic of raw emotions, experiences, and possibilities. I write with the intention of someone reading it and loving it. I write for you.

# ABOUT THE AUTHOR

As a reporter and community editor, Stephanie Carroll earned first place awards from the National Newspaper Association and from the Nevada Press Association. Stephanie holds degrees in history and social science and graduated *summa cum laude* from California State University, Fresno.

Her dark and magical writing is inspired by the classic authors Charlotte Perkins Gilman (*The Yellow Wallpaper*), Frances Hodgson Burnett (*The Secret Garden*), and Emily Bronte (*Wuthering Heights*).

Stephanie blogs and writes fiction in California, where her husband is stationed with the U.S. Navy. Her website is www. stephaniecarroll.net.

*A White Room* is her debut novel.

CPSIA information can be obtained
at www.ICGtesting.com
Printed in the USA
BVHW042155041022
648707BV00004B/10